STRANGERS AND FRIENDS

Strangers and Friends

A new exploration
of homosexuality and the Bible

Michael Vasey

Hodder & Stoughton

British Library Cataloguing in Publication Data
A record for this book is available from the British Library

ISBN 0 340 60814 5

Typeset by Hewer Text Composition Services, Edinburgh
Printed and bound in Great Britain by
Cox & Wyman, Reading, Berks.

Hodder and Stoughton Ltd
A Division of Hodder Headline PLC
338 Euston Road
London NW1 3BH

Contents

My song is love unknown,
 My Saviour's love to me,
Love to the loveless shown,
 That they might lovely be.
  O who am I,
   That for my sake
   My Lord should take
 Frail flesh and die?

Here might I stay and sing,
 No story so divine;
Never was love, dear King,
 Never was grief like Thine.
  This is my Friend,
   In whose sweet praise
   I all my days
 Could gladly spend.

Samuel Crossman
c. 1624–1683

A brother asked an old man, 'How does the fear of God come into the soul?' And the old man answered, 'If a man has humility and poverty, and if he does not judge anyone, the fear of God comes to him.'

Wisdom of the Desert Fathers
(from Fairacres Publications 48, 1975
trans. Sister Benedicta Ward, p. 2)

Not that we lord it over your faith;
but we work with you for your joy.

St Paul
2 Corinthinans 1:24

Acknowledgments

In writing this book I have often felt the loneliness of the explorer. Sometimes it seemed as if I had two incompatible maps of the same territory; sometimes there seemed to be none at all. On reflection I realize that, like any theological or academic writer, I have numerous intellectual and personal debts. Some of my intellectual debts are acknowledged in the footnotes. If I have overlooked some generosity or friendship in the list below, I hope those concerned will forgive me.

I would like to acknowledge a deep personal debt to the late Francis ('Frank') MacCarthy Willis-Bund, one time Dean and Chaplain of Balliol College, Oxford, whose friendship helped me to come to terms with the challenge of evangelical Christianity, to turn expectantly to the tradition of the church, and to see heaven as the goal and touchstone of Christian life and doctrine.

My thanks are due to Hodder and Stoughton for their confidence in commissioning this book, and to St John's College, Durham, for a sabbatical term that allowed me to get started. Two friends and colleagues, Margaret Masson and Robert Song, have not only believed in 'the book' but have gone to great lengths to support and help me in the writing of it. From other colleagues and from many ordinands I hope for forgiveness for the impatience and neglect which they have often had to endure while the book was being written.

I am grateful to David Attwood for letting me have copies of Paul Ramsey's articles on Augustine and Aquinas, to Phillip Tovey for drawing my attention to David Greenberg's *The Construction of Homosexuality*, and to Paul Williams for appearing out of the blue with such perceptive and well formulated questions.

At a more personal level, I should like to thank a number of people whose friendship has provided an important background to the writing of this book. Sean Lennox and Kevin Smith have, in different ways, taught me more than they can know – both by the friendship they have given me, and by the example of their courage. David Mann, a loyal friend for many years who will not even remember the chance remark that unlocked so many doors for me. Paul and Beverley Slater, for a friendship begun at a time of great vulnerability. Stephen Radley, for the great loyalty, kindness and thoughtful wisdom he showed me when the storms broke. Andrew Norwood, for the friendship and common sense that sorted out my house and study and got me to the point when finishing this book again seemed possible. I am aware too of a deep debt to friends, recognized and unrecognized, who have supported me in prayer.

The strangest part of writing this book has been the many moments when I have sensed the presence of God in the task. This is not to blame God for the many weaknesses that undoubtedly are to be found in the book, or to try to rescue its arguments and exegesis from careful and critical examination. Weaknesses and errors there will be, and they are my own. But to mention the presence of God is simply to testify to the strange friendship which the book itself struggles to articulate.

How to read this book

The aim of this book is to provide people with a map with which to make sense of the complex subject of homosexuality and how it relates to Christian faith. My hope is that it will give people a new set of perspectives through which to think about the subject, rather than to set out a precise programme for action. Because it takes a different approach at a number of points to those conventional in either 'conservative' or 'liberal' discussions of the subject readers may find it difficult to classify its position – I hope they will be patient and engage with what I have to say! Chapter 1 is intended to help different readers find their feet in the subject and in the perspectives from which the subject is approached. The book then falls into three parts:

Part 1 looks at sexuality, nature and culture, and at what is involved in making judgments in these areas

Part 2 discusses what homosexuality – mainly male homo-sexuality – really is and what the Bible has to say about it

Part 3 explores some life issues in the light of the positions developed in Parts 1 and 2.

For reasons discussed in chapter 1, the book can be seen as a continued attempt to hear and understand the Bible. Although the reader will not want to check every reference, scriptural passages are rarely set out in full and you will need to have a version of the Bible to hand.

My aim in writing has been to help both those who come to the subject fairly fresh and also people who are reasonably familiar with the complex arguments that the subject has gathered to itself. Because it is a map, it is always in dialogue with other much larger discussions and often there has only been space to give an outline of an argument or a wider debate. The extensive footnotes do not contain any of the argument of the book; they are intended to enable a reader to check the accuracy of my assertions and follow up in greater depth an argument or area that may interest them.

Introduction

Chapter 1

Starting Points

Burning questions are also complex ones. We
should have respect for the complexity of things,
listen, weigh them.

Pope Paul VI

The word of God is living and active, sharper than
any two-edged sword.

Hebrews 4:12

Mention the subject of homosexuality and feel the temperature
rise. In the most amicable of conversations there will be tension
as the topic resonates at many levels.

Some will be scandalized and feel that even discussion is a
step towards subverting the cultural and moral order. Others
will be irritated that 'they' are intruding once again. 'I do not
mind what they do in private so long as they don't rub my nose
in it.' Then there will be a quiet ambivalence amongst those who
know that a relative or friend is gay or who remember same sex
sexual incidents in their own lives. Openly gay people may still
be bruised by the hostility that they feared or faced when they
came out. They may still be haunted by the self-hate which they
absorbed during anguished earlier years. Those with a secret
gay aspect to their lives will know that, wrongly handled, this
is a topic which could expose them to explosive consequences
that may threaten both friendships and employment.

Christian believers are likely to sense yet further resonances.
They may recall powerful 'myths' from the Christian tradition
in which homosexuality is a sign of a culture's degradation or a

potent symbol of the rebellion that provokes God's judgment. They will be aware of condemnations of homosexuality in the scriptures and may fear that acceptance of gay people will move the church from a clear trust in the authority of the Bible. They may be affected by influential concepts which shape contemporary Christianity, and with which loyalty to the Gospel is often identified, such as the family, freedom or compassion. They are likely to be puzzled or offended by the strident protests of sections of the gay community or by evidence of a defiant, even extravagant, promiscuity on the part of some gay people.

Much of the heat generated by the topic of homosexuality arises because of its ability to threaten the symbolic ordering of human life. In classical Christian thought, sexual acts between people of the same sex are on a par with masturbation, itself traditionally seen as a serious moral fault. In the broad consensus of modern Christian thought, such acts are on a par with premarital sex or casual fornication. But neither masturbation nor non-marital sex has the power to generate the outrage or anxiety created by the public revelation of homosexuality.

In an earlier study, *Evangelical Christians and Gay Rights*,[1] I carefully avoided any discussion of the moral question of the status of sexual acts between people of the same sex. My reasons were twofold.

Firstly, in the highly polarized atmosphere of contemporary debate, many people might treat the booklet as a busy reader treats a boring thriller: turn to the end, identify the murderer, and then continue life as before. Judging people by their answer to this keeps the reader on safe territory. It distances them from what they read. They are protected from facing questions that the controversial nature of homosexuality may raise about their own life or stance. If the scandalous quality of homosexuality arises not from its moral character but from its symbolic power, then the non-gay reader is as much in the dock as the gay person whose lifestyle is under discussion. The potency of the feelings that surround homosexuality reveals that the symbolic systems of non-gay society are under challenge. Neat moral answers supplied too soon subvert genuine moral reflection.

Secondly, the moral status of same sex sexual acts is only one of a series of moral questions which homosexuality throws up. For church and society it cannot be separated from other questions such as: What respect is to be given to individual conscience in sexual matters? When, if at all, is the criminal law an appropriate instrument in regulating sexual behaviour? How much sexual abstinence can society ask of people in a fallen world? How are moral or religious dissenters to be treated in society? How is violence against gay people to be discouraged? Should gay people be disadvantaged when it comes to housing or employment?

For gay people the morality of same sex sexual acts stands alongside other questions: With whom do I make friends? How can I express my love? Where can I find human touch? What makes physical contact sexual? Are isolation and masturbation the best that God plans for me? How important to God is genital behaviour? What responsibilities do I have to gay partners, friends or to the gay community at large? How should I plan my middle years? To whom do I leave my house or money? What do I tell my employer/family/church/friends? How do I share the good things that have come to me through being gay?

This book aims to help the reader make sense of the cultural significance and symbolic potency of homosexuality, as well as to throw some light on the range of moral issues that it raises. An attempt to write from a Christian perspective properly focuses on two further areas. The first is the issue of where God is in this debate. Whose side is he on? What is he saying? What is he offering? What does he require? The second area is the impact of the scriptures. To whom do they belong? Have they more to contribute than a handful of condemnatory proof texts? On whom do they cast their light, and to what effect?

The homosexual debate today

Any discussion of homosexuality takes place in a particular context. On both sides of the Atlantic homosexuality is more than an armchair topic. In his appeal to 'family values' George Bush sought to harness anti-gay feeling in his unsuccessful attempt to keep the Presidency. During the run-up to the 1987 General Election in Great Britain, a sustained campaign in the pro-Conservative tabloid press denounced the opposition for its alleged support of gay groups and causes.[2] The

furore that surrounded Mrs Thatcher's Government adoption
of Section 28 of the Local Government Act 1988 illustrated the
symbolic significance of homosexuality within British culture.[3]
The section reads:

A local authority shall not
a) intentionally promote homosexuality or publish material
   with the intention of promoting homosexuality:
b) promote the teaching in any maintained school of the
   acceptability of homosexuality as a pretended family relationship:

The strict legal effect of this is very limited.[4] Its real impact
has been in intimidating local authorities, depriving gay groups
of public space or support, and suppressing the presentation
of a gay perspective in schools. In the marginal constituency
of Ipswich, which had a small Conservative majority, the Act
was used to prevent a lesbian poet appearing at a poetry
reading sponsored by the Council.[5] Devon County Council
cut £10,000 from the Exeter Arts Centre after they staged
a play about AIDS: this was part of a series of actions that put
the survival of the respected theatre company Gay Sweatshop
in doubt.[6] The North Yorkshire library service removed, on legal
advice, various items from an exhibition, such as an article from
the *New Internationalist* on coming out.[7] Robert Nicholson, a
Quaker heterosexual teacher in Birmingham, was dismissed
with significant loss of pension rights for a lesson that used
the Kinsey Report and his experience as a Samaritan counsellor
to illustrate the spectrum of sexual orientation.[8] Such events,
of course, create a climate that inhibits the presentation of
gay perspectives. However, the most significant result of the
passing of Section 28 was the strengthening of gay activism in
the United Kingdom.

Many of the major Christian traditions in the West are in
turmoil about homosexuality. The Roman Catholic Church,
the Presbyterian Church (USA), and the Church of England
are among those who have published major documents and
experience continued controversy. In the Church of England
the 1987 General Synod debate, which was initiated by Tony
Higton and coincided with the pro-Tory tabloid campaign against

gay people, established an atmosphere of fear which still prevails.

The practical focus of these church debates tends to be whether gay people who are in visible and stable relationships should be accepted in the ordained ministry. Through this medium three issues are in fact being discussed: Are openly gay people welcome in the church? Are 'practising' gays acceptable to God? Do the churches, as guardians of the Western cultural and religious tradition, stand by their portrayal of homosexuality as the symbol of rebellion against God and the godly social order?

These controversies in political and church life have led naturally to highly polarized stances on homosexuality. The concern of those who oppose the acceptance of an openly gay social identity may be crystallized as a defence of *integrity*: the integrity of a national ethos or a family ideal, of a Christian culture or the Christian message.

At the other pole the crucial concern is *survival*. Bishop William Swing of California has said, 'We have a homosexual ghetto as a monument to families all over the USA who cannot deal with their homosexual children.' Gay people differ from other cultural minorities in that they start out on their journey alone. 'It takes two straights to make a gay.' In a society which has no positive or overt understanding of same sex sexual attraction, the journey starts in unnamed darkness and involves considerable pain.

Finding the space for self-exploration, never mind acceptance, involves emotionally isolated young people in one of two drastic strategies. The first is the construction of a divided personal identity: I conform to an expected stereotype and secretly establish an alternative being. The second is a more open self-revelation which often precipitates expulsion from the family, rejection by 'normal' society, and violence. Individuals may have little choice in deciding which strategy to follow, and may find themselves propelled from one strategy to the other.

Before a person with homosexual tendencies can think through the issues that homosexuality raises, they have usually had to formulate a strategy for survival. This involves the discovery or creation of *social space* in which to be themselves and the search for a *name*.[9] Both, of course, prove controversial and often continue to be contested by the society in which they live.

Whatever distortions this process may give rise to, it is the precondition for serious thought about homosexuality. 'The one who first states a case seems right, until the other comes and cross-examines' (Proverbs 18:17). Without visibility and social space neither true understanding nor the wise and godly way to live can emerge. In the Western secular tradition, social space for such a quest is created partly through the language and complex philosophical tradition of human rights.

In the churches, establishing the conditions for such a search for wisdom has always proved more problematic. The difficulties are partly theological: the absence of a compelling apologetic for open debate, and an over-eager identification of present understanding with God's truth. They are also sociological: Christians, battling to hold their own in an uncomprehending society, value the received truth of the community above the disturbing insight of the person on the edge. Clergy see their role as guarding the flock rather than discerning the truth, and tend to hold the monopoly on the resources for, and terms of, theological discussion.

In the 1987 debates in the Church of England, Tony Higton argued for the removal from office not only of 'practising' gays but of any ordained person who declined to support his view of the morality of same sex genital contact.[10] The suppressed 1990 'Osborne Report' to the Church of England House of Bishops made few recommendations beyond advocating that the Bishops adopt a clear and pastorally informed policy. It was controversial because it gave space to the articulation of gay perspectives.

In 1992 the Anglican publishers, SPCK, decided, after consulting the Archbishop of Canterbury, not to publish a collection of prayers by and for gay and lesbian people which they had earlier commissioned.[11] The text was controversial because it was more than a book about homosexuality; it gave voice to gay people. To publish the prayers of gay and lesbian people is to admit that God may be with them, that they may have something to teach the rest of the church on the subject of homosexuality.

While social space for gay people in the church remains so

heavily contested, the barrenness of much theological reflection on homosexuality within the Christian church is hardly surprising. However, the impact of Christianity remains an important strand within broader cultural and political exploration of homosexuality. This wider process itself follows two significantly different paths.

The first has been the search for social space and for a name. Within the mythology of the gay movement itself riots in New York City at the end of June 1969, following a police raid on the Stonewall Inn, marked the emergence of a new, unapologetic gay identity and a different model of self-understanding for many gay people.[12] They ceased to look for public acceptance on the basis of a particular psychological or medical condition – a model associated with the term 'homosexual' and dominant since *c.*1860. Instead they adopted a social identity as an oppressed cultural minority. Faced with a society in which personal meaning and identity are increasingly associated with sexual feelings and relationships, they borrowed the same social idiom as a way of asserting their right to dignity within the community.

Readers with little direct contact with gay people can easily be misled by the public image of the gay movement. The first thing to grasp is that it is a complex and diverse world, consisting of many self-generating subcultures; it is not a single monolithic 'conspiracy'. Major disagreements in cultural stance, moral or religious judgments, or political approach tend to be obscured by a tendency of both gay and straight worlds to treat the gay world as one. The second is to realize that the lives of gay people are more ordinary, and less preoccupied with sex, than the images projected by the media, either straight or gay. It would be equally unwise to identify Western society with its TV adverts.

Non-gay readers may need to face their fears of embarrassment or contamination and take some steps to understand the lives of gay people from within. One such step would be personally to buy and read a responsible paper like the *Gay Times* for a year. Christians will need to be aware that gay experience within the churches is often heavily muted or distorted; a range of non-Christian gay friends will generally provide a more balanced picture.

The second path that contemporary exploration of homosexuality has taken is a critical re-examination both of homosexuality and of the culture that reacts to it. The literature here is vast and rapidly expanding. Even such a judicious and wide-ranging study as Peter Coleman's *Gay Christians* (SCM 1989) hardly touches on the issues raised by this developing discussion. My own understanding of this aspect took a quantum leap in 1987, through the somewhat daunting experience of attending a conference entitled 'Homosexuality, Which Homosexuality?' held at the Free University of Amsterdam and attended by about 500 people.[13]

Among the questions raised in this discussion is whether homosexuality is a transcultural psychological condition – the essentialist view – or a series of diverse, historically conditioned stances more akin to ethnic or national character – the constructionist view. If the former is correct, social and moral questions will concentrate on how individuals are to adjust to their condition. If the latter perception is valid, then homosexualities need to be understood as part of an ongoing discourse within society: gay people are not so much sick or immoral individuals as significant players in a society's search for wisdom.

There is an inevitable tension between the two paths that contemporary exploration of homosexuality has taken.[14] The costly struggle for social space represented by the gay movement has needed to identify a single core gay identity. The constructionist reappraisal of questions of sexual identity has tended to undermine this assertion. The interaction between the two paths is complex and developing.

The Christian faith is unlikely again to control public understanding of homosexuality; Christians, both straight and gay, will need to learn to navigate in uncharted waters.

Locating the writer

This book is inevitably shaped by the history and location of its writer. A reader may be helped by knowing some of the perspectives that I bring to its writing.

1 Jewish

My mother was a German Jew who lost her parents and two of her four sisters at Auschwitz. Although I warm to much of the beauty and goodness in the culture that the Christian faith has created in the West, I cannot forget that the same faith was used to fuel a murderous hostility to a non-conforming people. Central themes of the faith, such as the Cross and baptism, were taken up by the culture, subtly distorted, and turned into weapons against God's own people. The Church, like the society it sponsored, became a society for Gentiles only. Even amongst educated and sophisticated people a lingering cultural memory permitted collusion with unbelievable barbarism. The Holocaust remains an important unveiling of something deeply present in the enlightened, and partly Christian, culture of the West.

A Jewish background has affected me in many ways. It has given me a sense of the richness and development of tradition – both Jewish and Christian – as well as a love for the scriptures. It has given me the experience of belonging to a people for whom conventional expressions of the Christian faith have been, at the very least, dangerous. It has programmed me to ask how life is experienced on the edges of the world that the church, or a society claiming to be Christian, sees as its own.

There are close parallels between the experience of Jews and gay people in Western society. At least since the fifth century moments of danger for Jews have also been times of active hostility towards gay people.[15] Christians cannot dissociate themselves too quickly from the fact that both Jews and gay people found a common fate in the Nazi concentration camps.[16]

A historic pattern was repeated when, in the same week in March 1992, the Archbishop of Canterbury declined the patronage of one of the Church of England's oldest societies, the Church's Ministry among the Jews, and successfully opposed the publication of a prayer book for lesbian and gay people.

2 Evangelical

Particularly in North America, the word 'evangelical' is often used to refer to a style of Christianity which has fused together a strand of the Christian faith with uncritical nationalism, a narrow, somewhat self-righteous morality, and a literary and philosophical naivety. To me this is a sad caricature of an important movement in Christianity which I have often experienced as something altogether richer and more attractive. Its characteristics include a cultural adaptability, an active concern that others should come to a confident personal faith in Jesus Christ, and a vision of mature and well-instructed lay discipleship.[17]

Evangelicalism, as I see it, finds its roots in some important theological emphases: the recognition that the human race is caught up in a profound and destructive rebellion against God; the active and unmerited grace of God working in the world for humanity's salvation; the tender identification of Jesus, as God incarnate, with human vulnerability and sin – both in his very human life and in his awesome and lonely death; the creative and untamed activity of the Holy Spirit of God, both in the world and in believers, imparting truth, faith and goodness; and a lively expectation that God speaks through the Bible.

An evangelical approach to the scriptures will influence this book in many ways and deserves some expansion. To many readers, including Christian readers, it will appear quaint, obsessive or casuistical. Obviously, I hope that some will discover a more positive assessment of this approach as they read on. However, even for those for whom it remains pre-modern, sick or bizarre, the experience may retain some value. For better or worse the evangelical form of Christianity is very influential today; it is also one of the most hostile cultural forces experienced by gay people in the West. An attempt from within this tradition to re-examine the validity of this hostility may therefore have some interest even to those who do not share its presuppositions.

Evangelical Christians characteristically speak of the Bible as infallible and authoritative. I accept both these descriptions but do not think that they communicate very accurately the heart of the evangelical attitude to the scriptures. The Bible, of course, consists of sixty-six extremely heterogeneous, strange and often difficult books. As an exercise in divine communication God's use of scripture is almost as bizarre as his taking flesh at a particular moment in history, or his entrusting a saving message to a corrupt and fallible church. At the same time there is something liberating in his choosing to provide the normative instrument and record of his communication in this form rather than as doctrinal statement or legal and moral code.

There is, in an important sense, no definitive external guide to the scriptures. There are great truths which emerge from its pages. There is a mysterious and captivating person who steps out to meet the listening community or individual. There is an impressive consensus as to its meaning at many points. There are twenty centuries worth of illuminating commentary and reflection. But there remains in a certain sense no centre; there is no right place to start, no definitive key to this book. It is, as the writer to the Hebrews says, a two-edged sword in the hand of God himself. It cuts both ways. There is no defining fulcrum outside scripture which gives one person the right to wield this mystery against another. In the current controversies, few things do more disservice to the evangelical respect for scripture than its use as a source of proof texts to hammer others into submission. We may argue and fight but we have to leave space for God to speak to his own (cf Romans 14:4).

It may be helpful to articulate certain characteristics of my approach to scripture. I am intensely interested in the flow, literary form and background culture of the scriptures. I am more sceptical about many orthodoxies of scholarship than about scripture itself; at some points, but not others, this makes me conservative on questions of date or authorship. St Paul, I think, wrote the Pastoral Epistles; quite possibly St John wrote John. At the same time I think modern evangelicalism often has the Bible wrong – not least in its contempt for ritual and in its easy acceptance of amoral economics. In the area of sexuality, evangelicalism suffers some serious delusions – both in what it thinks the Bible says and in its confidence that its own views are those held by the historic Christian tradition. The situation is more intricate than popular presentations tend to reveal: evangelicalism is both nearer to scripture than Aquinas or Augustine and further away.

Although he is not well known outside evangelical circles, my most revered, modern biblical commentator remains the conservative Old Testament scholar, Derek Kidner. He brings to the particular text of scripture an exact and theological mind and a beauty of literary precision. Only Kidner could comment on the mysterious figure of Shabbethai the Levite (Ezra 10:15, RSV) and the three others who questioned Ezra's drastic action against mixed marriages, 'the harshness of the remedy and the lack of any obvious legal requirement of it could have stirred the same misgivings in them as in a modern reader'.[18] Such humane precision serves as one model in my attempt to rethink an evangelical approach to homosexuality. Evangelicalism, like any movement, includes its own disagreements.

Two stances, which some would associate with my Anglicanism, will affect the approach of this book at various points.

The first is the conviction that God also makes his way known outside the church in the human quest for truth. Christians have no monopoly on truth. 'Wisdom cries out in the street; in the squares she raises her voice' (Proverbs 1:20). What is known as the wisdom tradition in scripture is evidence of the respect in which the ancient quest for wisdom was held. It was a quest in which Israel was happy to share and to which she made a striking contribution. This involved engaging with a community of learning, a developing intellectual tradition and an inductive approach to human knowledge. Jesus himself adopts many of the idioms and approaches of a teacher in this tradition. It can be no coincidence that when the first Christians called themselves 'the Way' they adopted a term from this tradition (cf. Acts 9:2; 9:23; 22:4).

The second conviction affirms the place of the church in God's ongoing purpose of salvation. In St Paul's words it is God's purpose 'that through the church the wisdom of God in its rich variety might now be made known to the rulers and authorities in the heavenly places' (Ephesians 3:10). The church is more than upright evangelicals – it is a diverse people, identified by faith in Christ and baptism. This conviction finds an outworking in an enjoyment of diversity, a concern for unity and integrity, and in an expectation that Christians of different times and places have much to teach. It matters what Aquinas thought although he may be wrong; it matters what gay believers experience, and they may be right.

3 An English male
The poems of A.E. Housman at one time played an important part in my life. His first collection *A Shropshire Lad* was

published in 1895 and was carried by many a young Englishman as he went to die in the trenches of the First World War. His poems articulate an affection for the English countryside and also the various emotions of young men called to war. The so-called Great War exposed the bankruptcy of confident, Christian, Victorian society; it set in process the very mood of modernity among ordinary people in Britain. The war also saw in the young men going to slaughter a great flowering of passionate male friendship. In Martin Taylor's collection *Lads: Love Poetry of the Trenches*[19] it is impossible to tell from the poems themselves which young men were gay and which were straight. The tone of intense feeling mixed with a certain reserve was the same; the poetic idiom owed much to Housman.[20]

Housman himself was gay and his life was blighted by an unrequited love for a university friend.[21]

> He would not stay for me; and who can wonder?
> He would not stay for me to stand and gaze.
> I shook his hand and tore my heart in sunder
> And went with half my life about my ways.

Housman understood well what stood in store in his day for this form of same sex love:

> Shot? so quick, so clean an ending?
>   Oh that was right, lad, that was brave:
> Yours was not an ill for mending,
>   'Twas best to take it to the grave.

His response to the trials and imprisonment of Oscar Wilde in 1895 is worth setting out in full.

> Oh who is that young sinner with the handcuffs on his wrists?
> And what has he been after that they groan and shake
>   their fists?
> And wherefore is he wearing such a conscience-stricken air?
> Oh they're taking him to prison for the colour of his hair.
>
> 'Tis a shame to human nature, such a head of hair as his;
> In the good old time 'twas hanging for the colour that it is;

Though hanging isn't bad enough and flaying would be fair
For the nameless and abominable colour of his hair.

Oh a deal of pains he's taken and a pretty price he's paid
To hide his poll or dye it of a mentionable shade;
But they've pulled the beggar's hat off for the world to see
    and stare,
And they're haling him to justice for the colour of his hair.

Now 'tis oakum for his fingers and the treadmill for his feet
And the quarry-gang on Portland in the cold and in the heat,
And between his spells of labour in the time he has to spare
He can curse the God that made him for the colour of his hair.

I have not found Housman a satisfactory resting place in understanding homosexuality, although echoes of his world may still persist in my thinking. His poems cast a revealing light on a moment of historical transition. They show that Western homosexuality takes its place within a long cultural tradition of male friendship. With a certain austerity they face us with the consequences of how one form of male love has traditionally been interpreted.

For me, as for many people, other perspectives have emerged. New ways of perceiving or expressing personhood and love have been discovered. The First World War has changed the way in which women participate in the culture. Germaine Greer's acid comment that 'English culture is basically homosexual in the sense that men only really care about other men'[22] is becoming progressively less true. A new dialogue with the feminine challenges both secular and Christian thought. The feminist movement has precipitated a new exploration of masculinity[23] and has influenced the way both female and male homosexualities understand themselves[24].

Many factors, including the different location of lesbian and gay people within the culture, make it dangerous to extrapolate from gay to lesbian issues. This book includes some markers on how its argument affects lesbians. I hope they will forgive the real weakness that remains. To go further would for me have been the 'bridge too far'.

Where is God?

'He can curse the God that made him for the colour of his hair.'
The question of where God is in current controversy about
homosexuality remains a crucial one. In the New Testament,
Jesus is portrayed as the 'friend of sinners' (Luke 7:34). This
meant not that he had a remote concern to make people moral,
but that he enjoyed the company of those beyond the pale of the
moral law or the standards of righteous society. His behaviour
scandalized the religious people of his day (Luke 15:2)

It is hard not to feel sorry for the Pharisees, and modern
scholarship has gone a long way towards rehabilitating them.
They were not the old, compromised religious establishment.
They devoted great energy to understanding, doing and defend-
ing the will of God. They were zealous in spreading the word of
God as they saw it (Matthew 23:15). They were confident that
they understood God's righteousness and saw themselves as
the true heirs of Israel's religious heritage. They were careful
to keep their distance from all taint or compromise.

With Jesus it seemed they could not win. When they were
morally strict, Jesus dismissed their righteousness as scrupulous
and self-interested; when they were lenient, as on divorce,
he exposed their casuistry as a neglect of God's will. Their
confrontations with Jesus drove them into an alliance with the
sceptical national establishment they despised. What appeared
at first to be a well-worked out and scriptural stand of faith,
a commendable righteousness (Matthew 5:20), was gradually
exposed as shallow worldliness (Luke 16:14).

The disconcerting fact was that God was doing something
new and had chosen to start elsewhere. Jesus found a congenial
welcome among those whom the righteous despised. The new
order that this strange friendship created was not the restoration
of the old moral and social order for which the religious hoped.
In many ways it led to the collapse of the structure of life as
they knew it. Jesus's friends were, of course, changed by their
friendship; but the new world that emerged owed much to what
they brought to it.

In 1991 I wrote, 'Would the Jesus of the Gospels have had gay
friends and have been at home in a gay bar? The answer must be
Yes.'[25] An evangelical leader, whom I respect, denounced the

Daily Mail

remark to the press as blasphemous.[26] But God is not a moral
policeman; he is a strange and unpredictable player in human
history. Any discussion of homosexuality must leave room for
the possibility that Jesus is making significant friends beyond
the pale of 'righteous' society.

Moreover friendship has its own logic. To make a friend
you take a risk and move within the other's world. Thomas
O'Neil's poem 'Jesus is seen at a gay bar' may not be far from
the mark.[27]

> I caught
> sight of Him that night,
> looking sexy in His sackcloth
> and ridiculous in a Groucho Marx disguise,
> there in the corner behind the *David* statue,
> listening intently to the angel-faced
> tramp who knows how to dish with the best of 'em.
> Too bad Madonna
> was belting out 'Papa Don't Preach'
> so damned
> loud we couldn't overhear them.
> The tramp actually looked like he was
> putting the moves on the Almighty One,
> but Jesus just played it cool
> while he chatted over His glass of Perrier
> later seen, magically,
> to be filled with an amusing
> off-year Medoc.
>
> 'What the hell
> does He want from us?'
> some queen
> snarled that night over his pinot noir.
> 'Christ, we're not exactly the choirboys
> of the Holy Seraphim having their Christmas party.
> And, by the way, Jesus, we got St Paul's letter,
> again, just the other day: addressed
> to the insolent slanderers who exchange
> the Truth of God for a lie,
> deserve death,

and must forfeit the Kingdom.
There was no return address.'

But it was a night to remember,
Jesus joined us in a few choruses
of 'Over the Rainbow' around the jukebox
and disappeared before Last Call.
He left His keys on the bar.

Part 1

Thinking Straight

Chapter 2

Sexuality and Social Order

If two lie together they are warm; but how can one
be warm alone?

Ecclesiastes 4:11

Jesus said to them, 'Those who belong to
this age marry and are given in marriage; but
those who are considered worthy of a place
in that age neither marry nor are given in
marriage.'

Luke 20:34,35

What you see depends in part on where you are standing and on
what you expect to see. When people think about homosexuality
or read the Bible they often bring to these activities strongly-
held presuppositions. The familiar term 'presupposition' has
been criticized by contemporary scholars for its implication that
people's pre-understanding necessarily involves 'rooted beliefs
and doctrines . . . which can only be changed and revised with
pain, or at least with difficulty'.[1] While this implication is true
for some aspects of people's thinking about sexuality, in other
respects the ways in which a person's perspective limits their
ability to hear the scripture may be more innocent and more
open to change. Anthony Thiselton follows the philosopher
Hans-Georg Gadamer in preferring the term 'horizon': horizon
may not imply settled conviction; horizons change as people
move; horizons are changed as new worlds come into view.
One of the more bewildering features of listening to scripture
on subjects like sexuality is the discovery that its authors use

very different categories from those that modern Westerners take for granted.

Consider two questions. Is it natural for men to sleep together? Do gay people need healing? The answer 'No' to the first and 'Yes' to the second will seem obvious to many people and will affect both the way they see the world and the way they read the scriptures. The reality is somewhat more complex and culturally conditioned. Take each question in turn.

A pioneer missionary working in Indonesia writes, 'I . . . collapsed into an enormous bed, rolling right over against the wall to leave room for Rufus and Mawardi.'[2] Despite its frequent use in wedding sermons the text from Ecclesiastes 4, quoted at the start of this chapter, does not refer to a married couple but to two people of the same sex.[3] The same is true of Jesus's warning, 'I tell you, there will be two in one bed; one will be taken and the other left' (Luke 17:34); the translators of the Authorised Version thought it natural to render this 'two men in one bed'. Outside modern Western culture people of the same sex have often shared beds. For example, in the sixteenth and seventeenth centuries unmarried and even married men often shared a bed with their servants. In Shakespeare's *Othello* Iago speaks of Cassio caressing him in his sleep while dreaming of Desdemona.[4] 'Sleeping together' need not have the connotations that it usually does today.

The assertion that gay people need healing also carries with it strong cultural conditioning. Three particular ideas that underlie such a statement are worth identifying. First, there is the view that 'heterosexuality' is the healthy norm to which human beings should conform. This contrasts with Romans 1:24 which clearly indicates that all human desire is profoundly disordered: 'dishonouring of their bodies' refers to activity between men and women. Secondly, the notion of healing points to an assumption that homosexuality is a medical condition that inheres in the person. In this it draws on a reconceptualizing of homosexuality in the mid-nineteenth century. Thirdly, the statement appeals to a 'medical' model of salvation and gains some of its power from the fact that modern people perceive the medical approach to life as more humane than the legal or economic.

The aim of these three chapters is to look again at some

of the background ideas that people bring to their thinking on homosexuality. This will involve examining traditional and modern understandings of such concepts as sexuality, nature, family, and the meaning and purpose of sexual acts. It will also mean looking at the place of desire and law in God's dealings with fallen and broken humanity.

Sexuality

Sexuality is not a term used in the Bible; it is an overarching interpretive concept that has arisen in modern culture and serves to organize human experience in a particular way. '"Sexuality" is an historical construction which brings together a host of different biological and mental possibilities – gender identity, bodily differences, reproductive capacities, needs, desires and fantasies – which need not be linked together, and in other cultures have not been.'[5]

The point is not merely that a number of different activities or dimensions of human life are bracketed together. It is that the way they are linked itself creates a framework through which life is understood and organized. People think and live using language and social structures which have already been shaped by others; the power exercised by a single individual is limited. Understanding and organization are social activities; they constrain the individual and are subject to control by powerful groups or forces in society.

One influential thinker in analysing the notion of sexuality has been Michel Foucault who asserts that sexuality does not exist as an objective entity; it is a created concept that is deployed in the relationship of people in society.

> Sexuality must not be thought of as a kind of natural given which power tries to check, or as an obscure domain which knowledge tries gradually to uncover. It is the name that can be given to a historical construct.[6]

The concept of sexuality includes a number of separable elements: interaction between men and men, women and women, and men and women, and the way these interactions are conceptualized: the body and various bodily activities and the way these are conceptualized; various forms of social organization and the way they are conceptualized; and the way in which human identity and personhood are themselves conceived.

One result of bringing these elements together under the inclusive concept of sexuality is that aspects of human life, which other cultures have seen in a different way, are drawn into the focus or arena of the sexual. For example many pre-industrial cultures have given extensive recognition to strong passionate attachments between men without perceiving them as sexual. One reason for this is that many cultures have not perceived certain bodily or genital acts as the symbolically focal points of a sexual project in the way that we do. Obvious examples are kissing and dancing which the West usually perceives a part of the human project we call 'sexual' but which belong in many cultures to other perceptual spheres altogether.

Even genital acts are not always seen as part of the sexual project. It may be helpful to give some examples. Havelock Ellis, an influential writer on sexual psychology, cites the following case:

> A married lady who is a leader in social purity movements and an enthusiast for sexual chastity, discovered through reading some pamphlets against solitary vice, that she had been practising masturbation for years without knowing it. The profound anguish and hopeless despair of this woman in the face of what she believed to be the moral ruin of her whole life cannot well be described.[7]

Again, Ingrid Foeken gives an example from West Africa in 1976 where a woman saw activity which we would describe as lesbian sexual contact as uncontroversial friendly comfort.[8] In the sixteenth century there is substantial evidence that men engaged in sexual activity without giving it a name or seeing it as sodomy.[9] At a less striking level, genital contact by or between adolescents is frequently perceived as less than fully sexual. Even in our culture many adult men have sex with other men without seeing themselves as gay or their acts as truly 'sexual'.

One factor that shapes this different assessment of some genital acts is that pre-modern culture has generally associated the sexual with the demanding human project of procreation. The effect of this is to emphasize male emission of semen and female fertility. In Christian circles this led to the classic understanding of the Christian tradition that the essence of the sexual act was the transmission of seed. On this basis Aquinas classified masturbation, contraception, homosexual acts and bestiality as equally 'sins against nature'. This classic Christian tradition will be examined in more detail in the next chapter but it is important to note here that the comparatively recent Christian acceptance of contraception was extremely controversial and has precipitated a major shift in the way in which sexual activity is perceived. Among the changes have been a more positive attitude to sexual pleasure, a rediscovery of feminine sexuality, a shift in the social role of the family, and a significant widening of the domain that we classify as sexual.

Christians in contemporary society may wish to unpick the whole package implied by modern concepts of sexuality. They may wish to take a stand against particular aspects of behaviour or social organization. However, they are not in a position to step out of their culture altogether. In the main they have little choice but to live with human experience understood and organized through the concept of sexuality.

The family and the city

Sexuality sounds dangerous; family feels safe. Understanding the interplay between them involves looking at the meaning of family in ancient cultures and in modern society.

The Ten Commandments are commonly viewed as the foundation principles of the biblical law codes. They do not actually seek to regulate sexual or bodily acts in their own right. The seventh commandment, 'You shall not commit adultery' (Exodus 20:14) treats sexual behaviour in the context of regulating social relationships within society.

At first sight the commandment may seem to endorse popular Christian assumptions about the underlying basis of sexual morality. However, further exploration rapidly leads the enquirer into very unfamiliar territory. The commandment does not rest on a belief in lifelong monogamous marriage recognized by the state or a conviction that this is the only appropriate context for sexual relations. It does not forbid a man having sex with an unmarried woman. It does not preclude polygamy or also having a female slave as a concubine. The same law codes provide that if a single slave marries and leaves his master's service he must leave his wife and children behind (Exodus 24:4,5). While modern thought treats consent as the basis of marriage, the biblical law codes state that, if a man rapes an unbetrothed woman, he has to marry her with no possibility of divorce (Deuteronomy 22:28,29).

The primary concern of this network of laws is the maintenance and continuity of the clan, itself a web of related households that includes slaves and relatives. Adultery is singled out because it endangers the continuity of the patriarchal line and destroys or confuses relationships within the household and clan. The retaining of a slave's wife within the household makes clear that the household is set above any relationship created by sexual intercourse. The raped woman is at least protected from the isolation of not belonging or the shame of not bearing children.

The culture reflected in these laws and in related strands of the Old Testament shows certain characteristics: it pays no explicit attention to the woman's experience or expectation in sexual intercourse; it recognizes and creates space for male need for sexual expression; it focuses its ethical concern on procreation. Its emphasis on continuity reflects both a tribe's concern for survival and also an awareness that God's promise was linked with physical descent in the line of Abraham.

The Bible does not view the semi-nomadic pastoral culture in which these commandments took form as the ideal to which all cultures should conform. One of the major movements implicit in scripture is the move from the clan to the city. This is expressed, for example, in the idealization of Jerusalem in both the Old and New Testaments. The city is seen as the creation of human rebellion, characterized by pride and violence; it is also seen as the place where human capacity for creativity finds its proper realization. In the family structure of a pastoral tribe, familial and civic roles are conflated – not least in the role of the father. With the emergence of the city, roles and relationships become separated and diversified in the more complex world that the city makes possible.

The separation of family from city in urban life changes the way in which social relationships are perceived and regulated. The book of Proverbs reflects a more urban culture. The 'son' in Proverbs (cf. Proverbs 2:1; 3:1; 3:11 etc.) is a young man making his way within the court and civil service of the ruling class.[10] Although there is some continuity with his familial home (cf. Proverbs 5:20) the primary social context of the book is a sort of cross between office, school, university, and public forum. The frequent use of the term 'son' to portray the relationship of learner to mentor indicates that there is a gendered emotional tone to this relationship. In the main, Proverbs is concerned with a male and public world but it gives important glimpses of a complementary realm for the women of similar social standing in its society (cf Proverbs 5:15ff.; 7:4,5; 8; 9:1–6; 31:1–8; 31:10–31). From these passages it is clear that these women were educated, lived in a positive relationship with the male world, and were not necessarily patronized; they operated from a social base which gave great scope for their ability. The little Proverbs has to say about sexual behaviour has a different tone from the semi-nomadic focus on procreation and the purity of the tribal line; it has more to say about play and delight – and about what we would call 'relationship'. Foolish sexual behaviour endangers personal wealth and domestic stability (Proverbs 5;7) rather than the ordering of society around the safe transmission of the male seed.

The picture that Proverbs gives of two complementary gendered social worlds points to a characteristic of most societies, tribal or urban, before the emergence of modern industrial capitalism. It meant that an individual had to negotiate his or her relationship with two social worlds, both gendered. Human sin and unequal power relationships led, of course, to abuse, but between the sexes 'mutual dependence set limits to struggle, exploitation and defeat'.[11] One is reminded of Lord Hailsham's description of marriage as 'a set of interlocking dictatorships' except that this was true not only of marriage but of the whole of social life. In these societies men and women related at a deep emotional level to their own sex as well as the other. At various points an ideal of 'companionate' marriage emerges: examples include Elkanah and Hannah (1 Samuel 1:4–8), the ideal operating amongst sections of the Roman aristocracy,[12] and the emphasis by the Reformers on companionship in marriage. But even when this view of marriage surfaced, it was not seen as the only or even the major gender-toned relationship with which individuals were involved.

When the sixteenth-century Reformers expounded the fifth commandment, 'Honour your father and mother' (Exodus 20:12), they pointed to a person's continuing duty to the wider community as well as to the household. So Luther could write, 'in this commandment he has ordained and provided for the increase and preservation of the human race, that is for the households of home and state . . . upholding and preserving both home and state, commanding obedience to children and subjects.[13] The duty to parents extended beyond childhood and continued in the non-residential extended families that replaced the shared homes of other cultures.[14] This view of the family or household as a microcosm of the city was common to the Hebrew, Greek and Roman cultures from which the Christian faith emerged and in which the church first grew.[15]

The modern perspective

Western people live in a culture that operates on very different assumptions. It is unclear whether these derive from changing philosophical convictions, from the pressure of changing social and economic structures, or from some interaction between the two. Modern industrial society is based on what Ivan Illich has called 'genderless economics'.[16] Much human creative activity has been removed from the home into a public realm ruled by economic considerations and in which individuals are treated as genderless units of labour. The logic of this development was followed in the early days of industrialization when women and children as well as men worked in the factories and the mines. The resultant dehumanization led to a social strategy that has significantly altered the way in which the family is perceived.

Nineteenth-century social reformers, including evangelical

Christians, sought to rescue women and children from the industrial machine. In attempting to restrict the use of women and children as industrial labour, they created a new concept of the family as not so much a microcosm of society as a humane refuge from it.[17] This strategy had an understandable rationale but many unforeseen consequences. It has contributed to a polarized attitude between public and domestic life. Domestic life is seen as the place of religion, emotion, culture and humanity; public life is delivered over to rational, scientific and economic 'reality'. The movement of much creative labour from the home created a diminished sphere for women, an arrangement which the various women's movements of the twentieth century have understandably tried to overthrow. Enoch Powell has spoken of a continuing social experiment within which we may 'gropingly find the bounds of the potentialities of the two sexes'.[18] In this complex process of renegotiation their location in society means that feminist and gay movements have special insights to contribute.

The ideal of masculinity itself has been significantly changed by industrialization and by the attempt to create the humane refuge of the family. This has meant that not only are certain qualities associated with masculinity, but also, what was once seen simply as the male realm increasingly came to be perceived as the norm for humanity. Men came to see themselves as the 'normal' human being. St Paul, as part of the complex argument of 1 Corinthians 11, is keen to assert the complementarity and interaction of the sexes in the social realm (1 Corinthians 11:11,12). 'Headship' here is not about power, but nor is it limited to marriage; male and female discover their reality by interdependent interaction. This interaction belongs to the social sphere, not just to the home. The power relations in capitalist society fall short of this dynamic interplay; man has come to see himself as the norm, with woman as an ancillary supporter. The interaction of men and women as gendered beings is relegated to the domestic realm. One effect of this has been to produce an isolated, frozen and alienated masculinity. Outside the home, men's commitment to a world of 'work' dominated by 'rationality' has shaped and distorted their emotional and imaginative lives. Within the home, in Roy McCloughry's telling phrase, 'The absent father became the distant father'.[19]

This argument finds visible expression in the way in which prosperous men in the West dress. For the city they wear dark and restrained clothes; they dress for other men and their clothes speak of power rather than passion or art. For leisure and the home they dress in a more vivid and creative way; here they are in a more humble exploration of the mystery of their own masculinity and dress for men and women as well as for themselves. It can be no accident that gay men, who are both alert to masculinity and socially vulnerable, have played a significant part in the developing world of male fashion.

The apparent removal of gender from the public realm plays an important part in the shaping of the modern notion of sexuality. As the public realm is deemed (wrongly) to be gender-neutral, gender is relegated to the home, even to the bedroom. The result is that an awareness of gender and the feelings and art linked with it are seen as focused on domestic and personal identity – part of the sexuality package. Sensitivity to male beauty and emotional attraction or tenderness between men are directed to the residual realm in which they can be explored, to the sphere of sexuality – home and bed.

The new 'family' that has emerged since the seventeenth century differs in many ways from the ancient family that the New Testament designates by the word *oikos*, house or household. Its self-rationale rests on biology – sex and blood; servants are replaced by machines. It has created new barriers against the wider community – often even against the non-residential extended family. It has claimed a privileged status as the true place of personal value and intimacy. (The recent exposure of widespread domestic child abuse has raised questions about how healthy this development has been.) It has led to social identity being based on sexual attraction and relationship. Constructed as a place of refuge from the economic market-place, it has become a very effective player within it. Contraception has contributed to further developments in this concept of the family.[20] The ability to limit the number of children has helped to give the family an important new function: a structure to defend the living standard of the small group over against the wider culture.

One result of this recent history has been to create in the minds of many Christians a strong sense that support for

Christianity means support for the family. Some of the impetus for this has come from the part evangelicals played in promoting the family as a refuge from society. It can equally be argued that identifying the church with the modern family undermines the church's capacity for mission and evangelism. The point is not simply that most people do not live in an 'ideal' nuclear family; if people join the church as a refuge they will find it harder to engage with the city from which they are escaping.

The family / church shouldn't be a refuge

The new creation

The strangest feature of the contemporary alliance between evangelical Christians and so-called 'family values' is a lack of awareness that conflict between family and Christian faith has been part of Christianity since the New Testament. Not only did Jesus not marry, he repeatedly made clear that discipleship involved alienation from the family.[21] St Paul is equally insistent that Christian discipleship involves distancing oneself from the claims of family: 'Let those who have wives live as though they had none' (1 Corinthians 7:29).

NT critical of family

This strand in the New Testament was strongly taken up in the early Christian centuries, not least in the monastic movement. It is discounted by many modern Christians. Either they attribute it to a misguided rejection of sexual desire itself or they explain it away as based on a false expectation of Jesus's immediate return. A rejection of sexual desire did undoubtedly become part of the Christian tradition in post-apostolic times. But these dismissals fail to grasp the ambivalence towards the family in Jesus, St Paul or the early church. For them the family was part of the present world order which was characterized by rebellion against God; furthermore it found its hope in the face of death in the birth of children. Jesus's coming represented the arrival of a new order which rested not on marriage, nor on the birth of children, but on God's new creation. The new society that Jesus was creating was one in which membership was based not on marital, ethnic or social status but on adoption into the new humanity forged by Christ himself. In the new society all received the Spirit of God regardless of gender or social standing (cf. Acts 2:17,18; 2 Corinthians 5:16,17; Galatians 3:28). Hope in the face of death lay, not in the birth of a new generation, but in the resurrection.

Withdrawal from the social institutions and responsibilities of marriage and the family was a step into Christian freedom. It allowed people to take on their freedom as God's children rather than continue as slaves within the present transient social order. In the early centuries this was of particular importance for women and for struggling peasants, as well as for those like St Augustine caught up in the demands of imperial society.[22]

New Testament ambivalence towards the social institution of the family arose precisely because the church found itself simultaneously part of the old order and the new. As part of the old order, Christians were called on to respect the structures of society and to live in a way that would commend their way of life to those around them. This explains St Paul's concern for good order in the churches and his attempts to restrain the new-found liberty of women where this could bring the church into disrepute.

This ambivalence brought a complexity to Christian decision-making about the ordering of their communities which can be seen with particular clarity in 1 Corinthians 11:2–16. This passage, with its strange references to hair and veils, seems to be a source of almost universal embarrassment. However, it is precisely because we see the apostle wrestling with the interface of ethics and culture that it remains important; we shall return to it again. Here it is worth noting four strands that he weaves together in his attempt to find a way forward for the church. The four strands may be characterized as new creation, creation, pragmatism and culture.

1 *New creation*. St Paul holds on to the new liberty of Christians in Christ. Women are to prophesy. The new Christian reality may be constrained, but it is not to be denied.

2 *Creation*. He takes seriously the order of creation as manifest in the difference between the sexes, while being careful to honour the dynamic interdependence inherent in this.

3 *Pragmatism*. He makes allowance for the possibility that some exercise of Christian liberty may endanger the good

name or well-being of the church (vs. 10,16). The angels in verse 10 are the guardians of the transient social order – compare Deuteronomy 32:8.

4 *Culture*. St Paul was aware of local cultural options which did not view long hair for men as shameful.[23] His commendation of short hair has to be seen as part of his generally positive assessment of the Roman Empire and his desire to align the infant church towards it.

Two debates

In the light of this overview it may be illuminating to turn briefly to two contemporary debates about the limits and character of sexual relationships that are not immediately related to the question of homosexuality.

1 Polygamy

David Gitari, a distinguished evangelical and leading Anglican bishop in Kenya, has been instrumental in causing a re-examination of the church's stance on polygamy.[24] Prior to his intervention, the Anglican Church in Kenya regarded divorce as a pastoral matter to be treated with compassion and flexibility, and polygamy as a disciplinary matter that crucially affected a person's standing in the church. Bishop Gitari has little difficulty in showing that this difference flows more from cultural sympathy by European missionaries for their own society's form of 'serial polygamy' rather than from any careful reading of scripture. He draws attention to the comparative cruelty of the Western practice of serial polygamy in that all relationship with the first wife is severed. It is probably precisely this possibility which underlay Jesus's opposition to Pharisaic leniency on divorce.

There is certainly a contrast between the number of biblical texts that oppose divorce – a practice widely accepted among Protestant Christians – and the paucity of texts which forbid polygamy. Bishop Gitari has little difficulty in documenting substantial scholarly opinion that 'one flesh' (Genesis 2:24, cf. Mark 10:8 etc.) means essentially one clan or one social unit and does not preclude polygamy.[25] Even 1 Timothy 3:2 and Titus

1:6 ('husband of one wife') are probably more concerned with responsibility than monogamy. They form the basis of the new Canon Law in Kenya which prohibits polygamists from holding office in the church.

The Church of England Report *Issues in Human Sexuality* rests its argument against polygamy mainly on the idea of 'an evolving convergence on the ideal of lifelong, monogamous, heterosexual union'.[26] Bishop Gitari himself remarks, 'the New Testament says nothing definite against it [i.e. polygamy]'.[27] It may be that an argument for monogamy could be developed from the new attitude to women embodied in the Christian dispensation. Without pursuing the matter further it should be clear that a sexual arrangement, which most Western people would probably regard with abhorrence, can find a strong Christian defence when its own social context is properly understood.

2   Adultery and Rape

Professor William Countryman, in an important book, *Dirt, Greed and Sex*,[28] sees one of the concepts round which biblical sexual ethics are organized as the notion of sexual property. So, for example, in the contexts of the Old and New Testament, adultery is wrong because it offends against the rights one person has over another. Professor Countryman argues that the notion of sexual property defends my neighbour against me as well as me against my neighbour. Later, he addresses the question of how these biblical principles are to be applied in our own very different context. Two quotations will give the thrust of one strand of his argument:

> Where, in late antiquity, sexual property belonged to the family through the agency of the male householder, in our era it belongs to the individual (p.241).

> If in antiquity, given the existing concept of family, adultery was the characteristic violation of sexual property, in our own age it has become rape (p.248).

It may be that the metaphor of property puts the underlying issue somewhat too starkly, but one fundamental issue raised by his argument is to what extent should cultural assumptions govern our ethical assessment of behaviour. Probably many readers would share Professor Countryman's strong disapproval of rape and may have felt some embarrassment at the treatment of rape in Deuteronomy 22:28,29 quoted above. However, it cannot be adequate to rest our abhorrence of rape simply on the authority of a particular culture's whim. Nor is it entirely satisfactory to leave unchallenged the radical individualism implicit in his argument at this point. His illuminating analysis leaves unanswered an important question about whether there are intrinsic values present in God's creation which make both rape and radical individualism wrong. At the same time, the fact that we would not contemplate implementing Deuteronomy 22:28,29 as current law, reveals the degree to which we are willing to operate on different cultural assumptions – and to believe that we are right to do so.

Evaluating homosexual behaviour

Clearly there is a case to be made from scripture that sexual behaviour should be assessed in the light of the social structures or relationships in which it is set and to which it contributes. Furthermore, the recovery of gender-toned bonding between men in modern culture, to which the gay movement obviously bears some relationship, can be related to cultural forms well accepted in the biblical texts.

Before further evaluation is possible, some account of the phenomenon of homosexuality needs to be given (see Chapters 5–7) and some evaluation of particular scriptural texts made (see Chapter 8). However, prior to this, three important questions need to be discussed.

1 What does the Christian tradition teach about the significance of the body in sexual behaviour?
2 What is the relationship between cultural norms and the order of creation?
3 What is the status of particular biblical laws or commands in evaluating Christian behaviour?

These will be addressed in the next two chapters.

Chapter 3

Sex and Symbolic Meanings

Does not nature itself teach you that for a man to
wear long hair is degrading to him?

1 Corinthians 11:14

The last chapter explored a strand in scripture which suggests
that sexual behaviour is to be assessed in terms of the social
structures and relationships to which it contributes. This, of
course, is not the usual way we think about sexual matters. Sex
is about bodies and images, about relationships and intimacy,
about pleasure and desire. The idea that the morality of a
sexual act is to be judged by such 'external' criteria as the
social network to which it belongs may, at first sight, seem
fairly strange. Sex, we feel, is not simply about something as
superficial as social arrangements; it is about something deep
that we call nature.

What is this nature? How do we discern its demands upon
us? Many modern people tend to organize their thinking around
two poles of thought. At one pole there is nature which is fixed
and associated with the physical, biological and scientific; for
Christians this tends to be associated with what God has given
in creation. At the other pole there is society which is variable
and linked with a shifting kaleidoscope of social arrangements,
cultures and fashions; for many Christians this is the realm in
which sin is operative, corrupting God's good creation.

The surface structure of contemporary thought assigns sex
to the pole of nature and associates it primarily with physical
pleasure and relationship. Jobs and houses, although important,
belong to the field of market forces or of social policy, depending

on your political predilections. I often attend the weddings of young Christian leaders who choose or write their own prayers; frequently there is no prayer for children. At this point the two realms remain remarkably separate; their closer interaction through the arrival of children, or the possible pain of childlessness, lies in the remote future.

Family is somewhere near the intersection of these two conceptual spheres. Politics is widely perceived as part of the social or artificial world in which individual judgment rightly reigns and which Christians understandably avoid because of the taint of sin and the impossibility of moral certainty. Family is nearer the uncorrupt realm of nature. In its defence Christians may even be called to enter the dangerous, and possibly satanic, realm of political activism. This, of course, is caricature but it helps to explain occasional evangelical campaigns on gay issues. Gay people are a 'natural' assault on family values and seem therefore to be a clear target. The forces which really corrode domestic and public life, in particular unbridled individualism,[1] belong to the more ambivalent realm of social philosophy. The 'natural' family is, in reality, shaped and corroded by the ideas and 'political' choices of society.

The idea of the natural as fixed and the cultural as variable is too simple. Concepts of fixed and natural norms are quickly threatened by any comparison between different societies. The Chinese eat dogs and the French horses; most English people would categorize such behaviour as unnatural. In the realm of sexual practices the same variety quickly appears. Many people in the West view deep kissing, contraception or oral sex as part of the natural repertoire of human sexual behaviour. ('The National Survey of Sexual Attitudes and Lifestyles' indicated an increasing practice through the twentieth century of oro-genital contact between heterosexual partners.[2]) For each of these practices cultures can be found which see the activity as profoundly unnatural. Cultures differ greatly in their attitude to the privacy appropriate to sexual contact; the modern West expects more privacy than many traditional societies have offered. Attitudes to human nakedness and to where nudity is natural also vary widely. Cultural diversity as to what is natural reaches even to the body.

In 1 Corinthians 11:2–16 St Paul is writing about the way

in which men and women present themselves in the Christian assembly. The passage deals with the presentation of the human body through dress and hairstyles. Archaeological evidence shows that Roman society was familiar with men who covered their heads, with respectable women who did not, and with cultures in which men wore their hair long.[3] St Paul's attempt to guide the practice in the church does not rest on a cultural blindness or a mistaken view of human biology. It assumes a subtle and complex dress code in Roman Corinth which is not completely accessible to us, and then tries to use this to locate the church within Corinthian and Roman society. St Paul's appeal to nature only strikes us as odd because our 'scientific' view drives a wedge between nature and culture. For St Paul nature is a construct of biology and culture. He also appeals in his argument to God's will in creation (vv. 9,11,12).

Before examining the relationship between the three categories of nature, culture and creation, it may be helpful to look in more detail at the symbolic use and treatment of the body and its relationship to genital – or as we call them, sexual – acts.

Bodies and boundaries

On a number of occasions St Paul takes the human body as a metaphor for the community of the church.[4] Ephesians 4:25 uses the body as a metaphor for the relationship of human beings in society. The idea is a common place of social theory from ancient times. However, it has taken the discipline of social anthropology to help us recover an awareness that human beings follow the same process in reverse.[5] Human societies use bodily processes and states to symbolize the ordering of their social world. Highly complex patterns of behaviour come into existence, and then develop and change. Their effect in patterning human behaviour can be profound even though individuals and groups may have little conscious understanding of their 'meaning'. Although they take their raw material from the major physical processes of social and personal life, much of the symbolism is arbitrary. The most conventional dress for English men of a certain class is dark grey suits and blue spotted ties. It could have been different; the blue spotted tie imitates the colours of a popular nineteenth-century boxer. The main symbolic codes or systems for modern Western people are associated with hygiene, fashion, personal grooming and eating. (To grasp this, start by reflecting on your and other people's attitudes to deodorants, or male earrings, or the social image of certain foods, or the conventions of hospitality.)

A fairly accessible example from the biblical era is the complex food laws of the Old Testament. One of the main functions of the levitical distinctions between clean and unclean animals is to express the distinction of Israel from the nations.[6] The attempt to force Jews to eat and sacrifice pigs in the Maccabean period gave pork its particular significance for subsequent Jews.[7] The abolition of these food taboos in the New Testament era expressed in a vivid way the abolition of the barrier between Israel and the nations.[8] At a less heavily symbolic level, Jesus portrays table behaviour as a revealing key to social attitudes.[9]

If a modern reader wishes to get the feel of some of the complex ritual passages in Leviticus he or she should imagine trying to write a systematic account of the dress codes through which we organize our relationships with each other. A study of the development of men's fashions has many surprises in store. The three-piece suit made its arrival in 1666 with a rich but fairly restrained coat and a more ornate vest – the precursor of the waistcoat – reaching to just above the knees; it represented an official reaction against both Puritan dress codes and the first excesses of the Restoration.[10] The shortened waistcoat appeared in the 1770s. It revealed an area of the breeches (trousers) that had not been seen since the codpiece was hidden a century or two before;[11] the change was influenced by neo-classical revival of interest in the human form. The story can be traced with equal detail into the twentieth century. Bowler hats were strictly country garb, whose introduction into the city was strongly opposed.[12] King George V insisted on the modest frock coat for court dress; Edward VIII and George VI banned the frock coat, preferring the more daring cut-away morning coat.[13] Those daunted by Leviticus should try exploring the history of the trouser crease![14]

Imagine the vicar arriving in the vestry and saying that he could not preside at communion that morning because he had had a wet dream. The idea would be bizarre if not offensive. However, in some Christian cultures of the past and present it would be expected and understood.[15] The question of whether women can receive communion during menstruation was a matter of great controversy in the early centuries[16] and remains a deeply felt issue in some non-Western churches. What is happening in all this is the imparting of symbolic and social significance to 'bodily discharges'. It is precisely the thought world of Leviticus 15. Gordon Wenham, in his illuminating commentary on the chapter, follows Mary Douglas as seeing bodily discharges as 'symboliz[ing] breaches in the body politic'. 'When rituals express anxiety about bodily orifices the sociological counterpart is . . . a care to protect the political and cultural unity of a minority group.'[17] We not only have difficulty in understanding such symbolic systems; we also have difficulty in locating them in relation to our own different systems. Perhaps their nearest counterparts are the symbolic systems we construct around hygiene or sex, but either of these associations remains somewhat misleading.

The oldest and most basic provision of English secular law as it affects gay people makes it an offence under both common and statute law to bugger another person, whether male or female.[18] What the 'liberalizing' Sexual Offences Act of 1967 did was to exempt men over twenty-one from this offence, provided the act was committed with consent and in private. Buggery here means anal intercourse, and until the 1994 Criminal Justice Act a man could still be sent to prison for life for having anal intercourse with his wife with her consent. What at first sight seems a familiar and comprehensible prohibition of homosexual acts turns out to be formulated under a very different conceptual framework. Until 1826 the crime of buggery required proof that emission had occurred.[19] It was not until 1885 that other genital contacts between men fell under the explicit prohibition of the criminal law.[20]

We shall return later to questions of law and the changing symbolic significance of buggery or sodomy. The point to notice here is that the law was not targeting certain sorts of affection or affectionate acts between people of the same sex but rather certain bodily acts as understood within a symbolic system. A variety of such symbolic frameworks have existed in the past. For example, within the well-ordered hierarchy of Roman society, sexual acts were judged by whether they violated the social hierarchy, not by questions of gender in the participating parties.[21] A superior position in the social hierarchy implied an 'active' role in sexual intercourse; thus Roman society viewed with particular disapproval a slave taking an 'active' role in oral or anal sex with a citizen.[22] The point is not, as some accounts appear to imply, that Roman society was not aware of the different affectionate dispositions or preferences of individuals, nor that people always took a positive view of such affections or relationships. It is that these bodily acts were perceived within a very different symbolic framework to our own.

Two Christian views of sex

The symbolic system underlying the prohibition of anal intercourse in English law is the classical Christian understanding of sexual behaviour. This is sufficiently different from the view held by 'conservative' or 'orthodox' Christians today to need to be set out with some care. We mean by the classical view, the understanding of sexual behaviour held particularly in the West from about the fifth century and expounded influentially by Augustine and Thomas Aquinas. It effectively held sway as the prevailing opinion of serious Christian moralists until the early part of the twentieth century. A full history would have to take account of various eddies and byways which might confuse the picture but, within this variety, three constants of the classic view can be identified: its view of the purpose of the sexual act, its understanding of sexual desire, and the significance given to sexual 'purity'.

On the traditional view sex is about procreation; the essential nature of sexual intercourse is the transmission of seed with the possibility of procreation. Sexual acts which do not have this possibility are 'sins against nature'. Aquinas identified four 'sins against nature': bestiality, homosexual sex, non-procreative heterosexual sex, and masturbation.[23] Being sins against nature they are sins against God himself and a more direct form of rebellion than sins against neighbour, they are more serious than sexual sins within the natural order such as adultery, seduction and rape. This tradition has fed the profound horror with which masturbation has been regarded in the most vocal Christian tradition of the West; this was justified by an appeal to nature and by reference to the sin of Onan (Genesis 38:9, 10). This view of sexual behaviour gives little attention to the experience of women and so contributes to the comparative silence of both the church and the law on this subject.

According to this tradition, contraception is, like homosexual sex, 'sin against nature'. It is wrong both because it thwarts the purpose of the natural act and because it uses human artifice to do so. Galatians 5.20 lists *pharmakia* (RSV 'sorcery') as one of the works of the flesh; this was taken as a standard proof text against the use of artificial means to secure contraception.[24] It is difficult for Christians today to grasp how recent is the widespread acceptance of contraception. Its introduction was resisted with great ferocity in both church and society.[25] Only in 1930 did the Lambeth Conference agree – with considerable dissent – to birth control within marriage 'where there is a morally sound reason for avoiding complete abstinence'.[26] A more positive Lambeth statement had to wait until 1958.

The second constant of the classic tradition is a suspicion of sexual desire; this underlies, for example, the Book of Common Prayer's statement that marriage 'was ordained for a remedy against sin'. This tradition is indebted to Augustine, although his contribution is commonly misunderstood.[27] As has already been mentioned, early Christian tradition tended to see marriage as a form of worldliness; this was not a disapproval of sex or sexual desire but of the whole treadmill of life. Some Christians, like Clement of Alexandria, were keen to emphasize the importance of harmony and order in the Christian life and were disturbed by the element of frenzy or ecstasy in sexual intercourse.[28] Against this background Augustine insisted on the goodness of marriage, and against the thought of his day, taught that Adam and Eve had sex in Eden before the Fall. However, Augustine saw the heart of humanity's inner life as the tranquil rule by the reason over the emotions. He noted the ecstatic and disruptive nature of sexual desire and saw this ecstatic element as the direct result of the Fall. The loss of self-control in sexual intercourse was God's judgment on humanity's rebellious will and therefore symbolic of the dislocation of human nature through the Fall.[29]

This gave sexual desire a central and negative place in Christian anthropology. Even in marriage, sexual desire was a permanent reminder of humanity's subjection to sin. The primary purposes of marriage were procreation and the extension of bonds of affection within society by, for example, linking different families; a secondary purpose was to make available a permitted outlet for disordered sexual desire. So Aquinas was to teach that each partner in a marriage owed it to the other to provide them with the sexual outlet they needed; there was an element of moral fault if a spouse initiated intercourse because they themselves desired it rather than because they sensed their partner's need. There is no sense in this account that one reason for sexual intercourse is the strengthening of the bond between the couple. In the Roman Catholic Church this did not become a part of official teaching until the 1960s; it is first officially expounded in the document *Gaudium et Spes* from the Second Vatican Council and in Pope Paul VI's controversial encyclical against contraception, *Humanae Vitae*.[30]

The third constant of the classic tradition is the tendency to make sexual behaviour the touchstone of Christian discipleship. Three causes may be singled out. The first is the cultural pluralism of the early church. Unlike the Jews or other groups the early church lacked a distinctive ethnic or cultural code of practice to identify the community: 'strict codes of sexual discipline were made to bear much of the weight of providing the Christian Church with a distinctive code of behaviour'.[31] The second is Augustine's teaching on the symbolic significance of sexual desire. The third is St Paul's use of the term 'flesh' to portray human nature in rebellion against God. For the apostle himself the flesh is much more than sexual desire; it speaks of a world ordered in proud rebellion against God (Galatians 5:16ff.; Romans 8:1–15; cf. Isaiah 31:3). Once sexual desire had gained a new symbolic significance the term 'flesh' was easily taken captive to this view.[32]

This classic Christian tradition is a particular distillation of the more complex and dynamic views to be found in the scriptures and in early Christian thought. Although some of its roots lie outside scripture, it draws particularly on the emphasis on procreation in early Israel and on an interpretation of 1 Corinthians 7 made possible by this chapter's pragmatic approach and its emphasis on the transience of this present age.[33] Although it remained the dominant influence on church teaching until the early years of this century, alternative views were often present in other parts of church life.

The classic tradition focuses primarily on a male perspective and is addressed primarily to men; there is every possibility – and some evidence – that different perspectives prevailed in the separate world of women. John Boswell's *Christianity, Homosexuality and Social Tolerance* is important for its extensive documenting of widespread acceptance of homosexual desire and behaviour among Christians until about the thirteenth century despite official enactments. The Gaelic euphemism 'the friendly hand' for masturbation points to the presence in some circles of an alternative to the official view.[34] In the post-Reformation period different views of masturbation existed side by side.[35]

The Reformers' concern to allow the Bible to correct tradition and their promotion of a companionate view of marriage did not so much correct the traditional view as colour it. The domestic ideology promoted over the last 150 years[36] was also initially held alongside the classic Christian symbolic framework for interpreting sexual acts.

However, the twentieth century has seen the creation of a radically different symbolic system for understanding sexual acts and relations; a major catalyst for this change has been contraception. This new perspective sees sexual activity as essentially good and associates it primarily with relationship rather than procreation. It has had profound, and sometimes paradoxical, results. Sexual feeling is viewed more positively. There is a wider acceptance of sexual needs and activity. There has been a rediscovery of feminine sexuality. Sexual practices such as masturbation and oral sex are no longer disapproved of. The link between sex and relationship, taken with the economic market's erosion of other social bonds, has led to sexual attraction becoming the major basis for domestic life.

Although much remains controversial and unclear, the changes have affected both the church and the wider culture. Christians now recognize the ways in which scripture affirms the body and sexual feeling and take for granted the link between sexual intercourse and relationship. Even Pope Paul VI's controversial encyclical reaffirming the traditional prohibition of contraception rephrases the argument in order to give space for this view of sexual intercourse.

This new symbolic system is part of a new cultural vision which is attractive to many Christians. They see in it new possibilities in which passion and affection are being rescued from the strait-jacket of power relationships. Many hope for a new gentleness that can arise when people are *with* others rather than *over* them. Leonardo Boff traces the attractive quality of St Francis to precisely this renunciation of power.[37] This is not difficult to relate to the New Testament. Despite a common caricature which treats St Paul as a repressed emotional tyrant, he shows in his letters precisely this quality of tenderness, open emotion and gentleness; there is a link between this quality and his well-known preference for compound words with the prefix 'with'.

It would be simplistic to imply that the classical Christian tradition was wholly wrong and that the new conceptual framework is wholly correct. However, clear thought about homosexuality does involve recognizing the extent of the shift that recent Christian thought has made and in which 'conservative' Christianity is thoroughly implicated. This may be one reason why the subject of homosexuality causes so much anxiety. The Church may be facing not so much a dreadful tear in the seamless garment of Christian morality as the disappearance beneath the waves of the last visible peak of a sinking continent.

Chapter 4

Culture, Creation and Grace

> We have the mind of Christ
> 1 Corinthians 2:16

If bodily and sexual acts have to be understood in the light of the social structures and symbolic systems that give them meaning, then Christians cannot simply read off rules of sexual behaviour either from the text of scripture or from the 'facts' of human biology. Attention has to be given both to the various cultures in scripture and to modern conceptual frameworks. Furthermore, in the ethical assessment of homosexuality the evaluation of particular bodily acts, of certain relationships, and of the cultural projects in which both may be located, are theoretically separable. Are oral sex or masturbation wrong in themselves as the older tradition believed, or only wrong when done between two people of the same sex as the modern 'conservative' position appears to imply?

Many will fear that the introduction of such complexity will mean the end of objective sexual ethics. Complexity in life is unavoidable but great care needs to be given to the question, How does one decide that either a particular practice or a whole cultural system is contrary to the will of God?

For the Christian this question takes two basic forms. The first is, How am I to assess this practice or culture in the light of certain great truths of revelation – in particular the goodness and order of creation, the fact of human sin, and the good news of the new creation in Jesus Christ? The second is, How am I to relate this practice or culture to particular texts of scripture? Later chapters will look in some detail at the phenomena covered by the term 'homosexuality' and at some of the relevant passages of scripture. The rest of this chapter seeks to identify some of the principles that must operate in addressing these basic questions.

1 Nature and culture

The popular contrast between nature and culture does not do justice to the biblical doctrine of creation. The biblical doctrine relates 'Man' – the human race personified as an individual – to God and to the rest of creation. 'Man' is part of nature and at the same time a little 'god' within it. It is part of our nature to order, understand and to create. Nature (creation) waits for humanity's creativity to bring it to perfection, falls into decay as humanity abandons its divine calling, and views the coming of Jesus with joy and hope.

Scripture expresses this beautifully with two examples from the physical creation: the garden and the jewel. These figure in Genesis 1–3 and in Revelation 21–2. Nature waits on humanity to attain its beauty and perfection. This idea is equally present in the scriptural account of social life, for example, in the biblical picture of the city. This means that human culture is not to be contrasted with nature; although it may be dreadfully marred by sin, it is part of the nature (creation) that God has made.

2 Blueprint or corporate art-form?

This view of humanity's creativity means that neither nature nor society are to be seen as an immutable fixed order to which human beings must conform. The order and vitality of both are more fluid and open-ended than this. Living out our divine calling is not about conforming to a predetermined cultural blueprint. It is more like a design that a community – and the individuals within it – make out of the colours and materials that the creator provides.

This is probably the right theological concept through which to think about contraception. We have a freedom as little 'gods'. This does not exempt us from a responsibility to seek to understand the mind of God and to attend respectfully to the physical creation.

3 Social nature of 'Man'

The doctrine of creation points to the social character of humanity. 'Culture' is an aspect of this social nature. Human beings attain their maturity within a community which has its own corporate commitments and customs. An individual learns a language – with all its inherent values, aspirations and distortions – and then uses it.

This corporate character to human nature finds vivid expression in scripture's practice of personifying the human race as an individual. St Paul speaks of us belonging to the old 'Man' (Greek *anthropos*, human being) or to the new 'Man' (Colossians 3:9,10, cf. Ephesians 2:15; 4:22,24). Some versions of the Bible translate *anthropos* as 'nature', possibly misleading the reader into thinking that each individual has a distinct nature rather than participates in a corporate identity.

How then does an individual's moral responsibility relate to that of the community of which they are a part? Scripture clearly treats both communities and individuals as morally responsible and accountable to God. Individual self-righteousness is an illusion, partly because we are all implicated in the rebellion and unrighteousness of our culture. The point is beautifully captured by the Latin American poet, Ernesto Cardenal, in a commentary on Jesus's phrase 'unrighteous mammon' in Luke 16:9,[1]

> In respect of riches, then, just or unjust,
> of goods be they ill-gotten or well-gotten:
> > All riches are unjust.
> All goods,
> > ill-gotten.
> If not by you, by others.
> Your title-deeds may be in order. But
> did you buy your land from its true owner?
> And he from its true owner? And the latter . . .?
> Though your title go back to the grant of a king
> > was
> the land ever the king's?
> Has no one ever been deprived of it?
> And the money you receive legitimately now
> from client or Bank or National Funds
> > or from the US Treasury
> was it ill-gotten at no point? Yet
> do not think that in the perfect Communist State
> Christ's parables will have lost relevance

or Luke 16:9 have lost validity
    and riches be no longer UNJUST
or that you will no longer have a duty to distribute them.

Individuals are accountable both for their individual wrongdoing
and for their assent to the sins of their community (cf. Jeremiah
5:1–5,30–1). Even when they are seriously constrained and
have to go along with the corporate action, an inner protest
is not without significance (Ezekiel 9:4). At the same time
the moral significance of many – perhaps most – acts derives
from the particular cultural constructs that give them meaning.
This emerges vividly in the story of Naboth's refusal to sell his
vineyard; his grounds for refusal are respected in the narrative
although they are as quaint to us as they apparently seemed
to King Ahab (1 Kings 21:1–7). The story turns not simply on
Ahab's unjust abuse of power but also on Naboth's old-fashioned
conservatism.

For many purposes the primary moral unit is less the
individual than the community. In the Old Testament the
prophetic denunciations of Israel and of the nations treat whole
communities as the moral agents. The same phenomenon is
found in the New Testament, for example, where Jesus weeps
over Jerusalem (Luke 19:41ff.) or denounces the Galilean towns
for their failure to repent (Matthew 11:20–4).

4 Discernment and scripture

'But doesn't the Bible say . . .?' is an understandable cry
when an unfamiliar moral stance appears on the horizon.
The appeal to particular 'proof texts' is a legitimate part of
Christian use of scripture so long as one realizes that the
practice crystallizes understanding rather than short-circuits
the difficult but necessary task of discernment.[2] A later chapter
will look at the meaning and significance of particular texts. At
this point it may be helpful to note four aspects of this process
of discernment:

Discernment is a corporate task. St Paul's well-known injunction, 'Do not be conformed to this world but be transformed
by the renewing of your minds, so that you may discern what
is the will of God – what is good and acceptable and perfect'
(Romans 12:2) is in the plural. Discerning the will of God is a

difficult task (cf. 2 Timothy 2:7) that we have to undertake with others. Different Christians will bring to the task of discernment both different gifts and different perspectives.

Christians may need help from outside the church – truth is not to be found in scripture alone. This point is, in a way, obvious. No one turns to the Bible for advice on how to repair a car or thinks they have nothing to learn from an unbeliever about, say, the ethics of life insurance. At the same time, in areas such as sexual morality, Christians can quickly imagine that their inherited tradition has a monopoly on moral insight. Many Christian couples who now use contraception are ignorant of the Church's ferocious opposition to its introduction. We are no different from Moses who had something to learn from Jethro, although the latter was a priest of Midian (Exodus 18:1,13–27).

Proverbs 8 portrays God's gift of wisdom as available outside the realm of religious knowledge (vv.2,3,15,16); this wisdom includes ethical discernment and not simply 'value-free' information (v.6). The chapter makes clear that such understanding demands disciplined attention (vv.6,10), commitment to goodness (vv.8,13) and patience (vv.33–5). This, of course, is not to imply that all secular opinion is correct (v.13). There are many indications within scripture itself that the believing community incorporated into its life concepts, insights and institutions fashioned in the wider community.

No group can claim a privileged position in the interpretation of scripture. (See chapter 1.) If the Bible becomes a weapon, used by one group of believers against another, the process of discernment is inevitably distorted. This means, among other things, that gay people are not to be excluded from the attempt to discern the will of God over sexual behaviour. They must play a respected part in the process of discernment and not simply wait for a gay-blind church to announce its conclusions.

The Bible is not simply a book of timeless rules. For most of scripture we are not the direct addressees. We – with our fellow believers – have the mind of Christ (1 Corinthians 2:16) and listen in to God's address to others. Sometimes the 'cross over' will be direct ('love your enemies'). Often it is not so simple, and principles have to be discerned and reapplied.

In the case of the Old Testament law codes, this distance

from the text is readily acknowledged. Some Christians treat only the Ten Commandments as having universal authority – despite the New Testament's abrogation of the sabbath commandment (cf. Colossians 2:16,17). More satisfactory is the venerable distinction – used, for example, by Aquinas and Calvin – between moral, civil and ceremonial elements within the Old Testament law codes.[3]

However, even with New Testament 'commands', Christians know that 'direct' obedience is not always what is being required. This seems to be the case with contemporary evangelical understanding on remarriage among Christians, notwithstanding its apparently unqualified prohibition in 1 Corinthians 7:10,11.

It is easy for a reader of scripture to be misled into thinking that the New Testament offers greater clarity on sexual behaviour than is actually the case. The Bible, of course, forbids adultery; however the acts included in the term are not quite the same as those in the mind of a modern reader. Another example is *porneia*. Translations of 1 Thessalonians 4.3 ('abstain from fornication', RSV, NRSV) do more than simplify by translating *porneia* as fornication. *Porneia* is certainly not a synonym for sex before marriage and its meaning in Matthew 5:32 is notoriously unclear. Its root meaning is 'prostitution' (cf. *pernemi* 'to sell'). In a useful discussion focusing on Acts 15:20,29 Countryman suggests 'harlotry' as a translation, because it catches the difficulty in deciding whether, in that context, *porneia* means idolatry or the offences of Leviticus 18 (a chapter which forbids sexual union between men and also intercourse with a woman during menstruation).[4] The sexual meaning seems more probable to this writer. The decision reported in Acts 15 cannot of itself set standards for Christian sexual behaviour today; the Council seems to be treated in the rest of the New Testament as a transient and unsuccessful stage in attempting to enable Jews and Gentiles to live together in one church. However, the discussion itself illustrates the fluidity of the term *porneia*. It clearly means sexual behaviour that breaches the proper relation between human beings. It does not follow that this will be the same in every culture. It can only be a beginning in discerning the significance of certain genital or sexual behaviour.

5   *Evaluating a culture or practice*

If neither nature nor scripture provide a simple blueprint for
human behaviour, how does one evaluate a particular practice
or culture? How does one discern the mind of God? Possible
questions that may help this process of discernment include the
following:

Does it respect the elements and texture of God's creation?
[A]
Does it respect the character and calling of humanity?
[B]
Does it take sin and its resulting disorder seriously and
penitently? [C]
Does it hear God's voice in creation, in the scriptures
and in his prophets, and seek to reflect his goodness?
[D]
Does it attend to the common humanity we share with all
human beings? [E]
Does it respect the purpose that God is unfolding in history?
[F]

Different questions may be useful for different issues. [A]
might provide a starting point for evaluating oral sex or sado-
masochistic practices. [C] and [A] are called upon in Bishop
Gitari's preference for African polygamy over against Western
divorce. [C] and [D] point to the difficulty of assessing the
overall movement of a culture: is God judging Western culture
for its idolatry of sex or rejoicing in our rediscovery of it? [E]
directs attention to the radical individualism reflected in many
practices of contemporary culture as well as the limitations of
purely sectional perspectives.

Some of the deeper issues raised by [F] will be looked at
below in discussing 'The shape of grace' but an example of
its relevance may be mentioned here. Do God's purposes in
history focus on preserving social order or on reaching out to
those whom a particular social order excludes? In a situation of
social change, is God a conservative? One form in which this
question meets the church is, Should its priority be opposing
the social acceptance of homosexuality or evangelizing gay
people?

6 Evaluating cultural dissent

The question of cultural dissent is obviously important in any assessment of modern gay movements but it is a question which Christians face in many other forms. A contemporary British form of the issue is raised by Government action against travellers. If a culture's social structures are a reasonable expression of humanity's need and calling as found in human life and taught in scripture, what right has an individual or group to adopt an alternative pattern?

The practices of one's community obviously have a claim on one's loyalty. This derives from the social nature of humanity and from respect for God's providence. However, this claim cannot be regarded as absolute. A number of considerations could legitimate the adoption of alternatives:

(a) promptings from fellowship with other cultures in the church. A society's particular conventions and arrangements are commonly identified with the absolute values of which they are partial reflections. The multi-cultural character of the Christian church tends to call such absolutes into question. (When Asian Christians abandon the traditional practice of arranged marriage are they embracing the freedom of the gospel, abandoning a noble tradition that properly locates marriage within the network of relationships in society, or simply exchanging one culture for another?)

(b) respect for individuals and groups on the margins of society, realizing that dominant groups can be (possibly unintentionally) oppressive (e.g. James 2:1–7). An interesting non-sexual example is the case that can be made for legalizing cannabis in Britain in the light of its use in Afro-Caribbean culture. Tolerating alcohol and tobacco (English vices) and outlawing cannabis (a non-addictive Afro-Caribbean relaxant) tends to criminalize a whole group in British society.

(c) criticism of the narrowing of human potential involved in a culture's choice of social pattern. An example here has been the women's movements' rejection of social roles in the familial structures of industrial society.

(d) where a social pattern is oppressive enough to threaten

the survival of certain groups and individuals, the formation of alternative patterns is inevitable.

7 Respect for creation

The echo of philosophical and scientific difficulties with the Christian doctrine of creation, combined with an awareness of cultural diversity, have made appeal to the pattern of creation difficult in modern discussion of a variety of gender issues. Respect for creation is obviously important in evaluating gay cultures and lifestyles but does not figure prominently in much discussion of closely-related issues. Major discussions of feminist and gay issues have tended to look to other criteria for discerning the mind of God.

The Presbyterian Church (USA) has published *Presbyterians and Human Sexuality 1991*, one of the most illuminating church documents on human sexuality. As a guide for exploring the current crisis about sexuality in church and society it is hard to beat. It consists of a wide-ranging majority report that explores the issues that face many groups in society (e.g. the old), and then a minority report that seeks to reaffirm the 'traditional' line on homosexuality. In my judgment the majority report's treatment of scripture is usually better than the minority report. However, much of its argument is put in question by the way it uses the concept of 'sexual justice'.[5]

It rightly notes the distorting effect that oppression by certain groups has on human experience of sexuality. It calls for 'an abiding and passionate commitment to sexual justice-love'. This includes 'gratitude for diversity. Sexual justice calls us to acknowledge and respect the diversity of age, gender, sexual orientation, colour, body size and shape, families and custom.' This part of the report could hardly express more vividly the way in which the exercise of power over others destroys the intimacy and creativity that are near the heart of both sexuality and humanity. At the same time 'sexual justice' cannot simply mean giving equal dignity to every human option – except cannibalism and misogyny – and then seeing what happens. Justice must involve giving attention to the patterns and polarities present in creation.

The failure to consider this point in the report leads to a number of weaknesses. It means that the argument that contemporary homosexuality fails to take seriously the order of creation is not properly addressed. It is also closely linked with a tendency to identify human fallenness with 'patriarchy'.[6] This is too easy. Women are not simply victims, they also use their power as women to oppress (cf. Amos 4:1–3). Sin is against God and against the creation, as well as being present in oppression between the sexes. In the misuse of the physical creation, a case can surely be made that men have often cherished the natural order – say, as shepherds or foresters – and women have often led the consumer demand that ravishes it. A simple appeal to equality fails to address the question of what allowance should be made for the difference between men and women, and also between straight and gay people.

In his magisterial work *New Horizons in Hermeneutics* one of the issues that preoccupies Anthony Thiselton is how one distinguishes between theological writing which simply uses rhetoric to promote a particular cause ('socio-pragmatic hermeneutics') and writing which provides authentic criticism from a particular perspective ('socio-criticial hermeneutics').[7] He traces this important issue as it effects different strands of black and feminist theology.[8] Clearly the question is equally relevant to any attempt to incorporate gay perspectives into Christian understanding. He proposes three keys in this process of discernment. The first is the need to balance an openness to new truth with a suspicion of mere self-interest. The second is an awareness of the eschatological goal of history when truth will be clearly seen.[9] The third is to look to the controlling pattern of the death and resurrection of Jesus Christ.[10]

Anthony Thiselton's third key has both strengths and weaknesses as an aid to discernment. It places Jesus at the centre of human life and thought and ensures that the Jesus so respected is the Jesus of the New Testament. It also raises a suspicion against any claim to truth which is not characterized by a willingness to serve humanity at personal cost. However, it could appear to be saying, 'If you want it, it must be wrong.' Marginal groups tend to be characterized by an element of self-hate, which talk of sacrifice may simply activate. This criterion fails at precisely the same point as the Presbyterian Report's concept of sexual justice. It gives no guidance on how an understanding of creation is to contribute to this process of discernment. Ethnic identity is partly formed by the particular location of a people in the creation; English and Afro-Caribbean people are shaped by their climate and their land. The helpful ferment created by feminism cannot avoid the question of what is to be made of the difference between men and women.

Respect for creation must include respect for, and exploration of, the complementarity of male and female. It may seem, at first glance, that gay subcultures and domestic partnerships are vulnerable at this point. This may not be the case. Gay people play an important role in society's rediscovery of the mystery of gender. A failure to embrace this given of creation is widespread. For example, the male of modern industrial society has excluded the feminine from public life and narrowed the sphere of domestic life. The fact that industrial society has had a strong and stereotyped commitment to the heterosexual nuclear family has not prevented this.

By contrast, many gay people and gay cultures play a very positive part in recovering and embracing gender and gender complementarity. One example is the sort of friendship that gay men often have with women. Another is the cultural exploration of gender identity in which gay and lesbian subcultures are involved and to which the whole of society is indebted. It is precisely nonparticipation in heterosexual marriage that makes this possible. Of course, misogyny does exist in certain gay male groups. It is not that common and may be a by-product of self-hate; it is particularly prevalent when gay men face severe social hostility.[11]

8 The method of grace

The classic Christian tradition on sex was right to relate the fallenness of humanity to the phenomena of sexual feelings and behaviour. It fell into error at two points. First it is not only sexual desire and behaviour that have been disordered by human pride and alienation; it is the whole of human life. If there is a characteristic symptom in scripture of the disorder into which sin has plunged us it is violence (cf. Genesis 4; 6:5–12; Psalms 10;55; Titus 3:3) rather than sexual desire. However, the fact of human fallenness means that sexual feeling and behaviour include some expression of human hatred as well as of human hope and love.

The intimacy of sexual contact exposes as well as heals human evil.

The second error of the classic tradition – at least as popularly understood – was to make absolute adherence to a set standard of sexual behaviour the bench mark of Christian discipleship. In other areas of life – say human relationships, anger, greed or economic justice – we do not expect instantaneous perfection in a Christian. The effect of this myth of instant perfection in the sexual area is damaging to everyone. It makes for hypocrisy in the church and prevents true growth in grace. It leaves some straight people with a false sense of self-righteousness and a shallow view of what is going on in their sexual relationships. It leads to an exaggerated sense of scandal when the disorder in some gay people's lives comes to public attention.

In this respect there is an obvious contrast with the scriptures which regularly show much greater realism about human sexual behaviour. The Old Testament makes explicit and implicit allowance for the fallenness of sexual desire; it encourages social institutions that mitigate and contain the results of human fallenness in this as in other areas. This is equally true of the New Testament. There is no evidence that Jesus gave any great priority to sorting out the sexual lives of the 'sinners' with whom he was associated. In the moving incident of the prostitute who bathed his feet with expensive ointment, there is no mention of her abandoning her way of life (Luke 7:36ff.).

The significance of some of St Paul's strongest statements on sexual behaviour is often missed. Romans 13:13–14 and 1 Corinthians 6:9–11 rebuke certain sorts of sexual behaviour. However, in order to understand them, it is important to look both at what they reveal about the church and at their place in St Paul's pastoral theology. They reveal a candour about sexual behaviour and a recognition of its presence that are in marked contrast with the public face of many modern churches. Whatever *malakoi* and *arsenokoitai* may mean in 1 Corinthians 6, it is clear that people associated with some sort of homosexuality were openly accepted in the church at Corinth. Romans 13:13 could be paraphrased, 'Let's have less sleeping around and less quarrelling.' Although St Paul struggles with the presence of all sorts of wrong behaviour in the church – of which sexual wrongdoing is but one example – it is only in rare and extreme cases that he looks to church discipline as a remedy. Where he does require public discipline in 1 Corinthians 5 it arises from a relationship thought particularly scandalous in the culture. Furthermore, there is clear evidence in St Paul of an element of pragmatism and compromise in his pastoral judgments in this area. For example, in 1 Corinthians 7, where St Paul is wrestling with an over-enthusiastic abandonment of the social institution of marriage, he still urges people not lightly to abandon their single state. However, in the more down to earth and practical 'church order' of 1 Timothy, he commends pressure on younger widows to marry as their most viable personal option (5:11–15).

St Paul's injunctions on sexual behaviour are set firmly in the context of what classic evangelical theology calls 'sanctification', that is the way in which Jesus brings about change in the personal and spiritual life of the Christian. The characteristic shape of St Paul's approach emerges particularly clearly in Titus 2:11–13:

> For the grace of God has appeared, bringing salvation to all, training us to renounce irreligion and unworldly passions, and in the present age to live lives that are self-controlled, upright and godly while we wait for the blessed hope and manifestation of the glory of our great God and Saviour Jesus Christ.

It is *grace* – God's personal initiative of love and acceptance, expressed in part in the life of the church – that *trains*; as a result *goodness* and *self-control* are established in believers as they gain the beautiful Christian quality of patient *waiting* for God's new reign of peace. Exactly the same pattern is found in 1 Thessalonians 4:1–8, where the focus is particularly on sexual behaviour. Again the apostle frames his injunction in terms of God's gracious initiative, of exhortation, and of learning; honesty in relationships is an important explicit addition. The sexual behaviour he commends springs not from innocence or denial, but is characterized by self-control learned in an atmosphere of grace. Growth in grace involves not blind obedience but a Spirit-led process of discernment and maturing.

This grace-led approach to sexual ethics has clear implications as to how sexual matters should be handled among believers, and points to an element of pastoral pragmatism. It implies a certain sort of penitent tolerance of some imperfection in what we call sexual matters. The question becomes not 'Have you crossed the line?' but 'As one struggling sinner to another, are you making progress in your growth in grace?' While the implications of this tend to be accepted in evangelical organizations that work with gay people, there is little grasp of its implications for the ordering of church and society.

9 The shape of grace

This grace-led approach also has implications for the process of discernment in matters of sexual practice. Discernment in sexual ethics cannot simply be the transfer of biblical *rules* of behaviour to present situations; it must emerge out of the process that St Paul describes. The question here is whether faithfulness to Christ involves doing exactly what the apostle told other people to do or by *imitating the process* that the apostle sets out in his exhortations.

Another way of putting this is to ask exactly what authority St Paul himself claims in these matters. It is not simply that of the legislator (cf 2 Corinthians 1:24; 1 Corinthians 7:10, 12). As the one designated by Christ to bring the Christian faith to the non-Jewish world, he has a continuing theological authority in mapping out the framework for this universalizing of the Jewish encounter with God (cf. Ephesians 2:11–3:13); this is reflected in the common practice among older Christian theologians in referring to St Paul as 'the Apostle'. St Paul also had immediate pastoral authority over the churches that sprang from his apostolic ministry (cf. 1 Corinthians 11:2, 34); as we have seen in earlier discussions of 1 Corinthians 11:2–16 there was a pragmatic and situation-specific element to the exercise of this pastoral authority. These two forms of St Paul's authority are in theory separable and impact in different ways on the modern church.

In assessing the implications of this for sexual ethics it may be helpful to spell out the different strands in St Paul's much-quoted and much-misunderstood aphorism, 'You are not under law but under grace' (Romans 6:13). This is not an injunction to avoid legal scrupulosity. It is, first of all, a declaration of the inadequacy of moral rules in themselves as a way of putting right the pervasive evil in human life. On their own they lack the power to penetrate the corruption of human nature; they create self-righteousness, indifference or despair. They cannot do justice to the variety or creativity of human life. God's method is grace – a generous and creative acceptance that has its own power to generate goodness.

Beyond this St Paul's words imply a criticism of the adequacy of the Old Testament law to embody the new life that the Spirit is bringing into existence. He sees the particular provisions of the Old Testament law as subject to some temporal or dispensational limitation. They were appropriate for a particular stage or phase of God's unfolding purpose of redemption (Romans 5:20, Galatians 4:2–5). (When he appeals to particular provisions of the law codes – as in the case of pay for church workers in 1 Corinthians 9 – he tends to support his argument by appeal to other considerations.) For all their beauty and wisdom (Deuteronomy 4:6) Old Testament laws were no more than partial expressions of God's will in particular social contexts (cf. Matthew 19:8 on Deuteronomy 24:1, 2).

The purity laws of the Old Testament form a symbolic system, designed to mark out Israel as a separate people and to embody a particular notion of the normal (Leviticus 20:22–26).[12] Thus they exclude the leper from the community (Leviticus 13:46) and the disabled man from the sanctuary (Leviticus 21:16ff.). Sometimes the implied definition of 'normal' strikes us as arbitrary: eating prawns is an abomination because the 'normal' fish has scales and fins (Leviticus 11:12).[13] The Christian church has often been tempted to reimpose this symbolic system within its life; the Canon Law of the Church of England explicitly states that those born outside marriage can be ordained (Canon C2.4) precisely because the medieval church incorporated Deuteronomy 23:2 into church law. St Paul is not alone in the New Testament in seeing that Jesus's coming overthrew this whole symbolic system (cf. Acts 11:15, Mark 7:18). In Jesus, God claims people from all nations. Quite specifically, he takes as his friends those who are outside the clean space marked out by the symbolic laws of purity.

William Countryman sees the New Testament's overthrow

of the purity laws as having radical implications for Christian sexual ethics. He argues that the category of an intrinsically impure act is abolished – 'only intent to harm renders a sexual act impure'.[14] The difficulty with this is that it appears to deny all significance to the human body and its symbolic expression. In his argument, Professor Countryman probably overstates his case in claiming that references to 'purity' in the New Testament refer only to purity of heart or to avoidance of idolatry. The human body remains important in New Testament thought (cf. 1 Corinthians 6:12–20). Thus, in 1 Thessalonians 4:4, *skeuos* (vessel) probably refers to the believer's body rather than his wife, as some modern translations imply. The setting aside of the purity laws of the Old Testament does not indicate the abandonment of any symbolic significance for the human body but rather its relocation in a radically different context. The body continues to play an important part in the symbolic systems of human cultures; the Christian's response to this is to be determined by the new shape given to human history in the coming of Jesus.

Grace, in St Paul's teaching, is not simply God's active and undeserved love; it means the coming of Jesus and the revelation of the true direction and goal of human history (Colossians 1:25–27; Ephesians 3:1–6). Grace does not signify the abolition of humanity but its re-creation (Ephesians 2:14, 15); it must therefore imply a new respect for the body and its meanings. But, with the coming of Jesus, grace has a shape, and this shape is radically different from that implied in the Old Testament law codes. It gives particular dignity to those who were on or beyond the boundaries of Israel's life and who were thereby counted unclean. The new humanity is one in which the gifts and values of every culture have a place. In addition non-normal (non-conforming) groups are no longer to be given a negative symbolic significance. This must have implications for evaluating bodily practices to which certain societies give negative symbolic meanings. It may be natural for many Christians to gravitate to Old Testament cultural norms; the New Testament not only undermines cultural absolutes but gives particular honour to the despised outsider.

10 Desire: Beyond biology

What moves the body in sexual intercourse? The instinctive view of many people today is that human beings have an innate attraction to the other sex which is physically or biologically determined. On this view the root human desire which finds expression in heterosexual coupling and which leads in the end to the creation of all human culture is heterosexual desire. This is a simplistic extrapolation from the facts of human procreation which is shared neither by Freudian thought, nor by the Bible, nor by classical Christian thought.

Freud saw human sexual energy as an undifferentiated force in the human infant which needed to be shaped and constrained if the individual was to take his/her place in human society.[15] It was the requirements of society and its need of procreation that made heterosexual objective choice desirable rather than any intrinsic direction in human sexual energy itself.

The scriptures themselves operate on an altogether broader understanding of the vitality that is human life and that finds its expression in human desire. The biblical account of human desire emerges in Psalm 63:

> O God, you are my God
>   earnestly I seek you
> my soul thirsts for you,
>   my body longs for you
> in a dry and weary land
>   where there is no water.

Human desire is primarily for God; this is equally true for a person's psychic vitality and their physical being. It is rooted in the physical reality which also provides the symbolic meaning by which it is described. Out of this innate vitality and desire springs the whole diverse range of human activity. It is intended to find its unity in the only fountain that can finally slake this thirst – God himself (Isaiah 55:1; John 7:37; Revelation 22:17) All desire has a physical aspect whether it issues in cities, works of art, acts of worship or physical expressions of love. Admiration for the male – as in the roll-call of 2 Samuel 23:8ff. – and love between people of the same sex – as in the love between David and Jonathan ('surpassing the love of women', 2 Samuel 1:26) or Ruth and

Naomi (Ruth 1:14–18) – are part of this vitality and desire and not a perversion of it.

The modern reductionist tendency to treat all human desire as displaced heterosexual desire reflects an understanding of humanity that concentrates on a particular aspect of human biology and on its social consequences. For all its emphasis on procreation the Old Testament has a much broader view. To start with, it assumes richer, more diverse and less biologically determined models of social arrangement than the modern idealized nuclear family. The biblical use of narrative and symbol makes clear that there are many potent images that evoke and shape human desire and not only those that we call sexual. Human intimacy is located not only in the sexual act but in other important moments in human experience such as the shared table (Psalm 41:9), shared worship (Psalm 42), and civic art and ritual (Psalm 68:24–27).

The modern treatment of attraction between the sexes as the core human desire can lead to the misreading of even such an overtly sexual book as the Song of Songs. Francis Landy, in his rich and evocative commentary on the book, develops the suggestion that it should be set alongside Ecclesiastes and Job as a critique of the complacent worldliness sometimes to be found in the wisdom tradition, and that this is one purpose of its ascription to King Solomon. 'If Wisdom, with its love of moderation, was implacably hostile to incautious alliances, the Song counsels abandonment.'[16] Its argument is not very far from William Blake's *Proverbs of Hell*, e.g.

Prudence is a rich, ugly old maid courted by incapacity.
He who desires but acts not breeds pestilence.
If the fool would persist in his folly he would become wise.
The wrath of the lion is the wisdom of God.

The Song is, among other things, an exploration or celebration of desire. It should not simply be seen as an advertisement for marriage; the desire it celebrates is not simply 'heterosexual' attraction. Its literary form is a narrative about two people, not the presentation of some ideal. The moment

of sexual consummation takes place in a garden (4:16–5:1),
a piece of symbolism that echoes the story of the garden
of Eden without the crass implication that desire is 'really'
sexual. There is much that is subversive in the desire that
the Song celebrates. Its vision of sexual union is not associated with marriage. The predominant perspective in the
poems is the woman's delight in male beauty. Desire brings
the beloved into conflict with the guardians of social order
(3:1–3, 5:7).

'Love is strong as death' is part of the Song's manifesto (8:6).
The yearning for immortality is present in all forms of desire.
Like so many of his sonnets, Shakespeare's 'Shall I compare
thee to a summer's day' seeks, in the face of death, to preserve
the beauty of the young man he loves:

> So long as men breathe, or eyes can see.
> So long lives this, and gives life to thee.

In other sonnets Shakespeare urges the young man to father
a child (e.g. 'Die single, and thine image dies with thee.') All
desire has within it a yearning for immortality, a movement
of worship, joy and self-offering, and a potential for creativity. These find tangible fulfilment in the birth of children
and in the resurrection hope of a world where there is no
marriage, but they are not limited to these. The ultimate
goal of desire is not secure domestic 'relationship' – as much
modern discussion implies – but God and the transformation of
humanity.

This broader vision of desire places much human passion,
and the physical expression to which it gives rise, away
from the sexual project with which it is often associated in
the modern mind. Do affectionate expressions or patterns
of human relationships change their moral status when their
culture interprets them according to the modern interpreta-
tive category of sexuality? Some of the suspicion with which
passionate attraction between people of the same sex – and
its outworking in friendship, creativity, physical affection and
social arrangements – is regarded is clearly fuelled by the
view that heterosexual attraction is the core desire in human
nature.

This chapter has had the limited aim of clarifying issues that may arise in trying to evaluate what contemporary culture calls homosexuality. Before any conclusions can be drawn, both the nature of homosexuality and the meaning of different biblical texts need to be examined.

Part 2

Understanding Homosexuality

Chapter 5

Identifying Homosexuality

I'm not gay. I go surfing. That's about as male as
you can be.

Jason Donovan

Homosexuality is a cultural as well as a personal phenomenon.
This chapter begins to look at the way this insight is influencing
contemporary understanding of homosexuality. The next two
chapters examine, in turn, the relevant conceptual background
in Western culture and the emergence of a gay identity in
modern Western society.

'Gay' and 'homosexual' are cultural concepts which carry their
own strong associations. Many men have sex with other men
but do not consider themselves gay. Many evangelical churches
would find Julian Clary an uncongenial addition to their life
without enquiring about the details of his sexual behaviour.
Again, the researchers who conducted the National Survey of
Sexual Attitudes and Lifestyles recognized the need to frame
the questions they asked about sexual behaviour with great
care in order to obtain answers uncoloured by terms such as
homosexual or heterosexual. In their introduction they explain
the theoretical framework within which they operate and which
they regard as widely accepted:[1]

Biological determinants of sexual behaviour cannot be ignored.
Any theory of sexuality will have recourse to an understanding of anatomical and biological potential and limits which
provide the preconditions for human sexuality. But while the
biological human sexual capacity is universal, its expression

is influenced by socio-cultural forces. Sexuality is defined, regulated, and given meaning through cultural norms.

The link between sexuality and culture has been a commonplace in the avalanche of scholarly writing on questions of gender or sexuality over the last twenty years. It has hardly impinged on much Christian writing on homosexuality which continues to think of the homosexual person as a distinct psychological type, probably shaped by some sort of defective relationship with one or other parent, whose affective disposition requires either cure or moral concession depending on your viewpoint. As will emerge, this understanding of gay identity or lifestyle builds on concepts of homosexuality framed in the nineteenth century, and is often wedded to a cultural allegiance to the scientific or economic assumptions of modern society. The goal of much Christian counselling of gay people is to use the tenets of therapeutic counselling and self-acceptance to help people back to, or on towards, 'normality'. This concept of normality often tends to be a sanitized and uncritical version of a certain ideal of the family: namely a return to the purity of the TV series *The Waltons*, further sanctified by romanticized and selective projection from certain biblical cultures – Abraham without the concubines.

This attempt to understand homosexuality suffers from two weaknesses. The first is its attempt to treat homosexuality apart from cultural context. The second is its lack of interest in the strange disappearance from Western culture of the ancient ideals of same sex passionate friendship. Both will be explored in this and the following chapters.

Same sex behaviour between men cannot be treated as an isolated phenomenon. Four different aspects of the way in which men relate to each other need to be looked at together: sex between men; affection between men; social association between men; society's ideals of masculinity. These exist in any society, but the way in which they are organized and conceptualized varies considerably.

At the risk of caricature, one could say that the so-called 'traditional' view – held by many evangelicals – has the following assumptions: sex is about relationship and pleasure; masculinity is about success at work; social association among men belongs with work, sport and maybe drinking; affection between men is a strange, occasional occurrence without recognized cultural space. None of these assumptions is actually traditional to the historic and 'Christian' cultures of the West. It is a matter for discussion whether they have their origin in intellectual movements of recent centuries or in the economic arrangements of industrial and post-industrial society. They provide the building bricks out of which most modern men attempt to construct their lives. This attempt often exacts a high price, leaving little time for reflection, and creating a strong sense of allegiance to the ideals of masculinity attained at considerable personal cost. In many respects these assumptions also provide the basic social matrix within which contemporary forms of homosexuality develop.

Modern scholarship on homosexuality

Over the last twenty years there has been an extraordinary flowering of academic studies of sexual behaviour between men and its social clothing. The term *homosexuality* has itself been subject to criticism for carrying the conceptual background of its nineteenth-century inventors and also for the possible implication that there is a single transcultural phenomenon called homosexuality. Where the word is used it might be more accurate to speak of *homosexualities*. There are close links between recent scholarship on male homosexuality and related studies on lesbians, on feminism and on masculinity. I am aware of the interrelatedness of these subjects and hope readers will forgive a concentration on male homosexuality and accept that this limitation may make for clarity.

Western intellectual life, at least since the sixteenth century, has had a profound gut horror of the 'sodomite'. Some of the causes of this will be discussed below. One result of this horror has been the absence of serious scholarly study of sex between men and its related emotional or social dimensions. Recent years have seen this academic silence breached. This is probably abhorred by some scholars but it has led to a flood of high quality writing and to considerable ferment as appropriate conceptual frameworks are articulated and contested.

Four strands of this academic writing can be identified. The first is academic study of the origins of the modern gay movements with their historical contexts and precursors.[2] This strand has often led on to wider studies of the conceptualization of sexual identity[3] and obviously interacts with related movements of cultural dissent – particularly the feminist movement. The second strand has been historical, focusing on the history of homosexualities and their conceptualization.[4] In the main, these have been careful studies of particular moments in Western or world history. Particularly important was the publication in 1980 of *Christianity, Social Tolerance and Homosexuality* by John Boswell, a historian of the medieval period and professor at Yale.[5] Evangelical Christian awareness of this book has tended to be limited to its lengthy and disputed treatment of biblical material; however, its continuing importance lies in what it reveals about the conceptualization of same sex desire in pre-modern Europe. The third strand of academic writing has been cultural and anthropological studies of sexual relationships between men; in this case a vast amount of this information and analysis is brought together in *The Construction of Homosexuality* (Chicago 1988) by David F. Greenberg, Professor of Sociology at New York University. The fourth strand treats homosexuality as a key ingredient in, or illuminator of, Western culture's continuing discussion with desire and social order, an influential example of this is *Sexual Dissidence* by Jonathan Dollimore.[6]

Both historical and anthropological studies reveal a great cultural diversity, both in sexual behaviour, in practice, in conceptualization, and in the way in which it is related to the prevailing social order. The package represented by the modern Western cultural framework on sexuality proves to be a very bad guide to the diversity of patterns to be found. For example, many cultures have seen sexual relationships between men, not as a denial of social masculinity but either as integral to it, as in some of the military cultures of ancient Greece such as Thebes or Sparta,[7] or irrelevant to it – as in medieval England's easy acceptance of the relationship between Richard the Lionheart and King Philip of France.[8]

Such diversity extends both to the social roles exercised by men who have sex with other men and to the way in which sexual acts themselves are conceptualized. D.F. Greenberg suggests a rough classification of four forms of homosexuality depending on the relative social status of the participants: '*transgenerational* (in which the partners are of disparate ages), *transgenderal* (the partners are of different genders), and *egalitarian* (the partners are socially similar)'.[9] He discusses the occurrence of each of these in different clan or tribal societies and also a fourth pattern, found in socially more complex societies, in which partners belong to different social classes.

Greenberg has little difficulty in showing that all three types of same sex relating are well-documented features of tribal societies as well as later, more 'advanced', cultures. The literature relates the particular form of such sexual relationships to other aspects of these societies – in particular the way they socialize the sexes and the ideals of masculinity demanded by the tribes' particular circumstances. However, there is considerable variety of practice between tribes with similar cultures; one culture may use oral sex between men and a related one anal sex,[10] one culture may revere men occupying the female social role, another may despise them.[11] Although it is impossible to do more than allude to the complex material assembled and studied by Greenberg, it may be illuminating to comment on each of the cultural forms of homosexuality that he identifies.

Cultures with a *transgenerational*[12] form of homosexuality are the most disconcerting to Western myths about homosexuality, because they treat same sex activity as the norm for men at certain stages of their life. In these societies sexual relationships between older and younger men are an integral part of initiation into the masculine role demanded by the needs of the tribe. This practice often exists where the male and female spheres of life are kept radically separate and young boys have to make the demanding transition from the maternal world of their early years. Such same sex activity cannot simply be explained by lack of sexual access to women; it is an integral part of the emotional and cultural formation of the masculine identity. Greenberg discusses a number of such societies, but the most widely known outside specialist circles is the New Guinea tribe called the Sambia (a pseudonym adopted to protect the tribe) which has been studied for many years by Gilbert Herdt. The Sambian practice of oral sex as part of a prolonged process of male initiation has been subjected to extensive theoretical reflection.[13] Herdt's first published study of this tribe was called *Guardians of the Flutes* and the same title was taken for a BBC2 documentary on the tribe, first screened in the summer of 1994. Somewhat to his surprise, this writer was struck by the resemblance to his experience of an English public school in the early sixties! This rests not primarily on the existence of sexual activity but on its presence as a sort of 'open secret' in parts of English culture and its relationship to the formation of a type of masculine identity required by the emotional demands of public responsibility.

Transgenderal homosexuality[14] is at first sight harder to relate to contemporary Western forms of homosexuality, although it may partly illuminate the presence of transvestite and trans-sexual roles in certain Mediterranean and Latin American cultures and to the extensive transvestite culture in Thailand.[15] Greenberg's study of this form concentrates on its presence in the Indian cultures of North America that were destroyed with the coming of Europeans. The term *berdache* is applied to men and women in these tribal cultures who adopted the social role of the other gender and were recognized and accepted in this role. A common feature of this cultural form of homosexuality is the recognition that an individual is not suited to the particular culture's form of masculine or feminine identity. Its relationship to sexual behaviour could be complex: some female berdaches married women and some men.[16] This pattern of alternative sexual identity can occur in surprising contexts. *The Independent* of 16 October 1990 reported from Pakistan the electoral candidacy of a man from the Khusra 'clan' as a protest against the failure of more conventional politicians; the Khusra clan is a self-identified grouping of transvestites and eunuchs who are mainly tolerated in the wider Islamic culture as entertainers.

Greenberg's classification of *egalitarian* homosexuality[17] relates to accepted sexual contact between people of the same sex, where the partners treat each other as social equals. Many forms of such homosexuality are widespread in traditional societies and are not treated as alternative to the important social roles of marriage or child rearing. In certain cultures they cease at marriage; in some the opposite is the case. In certain cases the male form of this homosexuality may be related to lack of access to women, but Greenberg does not find this credible as the major cause of this pattern. Three particular comments on this form of homosexuality are worth noting:

> egalitarian homosexual relationships are sometimes found among adults, but they are not usually institutionalised (p.71).
>
> in general, indulgence of homosexual play among pre-pubescent youths is found when adults accept rather than repress children's heterosexual interests (p.71).
>
> Male competitiveness poses a further obstacle to an egalitarian relationship . . . If men are accustomed to compete with one another for status, and conceive of sex in terms of domination, then egalitarian relations must be asexual if they are to continue (p.72).

In the more stratified and complex societies discussed by Greenberg, these three cultural forms of homosexuality recur but are overshadowed by new patterns that reflect the more complex social organization.[18] Thus he discusses the emergence of cult prostitution, of sexual relationships as an element in warrior societies, of master-slave relations and non-religious prostitution, and of castration and the social role of eunuchs. A number of these have been found and accepted within overtly Christian cultures.

What is the significance of this evidence of widespread acceptance of diverse patterns of same sex sexual activity, particularly in non-Christian and pre-Christian societies? For many Christians the answer will be simple: such behaviour is a sign of the degeneracy of cultures untouched by the grace of God. To be convincing, such an account needs to give some indication of how these forms of homosexuality have their origin in the idolatry of the cultures concerned rather than in humane aspects of their culture. A case can be made that modern Western Christian hostility to homosexuality is itself the product not of faith, nor profound biblical insight, but of an ingrained fear of the disruptive effect of sexual desire and affection, combined with a cultural exaltation of competition between males as the basis of economic and social well-being. Before such questions can be addressed, attention has to be given to the origins of developed Christian attitudes to homosexual desire and to the patterns of modern homosexualities.

When the uninitiated reader turns to recent academic writing in an attempt to address such questions, he or she is likely to become aware of certain philosophical or conceptual disagreements which often find expression in the major studies concerned. These theoretical discussions can give rise to considerable passion and make it more difficult to grasp the outlines of a framework of thought which is increasingly well established. It may be helpful at this point to isolate two questions that underlie these philosophical disagreements.

The first is the question of whether cultural patterns of social and sexual behaviour have their origin in the way in which behaviour is conceptualized or in the social arrangements to which they relate. A significant school of thought, associated for example with Michel Foucault, sees human social reality as the creation of human discourse. Another school of thought sees human social reality as the creation of the social arrangements that prevail in society – and in particular in the economic arrangements within which human life is sustained. Any attempt to arbitrate in this important debate is beyond the scope of this book. The instinct of this author is that an anthropology rooted in biblical thought would have a place both for the effect of conceptual frameworks and of social structures. In a useful chapter in *Sexual Citizenship*, David Evans identifies four competing claimants to control the patterning of sexual identity and self-understanding – the sexual 'scripts' available to individuals.[19] These are: the concepts used to articulate human life and identity; the symbols round which social order is conceived; the 'psychodynamic' analysis of human development and behaviour; the economic and social institutions such as capital, class and state within which human life is lived. It is important in any such analysis to take account not only of the current controlling frameworks but also of the importance of cultural memory.

The second question which dominated gender studies in a formal way for much of the 1980s was characterized as a conflict between 'essentialism' and 'constructionism'. This debate partly has its origin in the philosophical questions discussed in the previous paragraph. With respect to the study of homosexuality it can be distilled into two questions: Given the cultural diversity that surrounds same sex behaviour and socialization is there a core essence that one could identify as homosexuality? Given the same cultural diversity, does there run through the human race a distinct group of people whose sexual and affectionate preference is for their own sex? A late and illuminating expression of this debate can be found in a pair of essays by John Boswell and David Halperin.[20] While struggling to retain his philosophical footing this writer would wish to respond with two assertions. First, while it is clearly possible to speak in general terms of homosexuality, the different configurations and social functions of different homosexualities easily make such generalizations misleading. Secondly, while John Boswell would seem to be right that people with an emotional and affectionate preference for their own gender seems to be a constant in human culture, social diversity would seem to be such that an individual who is sexually conforming in one culture might have been sexually deviant in another.

Serious reflection on any form of homosexuality needs to consider it within its cultural context. Christian assessment of contemporary forms of homosexuality needs to take into account both presuppositions inherited from the past and the anatomy of the modern gay identity. These are examined in turn in the next two chapters.

Chapter 6

Same Sex Love: The Pre-modern Matrix

> I grieve for you, Jonathan my brother; you were
> most dear to me; your love for me was wonderful,
> surpassing the love of women.
>
> King David
> 2 Samuel 1:26

The love of friends

Alypius discouraged me from marrying a wife. His theme was
that, if I did that, there would be no way whereby we could
live together in carefree leisure for the love of wisdom, as
we had long desired.[1]

Affectionate male friendship is a constant feature of Augustine's
account of his Christian faith. In his *Confessions* he writes of
his struggle for sexual self-control and recounts his mother's decision to dismiss his long-standing concubine in the
conventional expectation of a socially advantageous marriage.
However, alongside this turmoil runs the constant theme of
male friendship: the emergency baptism of an intimate friend
first confronts Augustine with Christ's power; the sweetness
of friendship smooths his pathway into sin; the friendship of
Alypius forms a major sub-plot in this account of their common
journey to faith; when Augustine comes to faith he abandons his
secular ambitions in the imperial service and sets up a pious
household – the forerunner of Augustinian religious communities – that includes Alypius and his own son Adeodatus.
In all this Augustine is living out a well-understood ideal of
male friendship that he received from classical culture.[2] Such
passionate friendships were a recognized aspect of pre-modern
culture and provided a well-understood part of the emotional and

affectionate landscape. Affectionate intimacy between men was an accepted and important part of life. It is interesting to contrast this with the comparative embarrassment that passionate friendships cause modern biographers. Peter Hebblethwaite's fine biography of Paul VI deals with great delicacy with the young Montini's love for his soulmate Andrea Trebeschi.[3] Again, the revelation of the youthful Lord Reith's passionate obsession with a handsome younger man is a major theme of Reith's diaries and a source of scandal and fascination to contemporary readers.[4]

In the classical culture of the Mediterranean, love between men was an important part of philosophical and poetic discourse. *The Symposium*, Plato's great treatment of the character and metaphysical nature of love which has strongly influenced Christian thought and devotion, is cast in the form of a dialogue on love set at a dinner party that Socrates shares with male friends. Love, the dialogue implies, is 'the consciousness of need for the beautiful and the good'.[5] 'The love concerned', comments an authoritative introduction, 'is homosexual love; it is assumed without argument that this alone is capable of satisfying a man's highest and noblest aspirations.'[6]

This example from Plato makes clear that the pre-Christian classical tradition of passionate male friendship made no great distinction between friendship that involved sexual intimacy and love that focused on the physical and moral beauty of the beloved. The widespread acceptance of genital intimacy between men in Graeco-Roman society is well known. This was not uniform; attitudes to all sexual behaviour – and to sexual acts between men – varied both between individuals and in different parts of the Mediterranean. However, the categories through which sexual activity were understood were different from our own.[7] Sexual acts were seen not as expressions of relationships but as acts done to another person and reflecting the order of society; hence it was considered shameful for a free citizen to play the passive role in oral, anal or intercrural sex. Although some men were known to have a preference for sex with men or had long-standing and respected relationships with other men, the cultural assumption was that sex with women or appropriate men was interchangeable. Also, excessive addiction to sexual pleasure was seen as a serious and often comical weakness of character. Although much sexual activity was confined to sex with younger men lifelong love and loyalty between men was a feature of the social ideal[8] and various forms of publicly recognized same sex union were found.[9] The Emperor Hadrian's love for Antinous was honoured across the classical world,[10] Julius Caesar was despised for apparently having played the passive role in sex with the king of Bithynia.[11]

This strong cultural affirmation of love between men has left its mark at surprising places in later Western culture. Mention has been made of Plato's influence on the theme of 'love divine'. Theocritus, a pastoral poet of the third century BC, wrote poems celebrating the love between shepherds and their young male lovers. These were taken up in the seventeenth century in the tradition of pastoral poets with lyric portrayals of love between young men and women in the context of a rural idyll. Other poetic traditions of love between men continued to influence Western cultural tradition.

Same sex love in Christian tradition

The classical tradition of passionate friendship between people of the same sex continued as a major strand of the Christian culture that emerged after the triumph of the Christian faith. There is a continuous tradition, of which St Paulinus of Nola (AD 353/4–431)[12] provides an early example, in which passionate and intimate friendship is celebrated in a way that draws on the pre-Christian classical tradition. This was demonstrated not only in poetry but in serious and systematic writing on friendship. One of the most important expressions of this is *On Spiritual Friendship*,[13] written by St Aelred of Rievaulx (*c*. AD. 1110–1167) at the instigation of Bernard of Clairvaux and drawing on Cicero's classic text *De amicitia* as well as Augustine's *Confessions*. It is a beautifully crafted dialogue that deserves to be better known today.

More problematic is how this emotional and affective tradition related to sexual activity between men. It is the major achievement of John Boswell's fine, if flawed, book *Christianity, Social Tolerance and Homosexuality* that he demonstrates that for much of the period before the thirteenth century significant sections of the Christian world did not regard male desire for sex with men as strange, did not think it particularly worthy of moral censure, and did not make such desire a ground for stigmatizing certain individuals in society. While at certain points Boswell pushes his evidence too far,[14] he does establish that occasional ferocious laws (themselves of a piece with a cruel age) and fierce denunciation by great preachers do not provide an accurate guide to popular attitudes or practice. St John Chrysostom, by repute the greatest of the patristic preachers, shared the ascetic severity of much fourth-century Christianity. But even his preaching against homosexual activity provides evidence of a contrary understanding:

> Those very people who have been nourished by godly doctrine, who instruct others in what they ought and ought not to do, who have heard the Scriptures brought down from heaven, these do not consort with prostitutes as fearlessly as they do with young men . . . The fathers of the young men take this in silence: they do not try to sequester their sons . . .[15]

(Chrysostom also denounced the practice of applauding sermons – and was applauded for his pains!) While Greenberg's *Construction of Homosexuality* gives a more nuanced account of opposition to homosexuality at various points in the period, it confirms the impression and evidence provided in Boswell's groundbreaking study.[16]

The case of St Aelred of Rievaulx, where Boswell if anything understates his case,[17] illustrates many of Boswell's main assertions. Aelred was part of the same movement of spiritual renewal as the great Bernard of Clairvaux. His own writing and the biography by his disciple, Walter Daniel, provide ample evidence that erotic attraction to men was a dominant force in his life, that the sexual activity that preceded his call to the monastic life was with male friends at the court of King David I of Scotland, and that profound emotional friendships with men continued to be an integral part of his life. As a Christian teacher and monastic leader Aelred inspired great love, combining personal austerity with a gentle affection, and creating a religious community in which affectionate relationships were seen as good – even affirming the place of affectionate gestures in such celibate communities. Aelred treats love between men and love between men and women as good, as complementary, as part of God's will in creation[18] and as a reflection of the only love that can last, love for God.

> This type of friendship belongs to the carnal, and especially to the young people, such as they once were, Augustine and the friend of whom he was then speaking. And yet this friendship except for trifles and deceptions, if nothing dishonourable enters into it, is to be tolerated in the hope of more abundant grace, as the beginnings so to say, of a holier friendship . . . just as yesterday we said that the friendship of man could easily be translated into a friendship for God himself because of the similarity existing between them both.[19]

Not only does Aelred treat gay love in adolescence and in adult life without embarrassment, it is clear that he lived in a time when this caused no comment or difficulty. It may be significant that he was a contemporary of St Bernard, famed for his spiritual use of the Song of Songs. Both belonged to a Christian culture at ease with sexual feeling and imagery.[20]

Much more surprising is the evidence, published in 1994 by John Boswell in *Same-sex Unions in Pre-modern Europe*, of the widespread liturgical celebration of permanent non-monastic same sex unions. Prior to the publication of this latest book by Boswell I viewed rumours of such rites and practices with considerable scepticism. The case, however, seems now to be well established, although the interpretation of the rites will no doubt continue to be disputed. More than sixty manuscripts of such a rite exist both in Greek and Slavonic, dating from the eighth to the seventeenth century.[21] The liturgical texts were often bound with marriage rites and shared the choreography of marriage. (For example, their hands were joined over a Gospel book on the altar and bound with a stole; a kiss was exchanged; a feast – and possibly communion – followed; and so on.) The prayers refer to the example of St Sergius and St Bacchus, martyrs of the late third or early fourth century, who were members of the imperial court that formed one household[22] and to whom many churches were later dedicated. The use of these rites was forbidden to monks.[23] The practice was called the monks.[23] The practice was called the 'making of brothers,[24] the term 'brother' had wider connotations in ancient cultures and was regularly used with sexual overtones as the Song of Song itself illustrates.[25] A seventeenth-century Western editor of these texts was clearly embarrassed at their existence.[26] Boswell provides evidence of the celebration of such same sex unions not only from the Christian East but also from Ireland[27] and, in a poignant example, sixteenth-century Rome where Portuguese men united by such a rite were subsequently hunted out and burned.[28] It is probably not widely appreciated that specifically Christian marriage rites were slow to develop and early Christian practice seems to have been to sanctify with prayer relationships accepted by society. The existence of these same sex rites provides surprising evidence of such Christian pragmatism towards human relationships.

Discussion will continue as to how the unions established by such rites related to the prevailing understandings of kinship and marriage and whether they envisaged or condoned genital activity. The contemporary context was very different from our own: non-biological kinship was an important part of the ordering of society; marriage was about creating and extending bonds of affection in society and not about recognizing erotic desire; the goal of desire was not marriage but God. At the very least the rites bear witness to the social recognition of same sex affectionate bonding – and their subsequent fierce prohibition to a sea change in Christian attitudes.

The myth of sodomy

A profound and pervasive cultural hostility to gay sexual behaviour seems to have emerged in Western culture in the thirteenth century. The burning of the Portuguese men just referred to fits in with widespread secular legislation against homosexual acts from the thirteenth century;[29] the common punishment of burning being the origin of the slang term 'faggots'. What was previously seen as one of a number of sexual sins, liable to the usual ecclesiastical penances, attracts to itself a new horror associated with the sexual act and those who commit it.

John Boswell documents the rise of social intolerance of various non-conforming groups from the thirteenth century with Jews as the first victims – this is the era that created the yellow star – and heretics and 'sodomites' following rapidly in their train.[30] It established a cultural pattern that continued in the West, documented in many historical studies,[31] of occasional local campaigns against those involved in homosexual activity leading to the execution of those involved.

The rising intolerance was not without precedent in Christian culture. The later years of the Roman Empire had seen certain moves towards a stricter sexual code. The extent and causes of this are difficult to assess.[32] Possible factors included: an ascetic mood in the culture which both influenced and was influenced by Christians; the more provincial sexual morality of certain emperors; changes in political and economic life; the intense symbolic significance given to sexual behaviour as the church began to systematize its attitude to the body and bodily desire and to articulate an exclusively procreative view of the sexual act. Some of the severest of the imperial laws against homosexual acts are under suspicion of being framed to justify action against political opponents and were generally ignored. By the sixth century a pattern had emerged in which ecclesiastical teaching against non-procreative and homosexual acts was complemented by widespread, if sometimes patchy, social tolerance.

The origins of the profound shift in popular culture from the thirteenth century have been the subject of considerable discussion. Boswell himself attributes it to the increasingly absolute authority of rulers, to the attempt to create and regulate a more tightly-ordered society, and to social tensions arising from increasing urbanization. Greenberg's discussion of this latter contribution to the rising intolerance is more developed. Apart from the presence of themes in the official teaching of the church, he singles out three factors within the social changes of the period. One is the disruption caused by the attempt to introduce and enforce clerical celibacy; this both increased the symbolic link between sodomy and the clergy that Henry VIII, for example, was to use to such effect, and also made the sexual practice of the clergy an increasing concern of ecclesiastical authority. Another is the association of homosexuality with the aristocratic ruling class: the rising class of urban merchants took homosexuality as a symbol of the luxury that they sought to supplant. Closely related to this are the different social priorities of the second generation of the urban bourgeoisie, a group whose social and sexual priorities concentrated on the thrifty management of the small household. (Protest against the aspirations and selfishness of this group was also a major factor in the development of Franciscan spirituality.[33])

Associated with this new cultural hostility was the creation of the powerful and long-lasting myth of the sodomite. The Old Testament view was that citizens of Sodom were destroyed by catastrophic natural disaster for their pride, luxurious living and injustice (Ezekiel 16:49–50). Their judgment was decided upon before the attempted anal rape for which they were later notorious. In the early Christian centuries Sodom gave its name to the sin of anal intercourse just as Onan (Genesis 38:8–10) gave his name to the sins of masturbation and contraception. However, from the thirteenth century a society concerned with social order, and making the link common to much ancient thinking between social order and cosmic order – the order of society and the order of nature – found in the sin of sodomy a powerful symbol of all that threatened social well-being and stability. The classic Christian tradition that non-procreative sexual acts were 'sins against nature' clearly gelled well with the potency of this developing symbol.

The subsequent history of this symbol in Western and English culture is not simple, but two strands can be discerned.[34] One concentrates on the sexual act so that the secular legislation introduced by Henry VIII punished not sex between men but anal intercourse. Later legal opinion often took the view that guilt under this statute required not only anal penetration but emission; it was not until 1826 that anal penetration without emission became unambiguously punishable by death. The second strand concentrated not on the sexual act but on its potent association with the threats to the social order of heresy, treason and debauchery. Even within this second strand, subtle movements of thought can be identified from the beginning: Henry VIII's statutes are overtly political in their thrust; Edward VI's cast the crime in a more personal framework, adding to a cumulative cultural symbolism. Henry VIII's statutes were aimed primarily at providing grounds for closing and robbing the monasteries. Prosecution under the

Tudor statutes was rare and generally associated with people of influence who threatened the social order.

The intense symbolic weight of sodomy affected the way in which society reacted to people actually involved in sex with people of the same sex. Under ordinary circumstances people do not easily see their friends and neighbours as freaks of nature whose very existence threatens cosmic catastrophe. This helps to explain the cruel but episodic character of campaigns against gay people and activity after this period. It has another more curious result, namely that those involved in – or aware of – such sexual activity did not associate their behaviour with the terrible sin of sodomy.[35] In a well-documented case in 1630 a man on trial for having sex with another servant (in a bedroom they were sharing with a third servant) clearly has difficulty in linking his behaviour with the terrible charges with which he was faced and for which he was executed.[36] There is considerable evidence that in the climate created by the potent symbol of sodomy, sex between men continued – for example, between friends[37] and between masters and their male servants (who regularly slept together) – without those involved identifying themselves with the cosmic blasphemy evoked by the symbol.

The Nazi concentration camps of the Second World War provide a horrifying testimony to the continuing vitality of the cultural myths created in the late medieval periods. Large numbers of homosexuals died alongside the millions of Jews and Gypsies in the camps.[38] Homosexuals found themselves near the bottom of the hierarchy established in the camps and a particularly small proportion of those who wore the pink triangle survived. A further testimony to the power of this myth was that not only were these Nazi victims not properly commemorated after the war but the allied authorities sometimes transferred them to prison to complete their sentences on the ground that the period in the camps did not count.[39]

Untainted desire

The emergence of the cultural myth of the sodomite which has proved fatal to the lives and happiness of so many gay people did not immediately taint all same sex love or its recognition within English culture. In an elegant and closely argued book *Homosexual Desire in Shakespeare's England: A Cultural Poetics*, Bruce R. Smith maps out the way in which love between men was recognized and explored in the literary culture of the sixteenth and seventeenth centuries. 'Moral, legal, and medical discourse are concerned with sexual *acts*; only poetic discourse can address homosexual *desire*.'[40] Such poetic discourse can mediate between official and everyday reality. Smith identifies six myths or 'cultural scenarios' which recur through the literature of the period and provided 'the "imaginative vocabulary" that sixteenth- and seventeenth-century writers possessed for talking about homosexual desire – the repertory of character types, plot motifs, images, and themes that offered ways of conceptualizing homosexual experience and playing it out in imagination'.[41] The myths have their roots in classical literature but Smith has little difficulty in showing that the writers and poets of the period were keenly aware of the sexual content of the stories and of the knife-edge created by the stigmatizing of homosexual acts.

Five of Smith's 'scripts' are found in the public literature and entertainment of the day. Thus *Combatants and comrades* is present, for example, in Shakespeare in Coriolanus' bonding with his archenemy Aufidius ('Let me twine mine arms about that body'), in Iago's jealousy of Cassio, and in the recurring theme of two male friends set at odds by a woman – as for example Bassanio and Antonio in *The Merchant of Venice*. Another myth, that Smith calls *The Shipwrecked Youth*, occurs in those Shakespeare plays where androgyny and gender ambiguity are explored in exotic contexts. Puritan objectors to the theatre were clear that the themes explored on stage were not to be confined to their exotic context:[42]

> [T]hese goodly pageants being done, every mate sorts to his mate, every one bringes another homeward of their way verye freendly, and in their secret conclaves (covertly) they play *the Sodomits* or worse. And these be the fruits of Playes and Enterluds for the most part.

The sixth of these myths, *The Secret Sharer*, manifest in Shakespeare's 126 sonnets addressed to a young man, enters a new domain. The sonnets were written, not for publication, but for circulation in manuscript within an intimate circle, and mark a new and daring exploration of intimacy.[43] Their hesitant publication came later. They create a new explicitness in the exploration of same sex love: 'With certain of Marlowe's stage heroes and with the speaker of Shakespeare's sonnets, the fictional character who feels homosexual desire, and acts on it, has changed from "he" to "I".'[44]

> A Woman's face with natures own hand painted,
> Haste thou the Master Mistris of my passion,
> A womans gentle hart but not acquainted
> With shifting change as is false womens fashion,
> An eye more bright than theirs, lesse false in rowling:
> Gilding the object where-upon it gazeth,
> A man in hew all *Hews* in his controwling,
> Which steales mens eyes and womens soules amaseth.
> And for a woman wert thou first created,
> Till nature as she wrought thee fell a dotinge,
> And by addition me of thee defeated,
> By adding one thing to my purpose nothing.
>> But since she prickt thee out for women's pleasure,
>> Mine be thy love and thy loves use their treasure.

With this declaration in Sonnet 20 the writer moves from passionate admiration into the idealism and vulnerability of the lover:

> Being your slave, what should I do but tend
> Upon the hours and times of your desire . . .
>> (Sonnet 57)

On the threshold of the modern world the love between men not only retained the many voices it had from the past but was exploring new and dangerous territory. Modern Christian opponents of the gay movements sometimes bewail the emergence of 'a new homosexual culture'. The confident exploration of male same sex love to be found in the classical and Christian culture of the West invites a different question: Where is affectionate and intimate friendship between men to be found today?

Chapter 7

The Emergence of Gay Identity

Diversity is not a weakness to be suppressed but a strength to be harnessed.

John Major[1]

The origins of modern forms of homosexuality have been the subject of extensive scholarly debate.[2] While some disagreements over interpretation remain, the outlines of this development are now clear. The indications are that the end of the seventeenth century marked a significant change in the way in which masculinity was perceived in society. This was manifest both in the emergence of new ideals of masculinity and of embryo homosexual subcultures in large urban centres. Around 1700 a social pattern emerged which has remained characteristic of modern culture, although the names and symbolic systems within which personal identity and social role are articulated have continued to change.

A new pattern

In the late seventeenth century two particular male stereotypes were on offer in English society, the rake and the fop.[3] The rake was the image of lawless, assertive masculinity – execrated and admired. He had sex with women and boys indiscriminately:

Nor shall our love-fits, Chloris, be forgot,
When each the well-looked link boy strove t'enjoy,

And the best kiss was the deciding lot
Whether the boy fucked you or I the boy.
(John Wilmot, Earl of Rochester 1648–1680)

By contrast, the fop was regarded as effeminate. He wore elaborate clothes, loved soft ways and preferred the social company of women; he was only interested in sex with women.

In the late 1680s a new figure emerges, the beau, 'who combined the dash of the rake with the softness of the fop'.[4] The elegant beau cultivated the society of women in the more egalitarian relationship between the sexes that was emerging within the home. However, the beau was still likely to find a sexual outlet with young men as well as with women. The figure of the beau was itself a sign of changes in society as new familial and economic patterns developed. New ideals of masculinity were emerging within the domestic ideals of hard work and frugal discipline that were encouraged in better-off urban households.

Up to this point sex with young men, in which the older man took the active role, was not seen as a denial of masculinity; it was tolerated as part of the male world or denounced as part of the luxury and sedition that was sodomy. However, between 1707 and 1726 a series of raids on taverns or 'molly houses' in London revealed the existence of a network of men involved in a lively homosexual subculture.[5] In the words of Samuel Stevens, probably an agent for the Societies for the Reformation of Manners,

> I found between 40 and 50 men making love to one another as they called it. Sometimes they would sit in one another's laps, kissing in a lewd manner and using their hands indecently. Then they would get up, dance and make curtsies, and mimic the voice of women . . .

This series of scandals revealed the emergence of a new form of homosexuality in English culture. It was both a sign of – and a catalyst for – changes in the masculine ideal and in the connotations of the sodomite. Sex with young men comes to threaten the masculinity of the man about town. By 1749 the practice of men kissing when they met could be denounced as 'the first inlet to the detestable sin of sodomy'.[6] The symbol of the sodomite becomes associated with the cross-gender behaviour of the molly houses; the 'heterosexuality' of the fop rapidly becomes incomprehensible. The ground is prepared for the belief that the homosexual is a kind of third sex.

This emergence of gay subcultures in London is part of a pattern that is documented across Europe; detailed evidence often comes from the investigations and trials that took scores of gay people to their deaths.[7] As well as the taverns there is a pattern of open air meeting places where networks of men met in search of sex. Different accounts are given of what contributed to these developments, reflecting wider theoretical debates as to whether conceptual frameworks or social structures shape social identity. Alan Bray finds evidence of the Enlightenment notion of the individual: 'I think there is no crime in making what use I please of my own body,' declared one man in 1726 when he was arrested.[8] Randolph Trumbach relates the changing pattern to the emergence of the new egalitarian family.[9]

> The modern Western culture, in which we still live, had begun to emerge around 1700, and with it came a distinctive pattern of family structures, sexual behaviour and gender roles. The early 18th century saw what I have called the rise of the egalitarian family, and what Lawrence Stone has described as affective individualism and the companionate marriage.

Greenberg discusses the impact of the freedom possible in larger urban populations as well as the ambiguous influence of the rising middle classes who both defined and sought to restrict sexual expression.

Randolph Trumbach sees the homosexual subcultures that appeared in the eighteenth century as the re-emergence of a transgenderal, as opposed to a transgenerational, form of homosexuality (to use Greenberg's terminology). Although, for example, evidence of sexual contact between ordinary working class men continued to appear, the male homosexual was now seen as an alternative to the masculine ideal of the culture; the role was becoming available as a social identity for those who were ill at ease with the prevailing masculine ideal within the culture. The comparison with the adoption of the alternative gender role in some tribal cultures should not be pressed too far. The adoption of feminine roles and behaviour in the molly subcultures was only episodic, and was not universal among men who had sex with other men. It represented a borrowing of the cultural models for affectionate and sexual behaviour, as well as being a form of ironic criticism of the social order that was hostile to this form of same sex affection.

Consolidation

The pattern of homosexuality that emerged at the beginning of the eighteenth century can be summarized as follows. A social identity arises that both borrows the gender categories of the culture and also provides an ironic critique of them. It provides a cultural counterpoint to the domestic ideal fostered by the economic arrangements in society. This social identity provides a threatened but identifiable social space for certain men and is focused on certain social activities that give visibility and identity to male same sex desire. Although associated with sex, this social space also provides an environment for intimate male friendship and for the exploration of gender and sexual feeling that is elsewhere tightly controlled or suppressed. Considerable sexual contact between men continues to happen at various other places within the society but the identity celebrated within the episodic subculture comes to define the cultural identity of same sex desire. For those within and outside the subculture this public identity becomes a point of reference in the cultural expression of same sex male desire. While sex between men continues often to be quite divorced from the symbolic identity celebrated in the subculture, this symbolic identity becomes both a celebration of, and a threat to, same sex love – a celebration in that it is affirmed, a threat in that it is perceived as perverse.

While the outline of this pattern is already clear in the early eighteenth century, the nineteenth and twentieth centuries have seen both its strengthening, and its occasional repackaging as the symbolic systems around which Western culture is structured have changed and developed. Various moments or influences can be identified in the consolidation of this cultural pattern of homosexuality.

1   The free market

The early eighteenth century saw society come to be organized around the domestic ideal, the valuing of personal freedom, a symbolic link between same sex affection and perverse desire, and the expansion of the male sphere of life to become the dominant, even the normative, social reality. The industrial expansion that gained momentum in the nineteenth century has tended to consolidate each of these, and the primary social mechanism for this has been the free market. As a social mechanism and symbolic ideal, the free market has emphasized freedom of choice within the framework of law, and the home as the place of feeling and personal meaning. Controversy has surrounded the theoretical limits to the operation of this free market – as, for example, in nineteenth-century campaigns to prevent children being employed in factories or the mines, or occasional attempts to protect the market for particular goods. The notion of the free market has also been questioned when sections of the labour force have found themselves economically bound to acquisitive employers or when it has excluded whole sections of the community from having a meaningful part in the national life – as, for example, with the Victorian poor or the newly identified 'underclass'. However, these difficulties have not threatened most people's acceptance of the free market as the prime economic mechanism in our society and as a pervasive symbolic background to social relationships.

Structuring social relationships around the model of a competitive market has profoundly influenced personal expectations and the way in which personal reality is perceived. The economic mechanism of the free market has influenced the cultural expression of same sex relationships and homosexuality in four ways.

Firstly, it has had a strong influence on the experience and expectations of masculinity.[10] The market model affected the world of men in a number of ways. It valued the social virtues of discipline, restraint, self-reliance and pragmatism. It gave its primary recognition to the competitive element in male relationships. Where men cooperated, they did so in order to strengthen their ability to compete with other men. These processes create emotionally self-reliant individuals whose main experience of social bonding outside the home is based on competition – a mode of relating expressed, encouraged and disciplined in the cult of competitive sport. A further effect of the industrial market was the removal of work from the home so that women came to be excluded from an active role in the new world of work created by the market. Women came to be seen as essentially passive;[11] men became alienated from the feminine – in society and in themselves. Despite the impact of the women's movements, many men perceive the real world as male.

Secondly, because the 'serious' public realm is associated with the restraint of feeling, desire or gender, it is dominated by the qualities associated with the self-reliant and competitive male. Other aspects of human reality – love, desire, beauty, poetry – are relegated to the margins of serious life – the spheres of entertainment, religion and the home. This has led to a society in which personal feeling and its associated sense of identity are seen as belonging to the protected domestic sphere. Domestic units are created on the basis of sexual attraction. The home – and the bedroom – is the place where sexual identity and feeling can be explored. Personal identity and domestic location are intimately associated with sexual feeling. To put it crudely: you either sleep with people or compete with them.

The third aspect of the market's influence is its ambiguity. Nineteenth-century social reformers promoted the nuclear family as a humane refuge from the rigours of the market-place; ironically the modern nuclear family has become a very effective player within the same market. Similarly, the free market creates a form of masculine identity which has difficulty with affection and intimacy between men: the demands that the competitive market places on men contribute to a hostility to the 'soft' masculine qualities often associated with homosexual men. At the same time market 'neutrality' has played an important part in creating space for gay people and gay subcultures. The neutrality of the market has enabled gay people and organizations to own property, choose where they live, how and with whom they spend their leisure time, and so on. Gay individuals

and groups possess their own wealth and are therefore able to
operate effectively in the market. If there is money to be made
in meeting the needs or desires of gay people, then the natural
dynamic of the market will be to respond. The myth of the 'Pink
Pound' exaggerates the disposable wealth of gay people,[12] at
the same time the financial sector has become sensitive to the
impact of the gay market. 'What do you call 14 million gay men
and lesbians? A dream market.'[13] Furthermore, where the idea
of the free market is made a platform of public policy, it provides
a potent focus for gay people to assert their citizenship – they
earn money, pay taxes, establish households and businesses;
why should they be treated differently from others and not
also benefit from the public purse? It is significant that one
of the more powerful pressures for the public recognition of
gay partnerships in the European Community is the treaty
commitment to the free movement of labour: if gay partners
are not free to travel across community borders, then the free
movement of labour is improperly restricted.[14]

Fourthly, the dominance of the model of the free market has
helped to change the political ordering of society. For medieval
Christians such as Aquinas and Aelred, the bonds of friendship
were the basis of society. This was part of the created order.
These bonds implied both affection and obligations. St Thomas
Aquinas's assertion that one reason for God's institution of
marriage was the creation of bonds of affection *between* familial
groups seems to us fanciful. Medieval culture, like some of the
biblical cultures, saw human life as embodied in a complex set
of relationships; a person's life was governed by expectations
and obligations that were located and enforced within the
different networks in society. In a similar way in early Israel
the enforcement of obligations was distributed between various
bodies and individuals: near relatives (who, for example, dealt
with the punishment for murder – cf. Numbers 35:6,9–34), the
city elders, itinerant judges, the priests (as teachers of the Law),
the king.

The idea of the market has profoundly affected the political
environment by dissolving all social bonds except those of
the home and the commercial alliance. In the modern nation
state this has been furthered by the claim of the national
government (technically, in Britain, the Crown) to a monopoly

on the administration of justice. (We would regard the early Old Testament practice over the punishment for murder as dangerous lawlessness.) This has affected the ordering of sexual relationships in two ways. First of all, it has provided the background for the considerable increase in the State's detailed regulation of people's domestic and sexual lives since 1800.[15] At the end of the nineteenth century two pieces of legislation drastically extended the criminal law against gay men in England: the Labouchère Amendment to the 1885 Criminal Law Amendment Act which created the offence of 'gross indecency' – sexual acts between men not involving anal intercourse; and the 1898 Vagrancy Act that punished 'persistently importuning for an immoral purpose'.[16] (In both cases the primary legislation was directed against female prostitutes but has borne heavily on gay men. For men – but not women – 'persistently importuning' means any potentially sexual advance even if the resultant act itself would be legal!)[17] Secondly, this shift in the political order has affected the way in which a public gay identity has taken shape: a symbiotic relationship between commercial concerns and voluntary associations that serve the social and political interests of gay people.

2 Science – the new truth

The nineteenth century not only saw the triumph of the free market, it was also the era of science. The study of the order and causality of the physical world had a profound impact on the intellectual concerns of the century and, through its alliance with emerging technology, contributed to the economic growth experienced in Britain. In the late twentieth century we are more aware of some of the ambiguities of this development and have begun to become sensitive to the element of arrogant presumption hidden in technology. Despite the controversy in some circles about a six-day creation, Christians – including evangelical Christians – found the intellectual world view fostered by science a congenial one. Its emphasis on a comprehensible order inherent in nature cohered well with the biblical doctrine of creation. The anti-speculative strand among some more 'fundamentalist' Christians found welcome support in the more practical outworking of the scientific project.[18] The scientific enterprise itself was often clothed with a myth of objectivity and purity that only the late twentieth century has begun to question.

It was natural that the scientific outlook became part of the mind-set of nineteenth-century people and was applied to human behaviour as well as to the physical world. Greenberg sees a link between the development of the bureaucratic state and the rise of scientific interpretation of life[19] – both were concerned with information, order and control – and he relates this to what has been called the medicalization of homosexuality. The application of scientific categories to homosexual behaviour has had a profound effect on the conceptualization of homosexual behaviour and desire. The first steps arose through the desire to give a scientific account of criminal behaviour and, in particular, to categorize and deal with criminal deviant personalities.[20]

Nineteenth-century 'objective' scientific description incorporated into its theories three givens of the way homosexuality had come to be conceptualized in the culture of the time. Developments since the fourteenth century had presented homosexual actions as a crime as well as a sin; their perpetrators were therefore criminal deviants – in the terms of Victorian science a personality type to be studied. The cultural abhorrence of homosexuality associated with the myth of sodomy surrounded the subject with a sense of danger and fear. The emergence of homosexual subcultures at the end of the seventeenth century meant that close feeling between people of the same sex was perceived as a perversion of the desire between the sexes rather than an aspect of same sex desire. The result of this was that homosexuals were perceived as a distinct personality type; the term 'homosexual' was only coined in 1869 and took time to establish itself in the scientific literature.[21] A significant body of research material began to be collected and a substantial (if conflicting) body of scientific literature and theory established, often focused in departments of psychology and in specialized institutes.

There were important ambiguities in the scientific accounts of homosexuality from the beginning. While early theorists were fully aware of the cultural abhorrence of homosexuality, scientific commitment to objectivity tended to tame something of the visceral horror that the subject engendered. Scientific study of homosexuality attracted attention in particular from two groups in society. The first represented a long-standing but muted intellectual tradition – going back for example to the eighteenth-century philosopher Jeremy Bentham[22] – that sensed the irrationality of the late Western fear of homosexuality. The second consisted of those who shared homosexual desires and sensed that scientific study might offer some respite, and even help, in the face of sustained cultural hostility.

This scientific study had profound effects on the way in which same sex love and sexual behaviour were conceptualized in the succeeding hundred years. For gay people it offered a name and identity; it also offered a less hostile social category than the sodomite – who threatened the cosmic order – or the criminal – who threatened the social order. To be classified as 'sick' was to be admitted to the human community, albeit in a way that made you vulnerable to the attentions of the 'healthy'. The general categories of health and sickness have proved attractive to modern society as a way of reasserting the personal without the supernatural 'baggage' of traditional theology; examples of this are the ways in which the metaphor of sickness is used to mitigate the demands of the law or the intrusive claims of economic 'reality' (as in, for example, 'the sick note').[23] However, for gay people it allows the old fear of the unfamiliar to return clothed with all the vigour of modern anxiety about contagion.

The scientific category of the homosexual was invented both as an attempt at explanation and as part of a strategy for dealing with certain social deviants. In both respects it has proved highly ambiguous and has, in large part, been abandoned, although it continues to live on as one of the clutter of symbols that form popular culture.

Many gay activists dismiss the suggestion that the idea of the homosexual has helped gay people. However, this does not take sufficient account of the importance of finding a language through which twentieth-century society could attend to a highly stigmatized group of people. The category of the homosexual, with its associations of science and sickness, played an important part in helping a stigmatized group find a toe-hold in the conceptual world of the scientific and political establishment. The identification of a distinct group of people, for whom homosexuality was a given part of their lives, proved an essential part of the campaigns to shift the very heavy burden of social hatred and legal oppression. The psychological categorization of homosexuality played an important part in the partial decriminalization that gay people currently experience through the 1967 Sexual Offences Act.

At the same time the category of the homosexual has also proved profoundly oppressive of gay people. It did not prevent the passing in 1885 of the Labouchère amendment with its new crime of 'gross indecency'. The trial of Oscar Wilde in 1895, who was then charged under this Act, helped to re-establish a hostile stereotype of gay people.[24] In Germany the term was easily coopted by Hitler who filled it with all the traditional associations of sodomy – but now cloaked with the apparent endorsement of modern science. His early moves to power included the destruction of Hirschfeld's Institute of Sexual Science[25] and the use of the accusation of homosexuality to destroy his opponents.[26] The category 'homosexual', with the bureaucrats' chosen symbol of the pink triangle, took tens of thousands to their deaths in the concentration camps.[27] It was still alive to be deployed by Senator McCarthy in post-war USA.

However, the real difficulty with the term 'homosexual' lies with some of the assumptions built into it from its original coining in the mid-nineteenth century. In the popular mind it carries the suggestion of a sort of third sex that it derives from the stigmatization of homosexual subcultures since 1700. As an intellectual analysis of same sex desire and behaviour this concentrates on the gender projections of the early gay subcultures without recognizing the complex relationship that this form of homosexuality has with how affectionate relationships operate within and between the sexes. Its blindness to the question of cultural context and its ingrained assumption that attraction for people of the same sex represents the redirection of a biological drive towards the other sex make it a flawed instrument for accurate analysis. One result of its use has been the difficulty that many scientists have had in taking at face value the affection and relationships that exist between homosexual people.

The popular notion that homosexuality represents the misdirection of a biologically-driven instinct towards the other sex, derives its force not from psychological theory but from the cultural resonance created by the molly subcultures and their successors. At the level of psychological theory a more sophisticated view emerged with the thinking of Freud.[28] Freud noted the 'sexual' awareness of very young children and proposed an undifferentiated sexual instinct, whose ultimate direction was determined not by an inherent bias towards the other sex but by a process of personality development within the family. This view has the merit of recognizing that sexual identity is not something that inheres within the individual but something that emerges from interaction with the family (and, others would add, the culture). It also recognizes that the judgment that a heterosexual orientation is the proper outcome of personality development derives not from an inherent and identifiable biological or psychological mandate but from an external judgment that this is the 'intended' outcome of the social development of human personality.

The decisions of the American Psychiatric Association and the World Health Organization to remove homosexuality from the list of mental disorders are not the result of some 'liberal' conspiracy; they represent the recognition that there is nothing *intrinsic* to a homosexual orientation that makes it psychologically disordered. If homosexual people have difficulty functioning in society, this is not a result of their personal instability but of society's unwillingness to accept their orientation.

A view similar to Freud's underlies the influential teaching of Dr Elizabeth Moberley, an Orthodox Christian whose writing and teaching have strongly influenced evangelical ministries to gay people[29]. The core of her analysis is that a homosexual orientation represents an arrested personality development arising from a deficit in the relationship with the same sex parent. She therefore proposes that healing for gay people is to be found not in attempting premature relationships with the other sex but through tackling the continuing insecurity about same sex relationships of which inappropriate erotic homosexual desire is a symptom.

The questions of the origins and personal significance of a homosexual orientation will be addressed in Chapter 9. At this point three caveats about the term 'homosexuality' need to be noted. First of all, it is a term with a precise cultural history that many gay people perceive to have been profoundly hostile to their personal well-being. Secondly, the term was coined in a particular cultural context and against a background which showed little sensitivity to the cultural variations in same sex affection and sexual behaviour. Thirdly, despite the writing of a continuous stream of theorists, represented for example by Freud and Moberley, it carries the dubious connotation that homosexual desire represents a displaced heterosexual desire.

3   Finding a voice

The most important factor in the consolidation of the pattern of same sex sexuality and identity that emerged at the end of the seventeenth century has been the vitality, courage and creativity of the members of this emerging subculture. In the nature of things the story, particularly in its early stages, is not particularly well documented. Our earliest evidence comes from trials that frequently led to the deaths of those concerned. The contested character of gay experience has profoundly affected the way in which gay people see themselves, the ethos of the subcultures they create, and the way in which they present themselves to a hostile society. It has also contributed to the considerable difficulty that straight society has in understanding or accepting gay experience. Many straight people assert that they would not object to gay people if they would remain invisible. This, of course, fails to grasp what it means for gay people to live in a society tightly organized around the concepts of economic competition and heterosexual desire.

There are interesting parallels with certain aspects of the way Gypsy people relate to surrounding society. As travelling people, Gypsies find themselves in a difficult relationship with the settled communities among whom they live, sharing much in common and yet seeking to maintain a distinct identity. Anthropological studies have drawn attention to two features of Gypsy culture that reflect this difficult relationship.[30] The first is the contrast between the way in which Gypsies present themselves to outsiders – where they adopt a variety of strategies to alienate and confuse – and the highly ordered and even moralistic culture that characterizes their life together. The second is the way the vital distinction between insider and outsider is reflected in the complex ritual organization of Gypsy culture. The analogy cannot be pressed but the effect of contested identity on the two groups is interesting. (There is, of course, the further disconcerting parallel that both groups have often found themselves with a common enemy in Western culture, be it the Nazi regime in Germany or significant parts of the British Conservative Party.)

A scriptural insight into the character of gay subcultures can be found in the literary genre of the lament, itself a recurring feature of biblical religion. Suffering creates silence. Laments are costly attempts to break through the pain and to find hope again with God and within the human community. Fundamentally cries for justice and for divine vindication, they are often characterized by anger, exaggeration and the denunciation of enemies. The struggle to find dignity and the space to be creates its own cultural and artistic forms. Christians can hardly be surprised if the struggle of gay people to find a measure of dignity in Western society has rarely been cast in Christian vocabulary.

The adoption of the term 'gay' represented an important turning point in the history of same sex desire in modern Western culture. The word already carried the associations of 'wanton' or 'sexually dangerous and alive' and had been used as one term of self-designation by gay people at least since the 1930s.[31] The transition from 'homosexual' to 'gay' marks the assertion by gay people of the right to name themselves in the society of which they are a part. It also represents a shift from a pseudomedical category to a sexually defined social identity – the explosive realization that the human dignity of gay people is more accurately asserted by appealing to the language of human and civil rights than by relying on the patronage of the scientific establishment. A riot by gay people following a police raid on the Stonewall Inn in New York in 1969 is widely seen as the symbolic moment in the creation of this new identity. The reality, of course, is somewhat more complicated.[32] The transition represented by Stonewall was built on a developing political awareness among the inchoate gay communities of North America; it found its voice through the approaches honed within the American civil rights movement and built on American constitutional respect for the individual. It took its starting point not only from the reality of police harassment and social oppression but from a long history of costly and often apparently unsuccessful self-assertion.[33]

On both sides of the Atlantic the political assertion of

their dignity by gay people has had to take place within the prevailing political structure. In the USA and continental Europe the philosophical articulation of a framework of human rights provided an important base for action. In Britain the absence of any such general protection within the law meant that the quest for safe public space for gay people has tended to concentrate on winning round the political establishment.[34] The European Community's commitment to human rights has already led to certain changes and will remain an important focus for action in the future.[35] However, such political action depends for its effect on the existence of strong and effective expressions of gay identity and community. There is always the possibility of tension between those organizations that address specific issues of law and human rights and the continuing vitality of gay subcultures. While the focus of attention often rests on public battles over particular issues, it is the vitality and character of the gay movements and subcultures that continue to provide the base for gay identity.

The terms 'gay community' or 'gay subculture' may obscure the diverse and episodic character of the gay movement and the complex relationship that public expressions of gay identity have with the wider social organization of desire, affection or sexual relationships. The lives or public persona of certain gay activists, the activity of gay organizations, and gay places of entertainment may appear to be defined by a fixed gay identity. The reality for gay people and for the wider culture is that these function as focal points for a wider continuous social exploration of desire and gender. 'Gay' is not an isolated personal identity although the pressures of social conflict often present it as such; it is part of society's continuing engagement with the dynamics of gender identity and same sex desire. The public face of the gay world – 'the scene' – is never the sum total of a gay person's life concerns; it is a social mechanism that enables gay people to engage with aspects of their lives that society otherwise refuses to acknowledge.

The contested character of gay life and identity is the key to two important features of gay life. One is a perceived obsession with sex, the other is a gift for irony and style.

Gay pubs are no more – and no less – about sex than straight pubs. The lives of most gay people are concerned with the same humdrum routines of employment, companionship and domesticity as other people. The National Survey of Sexual Attitudes and Lifestyles published in 1994 indicates that most men involved in same sex sexual activity are not more active than their 'heterosexual' equivalents.[36] The sense that gay people's lives are obsessed with sex has a number of causes. It represents a failure to see the extent to which gender and heterosexual desire provides the organizing script for much of life in modern society: 'I need a girl to take to the party.' It may also reflect a high level of sexual anxiety where people suppress and deny the place of desire and the celebration of gender.

The frequent perception that gay people's lives are dominated by sex derives in part from the fact that gay people are socially visible and distinct precisely in this area of life. Cultural hostility to openly expressed same sex desire contributes to an overt sexuality. The celebration of gay sexuality, either socially or sexually, becomes an important way of asserting personal freedom over against an oppressive culture. The exuberance to be seen in Gay Pride marches is part of a necessary process by which people assert their intrinsic sense of personal value. The place of music and dance in the celebration and enjoyment of freedom is a common human tradition to be found, for example, in the traditions of black American culture or the practice of Christian worship.

Another factor may be the considerable difficulties that exist for gay people if they wish to establish settled domestic relationships. It is easy for gay people to find themselves in a state of perpetual courtship if they lack the context or social support to enable relationships to mature. At least some of the men who go cruising in public areas are 'heterosexual' men – often married – seeking male sexual contact or affection.

The other feature of gay life that reflects its contested character is its cultural sensitivity and capacity for irony. Any reader of the gay press will quickly become aware of a shifting kaleidoscope of fashion and artistic sensitivity. Gay sensibility has been at the cutting edge of popular fashion as well as some of the major movements of modern literary culture. Jonathan Dollimore, in an important book on the origins and direction of contemporary literary culture, sees the different approaches to the relationship of personal identity to culture – near the core of debates about 'post-modernism' – prefigured in the different strategies adopted at the end of the nineteenth century by two gay men, André Gide and Oscar Wilde: Gide accepting and adapting the social categories of conventional society; Wilde cutting beneath the half-truths of conventional social identities by paradox and irony.[37] George Steiner, widely recognized as a major cultural interpreter, has written,

> Judaism and homosexuality (most intensely where they over-lap, as in a Proust or a Wittgenstein) can be seen to have been the two main generators of the entire fabric and savour of urban modernity in the West.[38]

The cultural impact of gay sensibility arises because gay people find themselves in conflict with the prevailing idolatries of modern society – in particular with the attempt to enslave human desire, with its inherent sense of God and the mystery of human destiny, to the false gods of domesticity, nationalism, materialism and technology.

The gay capacity for irony and art arises from the stresses of living as an alien in society, of belonging and not belonging. It is not confined to high culture but is a recurrent feature of gay subcultures.

> How many gay men does it take to change a light bulb?
> Two: one to buy the art deco light bulb and one to say, 'Oh, it's marvellous!'[39]

Babuscio, according to a useful discussion by Evans, identifies four characteristics of 'camp': irony, aestheticism, theatricality and humour.[40] Gay sensibility not only involves a capacity for self-mockery; like the external projections of Gypsy culture it is part of a strategy for survival, both creating space and exploring the categories within which gay people have to discover a mode of being.

> How many psychiatrists does it take to change a light bulb?
> Only one, but the light bulb really has to want to change.[41]

Gay style and humour represent both a sensitivity to, and a distance from, the shifting and controlling images of the culture. Their strategic role in creating personal space – together with the underlying strain of irony – mean that they often carry multiple meanings and are easily open to misinterpretation from outside. This is particularly the case when gay subcultures are involved in the exploration of gender. For example cross gender behaviour by gay men is a complex phenomenon; it is more likely to represent engagement with ambiguous social status than to be evidence of misogyny. It can involve a critique of the suppression of feminine qualities in conventional stereotypes of masculine character. It (obviously!) does not indicate a lack of interest in masculinity. Gay men often set the male fashions in modern society precisely because of their sensitivity to masculinity.

The coming of age of a public gay identity has somewhat changed both the character of gay self-presentation in society and the symbolic systems that prevail in gay subcultures and relationships. At one level this can be seen in the abandonment of the adoption of male and female social roles that was sometimes found in harsher days. Another is the re-emergence of queer as an assertive self-designation, objecting that gay movements have been coopted and tamed by the socially oppressive norm.[42] More controversially the lessening of cross-gender irony is balanced in some circles by an exploration of the dialogue between desire, power and masculinity that lends an SM tone to some sections of the gay subculture. Strongly repudiated by other parts of the gay movement, like other manifestations of gay identity it is likely to be misread and the element of 'play' underestimated.

When they are at their most outrageous, gay men are often making their most serious statements – both about the humanity which they share with others, and about the images and fantasies which dominate 'normal' society. This deep cultural engagement has had its part to play, alongside more overt political and economic activity, in establishing a public gay identity.

Here to stay?

The emergence of an overt gay identity in Western societies is perceived by many people, including many Christians, as an affront to the moral order and a denial of the domestic ideal which they believe has its basis in the Christian tradition. One of the questions that those who take this view need to address is whether a public gay identity is now a given of Western culture as we know it. However puzzling or undesirable, is it a feature of society to which legislators and the Christian churches will need to adjust? Should an attempt be made by discriminatory legislation, social ostracism and church discipline to suppress this disconcerting feature of modern life? Has such an attempt much chance of success?

The inclusion by many secular employers of sexual orientation in their equal opportunities policies is evidence that acceptance of a gay identity is increasingly a given of modern culture. Although many, perhaps most, areas of gay life remain heavily contested, there are many signs that the social and intellectual climate has changed decisively. Examples in the public realm are the recent report on homosexuality by the European Human Rights Foundation and the 1991 decision by Amnesty International to include people imprisoned solely on the grounds of homosexuality within its mandate. At a more ordinary level, most young people are aware of gay contemporaries and find it difficult to recover the sense of profound revulsion which many in an earlier generation took for granted.

A sense of history should keep gay activists from any danger of complacency. The emergence of the pattern of homosexuality represented by the new gay identity has been punctuated by savage repression. Such repression has often been triggered by social stress or attempts to assert national identity. The eighteenth-century campaigns against Dutch homosexuals occurred against a background of natural disasters and economic difficulty (and were accompanied by a devastating pogrom against Gypsies).[43] Hitler managed to destroy a movement for the decriminalization of homosexuality which many saw as invincible. However, recent history also provides evidence of the strong, historical dynamic towards the emergence of a gay identity. Anti-gay campaigners will have to show the ruthlessness of Hitler and his earlier predecessors if they are to make a real impact. One of the main effects of the Tory anti-gay campaigns of 1986–88 was to revitalize organized campaigns for gay civil rights. The fact that in Europe and America gay people have had to bear the brunt of AIDS led Victoria Gillick to say, 'I regard most things gays do as a swansong, because there are not going to be an awful lot of them left in 20 years.' The reality is that the gay community has responded to this disease with an energy and maturity that have earned it the respect and affection of many outside its number.

Ironically, one of the main reasons why the social pattern of a recognized gay identity is probably here to stay is that it is the product of some of the most powerful social commitments of our culture: the adoption of a competitive model for public economic life and the cultural decision to identify human desire with sexual behaviour and the domestic ideal. Christians who are appalled by this new development are often unaware that they have baptized into their working theology precisely the same social ideals which have led to the emergence of a gay identity.

Christians who look with admiration to the sixteenth-century Reformation cannot fail to be intrigued by the emergence of this pattern within the societies shaped by the Reformation. At one level it indicates the way in which any new vision or 'myth' is assimilated and to some extent taken captive by the society that receives it. Another example, discussed by Jeffrey Weeks, is the way in which the British working class assimilated and took captive the ideal of the family being promoted by nineteenth-century bourgeois and Christian social reformers, wresting it from its inventors and making it serve their own interests: designed as a haven of religious faith, it was to become a bastion against established public religion.[44]

Two features of the Reformation served to constrain the social impact of the Protestant Churches: their abandonment of economics to secular thought – the autonomy of the market place – and their hostility to monasticism. The Reformation campaign against monasticism provides a curious spectacle in which high-minded preachers are made the instruments of acquisitive landowners. The price paid by Christian social witness was very high. It drastically undermined the idea that wealth was held for the community not the individual. It enslaved the church to the ideals and myths of the bourgeois family. It cut the nerve of any social affirmation or exploration of male same sex love. The effect of this was not only to disable effective Christian witness to those parts of society for whom the Christian family ideal was not a viable mode of social being, but also to remove any credible Christian witness that desire is good – and its ultimate goal is not earthly beauty nor domestic bliss but God.

The emergence of a public gay identity raises difficult issues both for the Christian churches and for gay people. For the churches the questions are not limited to the moral evaluation of certain genital acts or affectionate relations. They have to decide whether it is right or possible to exclude from active church life those who openly align themselves with a gay identity. They also need to face deeper questions about their own social and cultural alignment.

For gay people the questions are similar. What are they to make of churches wedded to a cultural tradition deeply hostile to the instincts and well-being of gay people? When they hear the mysterious and attractive call of Christ, how and where are they to respond?

Chapter 8

What Does the Bible Say?

If the present course of the abolitionists is right,
then the course of Christ and the apostles were
wrong. For the circumstances of the two cases are
. . . in all essential particulars, the same.

Charles Hodge on slavery[1]
1860

The question 'What does the Bible say?' is never quite as simple
as it looks. Broadly it invites two sorts of answers, both of which
are important. One attempts to fit the phenomenon in question
into an overarching scheme that does justice to the structure
of biblical thought. The second attempts to find relevant biblical
texts and discover their meaning by contextual exegesis.

At the risk of being frivolous, it may be helpful to look first
at the less emotive question, 'What does the Bible say about
cars?' One person might attempt an answer in terms of biblical
theology: the doctrine of creation teaches us to see cars as
an expression of the goodness and diversity of creation; the
doctrine of the Fall teaches us to see cars as expressing the pride
and disorder of fallen humanity and its relation to nature; the
doctrine of eschatology teaches us what? Perhaps that there will
be no cars in heaven – just as there are apparently no secondary
sources of light (Revelation 21:23)!

The second sort of answer probably begins by attempting
to find cultural equivalents: possibly the chariot or the horse.
This approach will quickly face questions as to what is primarily
important about cars. Is it their relation to human mobility and
locality? Or is it their relation to human technology and ambition
– about which scripture would appear to be ambivalent? The

question of identifying cultural equivalents can quickly draw the particular matter into a wider context. Thus Richard Bauckham has described the car as the 'modern sacrament of freedom' – a freedom that rejects all limits: 'There is no more pervasive symbol of this freedom and its destructive futility than the motor car.'[2] Others date the collapse of old-fashioned sexual morality in the American Mid–West to the arrival of the car: 'Pa, can I have the car tonight?' was the prelude to sex in the 'Chevvie' and enabled the sexual energy of the young, on this view, to escape the discipline of the community.

So far this discussion has assumed that the question being asked is, 'How are we to evaluate cars?' However, another set of questions could also be in the frame: 'Should we drive cars?' 'Who should drive cars?' 'How fast should we drive cars?' and so on. Again, these apparently innocent questions rapidly turn out to have wider ramifications. For example, what does the fact than nobody keeps – or is expected to keep – the strict speed limits reveal about the nature of law or political authority?

The question 'What does the Bible teach about homosexuality?' invites the same sort of analysis and subdivisions. As with cars, one dilemma is, where is homosexuality to be located in the biblical text? The question of identifying cultural equivalents has to be addressed – and may not be the same for different sorts of homosexuality. Should a scriptural evaluation begin with the shape of biblical anthropology or with certain scriptural texts? If the latter, which ones? The apparently simple question 'Are sexual acts ever OK between people of the same sex?' itself needs to be analysed further. For example, what is the status of oral or anal sex? Does this depend on the gender of those involved? Is there a significant difference between solitary and mutual masturbation? How do these acts relate to same sex love? Are such acts better or worse if those involved love each other? Are bodily acts to be judged by an acultural absolute or by their meaning and expression within a particular culture?

Evangelical presentations on homosexuality usually follow a fairly standard pattern. They begin with Genesis 1:27 and 2:18–25 – and possibly with Jesus's endorsement of these passages' relevance to marriage and divorce (Mark 10:2–9; Matthew 19:3–12) – and use this to assert that in God's plan the place for sexual union is within the marriage of one man and one woman for life. They then turn to the six or seven particular texts which apparently condemn some sort of homosexuality and so create a 'knock-down' argument that homosexuality and any sexual acts between men are always contrary to the will of God. This 'standard' pattern characteristically assumes that these passages exhaust the significant scriptural references to the subject of homosexuality. Each element in this standard approach needs to be evaluated.

The major weakness of the standard argument lies in its inadequate analysis of homosexuality and of the ways in which the two sexes join in ordering society and in raising children. It does not reflect on the cultural diversity found in human relationships. It imposes on scripture the domestic ideal of the nuclear family – a husband and wife with their children enjoying domestic bliss in protected isolation from wider society. It fails to recognize that homosexuality is itself a complex cultural phenomenon that has to be seen as a form of same sex desire mediated through concepts, social arrangements and bodily symbolism that are shared with the rest of society. Even when the standard approach is presented with careful argument and meticulous scholarship, it often leaves upholders of the 'traditional' view of same sex relations uneasy. In turning to scripture, particular care needs to be taken to address the question of cultural equivalents: exactly where is homosexuality to be found in scripture?

The appeal to Genesis

The early chapters of Genesis have the same relationship to the whole of scripture that the Ten Commandments have to the biblical law codes: they provide a framework within which the complex material that follows is to be understood. In starting with Genesis 1 and 2 evangelical writers can point not only to their place in the canon of scripture but also to the way in which Jesus and the New Testament refer back to these early chapters (cf. Matthew 19:3–12; Romans 5:12–21; Revelation 22). However, it is simplistic to see the story of Adam and Eve as providing a biblical mandate for the isolated nuclear family of Western culture. These great chapters are intended to provide the backcloth to the whole complex story of the ordering of human society. When the text says, 'Therefore a man leaves his father and mother and cleaves to his wife, and they become one flesh' (Genesis 2:24), it is implying not the isolation of a married couple from the wider society but the creation of a new unit within society, as noted in the earlier discussion on polygamy, 'one flesh' refers to the creation of a new kinship group (cf. Genesis 29.14).

The difficulty with seeing these chapters as providing a biblical mandate for lifelong monogamy, as presented in the modern domestic ideal, is that this interpretation is not confirmed by the rest of scripture. In seeking a biblical basis for its commendation of monogamy the House of Bishops' report *Issues in Human Sexuality* can do no better than speak of 'an evolving convergence' in scripture.[3] The complex patterns of the Old Testament cultures have been discussed in earlier chapters. Even when something like the intimacy of modern companionate marriage occurs – as in Elkanah's tenderness towards Hannah (1 Samuel 1:8) or the warnings against irresponsible sexual liaisons in Proverbs (5:15–23) – the context is very different from the modern social pattern. The first example occurs in a polygamous marriage; the second in a culture which provided social arrangements that strongly affirmed emotional relationships within the two sexes. What the Old Testament portrays is not a flawed quest for the ideal of the nuclear family but a complex society in which both genders richly participate. The power of Old Testament narrative often comes from the way it engages with the potent images of gender and portrays the passion and wickedness of which human beings are capable. However, its goal is not the domestic bliss of an ideal TV family from the 1950s but a mysterious new creation, which the most powerful gender images are needed to describe (cf. Isaiah 61:10; 66:7–11). When elements of domestic nostalgia do appear – as in the refrain 'every man under his vine and under his fig tree' (1 Kings 4:25; Micah 4:4; Zechariah 3:10) or the domestic happiness of Proverbs 5 – these are quickly revealed as mere resting-places in a story with a different ending.

The New Testament's treatment of Genesis 1 and 2 follows a similar pattern. Jesus uses the primal vision of Genesis 2 to expose the contempt for women implicit in the Pharisaic approach to divorce (Mark 10:2–12, Matthew 19:3–12; Luke

16:14–18). Wives are not disposable adjuncts to male life; man and woman are created by God to be partners in the one society. The search for convenient legal justifications for putting a wife aside fails to embrace the duality of gender in God's creation; it does not take seriously either the importance of women or the quality of relationship to which human beings are called. However, the New Testament does not treat the domestic ideal of marriage as the goal of human aspiration. Jesus's mission is not about the establishing of stable marriages or secure and happy homes. He himself did not marry. It is precisely the passage in which Jesus quotes Genesis 2:24 that commends the renunciation of marriage. His primary thrust is the creation of an affectionate community within which marriage is almost an irrelevance (cf. Mark 3:14–19, Luke 8:1–3; Mark 1:16–18,29–31; 1 Corinthians 9:5; Romans 16:1–23; 1 Timothy 5:1,2). When the final book of the Bible picks up again the great themes of Genesis 1 and 2 in its vision of the goal of history it has nothing to say about the ideal of marriage, although it harnesses the imagery of gender with great power (Revelation 12; 14:4; 19:7–9; 21:2).

In a curious way, the confident assertion that Genesis 2:18–25 is simply about monogamous marriage itself reflects the way that modern society has limited affectionate relationship and the celebration of gender to domestic life. When St Aelred discusses the text 'It is not good for man to be alone' (Genesis 2:18), he sees it as affirming the friendship that is the basis of all human society – an affectionate generosity which human sin has corrupted.[4] It is because Aelred shares in a general consensus that God intends human beings to live in a society bonded together by friendship that he can turn naturally to this passage to show that same sex friendship is part of God's will in creation. The modern 'intuitive' sense that same sex love is somehow contradicted by Genesis 2:18–25 arises from the cultural invisibility of same sex affection outside the family and the complementary conviction that the visible same sex affection in gay subcultures is a perversion of heterosexual desire.

Genesis 1:27 and 2:18–25 are about the social nature of humanity and the mysterious duality of gender. The powerful images of these passages find their outworking in the ordering of human society and in the various forms of male/female union

which we lump together under the term 'marriage'. It provides
a framework for the gendered ordering of human society. It
may challenge the way in which particular societies recognize
the partnership of the sexes in their common life. It does not
provide a blueprint for the way in which a particular society or
culture is to order its public or domestic life. It does not of itself
preclude the possibility that certain individuals in a society may
not fit the general pattern and may respond in a different way
to the mysterious duality of gender.

Finding homosexuality in the scriptures

Conversations about what the Bible has to say about homosexuality tend to move quickly to discussing the classic 'anti-gay'
texts. These will be considered in the next section of this
chapter. However, it is important first of all to ask whether
there are other passages which need to be considered. This in
turn involves recognizing that the term 'homosexuality' covers
a variety of different emotional and social 'packages'; what we
are likely to find in the scripture are not exact replicas of the
modern gay lifestyle but individuals or groups who share some
of the characteristics that our society associates with a gay
identity. Among the passages that need to be considered are
those in which gay people find an echo of their own experience
and relationship with Christ.

1 *Where are the gay people?*
Were there gay people in Israel? The common assumption is
that the severe prohibitions of the Levitical law and the cleansing
effect of God's presence meant that there was no homosexuality
in Israel except where it was associated with the corruption of
the idolatrous Canaanite cult. A curious phrase in 2 Samuel 3:29
may indicate that things were not so simple. There are many
ways in which the historical books show that accepted practice in
Israel differed from what one might deduce from the law codes.
An obvious example is that David, as the recent descendant of
a Moabite woman, should not – according to the law recorded in
Deuteronomy 23:3 – have been allowed to worship with Israel.
John Boswell's timely warning that law codes are a bad guide to

either social reality or popular ideals finds many echoes in the historical books of the Old Testament.

The context of 2 Samuel 3:29 is King David's denunciation of the treachery of Joab, his chief of staff, for the murder of Abner, a general who had supported David's rival for the throne. David curses Joab in these words,

> I and my kingdom are for ever guiltless before the LORD for the blood of Abner son of Ner. May it fall upon the head of Joab and upon all his father's house; and may the house of Joab never be without one who has a discharge, or who is leprous, or who holds a spindle, or who is slain by the sword, or who lacks bread.

The first two categories in David's curse refer to people who would be perpetually unclean under the laws recorded in Leviticus. The term 'who holds a spindle' sounds like a term of contempt and would appear to refer to a male who fails to conform to the male stereotype of this fairly macho culture. Babylonian and Assyrian texts refer to effeminate men who were probably male prostitutes in the temple service of the goddess Ishtar; they were often portrayed as carrying a spindle.[5] In the case of the text in 2 Samuel there is no suggestion of an idolatrous context. The words appear to be a harshly contemptuous reference to a young man unable to adopt the masculine identity of his culture. If the expression 'who holds a spindle' is derived from non-Israelite culture, it may be an example of the common pattern whereby societies attribute non-conforming forms of homosexuality to foreign influence. (For example, eighteenth-century England tended to blame homosexuality on contact with Italians.)[6]

This curious verse does not necessarily correspond to what we would call a gay identity. Nor does it absolutely prove that such contemptible men were involved in sexual activity in Israel – although the evidence of other cultures with despised transgenderal homosexuality would suggest that this is likely. But it does point to the presence of a despised but tolerated group of men who could not conform to the sexually aggressive masculinity of the culture of the early monarchy (cf. 1 Samuel 21:4,5). Bracketed with two groups whom the Levitical law

declared unclean and whom Jesus explicitly declared clean
(Mark 1:40–1; 5:25–34), such men might have expected a
better deal under the gospel dispensation.

The New Testament account of the healing of the centurion's
servant provides an interesting contrast (Matthew 8:5–13; Luke
7:1–10). The centurion whom Jesus commends for his faith
comes to Jesus moved by deep concern for his servant. The
Greek text calls the centurion's servant his *pais* – his 'boy';
it is a standard term for a servant, but also an affectionate
diminutive often used in homosexual relationships.[7] The possible gay subtext in this passage is brought out by the New
Testament scholar, Gerd Theissen, in an imaginary dialogue
with a disapproving Jewish teacher.[8] The Jewish teacher is
speaking:

> 'One day a Gentile centurion living here in Capernaum came to
> him. He asked him to heal his orderly. Of course you have to
> help Gentiles. But why this one? Everyone knows that most
> of these Gentile officers are homosexual. Their orderlies are
> their lovers. But Jesus isn't interested in that sort of thing.
> He didn't ask anything about the orderly. He healed him – and
> the thought didn't occur to him that later someone might think
> of appealing to him in support of the view that homosexuality
> was permissible.'
>
> 'Are you certain that the centurion was homosexual.'
>
> 'Of course not, but everyone must have their suspicions.
> Jesus wasn't at all bothered. At this point I would advise more
> caution.'
>
> 'All right, perhaps it was ill-advised. But was it forbidden?'
> 'No, I couldn't say that . . . '

Although there is an element of speculation in this interpretation,
the scenario proposed by Theissen is certainly consistent with
the way Jesus is presented in the Gospels.

2 David and Jonathan (1 Samuel 18:1–5; 20; 2 Samuel 1:17–27)

Gay people have often felt a natural sense of rapport with the
passionate friendship recorded between David and Jonathan and
with David's affirmation that this love was 'surpassing the love

of women' (2 Samuel 1:26). The homoerotic strand of this story was even more obvious in pre-modern cultures which did not see homosexual desire as excluded by marriage. The love between these two men is portrayed as a fine and heroic passion that transcends the conflict in which both men are locked. In an intriguing study, David Halperin notes points of similarity with other heroic same sex friendships in ancient literature.[9] Jonathan's love for David transcends the social structure and is a sign of the emerging ascendancy of the handsome David, a marginal figure chosen by God to supplant Jonathan on Israel's throne. The covenant the two men make together confirms the social bonds created by their love.

In 1 Samuel 20:30 Saul denounces Jonathan's love for David as perverse and a source of sexual shame (cf. Leviticus 20:17–21). There is no suggestion here of a genital relationship between the two men; this makes it even clearer that Saul's sense of outrage arises from the concepts around which the sexual project was organized in early Israel. He saw Jonathan's love as shamefully unnatural because it ignored the heart of the sexual ethic of his culture: the continuation of the male line. It is part of the drama of the story that this unorthodox love is a sign that God's favour rests on David. Although out of the ordinary it is not seen as unmasculine. It fits easily with the macho culture of David's circle which admired the qualities of the male hero and rejoiced in close relationships established within a band of warriors (2 Samuel 23:8–39; 1 Samuel 14).

3 Jesus and friendship

David's love for Jonathan and the friendship that bonded together the band of outlaws that provided the core of his support (1 Samuel 22:1–2) prefigure the place of friendship in Jesus's life and ministry. Friendship – the formation of easy, affectionate bonds between social equals – is one of the clearest characteristics of Jesus in the Gospel accounts. Those who travelled with him functioned as a company of friends (Mark 3:13–14; Luke 8:1–3). His embodiment of divine grace which caused such continual offence was characterized as friendship with sinners (Matthew 11:19; Luke 7:34). The intimate relationship with God to which he sought to admit his disciples is movingly described in terms of friendship (John 15:15).

This obvious feature of Jesus's life rests on two aspects of his culture to which many modern people, at least in Western middle class society, have little access. The first is publicly accepted same sex social groupings. Jesus's choice of twelve men to form the heart of the apostolic band is a slight source of embarrassment in these days of equal opportunity policies. However, it reflected a common feature of much pre-modern society and is part, for example, of the social background to the book of Proverbs. Few aspects of traditional English society seem more quaint to us than the gentlemen's club. Hostility to such arrangements reflects not only the understandable sense that such groupings are used to exclude women from power in society, but also a cultural understanding of masculinity which has little place for affectionate association between men. It is interesting that while Jesus stood against the cultural oppression of women and freely included them in his circle (Luke 8:1–3; John 11; Mark 15:40–41) he continued to work with same sex social groupings.

The second cultural basis for the friendship upon which Jesus based his emerging movement was the general respect for friendship. Many Christians are influenced by the distinction that C.S. Lewis draws in *The Four Loves* between *philia* (friendship) and *eros* (desire). C.S. Lewis portrays friendship as the disinterested but affectionate pursuit of a common goal. This fails to do justice either to the intimacy or the erotic potential of friendship as ancient people understood it.[10] The account of Jonathan's first love for David has a note of passion that would be at home in any romantic novel (1 Samuel 18:1–4). Friendship had about it an egalitarian freedom not present in other relationships. At the same time it created social bonds akin to kinship. This is present in David's reference to 'my brother Jonathan' and underlies much of the personal warmth in the Christianity of the New Testament (Hebrews 2:11–12; 1 Timothy 5:1,2)

Friendship is not a minor theme of the Christian faith but is integral to its vision of life. The church's failure to attract newcomers often reflects precisely the distance between its life and Jesus's gift for friendship. Its capacity for friendship is often undermined by the temptation to see itself as the guardian of public morals or the servant of the domestic ideal.

Gay people often contribute to the life and mission of the church precisely through a gift for accepting friendship. Jesus's capacity for friendship has three outworkings that have been particularly evocative for gay people.

The first is his close friendship with the apostle John, 'the disciple whom Jesus loved' (John 13:23; 19:26; 20:2; 21:20). This is described in St John's Gospel in terms of deepest intimacy. At the Last Supper John reclines on Jesus' chest and is naturally the recipient of his every confidence (John 13:23). At Calvary the intimacy leads to Jesus' immensely poignant charge to Mary and John (19:26–7) – the love of friends creating bonds of kinship. On the morning of the resurrection John needs no one to tell him the meaning of the empty grave-clothes; he has an intuitive sympathy with his intimate friend (John 20:8,9). This strong theme of emotional intimacy does not necessarily contradict the more headstrong picture of John that emerges in the Synoptic Gospels (Mark 3:17; Luke 9:54) – as the biblical example of Jonathan's courage in war illustrates (cf. 1 Samuel 14). If the evidence of Irenaus and Polycarp is correct that St John died around the year AD 100 then at the time of the Last Supper Jesus was about thirty-three and John about nineteen. The Synoptic Gospels provide little evidence of this friendship, although they indicate that there was an inner group of three in the apostolic band (cf. Mark 14:33). Scholars who are sceptical about the historical basis for the fourth gospel are able to treat the intimacy between Jesus and John as a sort of code for the spiritual relationship being offered to the disciple or for special knowledge being offered to the Johannine community. However, the natural reading of these texts – with their detailed portrayal of great intimacy between two unmarried men – provides a natural echo with the love that many gay people share. It also raises questions about attitudes to intimate friendship in the life of the church.

The second aspect of this theme of friendship that rings bells for gay people is the easy and accepting friendship that Jesus offered to those whom society regarded as beyond the pale. For people who have a gift and need for friendship, and who know that they are potential outcasts in their society, the theme of Jesus the friend has particular power. The Gospels' portrayal of Jesus' capacity for friendship leads to a devotion to Jesus the friend which is sometimes almost homoerotic in tone – as in Samuel Crossman's hymn 'My song is love unknown'. This emerges starkly in a beautiful poem on prayer by Thomas O'Neil,[11]

> Jesus, forgive me,
> for these nights spent in the arms
> of the other boy I love.

The third outworking of this theme of friendship that resonates for gay people is to be found in the New Testament letter known as 1 John, with its simple assertions that 'God is love' (4:16) and 'love is from God' (4:7). There is much in the text of this letter to counter any purely sentimental or amoral understanding of the word 'love' (3:6,10,16). At the same time the primacy given to the idea of love resonates with the use of this idea in St John's Gospel (John 13:23,34–35; 15:12–17) and cannot be reduced to a code-word for orthodoxy. The Johannine literature makes it very clear that the love being spoken of here has a strong emotional tone. Aelred's *On Spiritual Friendship* is not making an impossible move when he explores the formulation 'God is friendship'[12] and takes this as the basis for his careful exposition of the path from carnal to spiritual love. Straight people are quick to see in the love and intimacy they experience a pale reflection of divine love. It is difficult to see why gay people should not be allowed the same freedom.

The seven texts

Earlier chapters have dealt in some detail with much of the background to the classic 'anti-gay' texts. In some cases careful consideration has already been given to how they are to be interpreted and used. It should be clear that the modern reader should not too easily assume that he or she shares the conceptual framework of the original texts. It is also important to bring to these texts a conceptual understanding of homosexuality and a disciplined concern to discern points of cultural similarity and difference.

Genesis 18:26–19:29

The fate of Sodom and Gomorrah was already sealed before the attempted rape of the angels that came to visit the city. There is no suggestion in the Old Testament that the practice of homosexuality was the reason for God's fiery judgment. Various prophetic warnings to Israel imply that it was sins she shared with Sodom that might bring her to the same fate (cf. Isaiah 1:10; Amos 4:11). Ezekiel explains the guilt of Sodom:

> she and her daughters had pride, surfeit of food, and prosperous ease, but did not aid the poor and needy. They were haughty, and did abominable things before me. (16:49–50)

The context makes clear that 'abominable things' refers to idolatrous worship. When Jesus refers to the fate of Sodom he has in view not their sexual practice but their refusal to hear God's messengers (cf. Matthew 10:14–15;11:20–4).

The attempted rape of the visitors is evidence not of sexual deviance but of an arrogant and violent society. On both the occasions in scripture when such rape is threatened, the gender of those targeted seems irrelevant (Genesis 19:8; Judges 19:23–5) except that the primary humiliation desired was of the socially more significant males. With one possible exception that will be discussed below, there is no trace in biblical literature of a symbolic link between Sodom and homosexual sex. The link that arose in subsequent centuries gained its force from the drama of the story and a cultural fear of homosexuality.[13] Given the role that the term 'sodomite' was to play in Western society in taking thousands of gay people to a cruel death, it is inexplicable that the NRSV should use the word to translate the unrelated Greek word *arsenokoitai*.[14]

This evocative passage has no light to throw on the practice of homosexuality – except to condemn male rape as a means of humiliating outsiders. However, it has much light to throw on the dangers of the careless use of symbolically potent parts of scripture. Like certain New Testament texts that have often been used to justify anti-semitism,[15] it remains a warning of the way profound, irrational fears can arise within a culture and take captive even the scriptures. Careless exegesis costs lives.

Leviticus 18:22; 20:13

These two verses in Leviticus are central to the very strong
Christian tradition that anal intercourse between men is absolutely incompatible with Christian discipleship. Earlier chapters
have attempted to locate them within the symbolic system of
Israel's culture and within the wider question of the Christian
use of the biblical law codes.[16] In reflecting on the way they
should be interpreted, three questions need to be addressed:
To what extent are they binding on Christians? How is their
content to be interpreted? How are we to relate to the symbolic
climate that they represent?

Few modern people, Christian or otherwise, are used to
thinking much about the law codes to be found in the early
books of the Bible. In many ways this is a pity – not least
because they contain rich insight on questions of justice, social
order and economics. This ignorance makes the question of their
status more difficult for Christians to handle when a subject as
emotive as homosexuality is concerned. Although there have
been periods in history when biblical laws have been taken as
the basis for secular law, this finds no justification in the New
Testament. Attempts to treat the commands of the biblical law
codes as directly applicable today ignore the fact that they have
to be read through four different filters: they arose at a particular
period in Israel's history and were not treated as immutable
when social conditions changed;[17] they are presented to us as
part of larger theological works and should be seen not simply
as laws but as elements within the total message of a book; their
context is a particular stage in God's unfolding dealings with his
people, so that their meaning today must be determined in the
light of Jesus's teaching and example; they are part of a symbolic
system which does not apply to Christians.[18]

All this means that careful consideration has to be given to
why these verses prohibit sexual intercourse between men.
This law is set within a complex symbolic system that gives
a clear symbolic meaning to bodily discharges and is concerned
to preserve both the stability of a clan-based society and
the distinctness of Israel from the surrounding nations. This
symbolic system works by creating a strong respect for the
ordered and the normal as a way of inculcating an ordered and
uncompromising allegiance to Israel's God. Within this context

this law can be understood in one of three ways. Firstly, it can be seen simply as part of an arbitrary purity code abrogated with the coming of Christ – a purity code aimed at creating a sense in Israel of the ordered norm of God's way as, for example, in the prohibition of eating prawns and the exclusion of lepers. Secondly, it can be viewed as a witness to an unchanging creation pattern for human genital acts. Thirdly, it can be regarded as some sort of combination of the two.

Those who take the second of these views will regard these verses as the basis of an absolute moral rule prohibiting genital contact between men. If the third interpretation is adopted, two questions will need to be asked in evaluating sexual acts or relationships between men today. Is the acceptance of such people within the Christian assembly consistent with the understanding of God that we have through Jesus Christ? How do such acts and relationships honour the patterning of God's creation? These two questions would at the least leave open the acceptance of certain sorts of sexual activity between men. The Father of Jesus Christ is a God who welcomes into fellowship those whom society regards as outcast and unclean. The duality of gender is respected both by those for whom the gender stereotypes of their culture provide viable structures for personal life and also by those for whom they do not. Gay people are involved in a painful dialogue with their society's reception of gender. This does not imply a rejection of the duality of gender – within the social processes of society they often play an important part in the rediscovery of the potency of gender.

The question of how the Levitical laws might apply in modern society can be seen with greater clarity over the question of oral sex. Oral sex is not mentioned in the biblical law codes. The reason is almost certainly that such sex was so abhorrent as not to need prohibiting.[19] This is to be understood against a culture or symbolic system that associated semen with the transmission of the male line – it was seed to be planted not swallowed. Does this mean that modern Christians who seek the mind of Christ through scripture should absolutely repudiate – and teach against – oral sex, because it is contrary to the mind-set of this Old Testament sexual ethic? Or does it mean that they should sigh with relief that on this matter there is no explicit law with which they need to wrestle?

The prohibition of anal intercourse between men in Leviticus is part of a symbolic system which creates a cultural resonance that is hostile to gay people. This is reflected in 2 Samuel 3:29 and in the cumulative negative symbolism of Jewish culture that came – despite the ambivalent story of David and Jonathan – to regard homosexuality as the characteristic vice of the Gentiles. Gay people are not unique in encountering a cultural hostility to their way of life in the cultures of the Bible. Other examples include: a negative symbolism for the sea – compare 'the sea was no more' in Revelation 21:1; a pervasive hostility to non-Israelite semitic people such as Edom,[20] and a relentlessly negative view of dogs.[21] Seafaring peoples have to comfort themselves with the sailors who were more god-fearing than Jonah (Jonah 1) and the massive nautical detail of Acts 27. There are no positive references to dogs in scripture, and the negative view is echoed by both Jesus (Matthew 7:6;15:26) and Paul (Philippians 3:2). In the case of dogs English people do not seem to find cultural re-adjustment too difficult!

Deuteronomy 23:17,18
This verse prohibits cult prostitution in Israel.[22] In verse 17 the Hebrew words used for female and male cult prostitutes, *qdeshah* and *qadesh*, both mean 'set apart' or 'holy'. The King James Version revealingly translates them as 'harlot' and 'sodomite'. In verse 18 the word 'dog' is used for the male cult prostitute; this may simply be a term of contempt or may refer to the position adopted in intercourse.[23] Cult prostitution seems to have been a perennial danger in pre-exilic Israel (cf. 1 Kings 14:23–4; 15:12–13; 2 Kings 23:5–7); it was linked with the worship of the goddess Astarte and was probably associated with the quest for fertility. As such it was part of the idolatry that Hosea and Jeremiah persistently denounced as harlotry and adultery (cf. Hosea 2; Jeremiah 3:1–14). Cult prostitution was denounced for its idolatry and for the implied attempt to gain divine blessing through the offering of sexual energy. There is no reference to male cult prostitutes in the related prophetic oracles; the focus of their denunciation was on the deification of sex.

There is a passing reference to the life experience of the *qadesh* in Job 34:16, accurately translated as 'short-lived as male prostitutes' (REB). In Revelation 22:15 the exclusion of 'dogs' from the heavenly city occurs in a list full of Old Testament allusions and highlighting the evils of false worship; it may carry the resonance of a cultural contempt for dogs and effeminate men but its primary reference is to the consuming worldliness that draws people from the worship of God.

Romans 1:18–32

This great passage is important both for the part it plays in the argument of St Paul's most influential letter and because of what it seems to say in verses 26 and 27 about the origin of homosexual desire. The meaning of the passage, and of these two verses within it, have been the subject of extensive scholarly discussion. There is only room here to give the outlines of this discussion and to begin to show its relevance to the interpretation of verses 26 and 27.

These two verses need to be seen within the context of the whole passage. St Paul's central thesis in the passage is as follows: God's judgment is active in the social processes of society. Humanity's failure to respond to the power and goodness of God, visible in creation, by appropriate worship and thanksgiving results first of all in an intellectual futility (vv.21,22) that leads on to idolatry (v.23). This in turn leads to disordered and destructive sexual desire (vv.24–7) and then to a social disintegration characterized by greed and violence (vv.28–32). Its relevance to modern life is obvious – although the mechanism by which idolatry results in personal and social disorder needs careful exploration.[24]

Modern scholars tend to take one of two starting points in discussing the place of this passage in St Paul's argument. Some see it simply as his restatement of the reality of the fall, recounting a process that can be seen in both Jewish and Gentile culture. Others note that St Paul has primarily the Gentile world in mind. On this approach these verses have to be seen in the light of the issue that lies behind many of his letters and that was a recurrent source of conflict in the New Testament church: the relationship of the first Christians to Jewish identity and the Jewish law. Such writers point to the repeated use of 'they' and 'them' in 1:18–32, the direct 'you' addressed to Jews and Jewish believers in chapter 2, the 'our' of 4:1 where St Paul assumes that he and the imagined hearer share a common Jewish origin, and the substantial references to tensions between Jewish and Gentile Christians in chapters 9–11 and 14:1–15:13. So, it is argued, Paul's aim is to engage with these tensions by addressing the theological questions of law and identity which underlie them.[25] Paul speaks from his identity as a Jewish Christian to expose the inadequacy of relying on the distinctive marks of Jewish identity required by the Old Testament law. This does not exhaust the argument of 1:18–32 but it shapes the form it takes.

An approach to biblical interpretation called rhetorical criticism[26] notes that the meaning of a passage often lies less in its content as 'simply a statement of truths' and more in the role that it plays within a persuasive argument. Behind the argument of Romans 1:18–32 lies a conventional Jewish critique of Gentile society that sees sexual disorder as the outcome of idolatry: Paul is making conscious allusions to Psalm 106:19ff. and to a later text, the Wisdom of Solomon 14:12ff.[27] The function of this passage is not only to spell out the way in which failure to worship the true God leads to social disintegration but also to draw the notional Jewish hearer (cf. 4:1) into the argument by presenting them with a familiar and congenial statement of this theme. Before looking further at whether this rhetorical purpose affects the interpretation of verses 26 and 27 it is necessary to look more carefully at the detail of St Paul's argument.

St Paul's argument in verses 24–27 is certainly not a simple affirmation of heterosexual desire. It is that all sexual desire is profoundly corrupted by the false worship that has marred our nature: 'dishonouring their bodies' (v.24) is used of sex between men and women. His subsequent reference to homosexual desires and acts places them within the general disorder of human desire that is our fallen condition. It is not clear whether 'dishonouring their bodies' refers to certain sorts of sexual acts – say, oral and anal sex – or to the current of ruthlessness and selfishness that characterizes such desire.

In making his points about the disorder of sexual desire and practice St Paul uses the same terms – nature (*phusis*) and dishonour (*atimia*) – that he uses in 1 Corinthians 11: 'Does not nature (*phusis*) herself teach you that for a man to wear long hair is degrading (*atimia*) to him?' Contemporary discussion about Romans 1:26–7 has focused on the implications of St Paul's remarks about nature. One position that recurs in different forms argues that the passage excludes those whose individual nature is homosexual: Greenberg quotes a popular expression of this view from seventeenth-century Italy;[28] it is present in Sherwin Bailey's influential use of the distinction between *invert* and *pervert*;[29] it was argued by John Boswell in his treatment of St Paul[30] – and has distracted attention from the real strengths of his important work. The difficulty with this position is that St Paul is clearly not speaking of an individual's nature but of some sort of recognized natural order which his argument relates to the order of creation.[31] Other scholars, such as James Dunn and Charles Cranfield, assert that Paul is unambiguously reaffirming the Jewish abhorrence of homosexuality as contrary to the pattern of creation.[32]

Professor Cranfield accepts that St Paul is using *phusis* in the same sense in Romans 1:26–7 and 1 Corinthians 11:1–16. This latter neglected passage provides an important commentary on St Paul's understanding of nature. It has already been discussed in chapters 2 and 3.[33] His argument is complex and not completely accessible to us; it is not, however, incoherent but is part of his attempt to find a social location for a vulnerable church that will enable it to gain a hearing and so serve God's mission. The term 'nature' for St Paul is not a simple reference to an acultural biological order but is an explicit construct of biology and culture. This is not to imply that 'nature' is merely synonymous with amoral fashion: it represents a social response to the created order – Cranfield proposes 'the very way God has made us' as the meaning of 'nature' in 1 Corinthians 11:14. The 'natural' is a real but culture-specific response to the order inherent in God's creation. When St Paul speaks of something as natural, he speaks from his cultural position as a Jew within the Roman empire – and convinced that the future of the gospel is best served by aligning the church with a certain strand in Roman society. One might compare his injunctions to honour the imperial order (Romans 13:1–7; cf. 1 Timothy 2:1–7) and to accept the institution of slavery (Colossians 3:22–25). St Paul's view of the demands of nature is shaped not only by his doctrine of creation but by a sort of missiological pragmatism.

Another question that needs to be asked is what light St Paul's argument throws on the sort of homosexuality he had in mind. The practices that he denounces have their origin, as he sees it, in an idolatry that refuses to honour God and gives its allegiance to the creature rather than the creator. They are passions that spring from the exaltation of self, the material world, and personal desire that is above the proper claims of God and neighbour. Those who see in the emergence of the contemporary gay identity the outworking of such idolatrous pride need to show how the rise of this movement has its actual origin in such idolatry. Given the fallenness of human nature all relationships are, of course, tainted by the temptation to a proud and destructive idolatry. But more than this needs to be established if the emerging gay identity of recent years is to be located within the structure of St Paul's argument. The analysis of earlier chapters suggests that the gay movement has its origin as a defence of certain humane perspectives inherent in the created order that are under threat in wider society – including an expressive rather than brutalized masculinity. It can be seen as the adjustment that certain individuals make to the emotionally hostile environment created by society's idolatry of the competitive market and the bourgeois family. Those who wish to locate contemporary forms of homosexuality within St Paul's argument face the challenge of demonstrating its outworking both in the culture and in the individual life stories of gay people.

A different way of attending to Romans 1:26–7 is to ask what sort of homosexuality St Paul had in mind in these verses. The obvious answer is that it was the public face of homosexuality in the Roman Empire as it appeared from the perspective of a cosmopolitan Jew. This form of homosexuality was strongly associated with idolatry, slavery and social dominance.[34] It was often the assertion of the strong over the bodies of the weak. Although there is evidence of an affectionate, egalitarian homosexuality – the tender physical expression of friendship – this was not the primary way in which sexual activity between men was perceived. As Richard Hays comments, 'the usual assumption of [Jewish and Stoic] writers during the

Hellenistic period was that homosexual behaviour was the result of insatiable lust seeking novel and more challenging forms of self-gratification'.[35] Romans 1:26–7 reads as if it is addressing the defiance of the seventeenth-century rake rather than the vulnerable but demonized gay subcultures of the twentieth century.

Anthony Thiselton helpfully emphasizes the importance of taking into account a writer's horizon – the provisional working assumptions and expectations which are implicit in their argument; the experience of the world and awareness of possibilities which they take into account in what they say.[36] We hear in St Paul's savage aside about the Jews, 'God's wrath has come upon them at last!' (1 Thessalonians 1:16) something that he did not intend, because we are aware of a long and cruel history of persecution and suffering. In the nineteenth century, Christian defence of slavery often appealed to St Paul's acceptance of slavery;[37] we neither accept slavery nor feel embarrassed by St Paul's accommodation to it because we are aware of his different horizon – and of the priorities and options that this horizon gave him. This invites the question of what relation the homosexuality of the modern gay movements has to the cultural form of homosexuality with which St Paul was familiar, and which he could plausibly present as the direct outworking of a proud idolatrous wickedness.

There is certainly an argument to be made that the man we know from his letters might be more at home today in gay rather than non-gay society. He shared Jesus' non-familial emphasis and lifestyle (1 Corinthians 7:25–35; 9). He treated no group or person as inherently unclean. His letters show a quality of tenderness, open emotion and gentleness (cf. 2 Corinthians 10:1) that is far removed from the heterosexual masculinity of our culture. He was happy to use feminine imagery of his relationship with others (1 Thessalonians 2:7,8). He had strong non-sexual relations with women (Philippians 4:2; Romans 16). He had strongly emotional relationships with younger men (2 Timothy 1:1–8, 2 Corinthians 2:13). One might add that he experienced ostracism and desertion by the church (2 Timothy 1:15).

In the light of these various considerations it is at least possible that Romans 1:26–7 should not have the sort of absolute force that it has to modern ears – ears that have often been tuned by an ignorance of gay experience, a cultural hostility to affectionate male friendship, and a mythological fear of the 'sodomite'. Some of its content derives from St Paul's particular context – including his desire to include those influenced by Jewish cultural perspectives and his instinct to align the church with the ideals of responsible and sober citizenship in the Roman Empire. It does not necessarily follow that missiological priorities should be the same in the twentieth century. In a culture that shows signs of making Mammon its god, Christ may choose his friends from among those whose personal dispositions align them against the idolatries of their day.

This is not to suggest that this passage be ignored by gay or non-gay people today. Within the unfolding argument of Romans it is not about enforcing a moral code but about discerning the roots of tyrannous desire and social disintegration. Its summons to identify and repudiate the idolatries at work in our society[38] – including our idolatry of sex – make it a vital biblical text. Its implied promise is that in Jesus a disordered human nature is being transformed into something new. St Paul knew that the form of the new creation was beyond his imagining; there is not too much in scripture to suggest that it will be modelled closely on the heterosexual ideals of Western culture.

1 Corinthians 6:9,10

Some of the implications of these verses have already been discussed in Chapter 4.[39] Although they include a sharp summons to a godly and charitable life, they portray a style of church which would be more open to gay people than many modern churches. It is not a church which lifts its skirts against the moral reprobates of society but one which provides them with an accepting welcome in Jesus Christ. It is precisely this welcome that provides the basis for the transformation of life for which St Paul looks. This is not a church in which people have to pretend to be something that they are not in order to remain within its fellowship.

An important issue for a biblical evaluation of homosexuality is how the two terms *malakoi* and *arsenokoitai* are to be translated. The King James Version translates them 'effeminate' and 'abusers of themselves with mankind'; the RSV translates them together as 'sexual perverts'. The difficulty arises because the precise meaning of the terms is not known and people tend to translate them in the light of their existing perceptions of current or first-century homosexuality. One modern strand of interpretation has seen *malakoi* as a man who takes the passive role in sex and *arsenokoitai* as a man who takes the active role.[40] However, there is no real evidence for this and considerable evidence in the case of *malakoi* that it carried no precise connotation of sex with men. It seems better to translate *malakoi* 'wanton' or 'loose living';[41] Bagster's Interlinear Greek-English New Testament suggests 'voluptuous persons'. This view is supported by the fact that *malakoi* does not occur with *arsenokoitai* in 1 Timothy 1:10.

There remains the question of how *arsenokoitai* is to be translated. Here the division lies between those who argue that it refers to a group such as male prostitutes and those who assert that it is a generic term covering all sexual acts between males. The derivation of *arsenokoitai* is 'male + sex' – probably 'those who lie with males'. John Boswell argued that it was a coarse term for men involved in penetrative sex and therefore referred to male prostitutes serving either sex.[42] William Countryman suggests that it refers to attractive young men on the make.[43] An important article by David Wright has suggested that the term emerged in Hellenistic Judaism, possibly derived from the way in which the Septuagint translates Leviticus 18:22; 20:13;[44] 'it came into use . . . to denote that homoerotic vice which Jewish writers like Philo, Josephus, Paul and Ps-Phoculides regarded as a signal token of pagan Greek depravity'. From this David Wright concludes, 'We are justified in seeing in it a declaration that all male same-sex erotic relationships are sinful.'[45] Subsequent debate has questioned whether it is legitimate to read into *arsenokoitai* affectional preference as Wright's formulations imply.[46]

The problem remains that any translation is somewhat speculative. The suggestion that it was coined, whether from Leviticus or simply from its obvious roots, as a sort of general term for sex between men has much to commend it. However, it goes beyond the evidence to read into this a condemnation of all sorts of homosexuality and the dispositions that lie behind them. It would be more natural to see it as a term for certain forms of same sex activity that were known and disapproved of – possibly by the Jewish community if David Wright is correct, possibly by others if the term originated elsewhere. (Countryman's rather speculative suggestion might fit into this latter category.) David Wright's attempt to derive a wholesale condemnation of any same sex 'erotic' relationship or sexual activity from the etymology of the word tries to prove too much. A general term has hidden within it both the horizon and the organizing categories of those who use it. So 'homosexual' has a hidden psychological and cultural agenda that condemns a whole class of people while excluding many men who have sex with other men. Equally, whether it originated in the Jewish cultural context or not, *arsenokoitai* can only be understood within the cultural assumptions of the time It is likely that it carries those connotations of slavery, idolatry and social dominance that were associated with corrupt Roman society. It cannot in itself settle the question of how other homosexualities were to be judged.

1 Timothy 1:8–11

This passage figures in discussions of homosexuality because of the occurrence of *arsenokoitai* in verse 10. This has been discussed in the last section. However, these verses invite another question: 'Is it part of the church's calling to urge the enforcement of Old Testament laws?' Richard Hays comments that 'no direct appeal to Romans 1 as a source of laws about sexual conduct is possible . . . If Romans 1 is to function appropriately . . . it must function as a diagnostic tool.'[47] The whole thrust of Romans is that the church is called to receive and preach Jesus Christ rather than the Old Testament law (Romans 5:12–21; 6:14; 7:1–8:4). Any role the church plays in society is to arise out of its life in Christ. The gospel of Jesus Christ, according to Romans, is one that brings faith and love that spring directly from Jesus Christ (Romans 8:1–4; 10:17; 13:8–10).

These verses in 1 Timothy are about the function of the Old Testament Law and arose in response to teachers who were using the Old Testament to set up an elaborate speculative system which was aimed at promoting the interests of the teachers and exploiting the flock (1 Timothy 1:3–7; 6:3–5; 2 Timothy 2:14ff.; 3:5–9), and which St Paul saw as an irrelevant distraction, far removed from the love that is the outworking of genuine faith. Faced with antinomian teachers who used the Old Testament as a quarry for speculative angelology his response is, 'if you want the Old Testament try its moral teaching!' He then gives a list of undisputed wickednesses, which include the public face of homosexuality as he sees it.

These verses would be a slender basis on which to urge the church to a campaign for moral renewal based on Leviticus. An incident in 1641 from colonial Massachusetts provides an intriguing vignette of what this might involve.[48] Three men sexually abused two young girls who had been virtually abandoned by their Puritan father. As the existing laws did not specifically relate to child abuse, the magistrates sought the opinions of eminent preachers who devoted great energy to the exegesis and application of the relevant biblical laws as they saw them. As agreement could not be reached about how these offences related to the biblical laws, the men concerned were spared the death penalty and were sentenced to be whipped, imprisoned, to have their noses slit, to be further detained and to pay compensation to the father.

Before Christians pursue this line of argument they need to examine the terrain into which it might lead them. Few modern evangelicals advocate criminal prosecution for adultery – despite the death penalty required by Leviticus 20:10.

Jude 7

An unwary modern reader could easily mistake this reference to Sodom and Gomorrah 'going after strange flesh' (King James Version, cf. RSV 'indulged unnatural lust') as a reference to homosexual intercourse. However, the real reference is to attempted sexual intercourse with angels, as the context (v.6) and other passages indicate.[49] The background to this assumes a common interpretation that this was the sin that provoked the flood (Genesis 6:1–4). In this context the letter is making a coded reference to teachers who advocated sexual license as a rejection of the social order the angels represented. It may be a similar phenomenon to the false teachers denounced in the Pastoral epistles.

Some evangelical Christians see Christians who are sympathetic to gay people as an example of just such an aberration. However, what Jude and other parallel passages are describing is a radical antinomianism that claims a superior revelation, glories in the rejection of all authority, and arises out of an individual teacher's quest for a personal following. It is easy to project such an image on to those whom we fear; established Christian groups have often portrayed the mildest of social reformers in these terms. (Gay Christians may be tempted to see certain 'conservative' Christians in similar terms!) Discernment is made more difficult by the ease with which the irony and anger, which are part of the way gay people survive in a hostile environment, can easily be misinterpreted by their opponents as the rejection of divine authority.

Christian history is littered with accounts of the demonization of groups who were regarded as unnatural, unclean and dangerous. Pogroms against Jews and Gypsies and the burning of gays are only a small part of the tribute that such irrational fear has demanded over the centuries. Christians themselves experienced the same misrepresentation in the early centuries of persecution. St Paul's approach of mutual respect in disagreement (Romans 14) seems a safer starting point. The generosity that he alludes to in 1 Corinthians 13:4–7 suggests that people need to be listened to before being mythologized in this way.

Applying the scriptures

The Bible is not a weapon in a cultural war, but a source of wisdom offered by a gracious God to people who easily get the wrong end of the stick. We need to remember how often Jesus rebuked his confident followers for their failure to understand (cf. Matthew 16:8; 17:7). As gay and non-gay people wrestle with the phenomenon represented by the modern gay movement, they have to be open to the God of the scriptures and not try to reduce the mysteries of human life to a neat formula. The 'message' of the scriptures cannot be reduced to a few paragraphs at the end of a chapter. It takes place in life. It belongs in a continuing exploration as individuals and groups open themselves to others and to God. The weighing of what the Bible says about homosexuality – and about much else – needs to take place within a church which welcomes gay people and gives them an unthreatened place in discerning the mind of God.

It is possible to identify a number of approaches that the biblical material surveyed in this chapter might lead to. One position would be to treat the Old Testament's view of sexual acts as part of a universal natural law reflecting God's intention in creation. Those who take this view will need to widen their horizons far beyond gay people and, for example, address such matters as the prevalence of oral sex and anal sex in male/female relationships.

Others may take the approach that is often followed in young people's groups in evangelical churches and in the pastoring of married couples: try to make sure that relationships are conducted in a responsible, respectful and affirming environment and leave the details of sexual practice to be worked out by those involved without outside interference. This approach raises the question of why gay people are not entitled to the same courtesy and respect. If appropriate sexual activity is seen as the product of healthy relationships, why should the Holy Spirit be thought less able to impart his wisdom to individual gay Christians? This pragmatic approach followed by Christians in many other areas of sexual behaviour fits closely with the position explored in Chapter 2 that sexual acts derive their primary meaning from the social context in which they occur.

Within the broader framework of what scripture has to say about human society, about friendship, and about gender, attention naturally focuses on those biblical texts which specifically address some form of homosexuality. These have already been discussed in detail, but one particular issue deserves to be highlighted. In the cultural environment that shaped these texts, the public face of homosexuality was the hungry, idolatrous assertiveness of 'normal' masculinity. There may have been individuals whose homosexual activity had a different source but the conceptualization of same sex activity bracketed them with an out-of-control masculinity that refused to remain satisfied with sexual relations with women. The emergence of a public gay identity since the eighteenth century has created a very different situation. The public face of homosexuality is now associated with those who – for whatever reason – find themselves unable to accommodate to the robust 'heterosexual' masculinity of the culture, to the suppression of public affection outside the home, and to the culture's identification of desire and 'heterosexual' domesticity. Modern gay identity, on this reading, is not about proud rebellion against God but arises from the sensitivity of certain vulnerable individuals to certain truths of creation suppressed in the wider culture. The church then faces the dilemma that when it presents itself as the primary opposition to this public gay identity, it is opposing the form of homosexuality which is least easily identified with St Paul's strictures. It finds itself as an agent of oppression and social condemnation to a group of people whose ears may be open both to the mystery of God's creation and to the gentle call of Christ.

Some may reply that under no circumstances can the church compromise with a social institution which itself appears to compromise some of the deepest scriptural affirmations about human beings. One reply would be to quote St Paul's, 'Slaves, obey your earthly masters' (Colossians 3:22). New Testament ethical exhortation so accepted the imperfect social arrangements of its culture that many 'biblical' Christians were confident that the Bible supported slavery.[50] The biblical treatment of slavery witnesses both to the problems of applying scripture across different cultures and to the place of social pragmatism in working out obedience to Christ.

Chapter 9

'Why Am I Gay?'

When I would muse in boyhood
    the wild green woods among,
And nurse resolves and fancies
    Because the world was young,
It was not foes to conquer,
    Nor sweethearts to be kind,
But it was friends to die for
    That I would seek and find.
              A.E. Housman

Nothing is what it seems. This is certainly the case when discussing the cause of homosexuality. The difficulty lies not only with the question of what homosexuality is, but also with the assumptions, intentions and social influence of the questioner. It is well known that certain verbs decline in an irregular way: I inquire; you interfere; she intrudes. The assumptions behind a question reflect not only the categories into which a correct answer may fall but also the power and social role of the questioner. Questions of why a person is gay or homosexual tend to assume the categories through which such same sex behaviour is to be understood, and to be searching for a programme to 'normalize' the person. This, in turn, often implies a superior knowledge in the questioner, an uncritical definition of the 'normal' – and an implicit strategy for normalization.

John 9, one of the most sustained dramatic dialogues in the New Testament, starts with a question about the cause of a personal condition and provides an interesting point of comparison with the question, 'What is the cause of homosexuality?' Jesus's disciples asked him, 'Who sinned, this man or his parents, that he was born blind?' As the story unfolds it emerges that different people's understanding of the man's blindness expose their own fundamental life stances and their relationship to the mysterious figure of Jesus. The disciples (the church?) are almost an irrelevance, – echoing the conventional wisdom of the religious culture, preening themselves as religious experts, and viewing the blind man as a valuable case-study (vv. 1,2). Jesus's response changes the direction of the story: he refutes the conventional wisdom about causality, gathers the disciples into the movement of his own mission, and, by word and action, places the blind man centre stage (vv.3–6).

At the start the man's blindness is, for him and his parents, simply part of life. To the Pharisees, who saw themselves as the standard of faithfulness to God, blindness puts the man beyond the pale of godly society and deprives him of any possibility of insight about God (v.34). To Jesus the blindness, with all its social and religious consequences, makes the man a special object of God's loving attention. Jesus's gift of sight sets in train a process by which the man struggles painfully to a full realization of the one he has come to know, and of his own right to interpret the impact of God's grace in his life (vv.8–38). In his journey to believing self-confidence the man has to overcome the prejudice of those around him – including their tendency to treat him as socially invisible (vv.8–9) – his parents' embarrassment, and the hostility of the self-appointed guardians of religious values. By the end he believes in both himself and in Jesus his Lord.

The Pharisees' confidence that they represented faithfulness to God prevented them learning from the outcast who could lead them to Christ. Part of the irony of the narrative is that their refusal of the outcast who had experienced grace from Jesus turns out to be a refusal of all that they think they believe in. The question of the cause of the man's blindness – whether theological or scientific – is rejected by Jesus and disappears from the story. It is replaced by a counter-intuitive act of grace that turns a case-study into a witness, a man on the edge into a friend of God. The meaning of the man's blindness is personal; it is part of the hiddenness of his relationship with God. The story is not saying that blind people must be healed in order to know

God. Blindness is woven by human sin into a strait-jacket of social and religious oppression. It is in reversing this oppression that Jesus displays the works of God (v.3).

Straight people often want to focus discussion of homosexuality on its causes. To them this has the advantage of relating a symbolically potent subject to the secure world of objective science. To the gay person it can feel like opening negotiations with a shrewd and powerful oppressor. The question of what causes homosexuality – and of what makes an individual gay – is a legitimate one. Any attempt to answer it must leave freedom for people to interpret their own experience and be open to the surprises of an unpredictable God. 'Why am I gay?' is more likely to lead to truth than 'Why are they homosexual?'

Thinking about causes

The question of what causes homosexuality in an individual is notoriously complicated. Any attempt to summarize the current state of 'scientific' discussion has to acknowledge its transitory and speculative character and to recognize that 'science' has rarely occupied a neutral position in society's treatment of gay people. In many cultures people who do not conform to society's norms with respect to sexual and social behaviour are treated with incomprehension and hostility, and popular explanations of their behaviour usually say most about the social forces arraigned against such people. One of the most frequent explanations of socially unacceptable forms of same sex affection is to attribute it to foreign influence – be it Italian, French, English, Western or Eastern. Often one is dealing with little more than social anxiety and the prevailing myths or conceptual maps through which the culture understands its relationships. In addition, popular 'psychology', like popular religion, often draws in an incoherent way on different theories that have at various times been advocated in the culture. The conceptual world of modern Western society is littered with the debris of more than a century of different scientific theories of homosexuality, not to mention the folk memory of earlier days.

However, there is a deeper reason why discussion about the causes of homosexuality rarely rises to anything like coherence.

Homosexuality is a cultural phenomenon. Intimate affection and genital activity between men arise for different reasons in different cultures. What counts as sexual non-conformity depends mainly on what the prevailing pattern of relating between men is in that particular culture. Individuals whose personal make-up fits the social norm in one culture may well be under strong pressure to take up contested practices or a non-conforming social identity in a different cultural framework. Discussions of the causes of homosexuality need to give the same attention to the prevailing patterns of a culture as to the particular disposition of certain individuals. Furthermore, those who share the Christian conviction that human life is profoundly distorted by human alienation from God need to be especially open to the possibility that non-conforming individuals may be different because they are alert to aspects of goodness that the culture as a whole is neglecting.

1 Reflecting on the Sambia

It may be helpful to work through one example from what is at first sight a culture very different from our own.[1] Until recently the Sambia people in New Guinea lived in a state of perpetual vulnerability to attacks from their warlike neighbours. The survival of the tribe depended on the finely honed aggressive masculinity of the men who needed to be available to maintain the tribe's security and territory. The result of this was a culture in which the social spheres of men and women were strictly segregated. Young boys spent their early years in the world of women. Sometime between the ages of seven and eleven they made a dramatic transition to the male world and began a long process of formation into the masculine identity and social grouping which the tribe's interests required. This prolonged period of initiation involved isolation from the women in the tribe and had the task of creating a bonding among the men that needed to continue after they were fully initiated and had taken wives of their own. The formation of this masculine identity and the preservation of distinct male and female worlds among the Sambia are articulated in terms strange to us: the men perceive themselves as needing to guard their stock of semen and to ingest semen from other men during the long process of initiation and from a certain tree in the forest after initiation is complete.

From a more Western perspective the presence of oral sexual activity and related group bonding among the men undergoing initiation can be explained in terms of the task of creating and sustaining the form of masculinity that this society needs. For Sambian men oral sex, first given and then received, is a normal part of what it is to be male.

In 1979 the anthropologist, Gilbert Herdt, who had been studying these people for some years, took with him to New Guinea a colleague who was a psychiatrist in order to study the way in which sexual activity and relations were conceived among the Sambia and among certain individuals whom he had got to know very well. The resultant book, *Intimate Communications: Erotics and the Study of Culture*, includes an extensive account of two non-conforming individuals in Sambian society. One is Kalutwo who sees himself, and is seen by others, as an inadequate failure, unable to establish a proper masculine identity. He continues to have oral sex with young men beyond the normal period of initiation and is despised for doing so.[2]

More interesting for our purposes is Imano, who is described as 'gentle' or 'feminine'.[3] He stands out in this macho culture as a rare but recognizable type: he is shy and somewhat anxious, easily expresses his emotions, is never aggressive, is eager to please and to receive reassurance. A gentle and considerate person, Imano is more at home with women and children and ill at ease in the more public and aggressive world of men. He looks younger than his years. Imano comes from a strong and respected family. His father, who had an unusually close relationship with Imano's mother, was an important man in the tribe and a tough and fearless warrior. In terms of the prevailing culture, Imano is a reasonably popular figure. In terms of the tribe's gender roles, Imano is identified as sufficiently seriously aberrant as to be given a distinct social identity: *aambei-wutnyi*, 'gentle'. He is unwilling to take up the warrior role required in society. During the early processes of initiation he was extremely reluctant to be involved in oral sex and later, most unusually, never agreed to be fellated. He married at the earliest opportunity, soon took a second wife, and is known to be unusually interested in sexual relations with them.

This brief outline points to a number of issues. Some readers may be tempted to draw quick analogies with forms of male relationship in parts of our culture or to compare Sambian culture with some imagined normal or perfect society – maybe the Old Testament patriarchs, the Victorian middle class ideal, or the politically correct masculinity of the 'new man'. However, such cross-cultural analogies inevitably fail to respect the fact that the pattern of Sambian behaviour arises within a precise historical niche and reflects the particular tasks which this people face in that context. To require such a culture to change wholesale to what we would regard as something closer to biblical or western patterns would be as inappropriate as saying that the Maasai of Kenya should give up cattle herding and adopt the more settled farming life of the Bantu on the grounds that Bantu culture is closer to that of pre-monarchical Israel.[4] Particular cultures need to be respected for what they are as the response of whole human communities to the situation in which they find themselves. Any change in the masculine ideal of Sambian culture would have to be viable under the constraints of Sambian life. Similar issues, of course, occur in Western culture when churches require working-class men to adopt the more 'effete' culture of sedentary 'professionals'.

This case highlights some of the difficulties of discussing the causes of homosexuality. Homosexual behaviour on the part of Sambian men can be explained in terms of the conventions of their culture and is integral to attaining a socially necessary masculine ideal; it is clearly inappropriate to search for particular explanations in the biography of individuals. The continuing homosexuality of Kalutwo relates to his failure to attain the cultural ideal. Equally, the exclusive heterosexuality of the gentle Imano also represents an inability to attain to this ideal. While the latter's non-conformity is respected in Sambian society, it remains a vulnerable social identity that could not safely become the social norm. It raises the intriguing question of whether this quiet and sensitive man, with his inability to accept the masculine role required by his society, might not, within another cultural framework, have expressed his sexual non-conformity in other ways. Is it more than chance that missionaries discourage the traditional initiation practices of this society rather than pray for Imano's healing?!

2 Different patterns of homosexuality

Greenberg's classification of different social patterns of homo-sexuality[5] provides an interesting framework within which to speculate on possible 'causes' for different manifestations of homosexuality. Although drawn up as a way of analysing patterns in 'simple' tribal cultures, they provide a suggestive grid to place against same sex patterns in pre-modern and modern society.

In *Transgenerational* homosexuality, sexual activity occurs between 'normal' men in the society at certain stages of their lives. It tends to be part of the formation of the requisite male identity and to contribute to appropriate bonding between men. The bodily activity is of a piece with the transgenerational bonding that enables young men to assume an appropriate masculine identity in the society. Sambian society is one example of such a culture. Where similar behaviour occurs in more 'advanced' societies it is inevitably coloured by other values and projects of the culture. The homosexuality that was common in traditional public schools obviously has certain similarities with this pattern.[6] Its form sprang from the 'sexual' energy and ideals of these closed communities that were involved in forming the English ruling class. While this homosexuality was always an 'open secret' among the men in certain classes of English society, it has recently become less visible or comprehensible as the public face of homosexuality has been taken over by the gay movements, and 'adolescent' sexuality is now demonized under the catch-all phrase 'child abuse'.

Transgenderal homosexuality occurs in many forms but all have in common the inability of certain individuals who find themselves unable to identify with the major gender stereo-types of the culture. Greenberg's discussion shows the wide variety of forms that this takes in tribal society. Transgenderal homosexuals tend to form a more or less distinct group in their society; they may be more or less visible and may be revered or despised. The main feature of such homosexuality is that individuals adopt an alternative social role to the majority of their sex. Any attempt to identify the 'cause' of transgenderal homosexuality in an individual would need to relate the particular characteristics of the individual to the values and roles of the culture. This tribal form has certain similarities with the modern gay 'sexual minority'. Despite common assertions to the contrary, the idea that certain individuals may be innately homosexual is not limited to modern times but has occurred at various points in Western history.[7] Where this notion arises it is usually associated with some form of transgenderal homosexuality. In many cultures certain people are perceived as innately unable to adopt the predominant gender stereotypes of their culture and allowed to adopt alternative social patterns and identities. The 'cause' of such non-conformity clearly has to be related to the cultural stereotype as well as to the individual.

Egalitarian homosexuality is less closely related to defined social roles and tends to occur in societies that are at ease with sexual feeling and activity. As much as anything it approximates to a form of egalitarian friendship. An example among women are the sexual friendships that develop among married Nandi women in Kenya.[8] As noted earlier, Greenberg makes the interesting comment that among men, this form of homosexuality is inhibited by cultures which strongly emphasize male competitiveness. There is evidence that something like this pattern occurs in certain Western societies where there is a lessening of anxiety about sexual contact. Such patterns exist among sections of the gay community – and may also operate among certain groups of young people.

Greenberg identifies an additional pattern of homosexuality associated with societies which have sharply divided social roles. Part of the homoerotic background to the modern gay movements is the past 'eroticization' of certain aspects of class in which certain forms of beauty and some social roles – such as the labourer, the soldier or the biker – gained an erotic charge. These more complex forms of homosexuality may originate out of patterns of social domination or sexual frustration – certain men are available for 'use'. They may also reflect a complex relationship with the ideal masculine figures of a culture. Whereas in Sambian or ancient Greek culture the required masculine ideal combined physical and social qualities, more diversified or bureaucratic societies tend to relegate physical beauty and strength to groups other than the socially powerful males.

None of this is intended to suggest a precise aetiology for modern Western homosexuality. It is possible to see traces of each of Greenberg's patterns in the homoerotic sensibilities in Western culture. The complexity of the pattern should be sufficient to warn against over-simple identification of 'causes'. It should be clear that the homosexuality of individuals needs to be seen as one element within a wider complex social discourse. There is no possibility that its 'cause' can be limited to certain elements of genetic make-up or personal biography.

There is no inevitable progression from being arrested ('turned on') by a certain masculine image and responding to it in sexual activity, in the formation of an intimate relationship, or in both. The 'script' for turning desire into activity and relationship will also be derived from the culture. But the actual moment of desire remains important, although in the various forms of homosexuality described above, so-called sexual attraction may be more or less significant. The form that inspires such desire is going to be highly culture specific – and may not even be comprehensible across cultures. Herdt and Stoller show that the shape of a boy's mouth becomes a focus for sexual desire among the Sambia. The source of sexual charge associated with certain forms of masculinity is complex and relates to the prevailing images in the society as well as the patterns of social relationship and bodily intimacy that operate within the culture.

In the previous sentence the word 'image' is important. In attempting to identify the source of 'erotic' desire we probably need to recover the realization that there is a link between the stimulation of the body and the projection of certain images which become the focus of desire within the culture. The modern scientific 'myth' associates desire simply with the need of the species to procreate. Older understandings knew that these images can be seen as intuitions of the divine mediated through the body and through social ideals.[9] Dante recognized in the beauty of the young Beatrice a vision of the divine glory and call; he was to make this the basis of the greatest theological poem of Western culture. Such 'erotic' vision can find its outworking outside sexual activity. However, as embodied beings we do our imagining within a bodily existence and against the background of specific cultural 'scripts'. It is one of the weaknesses of the scientific myth about the biological origin of desire that it underestimates the role that certain images have in harnessing the energies and ideals of a culture. Plato was on to something! The images that dominate the desire of a culture will inevitably reflect both the beauty God has hidden in creation and the destructive idolatry of fallen human nature: they will play a significant part in determining the form that sexual desire takes in a culture. Certain people are gay partly because certain people are beautiful.

3 The voices of science

Modern discussion of the causes of homosexuality is dominated by the self-understanding of the modern scientific 'project' that blossomed in the nineteenth century and also by the particular cultural form of homosexuality which these scientists sought to explain.[10] The homosexuality that has preoccupied nineteenth- and twentieth-century science is the new pattern that began to emerge in Western Europe at the start of the eighteenth century. The image of this homosexuality is shaped by the new ideals of domestic affection and by the dominance of a competitive and emotionally restricted masculinity in public life. Emerging within an extremely hostile social climate, the men who came to the attention of the newly confident 'science' of this era were men who felt they had to adopt a counter-cultural identity despite the great dangers involved. There can be little doubt that their sexual non-conformity was not lightly assumed but signified a real inability to live with the social and sexual role offered them by society. It also meant that the homosexuals studied by the new science were highly stressed individuals, much of whose behaviour arose not from their 'sexual orientation' but from the stressful condition of their lives in an unsympathetic society. The 'scientific' study of this homosexuality has constantly been bedevilled by the failure to identify which behaviour arises from the person's sexuality and which from the contested character of their public lives.

The science that emerged in the nineteenth century was not in the main sympathetic to the gay people that it sought to understand. The late nineteenth century saw a considerable increase in anti-gay laws in the United States of America. The pressure for these laws frequently came from doctors, who were increasingly confident of their right to interpret society and who brought to this task of interpretation the outlook of busy professional people who themselves had often had to make emotional and sexual sacrifices to complete their professional training.[11]

Greenberg identifies a succession of theories which the physicians and scientists of this period deployed in their attempt to understand the deviant behaviour of homosexuals. It may be helpful, at the risk of considerable simplification, to list them and to identify the strategy for 'cure' to which the theory was thought to point:

(a) *Indulgence: homosexuality as the end-point of sexual indulgence.* At the beginning of the nineteenth century, masturbation was increasingly regarded as a serious evil that undermined manliness and was the gateway to the unmanly vice of sodomy.[12] Campaigns and precautions against masturbation continued through the century. The 1888 Indiana sodomy statute included within its scope, 'whoever entices, allures, instigates or aids any person under the age of twenty-one to commit masturbation or self-pollution'.[13] The penalty was imprisonment for between two and fourteen years.

(b) *Degeneracy theory: homosexuality as the outworking of hereditary degeneracy.* This theory gained ground from the middle of the century and attributed all sorts of medical and social problems (such as labour disputes) to the deterioration of the human body under the impact of an unhealthy environment.[14] Such degeneration could be transmitted genetically to offspring. As a theory about homosexuality and other forms of social disintegration, it served to distance the middle class from such degeneracy; it was also used in mitigation to protect such degenerates from the harshest applications of the law.

(c) *Darwinism: homosexuality as a fall back to a more primitive evolutionary form.* Darwin's theory of evolution led some physicians to see homosexuality as a reversion to the bisexual characteristics of primitive organisms.[15] This approach and the similar idea of degeneracy had profound effects on gay people in nineteenth-century society. Among the intelligentsia they served to give some scientific recognition to the homosexual condition and therefore contributed to the process by which gay people were recognized and allowed some public existence in society. At the same time this scientific account of human behaviour became closely linked with new ideas about social policy in which state intervention, properly guided by appropriate 'professionals', was a duty.[16] Linked with other social problems such as alcoholism, crime and labour strife, drastic measures were advocated against homosexuals. Significant medical figures argued for lifelong incarceration, the prohibition of marriage, castration and forced sterilization. Many states in the USA adopted compulsory sterilization procedures for sex offenders including homosexuals, as well as for habitual criminals and the mentally retarded. In Britain the related Eugenics movement, calling for social policies to strengthen the racial stock, found evangelical support in the Baptist preacher F.B. Meyer.[17]

(d) *Psychoanalysis: homosexuality as the consequence of patterns of emotional relationship within the family*. Building on the discovery of childhood sexuality and the observation that embryos have both male and female sex organs, this school identified newborn children as having an undifferentiated sexual nature. It located the development of homosexuality as one outcome of the formation of a sense of personal identity formed through the child's developing relations with its parent.[18] If degeneracy theory and Darwinism treated homosexuality as something intrinsically remote from the healthier middle classes, psychoanalysis brought homosexual desire in some form into the make-up of every person. Freud himself did not view homosexuality as a sickness as such, nor did he expect psychoanalysis to produce a heterosexual orientation but only to help resolve conflicts and eliminate unhappiness and inhibition. However, his view that a settled homosexual condition represented a developmental immaturity inevitably served to provide a new diagnostic tool among those who sought to 'cure' homosexuals.

As a theory, psychoanalysis has done much to shape the intellectual climate of modern society. It broadened the scope of the sexual to make it a pervasive concept for understanding personality. It owed some of its directions to the more positive attitude to sex emerging in prosperous early twentieth-century America.[19] One of its most powerful effects was to further the expectation that scientists and physicians could be trusted to unravel such disorders of the personality – giving the authority of 'objective science' to evaluations that often had a cultural or religious base. In terms of more recent scholarship, a major weakness of this school has been its failure to take account of sociological factors, and to consider that symptoms of 'dis-ease' in gay people may arise from the pressures of a hostile and uncomprehending society.

(e) *Behaviourism: homosexuality as a learned pattern of behaviour*. This school has set its face against the intangible psychological constructs of Freudian theory and views human behaviour patterns as forms of learned response that can be reconditioned and redirected through aversive reconditioning.[20] While this theory gives no reason for viewing homosexuality as a sickness, it has provided the basis for various attempts to cure homosexuals by electric or chemically induced shock treatment.

Two modern answers

Variations on psychoanalytical theory continue to have a fascination for many people in Western culture, because they address the impact of the duality of gender on the structuring of a person's inner life. This attempt to mediate between our outer and inner worlds gives such theory a popular appeal among those who want to understand their own or other people's emotional behaviour. It also attracts Western Christians who are influenced by an Augustinian tradition of spirituality that pays careful attention to inner motivation and desire. Attitudes among gay people to this tradition of thought are more varied. Many keep their distance out of a sense, probably well-founded, that such theory is fundamentally an attempt by hostile straight society to categorize and control the imagination of gay people. Other gay people, who for some reason seek or need to understand their mental state, turn for counselling to those whose theoretical framework is strongly influenced by this movement.

Anyone approaching the question of the origins of an individual's homosexuality through theories influenced by this movement needs to recognize that the theories themselves originate as part of the Western cultural 'project'. The possibility therefore exists that their underlying value system will reflect uncritically the interests of professional practitioners and the current preferred social arrangements in society. In addition, they are likely to bring to an individual's homosexuality the common stock of theories and stereotypes that nineteenth-century science attributed to a particular group of despised individuals who were not able or willing to accommodate to the accepted social behaviour of that society.

Given the continued appeal of theories in this tradition it may be helpful to look in turn at two modern examples which represent interestingly different approaches.

Richard Friedman's *Male Homosexuality* was published in 1988 and describes itself as 'A Contemporary Psychoanalytical Perspective'.[21] It represents a careful but critical restatement of psychoanalytical developmental theory in the light of recent study of homosexuality and the author's own investigations. Friedman provides an accessible summary of earlier studies of homosexuality which brought home to this reader the inadequacies of commonly-quoted studies such as those of Bieber.[22] In common with other scholars in this tradition he gives no direct attention to the cultural diversity of homosexuality and its possible relevance to his study. He gives some credence to evidence that genetic factors and experience of stress in the womb may predispose certain men towards homosexuality.[23] Friedman does not view homosexuality as a pathological condition that needs to be cured[24] or as incompatible with a well-founded adult masculine gender-identity. At the same time he recognizes that homosexual desire and behaviour may on occasions appear in otherwise heterosexual men whose sense of self-worth is under threat, either through personality disorder or external stress.[25]

Against this general understanding, Friedman addresses the question of why certain men – one should probably add American men – grow up with an erotic preference for their own sex.

He notes that there are two groups of young boys who are likely to emerge as gay when they grow up. One are boys whom are identified by their culture as 'sissies', boys who for various reasons seem to identify more with girls than boys in their early years.[26] Friedman devotes much of his book to a second larger group of boys who are not in any way 'feminine' in their early years and yet emerge as gay. His suggestion is that these boys turn out on examination to be 'unmasculine':[27] although their behaviour is consistent with normal understandings of masculinity, it is not recognized as such, and in childhood they perceive their masculinity to be unaffirmed by their fathers *and their peer group*.[28] Friedman takes the view that erotic preference is fixed in the very early years of childhood, somewhere between toddlerhood and the onset of puberty.[29] Erotic preference is the product of the fixing of the images of sexual fantasy at a fairly defined point in the pre-pubertal development of personality.

Although Friedman's theories stand firmly within the traditions of psychoanalytical development of personality, the process that he suggests for the formation of a gay sexual orientation does not rest exclusively or even primarily on emotional relationships with either parent. With his emphasis on the peer group he is effectively recognizing that certain Western men are gay partly because of their interaction with the culture's current ideals of masculinity.

A second theorist in the psychoanalytical school is Elizabeth Moberley, an Orthodox Christian who is widely involved in ministry to gay people who wish to change their sexual orientation. Her writings, particularly *Homosexuality: A New Christian Ethic*,[30] have become a major source for evangelical Christian groups seeking to change the orientation of gay people.

Moberley accepts the broad outlines given by the psychoanalytical school of the processes that lead to the formation of the sense of personal identity. However, against those who attribute male homosexuality to an over-close relationship with the mother, she locates the source of the emotional immaturity that prevents a person's attaining their intended heterosexual orientation in an unresolved deficit in the person's relationship with their same sex parent. This deficit, she argues, can be triggered in a variety of ways, but its effect is the same: a person continually seeks a strong affirming bond with a person of the same sex. Under the conditions of adolescence and against the background of current sexual attitudes, this same sex desire becomes eroticized and emerges as a gay orientation. She concludes that any pastoral approach to a gay person needs to begin with recognizing the legitimacy of their desire for strong same sex relationships. Accepting, as she does, the common Christian view that sexual relationships between men should never be countenanced, Moberley proposes a therapeutic programme for gay people wishing to change their orientation. This involves finding strong but non-erotic relationships with people of the same sex, escaping the sexual ambience of gay subcultures, and then attempting to address by appropriate prayer and counselling the blockages which have prevented the complete development of proper heterosexual desire.

This influential analysis has been well received amongst many gay people. It takes seriously the pain experienced by gay people in society, and respects and affirms their instinct that their own need is for strong same sex relationships. Its therapeutic consequences are a far cry from the more drastic strategies of imprisonment, aversion therapy, forced dating, or simply 'beating it out of them'. It is unlikely to be easy to discern whether these theories appeal to gay people simply because they promise reconciliation with an alienated father and a hostile society, or whether they do accurately chart the inner processes by which some Western men become gay.

Even more than Friedman, Elizabeth Moberley's approach ignores the possibility that there may be a cultural element to a gay orientation. Part of the evidence for her analysis is the common observation that gay men often have distant and uneasy relationships with their fathers. This observation is open, however, to an alternative explanation, namely that the fathers of gay men are unable to cope with sons who do not conform to the masculine stereotypes of the culture. An interesting study has compared the relationships of four groups of men with their fathers: men attracted to adult women, men attracted to young girls, men attracted to young boys, and men attracted to adult men.[31] The first three of these conformed to the recognized cultural markers for masculinity and were found to have similar strong relationships with their fathers. The fourth group did not conform to such markers and had more distant relationships with their fathers. The more natural explanation of this observation is that distant relationships between gay men and their fathers arise from the invasion by the culture's predominant understanding of the masculine stereotype into the father/son relationship. If gay men feel unaffirmed by their fathers, and by the typical males of their cultures, this is not necessarily evidence of a developmental malfunction in their personality. It may equally point to an element in the formation of the 'normal' masculinity of the culture which alienates 'normal' men from a male affectivity to which men who emerge as gay are responsive. Academic study of men involved in violence against gay men in the United States of America has shown that such violence is perpetrated by young men from good backgrounds who are perceived to be normal and well-integrated personalities.[32] A plausible explanation is that establishing the normal masculinity of American society involves the violent suppression of certain human qualities which are felt to be present in gay men.

Elizabeth Moberley's theories, and the therapeutic strategies attached to them, involve other commitments that need to be articulated and examined. Although those who are attracted by this account are often strongly critical of the hostility that gay people face in society, they fail to recognize that resistance by self-affirming gay people is a necessary part of the process by which such attitudes are to be countered. A social strategy that concentrates on conforming gay people to the current patterns of the culture colludes both with the alienated masculinity of the culture and with the hostility to gay people to which this is closely related. It fails to ask whether there are aspects of created masculinity to which gay men are sensitive and which the wider culture needs; affirming and supporting the contribution of gay men in society may be a better way of honouring the human potential of what it is to be male.

Moberley advocates the therapeutic value of strong, affirming same sex relationships within the Christian community without seriously contemplating that such relationships are already available to many gay people in gay relationships and within the wider network of gay communities. Her certainty that Christian faith can never countenance sexual relationships between people of the same sex commits individuals to a prolonged and painful journey within what is often a homophobic community when healthy relationships that sustain and discipline human personality are already available to them. Common to these approaches is a refusal to acknowledge what is good within the lives and relationships of gay people and communities. A misplaced confidence in the interpretation of certain biblical texts becomes the basis for ignoring significant cultural questions and for denying qualities and relationships which others recognize as healthy and even noble.

It is a commonplace of Christian thought that healing is an aspect and sign of salvation. The gospels often portray miraculous physical healing as a sign of the deeper restoration represented by the kingdom of God. In a similar way, sickness becomes a symbol of the more radical distortion and alienation that Christians call sin. Things may not be what they seem. What looks like healing may be a true sign or an escape from a deeper sickness. Jeremiah rebuked his fellow religious leaders with the haunting words, 'They have healed the wound of my people lightly, saying "Peace, peace", where there is no peace' (6:14). The stress experienced by gay people may arise from the malaise and alienation that afflict all human beings and all human relationships. It will certainly also reflect society's violence against those who are vulnerable and different. This is likely to focus on precisely those points at which gay people threaten the confident idolatries of straight society. All this points to the difficulty of what counts as true healing. Is it the maturing of human personality that occurs in the intimate relationship between two gay men who commit their relationship to God? Is it in the realignment of a person's affectionate life through friendship and sexual abstinence with the possibility of heterosexual courtship and marriage? Is it collusion with the society's ideals of masculinity and with the violence and misrepresentation directed against gay people? Is it costly confrontation with this violence, and its underlying idolatry, by self-affirming gay people pursuing an alternative vision of human society?

Healing this side of death can only be partial and occurs within a world still deeply alienated and scarred; it should cause no surprise if different people perceive healing in different ways. *You*

Don't Have To Be Gay describes itself as a book 'to help those who are not happy as homosexuals to change their identity'.[33] It consists of letters written under an assumed name by 'Jeff', who has escaped a gay lifestyle, to Mike who is suicidal at his inability to control or escape his homosexual desires. The book comes with the warm commendation of Elizabeth Moberley, and presents itself as a lively and down-to-earth application of her theories. 'Jeff' takes Mike very carefully through a process of distinguishing his sexual desires from his strong need for male affection, and helps him to establish a different pattern for maintaining affectionate relationships with straight men. The book is a powerful testimony to the commitment of these two people to escaping an intolerable way of life. The process of change it advocates is more than a move to greater self-understanding, it involves the thorough process of overcoming the envy and insecurity that affect Mike's relationships with straight men and a careful programme for adopting a new, more masculine, identity.

As impressive as the personal stories is what the book reveals about the society in which these two live out their lives. Jeff's journey to healing begins with the break-up of a four-year strong and loving relationship with Brian, which they abandon because they cannot face the hostility of family and society. Throughout the story it is unthinkable for both 'Jeff' and Mike that anyone outside the therapeutic process should know that they are or have been gay. Within the narrative of the book the only alternative for gay people is suicide,[34] which becomes the symbol of refusing the heterosexual way of Christ. The book has no place for gay people who do not have the personal resources or contacts to undergo such rigorous reprogramming, or who believe that other claims on their energy have a greater priority, never mind those who see being gay and Christian as compatible. It does not question society's hostility to gay people, and appears to see this as the natural outworking of Christian truth. The deep dishonesty to which this hostility gives rise, as well as the culture's underlying goals and values, are both taken for granted; the health of the prevailing pattern of male relationships in American society is never questioned. Is this healing or is it worldliness? What does it say about personal identity in Christ that the author cannot use his name?

The gift of freedom

'For freedom Christ has set us free; stand fast therefore, and do not submit again to a yoke of slavery' (Galatians 5:1). Freedom is one of the most beautiful words in Christian vocabulary. It is also one of the most abused, and cannot be simply the freedom to do what we want regardless of others (Galatians 5:13). When the idea of freedom is explored in the New Testament, the ancient institution of slavery is never far in the background. In St John's Gospel Jesus says, 'everyone who commits a sin is a slave to sin . . . if the Son makes you free, you will be free indeed' (John 8:34,36). It is easy to see the sin referred to here as a particular personal weakness such as anger, drink or sexual addiction. However, the scope of the freedom offered sets these personal enslavements in a wider context. What Jesus offers those who come to him is a new identity – with the free status of 'sons' (cf. Matthew 17:24–7) – in which people are no longer subject to the powers and values that govern a world in rebellion against God. This freedom is one that affirms the truest desires of the human heart (John 7:37,38), one that gives people an identity that springs from Jesus's deepest knowledge of who they are (cf. Revelation 2:17).

Christian freedom is easily lost – which explains the passion of St Paul's letter to the Galatians. In the difficult task of personal discernment the key to freedom lies with the life-giving love of Jesus Christ and not with the values and powers that dominate religious or secular society (Galatians 4:3–9, cf. Colossians 2:8,20). In 1 Corinthians 7:17–23 St Paul explores the question of how Christian slaves can be free: how is discipleship to be lived out under the hostile institution of slavery? The strange answer is that both accommodation and escape can be expressions of Christian freedom; in either case freedom comes within the human context in which Christ calls us. But at its deepest level the gospel of Christ turned out to be subversive of the ancient institution of slavery. Beyond the apparent acceptance of this anti-human social arrangement lay a deeper hope, expressed in the liberation of the human person into Christ and into a community where the unclean are made clean, the unloved know love, and the marginal share the spacious freedoms of royal status.

Who is free? The gay person who escapes a gay lifestyle to adopt 'norms' of a fallen and disordered society, or the gay person who opens their heart, with the human intuitions and gifts of friendship that are part of their gayness, to Christ? I owe to a good friend the evocative phrase, 'the unfathomable mystery of individual vocation' – the shape and goal of an individual life lies mysteriously in the unfolding purpose of God. Part of freedom in Christ is the inscrutability of this process of discernment. The form of the new creation cannot simply be read off the blueprints of past cultures. The individual has to face the question, what does the love of Christ want me to make of the gifts that lie hidden in my gayness? For the church, part of Christian freedom means respecting and supporting the answers to which a person comes. 'Who are you to stand in judgment on the servant of another? It is before his own master that he stands or falls. And he will be upheld, for the Master is able to make him stand' (Romans 14:4). The individual's task of discernment is certainly not made easier where the church that offers 'healing' colludes with society's idolatrous violence against gay people. Can gay people hear the voice of Christ through a church that requires them to be invisible – in which they may not even use the name by which Christ knows them?

Part 3

Life Issues

Chapter 10

Gays and Society

Apostate Christians, sorcerers and the like should
be drawn and burnt. Those who have connexion
with Jews and Jewesses or are guilty of bestiality
or sodomy shall be buried alive in the ground
provided they be taken in the act and convicted by
lawful and open testimony.

Thirteenth-century lawcode[1]

Gay men value friendship because until they find
their feet as human beings, and, let's face it, it's
not easy to be 16 and gay, friends are not *just*
friends. They're allies against the world.

Tony Warren
(Creator of *Coronation Street*)[2]

The following stories have been chosen almost at random.
Similar accounts can be found any month in the gay papers
and reflect the common experience of gay people.

Two gay men were desperate to escape a hate campaign
being waged against them by their neighbours in their block
of flats.[3] According to the Bristol Evening Post of the 11
December 1990, their flat had been burgled and sprayed
with obscene graffiti; they were insulted in the street and
afraid to go out alone. In their desperation to be rehoused the
pair hatched a plot to damage their flat. They planned a small
fire in the entrance hall, but misjudged and the whole thing
got out of control. They were lucky to escape the resulting

conflagration with their lives. The judge did not accept the harassment they endured as extenuating circumstances and jailed them for three years.

In summer 1992 three women were dismissed from their jobs at a Glasgow delicatessen by the manager, Raymond Scott, who was described as a 'born again' Christian.[4] The trouble started when one woman, a student, blew a kiss to her flatmate while working in the shop. Another staff member, Veronica, was dismissed when she protested against the sacking and admitted that she was also lesbian. A third staff member, Alison, was dismissed two days later on the false assumption that she was also lesbian; the evidence for this was that she had been recommended for the job by Veronica and shared a flat with her. The manager explained his actions to the press as follows: 'Everyone should read the first chapter of Romans. The word makes it clear where the Lord stands on homosexuality.' One woman described him to the *Pink Paper* as 'warped by religion. I was angry at first but now I feel sorry for the guy. He says homosexuality is a dark force.'

In 1992 a fourteen-year-old boy told his mother that he thought he was gay. She, horrified by her son's declaration, told him that he was disgusting, disgraceful and evil. The boy went quietly to his room and hanged himself. At the inquest, no mention was made of the boy's sexuality.[5]

At 8.30 a.m. on 2 June 1993 a secondary school teacher who taught maths and computing at an independent school in Hertfordshire was woken by police officers with a search warrant for 'videos, photographs and material attached to sado-masochism.'[6] Ten officers, including two who filmed the raid, took away videos (including *The Sound of Music*!), a camera, a computer, whips, canes, bondage equipment and dildoes. In seizing copies of *Gay Times*, *Capital Gay*, and *Zipper*, one officer said, 'This stuff cannot possibly be legal.' It seems that the police had obtained his name and address from the address book of a man whom he had met three and a half years ago who was under suspicion of being involved in child pornography. No charges were brought against the teacher and there was no evidence of any involvement or interest in paedophilia. Two weeks later the video of the raid was shown by the police to representatives of the school governors at the local police station. On 22 June he was interviewed by the headmaster and then dismissed.

In 1993 the Belgrade gay group Arkadi reported a systematic Serbian campaign against homosexuals: 'After the Croats, homosexuals are the Serb's biggest enemy.' Rados Smisanic – a leader of Serbia's Socialist Party – claimed that opposition met by Serbs in the current conflict was, 'under the influence of Western gay organizations. It is hard to imagine the force and power of these groups.'[7]

When I attended the conference *Homosexuality, Which Homosexuality?* in Amsterdam in December 1987, a surprising feature of the event – at least to this somewhat bemused Englishman – was an official reception for those attending the conference laid on by the Mayor and civic authorities of Amsterdam and the Dutch Minister of Welfare, Health and Cultural Affairs. Among the other guests was a small, neat clergyman distinguished by a dark suit and a very deep clerical collar. He turned out to be a Baptist evangelical pastor called Joseph Doucé who ran the Centre du Christ Libérateur (CCL) in Paris. The aim of the institute, he told me, was to help and witness to sexual minorities in France; it had an extensive programme of pastoral care, study and education. Pastor Doucé was closely involved with virtually every sexual minority and was the only person in France who had mastered the legal processes necessary to enable French lesbians to have children by AID. He was wearing his clerical collar to this event to demonstrate a church presence.

On 19 June 1990 two plain clothes officers of the French secret police (Renseignments Généraux) created a disturbance at Pastor Doucé's house before being scared off by uniformed police. There is other evidence that the RG was involved at the time in 'dirty tricks' against various groups and individuals and had attempted to infiltrate the CCL to obtain information about paedophiles. On 19 July at 8.30 p.m. Pastor Doucé left his flat with two men who claimed to be police officers. It is likely that he was strangled that night, although his body was not discovered in the forest of Rambouillet until 18 October.[8] No one has been charged with his murder.

Analysing the encounter

I am constantly surprised at how differently gay and straight people perceive society. To most straight people gay people tend to be invisible – an occasional and unexpected intrusion into ordinary life – possibly comic, possibly sinister. Gay people encounter the world as a place of threat and violence.

The various stories at the start of this chapter include many features which will find an echo in the lives of gay people, whether or not they are sexually active, and whether or not they are actively involved in the gay scene.

1 *Invisibility*
Gay people tend to be invisible to straight people. Unless they identify themselves as gay they are assumed to be unsuccessful or eccentric players in the straight 'game'. This invisibility has many results. It means that many straight people's image of gay people is created by the media and the more extravagant manifestations of the gay movement rather than by their gay friends. It contributes to an illusion of social uniformity: everyone is like 'us'. It heightens the shock and thrill of discovering that someone is gay – and therefore ironically makes homosexuality more visible: as if erotic attraction and sexual activity were otherwise absent from society! It introduces a hidden question into many friendships between gay and straight people: Will the friendship survive the uttering of the secret? Is the friendship conditional on the half-suspected not actually being uttered?

2 *'The dark force'*
Raymond Scott's behaviour attributes a sinister power to gay people that renders them incapable of selling salami or cream cakes without corrupting decent society. This is more than moral outrage and draws, as earlier chapters have shown, on three powerful cultural instincts. The first is the need of any social group to symbolize the forces that threaten the social

cohesion and welfare of the group. The second is the later Christian harnessing of the story of Sodom and Gomorrah which has cast gay people in this symbolic role in Western culture. The third is a pervasive sense of unease about the central institutions of modern society: the economic market and the nuclear family. This unease itself has two elements to it: fear that these institutions are in danger of disintegration, and an awareness that they are not delivering the humane quality of life which they appear to promise. The idols of our culture are under threat; how powerful must these people be who can escape their power!

3   Threat

The reality, of course, is that gay people are not powerful but vulnerable. Threat is an all pervasive element in gay experience. This hostility is not mere gentle mockery but something far more violent and invasive. It focuses on some of the deepest areas of an individual's sense of worth: their awareness of beauty, their hopes of friendship and domestic stability, their relationship to the ideals and primary images of the culture. What is at risk for gay people is domestic belonging and security and, beyond this, economic livelihood. Many young gay people fear rejection by their family and with good reason. Many homeless young people find themselves on the streets because of such parental rejection.

If ejection from home and family is one danger, the loss of a job is another, with all the consequent threat to housing and livelihood. At the moment the law in Britain, despite repeated resolutions of the European Parliament, gives a gay person no direct protection against being dismissed from their job for being gay.[9] An argument exists that the 1976 Equal Treatment Directive may preclude discrimination against gay people in employment,[10] but the point has yet to be established and the previous record of the courts is not promising. Once unemployed the stigma of being gay is unlikely to make finding another job easier. The gay person who is hiding their gayness from themselves and others is obviously most vulnerable at a time of crisis. Those who might offer support are likely to be in shock; the person is without moral support or the reliable advice available from gay organizations.

It is important to note that what is being stigmatized in these drastic rejections is not a person's sexual behaviour but some mysterious inner quality: the sense that they are refusing the pervasive ideals of the culture.

This sense of threat is often one of the earliest aspects of gay experience, frequently preceding any awareness of gay movements or the possibility of sexual activity. It contributes to a profound sense of insecurity and self-hatred which can form a major part of gay people's personal make-up. This sense of vulnerability and self-hatred explains the susceptibility of gay people to certain forms of destructive behaviour.[11] It also explains the defiant exuberance of aspects of the gay movement as gay people seek to reclaim their own imagination.

4 Violence

Violence against gay people is the natural extension of this hostility. Physical violence and verbal abuse against gay people are extremely common and are probably part of the experience of a good proportion of gay people. Two surveys by the Gay London Policing Group (GALOP) in the early 1990s found that 40 per cent of gay men and 25 per cent of lesbians had been beaten up by queerbashers at least once in their lives. During the same period another survey, funded by the Home Office Safer Cities Project, found that 45 per cent of gay men had been the victim of such violence. Not only is violence against gay people common, but those who assault or kill gay people are regularly treated with great leniency by the courts – particularly where assailants claim to have been shocked and horrified by the discovery that their victim was gay.[12] Furthermore, gay people know that if as victims of violence they go to the police, they are unlikely to receive a sympathetic hearing; they may well find themselves the subject of police investigation, while little or no attempt is made to pursue their attackers.

5 Hostile institutions

The comparative indifference of the courts and the police to violence against gay people is part of a wider pattern: the hostility to gay people by the public institutions of English society. The courts are able to treat gay people's lives as cheap and their interests as not worth protecting, because they are formed by a settled cultural tradition. An interesting study by Les Moran has shown the way that judges import into the administration of the law understandings of homosexuality derived from the Christian tradition and the medical tradition that emerged in the nineteenth century.[13] The tendency of judges is to portray gay people as at the opposite pole from decency: 'a particular perverted lust, which not only takes them out of the class of ordinary men gone wrong, but stamps them with a hallmark of a specialised and extraordinary class' (Lord Summer, 1918). A judgment by Lord Justice Lawton in 1973 shows the continuation of this tradition: he refers to the homosexual as 'disordered', 'depraved', 'wicked', 'revolting', 'damaged', 'effeminate', uncontrolled ('the driving force of lust'), 'corrupt', 'mentally ill' - skilfully weaving together both Christian and medical terminology.

The common experience of the hostility of the police has already been mentioned and is regularly documented in the gay press.[14] In major cities, such as London and Manchester, the police make occasional moves to establish better relations with the gay communities but these are frequently called in question by the realities of police practice.[15] Part of the known inability of the police to solve murders of gay people is the lack of trust of the police within the gay community.[16] The gradual adoption of an explicit gay equal opportunities policy among the police, pioneered by South Yorkshire police in 1991,[17] may eventually lead to changed attitudes as more police are known to be gay; the indications are that change will be slow. Part of the mistrust between the police and gay people arises from the vulnerability of gay people to criminal prosecution and the ease with which police can boost crime detection rates by acting against the victimless crimes of gay sexual activity.

The continued hostility of the actual law to gay sexual activity is probably not widely understood.[18] Public displays of affection may be prosecuted as conduct likely to provoke a breach of the peace.[19] It is a crime for a man 'persistently to solicit or importune a man in a public place for an immoral purpose'. The courts have ruled that this can mean any word or gesture which has a possible sexual intent. 'Persistently' means more than one invitation – possibly to different men on different days! 'Public place' means anywhere except a private home or hotel room.

The effect of this is to cast a veil of criminality over much gay socializing. The vagueness of such law gives plenty of scope for the police to victimize gay people. The tendency of juries to require hard evidence before conviction and to be more reluctant than magistrates to regard gay people as intrinsically immoral means that informed lawyers often advise clients to opt for jury trials – a right endangered by Government proposals to abandon trial by jury for such 'minor' offences. Equally an increasing tendency of juries to acquit gay people has led to an increasing reliance by the police and Crown Prosecution Service on local by-laws that can be dealt with in the more amenable magistrates' courts.[20]

The 1967 'liberalization' of the law against gay sex was strictly limited in its effect: it simply decriminalizes sex between men over twenty-one in private. The reason that the Home Office will not allow the distribution of condoms in prisons to avoid the spread of AIDS is that they regard prisons as a public place and sexual acts as unlawful. Having sex while another room in your flat is occupied is not private.[21] Introducing gay people to each other may be a breach of the law, even if the sex that may result is lawful.[22] In England and Wales the 1967 Sexual Offences Act was followed by a marked increase in prosecutions for gay sex between consenting men.[23] During the 1980s 2561 men were imprisoned for gay offences, largely consensual sex. Section 30 of the 1991 Criminal Justice Act is likely to lead to much longer prison sentences for crimes involving consensual sex.[24] Despite certain specific changes, such as the recent lowering of the age of consent to eighteen years, the intrusion of the criminal law into sexual and affectionate relations between men has tended to increase. The lowering of the age of consent is expected to lead to an increase in prosecutions with longer prison sentences for men in their twenties having sex with seventeen year-olds and with men under eighteen themselves being prosecuted.[25]

Another public institution that has proved increasingly hostile to gay people is the tabloid press. Press coverage of gay issues is dealt with carefully in a regular feature by Terry Sanderson in the *Gay Times*. In a wider discussion of the increasing virulence of the tabloid press against gay people, he attributes the change to three factors: the fear of AIDS, the 'right wing of the political establishment' realizing 'what a potent force homophobia is . . .

exploiting it to its own advantage', and economic pressure created by the vicious circulation war between these papers.[26]

6   The isolation of young gay people

Many lesbian and gay young people experience school as a time of loneliness and confusion. A report published by the National Union of Teachers in July 1991 reported that lesbian, gay and bisexual teenagers are 'frequently isolated, sometimes confused and are often subject to appalling victimization'.[27] A 1984 survey showed that 19 per cent of gay teenagers had attempted suicide once in their lives, a fact that is acknowledged in literature produced by the Department of Health.[28] This figure may be conservative; North American evidence suggests that young lesbian and gay people are 'two to three times more likely to attempt suicide than other young people – they may comprise up to 30 per cent of completed youth suicides annually'.

These figures are, of course, symptomatic of the wider problems faced by gay teenagers trying to negotiate the powerful stereotypes and pressures of their culture. In two important ways the British Government has effectively restricted the scope of support that can be given to such young people in schools. One is Section 28 of the 1988 Local Government Act, described to Sir Ian McKellen by one Government minister as 'a piece of red meat thrown to the wolves'. Another is the Education circular 11/87 which makes no provision for general teaching about homosexuality beyond certain strong negatives. The desire to 'protect' young people, which apparently underlies such provisions, has a curious air of unreality about it. Almost no one – least of all those who experienced the traditional public school – can imagine that sexual contacts in teenage years play any part in turning someone gay. The Government's refusal of any financial support to vulnerable and even homeless young people of sixteen and seventeen does not feel like concern. The realities of adult life impinge sharply on people in their mid-teens. The notion that sexual feelings can somehow simply be denied until the end of adolescence, or do not need respectful and sympathetic engagement during school years, is bizarre.

School is not the only place which is experienced as menacing by young lesbian and gay people. The law itself creates a context in which it is extremely difficult for young people to find advice or counselling. Nor is the threat of the law without teeth: of the 102 men imprisoned for gay offences in 1989, twelve were themselves under twenty-one and twenty-three were imprisoned for having consenting sex with men between sixteen and twenty-one.[29] Particularly serious is the plight of gay young people in care, as the immensely moving chapter by Ben Perks in *Coming on Strong* makes clear.

7 *The lack of recognition of gay people's primary relationships, whether sexual or not*

The notion that the community or the state should recognize and support significant social relationships other than marriage and the upbringing of children probably strikes most Westerners as bizarre. In tribal and traditional societies the exchange of money forms only a small part of the way by which people play their part in the life of the society and are supported within it. These broader forms of association are reflected in the New Testament in the institution of the household: a social and financial unit including many more people than the immediate biological family. Churches in the New Testament era adopted this pattern: they thought of themselves as a household (cf. 1 Timothy 3:15) and gave extensive financial, social and personal support to their members. Although in the West the economic market remains the dominant social mechanism on which our society relies to attend to the welfare of its citizens, many people find their well-being elsewhere. They depend on a network of friendships and support that is supplied by family, friends and various voluntary associations. These relationships not only contribute to people's viability and identity, they are also an essential part of the social and economic fabric of society. In the case of marriage and children, the economic regulation of society is adjusted to recognize the contribution that these relationships make – for example through tax allowances and pension arrangements. The refusal to extend such recognition to other relationships has a variety of causes. In the case of those responsible for the long-term care of the sick, elderly or disabled, it probably reflects the vulnerability of the carers themselves. In the case of gay people, cultural hostility and extensive ignorance of the reality of gay people's lives are probably additional factors.

8   *The danger represented by evangelical Christians*

The role of Raymond Scott in the dismissal of three women for being or befriending lesbians is not an isolated incident. Evangelical Christians often have a powerful sense of vocation that they are called to oppose the evil of homosexuality. The impact of this on individual gay people can be devastating. Sometimes it comes with undisguised violence, as in the interrogation of a gay RUC constable recorded in *Coming out of the Blue*.[30] Often it is reflected in a refusal to allow gay people to give their own account of their experience or to obtain information and help in a way that will allow them to come to their own assessment of their situation. One example is the reported reluctance of the Courage Trust to inform parents and young people about pro-gay parents groups.[31] Another is the reluctance of the organization CARE to allow the legitimacy of any alternative views of same sex relationships in its contributions to sex education in schools.

Two interpretations

Different explanations can be offered for the hostility and resistance that gay people experience in Western society. Some would want to argue that it is a sign of the unnatural character of the gay way of life: social difficulties are evidence of the disordered nature of homosexuality; society's treatment of gay people is the product of a deeply ingrained sense of the divine order. There are a number of difficulties with this view: its affirmation of the righteousness of the social order is naive and fails to take account of what the Bible says about the fallenness of human nature; it does not reflect on the cultural character of the modern gay movement; it refuses the moral challenge of addressing the violence experienced by gay people.

Before looking at an alternative account of the way gay people experience society, it may be helpful to outline the biblical understanding of idolatry. The essence of idolatry in scripture is not the worship of physical images; it is the tendency of human societies to create a reality, an image, to which they offer their service and from which they expect to receive the prosperity and happiness which their heart tells them are their true goals.[32] The irony of idolatry, as its many scriptural denunciations seek to demonstrate, is that the idol becomes a delusive and cruel master – corrupting the human spirit and leading to cruelty and injustice. One of the most illuminating applications of this sort of analysis to modern culture is that of the Protestant political thinker, Jacques Ellul, in *The New Demons*.[33]

At the risk of considerable caricature, this sort of analysis may provide an alternative explanation of why modern society is so reluctant to extend the ordinary dignities of human life to gay people. The controlling ideas and principles around which modern society is organized are economic competition and the sexual attraction between men and women. The myth behind this social arrangement is that the well-being of all within the community will be best safeguarded, as far as is possible in a fallen world, by locating affection and desire within social units created by the sexual attraction between men and women, and by leaving the creation and distribution of the resources of life to unrestricted competition between the individuals in society. This understanding of the social order stands in marked contrast with ancient or medieval world views in which society was conceived as a complex web of social relationships – each characterized by obligations of honour and service. The 'idols' of the modern social order are 'the economic market' and 'the family'. (These gods are served in turn by the lesser idols of the state and technology.)

The modern social 'myth' has had the effect of imposing a competitive and emotionally-restricted masculinity on the men in society. It has also sought to divert the human instinct for worship from God and the city of God – to use St Augustine's phrase – and redirect it towards the sexual attraction between men and women. The effective triumph of this social myth, and the social arrangements to which it relates, has been to weaken those intermediate social bonds which gave meaning to earlier cultures and social responsibility to the individuals within them. Despite its essential simplicity – and the energy which human technology and bureaucracy have devoted to its establishment since the eighteenth century – this social pattern carries within itself the seeds of its own destruction. It erodes the social relationships upon which the health of the wider society depends and it creates isolated individuals alienated from others. The symptoms of this weakness can be seen in the lack of economic prosperity for all, and in the failure of the nuclear family that it has created to provide the happiness and fulfilment that it promises. The outward signs of the twin idols' inability to deliver are, on the one hand, unemployment, the loss of creative enjoyment in work, and financial insecurity – and on the other, domestic violence, imaginative stagnation and child abuse.

Where do gay men fit in? (I hope the reader will continue to forgive my inability to include the lesbian and feminine perspective.) The interpretive scheme that this book proposes is that certain individuals, because of their response to the constructed forms of sexual desire which Western culture offers them, find it difficult to take up the scripts offered them by the idols of modern society. In particular certain men, by reason of their inherited make-up and social experience, find difficulty in adopting the distorted masculinity of the culture. Because such men are not able to become players in the game that the idols dictate they become the focus of hostility. The great biblical denunciations of idolatry make clear that those who resist the power of great idols not only suffer but are unable totally to avoid thinking in the categories which their society's idols dictate. In the same way gay people find themselves not only involved in a painful and defiant form of cultural resistance but also inevitably borrow – and attempt to rework – the categories of the prevailing culture. The important role that gay people have as critics of contemporary culture and the anger directed against them are both signs that they are touching a powerful symbolic nerve. Those who find themselves the enemy of idols cannot be very far from the mysterious presence of the true and living God.

If there is any truth in this analysis, then many of the polarizations of the contemporary debate may rest on powerful misconceptions. The sense among many people that the way to preserve society is to protect economic prosperity, to shore up the family and to oppose gay people is mistaken and rests on a deep collusion with the idolatry that is actually undermining society. The open inclusion of gay people into the fabric of society holds the promise of resisting this destructive idolatry:

it inevitably challenges the distorted vision of human beings that the idols impose on us; it has the potential to bring people into contact again with the springs of friendship, gentleness and desire which the present pattern violently suppresses. Real repentance is never quick or painless. The process of allowing gay people to take their place within the social order is inevitably characterized by conflict and passion. It also runs the serious danger that gay people will simply become assimilated to the present social order; that they will, in turn, become new clients of the idols. But, however messy the process may be, it holds the promise of introducing a creative element of penitence and humility into social relationships and the social order.

In his important book on St Francis, Leonardo Boff singles out gentleness as the quality that characterizes St Francis and which modern society lacks.[34] Boff relates the quality of gentleness in Francis to his refusal of power over others; it arises from a profound and penitent presence *with* those who were poor and vulnerable. Gentleness is an important quality in the New Testament's presentation of both Jesus (Matthew 11:29; 2 Corinthians 10:1) and Paul (1 Thessalonians 2:7; Galatians 6:1). In both cases it is intimately related to their refusal to dominate those to whom they came. Despite popular caricatures of St Paul as harsh, his own writing shows a quality of passion, tenderness and open emotion of which many Western men are simply incapable. This quality in Paul is intimately related to his love of compound Greek words that include the prefix *with*. It is interesting that Jesus, Paul and Francis all used feminine imagery of their relationships with those for whom they cared;[35] this self-committing generosity has the capacity to awaken the gentleness of men and the strength of women. Generosity rather than violent control is the way of Christ. Those who fear that allowing gay people to take their place in society will undermine its fabric may yet find that a new humility and generosity have the capacity to recreate a culture.

Making space for gay people

Not surprisingly, the initiative in the fight for gay people to be accepted in Western society as full citizens has rested almost entirely with gay people. Contrary to many people's impression, the movement for gay rights has not originated in highly politicized individuals but in the pain and spontaneous creativity of gay individuals and subcultures. As discussed in Chapter 7 a crucial step in a long story was the shift from a medical to a civil rights model of gay identity around 1969.

It is possible to identify a number of complementary strands in the pressure towards the wider acceptance of gay citizenship: the cultural creativity of gay people; the vitality of the commercial gay scene and community celebrations such as Gay Pride; the limited but real economic resources available to gay people (the myth of 'the Pink Pound');[36] community work that builds on gay awareness, particularly over issues where gay people are the victims of unfair treatment; careful political lobbying by respectable organizations such as Stonewall; 'direct action' by groups such as Outrage!; the dedication of the gay community's response to the HIV virus. Those familiar with the internecine strife that characterizes the Jewish and Christian communities will not be surprised to find similar quarrels among the various strands of the gay movement. Although such disagreements can be fierce they do not often reach quite the venom of which religious groups seem capable.

The agenda in the pursuit of gay rights is probably familiar to most readers, although in the nature of things, priorities change and new issues arise.[37] Concerns include: freedom from discrimination in employment and housing; freedom from harassment; repeal of laws on sexual matters where these are notably stricter than those applying to other citizens; respect for privacy; fair treatment by the police and the courts; open discussion of gay issues and options for young people; economic recognition of significant relationships for gay people through housing arrangements, pensions and tax allowances. In the pursuit of these aims, certain issues emerge as points of difficulty or concern, particularly for straight people or for Christians who are concerned to take a 'biblical' view of homosexuality.

1 The language of rights
The language of human rights is the major idiom in which the public discussion of justice is framed today. This tradition

was framed in an era which identified the need to defend the dignity and welfare of individuals against injustice and totalitarian rule, and is therefore well adapted to the attempt by despised groups to gain social space. In the case of gay people the enshrining of this ethical tradition in the law and institutions of the European Community inevitably means that these are called upon in the defence of the particular concerns of gay people.[38]

Some people find themselves uncomfortable with this tradition for various reasons: it appears to concentrate on the individual at the expense of the community; while it identifies particular issues with clarity it has less to say about how apparent conflicts of rights are to be resolved; it is comparatively silent about a social theory of justice; it is not always easy to link to the scriptural language and categories about justice. A number of these issues are more apparent than real.[39]

Justice and righteousness are major themes in scripture. Large tracts of scripture are devoted to declaring God's anger at the way religious and socially secure people oppress and exploit others. The basic concept that underlies the biblical idea of justice is that individuals are set within a web of relationships – to neighbour, to clan, to the rest of creation, to land, to God. Righteousness and justice consist of honouring and living 'rightly' within these relationships. Within this overarching concept the scriptures have a great deal to say about the importance of the individual, and about the special duty to protect the vulnerable and the outsider. These concerns are not far from those articulated in the ethical tradition of human rights.

Closely related in scripture to the theme of justice is the sin of violence. Violence is not a minor matter within the overarching scheme of scripture – it is the first and principal outworking in human relationships of rebellion against God (cf. Genesis 4:6,23,24). According to Genesis 6 it was because of the sin of violence that God destroyed the old world in the days of Noah. Violence and injustice are closely related in scripture (Psalm 55:9–11; Ezekiel 7:10–13; 28:11–16). Violence is not simply injuring the body, it is an assault on a member of the community and the relationships that sustain them. The evidence of violence is protest and lament (cf. Isaiah 5:7). Indifference to the personal and institutional violence experienced by gay people is not a light matter. It ought to challenge people – both individual Christians and churches – to engage with the issues of public justice for gay people.

2 Does 'immorality' have rights?

Those who believe that sexual activity and affection between people of the same sex are always wrong often feel that they must oppose the granting of any specific rights to gay people. Typical of this position is the 1986 Vatican *Letter to the Bishops of the Catholic Church on the Pastoral Care of Homosexual Persons* which attempts to forbid individual and church involvement in 'organizations in which homosexual persons associate with each other without clearly stating that homosexual activity is immoral'(#15). There are two difficulties with this position: it fails to address the causes of the emergence of a gay social identity, and it has no programme for addressing the injustice experienced by gay people.

Those who take this position often bemoan the emergence of a public gay identity and claim that the ordinary processes of justice in the community should be sufficient to provide justice for all citizens. This, of course, fails to notice that the main reason for the emergence of a distinct gay social identity is precisely the failure of these processes. It is the injustice experienced by gay people before the law, in employment and housing, and in personal harassment, that has given its present profile to the public category of gay.

'Conservative' Christian documents always include an obligatory paragraph deploring the hostility and injustice experienced by gay people.[40] Such statements lack credibility, partly because they include no analysis of the hostility and violence experienced by gay people, and partly because they never issue in any action that is likely to be effective in the public arena. Since 1986 I have carefully followed the media coverage of attempts to address justice issues for gay people or attempts to resist violence against gay people. To my knowledge, during this period no 'conservative' Christian body or individual has ever attempted any effective intervention on these issues. In the case of the bishops of the Church of England the evidence has been all the other way. While the report *Issues in Human Sexuality* decries the treatment that gay people receive in society, the actual activity of the bishops has been consistently hostile to the interests of gay people: the Archbishop of Canterbury intervened to stop SPCK publishing prayers by and for gay people,[41] the Bishop of Chester led the House of Lords' attempt to keep sex between men over eighteen as an imprisonable offence,[42] the Bishop of Worcester oversaw the decision of the Children's Society not to allow children to be placed with gay carers.[43] This last decision is curious, because the Children's Society agreed that it would often be in the best interests of a child – particularly an older child who had been abused for being gay – to be so placed. Their spokesman on the BBC Sunday programme appealed to the Bishops' Report to justify their stand and said that they would refer such children to other societies which would be able to act in their best interests!

Prior to the Second Vatican Council, the Roman Catholic Church found itself in the same position over the civil rights of those whose religious beliefs it condemned and espoused a political position summarized in the aphorism 'error has no rights'. The result of this was that the Roman Catholic Church would never act in a way that gave political rights to bodies or individuals that it believed to be in error. One of the most important achievements of the Second Vatican Council was to reverse this policy and to affirm the principle of religious liberty.[44] The Declaration bases this 'right of the person and communities' on the 'dignity of the human person'; the quest for a right and true response to God arises from the free dignity of the human person and must not be defended in a way that denies this dignity.

This important change of stance provides a model for how 'conservative' Christian bodies might relate to the issue of gay rights. To admit that '"Immorality" has rights' would be to affirm the humanity of gay people and their right and responsibility to discern and plan their own way in life. The alternative denies gay people the right to listen to God for themselves. To refuse to engage with the issue of gay rights is to deny, rather than to assert, the humanity of gay people.

3   The relation of law to morality
This has been a classic question of English legal and moral theory embodied in the famous controversy between Lord

Devlin and H.L.A. Hart. The question that impinges on gay issues is not the broader one of how law and ethics relate to each other but the narrower one of whether the criminal law is an appropriate instrument for regulating consenting sexual behaviour between human beings. During the 1986/7 public discussions on homosexuality, Lord Jacobovits proposed the criminalization of adultery. The 'biblical' case for such action is obvious (Exodus 20:14; Leviticus 20:10). The fact that our society does not bring heterosexual sexual activity outside marriage within the pale of the criminal law does not amount to a failure of moral nerve. It is based on an acknowledgment that the morality of sexual behaviour is better regulated within the normal processes of personal and community relationships. It amounts to a certain modesty about the role of the legal processes of the nation state. The various provisions of national and local government law that criminalize corresponding gay behaviour – despite the fact that such behaviour is very rarely as destructive as adultery – have roots in a cultural mythology that is profoundly hostile to gay people. The fact that this mythology has depended for much of its emotional power on a misreading of scripture (particularly Genesis 19) ought to mean that Christians zealous for the right understanding of scripture should be active in proposing change.

4 Gays and young people

The possibility of gay people having responsibility for the care of children is a highly emotional one. The stigmatizing of an unpopular and strange group as a danger to children is a recurring one in history. The first Christians were suspected of sacrificing children at their eucharists, just as Christians subsequently accused Jews of similar crimes. The reluctance to allow the fostering or adoption of children by gay people rests on two fears: the danger of sexual abuse and the fear that improper role modelling will distort the emotional growth of the child. The recent discovery of the extent of the sexual abuse of children in 'ordinary' families ought to have gone a long way towards undermining the first fear; it suggests rather that there is something seriously dysfunctional about the nuclear family that has emerged in the West. This is a dysfunctionality that gay people have often experienced and which gay people have an important part in helping the wider society address.

The issue of role modelling is equally irrational and rests on dubious assumptions as to the part parents play in the emergence of a gay orientation. It ignores the obvious fact that gay children emerge from straight families. If one of the contributory factors towards the emergence of a homosexual orientation is the distorted masculinity of Western masculine culture, then the impact of gay men in parenting roles is likely, if anything, to affirm the masculinity of gentle male children with the possible result that they will grow up straight!

The idea that the care of children should be limited to the heterosexual couple of the modern nuclear family sits oddly with the experience of other cultures. In tribal societies, and other cultures with extended domestic networks and households, the primary care of children often rests with adults other than the biological parents. The irrational fear of gay people being involved in parenting roles has one major result: vulnerable children are deprived of effective and generous care in childhood and often find themselves confined to destructive institutional care or to abusive households.

5 Domestic partnerships

The suggestion that domestic partnerships other than marriage should be recognized in law – particularly if those involved are of the same sex – probably strikes most people as bizarre. Such partnerships can now be legally registered in Denmark, Sweden and Norway and are under consideration in other European communities. Mention has already been made of the extensive evidence for the liturgical celebration of permanent same sex unions in parts of the ancient Christian world.[45]

Two aspects of the wider argument of this book have a bearing on the evaluation of such proposals. While modern industrial society structures itself around competition between nuclear families, medieval Christian culture saw friendship – with its corollaries of affection, loyalty and mutual obligation – as the basis for human society. What made marriage unique was its capacity for procreation and the stark encounter of the distinct social worlds of men and women. One expression of this understanding of society is to be found in the complex obligations created by taking the role of godparents at baptism.[46] Another is that St Thomas Aquinas saw one of the purposes of marriage not in the creation of a bond of love between the couple but in extending the bonds of affection in society by bringing two families into relationship with each other. This is probably the background against which the same sex unions described by John Boswell need to be understood.

The notion that friendship rather than competition is the true basis for a healthy society has great attractions to it. One of its consequences would be a positive attempt to encourage the recognition and support of affectionate and loyal relationships within society. Against such an understanding the recognition of gay relationships within legally registered domestic partnerships might seem less alien.

6 Overt sexuality

Overt gay sexuality is clearly disturbing to many people. In part this arises because modern Western culture has preferred to project an image of the male that concentrates on power and control rather than beauty, sensuality and feeling. The conventions of sexual display in popular culture enjoy extensive female nudity but have until very recently found the portrayal of male genitals profoundly shocking. Despite the Song of Songs, Christians have rarely been at ease with explorations of the erotic or the sexual. Part of this nervousness arises from the assumption that the primary goal of such exploration is sexual activity. This is too simple. Sexual imagery and display fulfil a much wider function in renewing the culture's imaginative engagement with the mystery of gender. Much of its purpose is not the justification of sexual activity – which would happen anyway and often in ways unrelated to the erotic images celebrated in the culture. It is this wider function that makes popular discussions of heterosexual pornography so difficult. Alongside the clear dangers of exploiting individuals, encouraging delusive fantasy, and endorsing male abuse of women, there is the legitimate agenda of celebrating desire. Sometimes this is discussed in terms of a difficult distinction between pornography and erotica. The scale of Western pornography reflects not only the culture's obsession with the sexual but also the isolation from human contact that its social arrangements encourage.

Within this wider context the character of overt gay sexuality needs to be understood in the context of the particular pressures and social role of gay culture. Overt gay sexuality is partly a form of cultural resistance: an attempt to reclaim social space and imaginative freedom. It also relates to the particular role that gay subcultures have in the West of exploring a more sensual rather than merely dominating understanding of what it is to be male. The social dynamic of Western homosexuality also means that gay erotic material is comparatively free from some of the charges levelled against heterosexual pornography: exploitation of individuals and the endorsement of male social dominance. In this complex area people's judgment will clearly differ. Any discussion needs to make some allowance for the differences between gay and heterosexual erotica.[47]

Why society needs gay people

'We are members one of another' (Ephesians 4:25). When St Paul gives this reason for public truthfulness he is not speaking only about the church. He is drawing on a common ancient understanding of human society. Human beings relate to each other in society in the same way as the different parts of the body. As a political model this ancient description has a number of strengths compared to some of those more usually articulated in modern society. In particular it emphasizes both interdependence and diversity. Much of the hostility that gay people experience in society arises not from particular moral judgements on certain genital acts but from a hostility to a form of human diversity that has gained a certain symbolic charge within the culture.

The image of human society as a body has the potential to affirm the diversity within human communities. Society needs gay people because they are human – they belong. It benefits from gay people precisely because they are different – whether as social critics, as explorers of gender, as models of different approaches to gentleness and strength, as the inheritors of the ancient cultural traditions of same sex affection and friendship, as people skilled in creating social networks based on grace and acceptance, as exemplars of a less predatory way of males relating to women, as those able or willing to exercise social functions that other members of society find difficult. The quest for a new relationship between gay people and society finds part of its key in an understanding of the role of diversity within the beauty and wickedness of human culture.

Chapter 11

Gays and the Church

I believe it is only fearful, insecure Christians who
avoid the positive encounter of dialogue and the
sharing of a common life together.

George Carey[1]

Friendship with the world is enmity with God.

James 4:4

'I am a widower,' the voice on the telephone said. The caller
was plainly terrified and refused to give his name. He explained
that he worked for an evangelical society and had recently read
an article by me in the *Church Times* criticizing an evangelical
campaign to force a gay man to resign from the General Synod.
The caller said that when he was young and before his marriage
he had a gay relationship which had meant a lot to him. Now that
he was older and alone he just wanted to sit again with a man
in his own home and hold hands. 'Is that so terrible?' My main
memory of the call is the man's terror: he was convinced that if
the organization he worked for had known of this conversation
or how he was feeling he would lose his job and his pension.

At first sight the clash between the church and the gay instinct
could not be sharper, whether it occurs in an individual's life
or in the public realm. Outside Westminster Chapel stands
a small group from OUTRAGE!, led by Peter Tatchell, a
one-time evangelical Sunday School teacher, holding a poster:
THE CHURCH CRUCIFIES QUEERS. Inside, a large Anglican
evangelical gathering sings 'Shine! Jesus, shine!' in order to
drown the voice of protest. Many in the evangelical movement of

the Church of England treat the question of homosexuality as the touchstone of faithfulness to Christ and to scripture. Significant evangelical leaders hint that 'compromise' on this issue might lead them to separate from the Church of England.[2]

Analysing the clash

At a public level the clash is between two apparently incompatible social stances: a stand for Jesus Christ and a stand for gay people. Choice and costly resistance are part of Christian discipleship. Jesus spoke of two 'ways', one leading to life and the other to destruction (Matthew 7:13–14). In many different ways the New Testament portrays the Christian way as turning from the way of the world – meaning not rejection of the good creation or of commitment to society, but a refusal of the idolatry and pride that undergird fallen human life. One of the recurring dilemmas for Christian movements is how to reconcile the twin claims of humanity and holiness. At any time there are voices advocating withdrawal and others urging involvement. Both the monastic movement of the early centuries and the evangelical movement that emerged in the eighteenth century have struggled with this tension; what some interpreted as a distancing necessary for effective service others have seen as withdrawal into a spiritual ghetto.

The most profound exposition of this tension remains St Augustine's great work, *The City of God*, which picks up the recurring symbolism in scripture of Babylon and Jerusalem. Augustine portrays the Christian life as the outworking of a dual citizenship: the visible church is not an alternative society turning its back on the world, but something more like a resistance movement – a company of people responding to the sweet but hidden tones of the love of God and at the same time an integral part of the 'earthly city', which is the current context of their lives and the place where they live out their love of God and love of neighbour. Human history, as Augustine presents it, is the outworking of two 'loves', two desires: love for God and love for self.

This vision of the Christian way has an inescapable political

dimension in that it demands a certain stance within the *polis*,
the city, within organized human society. As scripture, and
Augustine its great expositor, explore this theme, Christians
cannot escape confrontation with the powers and idolatries that
dominate fallen society. The prime forum for this confrontation is
not sexual morality, although the dramatic conflicts being played
out in public life are also reflected in the turmoil of the human
imagination and bodily desire. The choice that faces the Christian
is between the worship of God and that of Mammon (Matthew
6:24): between, on the one hand, the idolatry of the beast (Revelation 13) and, with it, the cruel pride and ruthless commerce
of Babylon (Ezekiel 28; Revelation 18), and on the other, the
hidden beauty and love of God that took flesh in Jesus and now,
in the streets and alleyways of Babylon, is preparing and refining
the haunting beauty and promise of the heavenly city.

Part of the beauty of Augustine's exposition of this theme
is the way he relates the desire of the human heart and the
public ordering of society. Christian life is marked not only by
certain outward signs and beliefs but by a movement of love.
This movement is expressed in part in affection and service
within the human community. It is also seen in Christian liturgy,
a corporate art-form which anticipates and models the beauty of
the heavenly city.[3] In the activity of worship not only are the
idols of the day kept at bay, but a renewed desire for God, in
a limited and transient way, creates glimpses and reflections of
true human glory. The forms of Christian worship are, then,
not simply occasions to teach but they make visible a hidden
current of life running in human history. The problem, of course,
is that these manifestations of love for God cannot trap the
movement of the Spirit that creates them, nor are they ever
pure. In different eras of the church's life, what some have
seen as signs of the heavenly city others have seen as the
captivity of the church to powers that seek to supplant God.
Was the splendour of fourth-century worship a celebration of
Christian freedom or collusion with imperial power? Is medieval
worship and art a hauntingly beautiful testimony to the way a
society's imagination can be captivated by Christ or an idolatrous
attempt by a powerful institution to grab wealth and power in
feudal society? Are the Reformation liturgies the recovery of
scriptural Christianity or the instruments of social control by

ruthless Tudor monarchs and their greedy courtiers? Is modern evangelical 'family' worship a sell-out to the myths of modern life or a potent form of resistance to it?

Despite the violent clash between Christian culture and an assertive gay identity, the two movements have some important elements in common. Both are attempts to deny the claim of the idols of modern society, to make contact with the creative springs of life and desire, and to assert the importance of love and affection over that of power and violence. These common roots are reflected in common elements in the experience of Christians and gay people. Both express their deepest instincts in song and art, and try to be communities of acceptance and affection. Both encounter misrepresentation and hostility from the media which partly arises from sheer puzzlement at what makes the particular movement tick. Both experience a sense of alienation and hostility from the dominant forces in the culture. The 'persecution' of Christians and gay people follows similar patterns: groups or individuals that are often accepted by their neighbours find themselves vulnerable to the hostility of individuals or to scapegoating in times of social stress. Both movements find themselves in an uneasy dialogue with the prevailing concepts and symbols of the culture. In both cases the pressures of an alien and debilitating environment lead on occasions to irrational bouts of internal warfare.

The quarrels between the two movements are in some respects like quarrels between siblings. As with many family quarrels the patterns of mutual recrimination, dependence and hostility have grown complex and bitter. Three particular moments from the past continue to resonate whenever the two movements meet. The first was the willingness of the church in the thirteenth century to allow the story of Genesis 19 to be coopted by a stressed society to demonize certain non-conforming groups within later medieval culture. The effect was to portray those who did not conform to the social order as threats to the cosmic order and the objects of God's wrath. Once born, the myth of the sodomite has remained available as a potent and scriptural image with which to clothe the unfamiliar.

A related moment arose with the attempt in the later medieval period to impose celibacy on the clergy.[4] This had the effect of increasing anxiety about sexual behaviour and contributing to a mental link, in certain lay sections of the church, between liturgy and homosexuality. This link has continued to operate at different points in subsequent Western Christian history. It was used by Henry VIII to justify the dissolution and plundering of the monasteries. It inserted into Protestant piety a suspicion of the God-centred art and devotion of the medieval period. This prepared the ground for an identification of Christian worship with domestic piety and commercial thrift which, in turn, encouraged later Protestant tradition to yield the public realm to hard-nosed 'science' and commercialization and to relocate desire for God to the home. Not everything in this development was harmful; there is evidence that, for a period, Puritan piety found a new reconciliation of the masculine and feminine in spirituality.[5] However, in the end this development led traditional Protestant Christianity to abandon the vision of affectionate relationships as the basis of society, the conceptual link between human *eros* (desire) and public art and culture, and any secure understanding of same sex friendship as a social and creative phenomenon.

The ground was thus prepared for the third moment in the emerging quarrel between the two movements, namely the alliance between the nineteenth-century evangelical movement and the new symbol of the 'family as humane refuge' which social reformers advocated as an answer to the brutality of mass industrial society. By these stages a church that had dreamed of heaven, given birth to communities of the poor and dispossessed, and created public art of great beauty, became a movement that withdrew from society except for occasional forays in support of 'family values'. It is interesting to note how in the years after the Second World War English evangelicalism had occasionally to relax its grip on some of these convictions in order to encourage the flowering of successful evangelism that this period was to see. Examples are the acknowledgment of adolescent sexuality in evangelical youth work, the affirmation of same sex friendship in the various camps for public school boys, and the recurring realization in parish evangelism that the sexual dimension in the lives of those on the edges of church culture must not be denied – 'When the Bible says sin it does not mean sex', etc.

Obviously this picture is too sharply drawn and does not, for example, have sufficient place for the extraordinary influence of William Temple's *Christianity and Social Order* in the middle years of this century. However, it helps to explain why the more 'catholic' wing of Anglicanism – with its romantic admiration for the humane values of medieval culture[6] – both attracted men with a gay disposition and was suspected by 'decent' Protestants of being a denial of sober and patriotic domestic virtue. Hence were born the potent intuition of English church life that all catholics are quasi-gay (or at least sympathetic to the unmentionable vice) and the equally false notion that 'true' evangelicals cannot be gay.

This tangled history has had profound results for the public interaction of the church with what one might call the gay cultural intuition. It has made it hard for Christians to recognize the significant elements of common cultural agenda that they often share with gay movements. In more recent years it has led the churches to oppose almost any attempt to relax the law as it impinges on any aspect of gay people's lives. It has meant that evangelicals have found it hard to recognize that gay people have much to teach evangelical culture about what it is to be male and female, or that the clash with gay movements exposes the extent to which evangelical culture has surrendered to some of the most powerful idols of modern society.

One of the most serious results of the alienation of these two movements is its impact on individuals. Precisely because of their lack of responsiveness to the heterosexual project, men with a disposition towards gayness are often susceptible to the underlying vision or spirit that stirs in church life – to the notion that the true goal of our sense of beauty and life lies in God, in a diffused social affection, and in art – and not exclusively or even primarily in marriage. While their contemporaries search for their first woman they are open to a different call. Furthermore, as they experience isolation and hostility in society, they naturally respond to the sort of friendship that Jesus offers. It should be no surprise that many gay people find their way into the church.

For many the next step is a cruel betrayal. They discover that the community to which they have been drawn lacks any realistic comprehension of how they can discover a viable affectionate and domestic life. It emerges that the church in which they have sought a home has public commitments that are profoundly hostile to their personal and social well-being. In addition it sends them strongly contradictory messages about the spiritual intuition that brought them to Christ: it is simultaneously an echo of the music of heaven and an unspeakable wickedness that threatens the community with God's wrath. Different people respond in different ways to this sharp turnabout from attraction to hostility. One outcome is the presence in the gay community of large numbers of people who went through a 'church phase' and are now either hostile or simply nostalgic about Christian faith. A member of one evangelical church in London commented to me that of eighteen gay people in the congregation at one time only two were still Christians. Another response is the adoption in some form or other of a divided identity; this can be more or less consciously assumed and may take more or less healthy forms. Significant numbers of gay people continue to live by the intuition that first drew them to the life of the church and to serve the liturgy and the community. The great danger is that they never focus on their own needs of affection, bodily affirmation, intimacy, or domestic security.

The drastic impact that this dual message has on the lives of many gay people who respond to Christ should be of major concern within the church. At the 1995 Evangelical Anglican Leaders' Conference Michael Baughen attempted to divert divisive discussion by speaking of 'a very vocal lobby representing a very tiny homosexual community in this country'.[7] Apart from Jesus's own words about the significance that God gives to a single individual (cf. Luke 15:1–10) such a comment fails to recognize the impact of a divided message on many gay individuals within the church. Whatever the situation in the national population, it is certainly the case that many of those who find a home in the church and serve it faithfully are gay. In 1990 Dr Ben Fletcher, who had previously published studies of stress in various other work contexts, published a detailed study of stress among clergy in the Church of England. His investigations led him to believe that about 15 per cent of the clergy in the Church of England are homosexual.[8] He concludes that this minority 'suffers very high levels of stress'.[9] There is no evidence that such a detailed and careful report by someone whose professional expertise lay in the area of analysis of occupation-related stress has received any serious attention within the Church of England.

It is understandable that many gay people perceive the church to be a hostile institution. However, again this analysis is too simple. The physical violence experienced by gay people may on occasion be fuelled by myths derived from the Christian tradition, but it gains in virulence from the isolation of individuals and the disintegration of the networks and social relationships in industrial society. If, God forbid, a really serious attempt to eradicate gay people from Western society were to occur again, it might use Christian language but it would derive some of its psychic force from the way our economic structure is disintegrating social bonds without delivering happiness or prosperity – the social disintegration described in Romans 1:29–32 or Titus 3:3 is not far away. Despite its history of hostility towards gay people the Christian church remains one of the social forces most likely to reverse the disintegration to which modern forms of idolatry are giving rise. There are three ingredients of church life which could contribute to this effect: biblical teaching that emphasizes the bonds that exist between all people in society, for example the ideas of 'the neighbour' or of society as 'a body'; the geographical location of churches which can make them a potent stimulus for local community; and the hidden presence of Jesus within their life. It is one of the ironies of the current controversies about the church and gay people that reconciliation with gay people could play a part in separating the churches from the idols of the society and enabling them to become again points of reintegration within the culture.

Rethinking the chasm

Clearly one of the main barriers that stands in the way of churches relating creatively to the gay people within and on the edge of their life is the profound sense that to do so would be a denial of Scripture. Earlier chapters have sought to expose some of the simplifications or misunderstandings which have contributed to this. More careful study of the Bible and its relation to the forces and movements of the culture must play an important part in any re-forming of the mind of the church.

Any serious attempt to rethink the chasm between the church and gay people must also pay respectful attention to the experience of gay people and to the way they hear and interpret the scriptures. Given the web of potent associations that the subject of homosexuality has accrued in Western Christianity and culture, genuine and prolonged encounter at a personal, theological and cultural level needs to take place. There is an arrogance in believing that clarity of thought about the question of homosexuality can be attained by excluding from the discussion those who are directly affected or by prescribing in advance the conclusions to which such discussion may come.

A number of St Paul's letters could provide interesting starting points in an attempt to re-examine the relationship of the churches to the modern gay movements:

1 *The answer of 1 Corinthians 11:2–16: Missiological pragmatism*. This important passage has been discussed at various earlier points in this book.[10] A line of argument that seems alien and difficult to many expositors has its roots in a simple reality: St Paul as a missionary leader sought to fix the social location of the church in Corinth in a way that would enable it to function with the grain of the social order of imperial Roman Corinth. What emerges starkly in this passage in fact underlies the argument of other important ethical passages in the New Testament. One example of this is the care St Paul takes to avoid destructive conflict with the authorities of the Roman Empire. Behind St Paul's commands to obey the imperial authorities lie a cultural judgment and a strategic missiological commitment. The cultural judgment was that the Roman Empire, for all its wickedness, was likely to continue as a fixed element in the political landscape and conferred a valuable degree of stability on the lands of the empire. The strategic commitment was to align the congregations for which he was responsible with the social order that the imperial authorities created.

What are often known as the 'household codes', the lists of ethical injunctions in certain New Testament letters, are another example of such missiological pragmatism. The Christian *identity* of the individuals and communities to which these letters are addressed rests firmly in the new creation in Christ expressed in baptism.[11] However, in setting out a pattern of *social behaviour* for these Christians, Paul and other New Testament writers are content to incorporate the social arrangements and accepted roles of the culture. While Colossians 3:5–17 roots the ethical injunctions of the letter in baptism, the specific injunctions of 3:18–4:1 address wives, husbands, children, fathers, slaves and masters. St Paul accepts the way society is ordered, and then brings the perspectives of the gospel of Christ to bear on the various social roles to be found within it. Probably the most remarkable aspect of this missiological pragmatism to modern people is St Paul's willingness to work with the social institution of slavery.

This apostolic example of missiological pragmatism could offer the churches an alternative approach to the emergence of a gay identity. If the cultural judgment is made that a public gay identity is now an inescapable element of the social landscape, it would be open to the churches to make the sort of adjustments that they have made to the economic arrangements of industrial society or to the prevalence of remarriage after divorce. Beyond this question of cultural judgment lies the more difficult discernment of strategic alignment. The process of discernment involves both prudential judgment and also sensitivity to the movement of the Holy Spirit. If the gay cultural intuition represents a form of resistance to the values and 'gods' that underlie the social disintegration of Western industrial society, then including openly gay people within congregations may help the church discern its vocation in such a society. Christians must discover whether the way of the Spirit lies in seeking to defend the ideals of the nuclear family – with a possible uncritical acceptance of the 'way of the world' – or whether it lies in establishing a more extended and diverse network of social relationships, a re-visioning of society as bound together by bonds of affection and friendship.

2 *The answer of Galatians: The radicalization of ethnic and sexual identity.* One of the most remarkable cultural shifts that took place in the New Testament church was the rejection of circumcision as a requirement for membership of the people of God. Few biblical exchanges are more savage than St Paul's invective against those who sought to impose circumcision

on Gentile believers: 'I wish those who unsettle you would muti-late themselves!' (Galatians 5:12). Circumcision was the most venerable of Jewish religious and cultural practices. Its effect was to imprint in the body and the psyche a characteristic ethnic and gender identity; it spoke of an identity that was formed by a particular cultural commitment and implied a view of masculinity that linked the hope of God's blessing with the expectation of children. St Paul's passionate resistance to any attempt to impose circumcision outside the Jewish community was made in the name of 'freedom' (Galatians 5:1–6; 6:11–17). While he was willing to go to great lengths to accommodate different groups within the congregations under his influence, he understood that any attempt to identify life in Christ with a particular ethnic or gender identity was to turn back from the newness of the Christian way (cf. 3:28; 6:15). The new creation of the gospel of Jesus Christ was of a new human identity, created not by the imposition of a cultural identity but by responding in love and faith to Jesus Christ. When Paul writes, 'I carry the marks of Jesus in my body' he refers not to circumcision but to the great hostility he encountered because of this refusal to link Christ to a particular ethnic or gender identity.

3 *The answer of Romans 14:1–15:13: Acceptance without agree-ment.* These two chapters address strong disagreement about what sort of food Christians could eat. It is not clear – at least to this writer! – whether the disagreement was over the Jewish food laws or something closer to the dispute reflected in 1 Corinthians 8–10 about meat that had been offered to idols. However, the broad outlines of the matter are clear: Christians were sharply divided over the interpretation of symbolically significant behaviour in a particular cultural context. The result was not only acrimony and division but a determined attempt by each group to dominate and impose their view on the other. There are three strands to St Paul's response. The first is to insist that agreement must not be made the condition of fellowship; welcome that reflects the warmth of Christ must provide the context in which the disagreement is explored. Secondly, he urges that restraint may be necessary in order to facilitate such discussion. Thirdly, he is confident that allowing those involved to come to their own personal decision without

hostile pressure and judgment from others will lead to a secure and well-founded faith.

This principle not only challenges the way in which many Christians wish to predetermine the outcome of discussions of homosexuality by making the acceptance of a particular view a condition of fellowship. It also illuminates the difficult relationships between gay Christians who take different positions on various ethical questions. It is inevitable that Christians with a gay disposition will come to different theological and moral assessments of homosexuality, and legitimate that they will form therapeutic associations and campaigning organizations that reflect these positions. However, the adoption of a particular position must not be made the condition of accepting another person in Christian fellowship. Those who reject the legitimacy of any genital activity should not simply be written off as traitors or 'homophobes'. Equally dubious is the practice of some evangelical groups of 'protecting' people from contact with more gay-affirming Christians. Alongside the passionate commitments that must accompany such controversial matters there is a need for places and contexts in which genuine acceptance is not conditional on particular interpretations or moral positions.

4 *The answer of 2 Corinthians: Vulnerability before reconciliation*. In this extraordinary letter St Paul is trying to restore a relationship with the church in Corinth that has all but broken down. He rests his appeal to these Christians not on a powerful assertion of his authority or his orthodoxy but on a vulnerability that sets himself alongside those from whom he is estranged. It is his sense of weakness and his experience of God's consolation in suffering that provides the basis of his approach. Despite the depth of his concern, and the seriousness of what he believes is at stake, the letter makes clear that the faith he seeks must result from a free response to Jesus Christ not from psychological or social pressure from a dominant authority figure.

Current church strategies

The emergence of a public gay identity in Western society has inevitably created turmoil within the churches. In the

1950s certain church leaders played a significant role in urging the decriminalization of homosexual acts.[12] Viewed from the perspectives of the nineties, the firm stand taken by the highest Church authorities in Britain in favour of the change may seem surprising. The difference does not lie in any so-called contamination by the 'permissive' sixties, a difficult charge to imagine against people such as Archbishop Fisher or Cardinal Griffin. At that time the issue of homosexuality presented itself to the churches in terms of the considerable suffering of certain individuals for whom the churches acknowledged some 'pastoral' responsibility. The churches are now encountering gay people as an assertive element in a changing culture, and have to contemplate the acceptance within their own life of lifestyles and cultural stances which run counter to the recent cultural commitments of the churches themselves. The resulting turmoil and disorientation are not surprising. A number of strategies for coping with these issues have emerged within the churches.

1 *Systematic rejection*

The position taken by recent Vatican documents on homosexuality, despite the careful adoption of a judicious and pastoral tone, resolutely rejects the emergence of a public gay identity. The 1986 *Pastoral Letter* not only reiterates that 'homosexual actions' are '"intrinsically disordered"', and able in no case to be approved of' (#3), but declares the church must distance itself from all those inside or outside its membership who ignore the teaching of the church. Attempts to articulate a positive understanding of committed gay relationships have 'a direct impact on society's understanding of the nature and rights of the family and puts them in jeopardy' (#9). It attributes violent attacks on gay people to the introduction of 'civil legislation . . . to protect behaviour to which no one has any conceivable right' (#10). A subsequent document,[13] made available in 1992, defends the 'legitimate concerns' of landlords 'in screening potential tenants' and asserts the propriety of discrimination against known homosexuals 'for example, in the placement of children for adoption or foster care, in employment of teachers or athletic coaches, and in military recruitment' (#11). One of the more curious features of this document is the statement that such discrimination is legitimate as it will not affect homosexual persons who do not publicize their sexual orientation (#14). Behind this paragraph lie the unwarranted assumptions that those who do not publicize their sexual orientation have more ordered sexual lives, that they are not subject to arbitrary discrimination, and that scrupulous secrecy – even duplicity – about such a significant aspect of one's personality is something that church and society have the right to require as the precondition of social acceptance.

Although such official statements make the questions surrounding homosexuality highly controversial in the Roman Catholic Church, its actual church life is inevitably more complex. The interventions from Rome reflect the extent to which sections of the Roman Catholic Church in the USA have faced up to the reality of the lives of many gay Catholics. The main headline of the *National Catholic Reporter* of 4 November 1994 read, 'He's not disordered, he's my brother', and set out one bishop's personal journey when faced with the shocking discovery that his younger brother was gay. According to the article, the clarifying moment came when the bishop was asked by his eighty-seven-year-old mother, 'Is Dan going to go to hell?'

Whatever the realities within the Roman Catholic Church, the position adopted by the Vatican is one to which many Christian individuals and organizations aspire. In the summer of 1994 a service organized by the International Christian Aids Network in Bangkok had to be moved from an Anglican Church because it insisted on advance assurance that no self-professed homosexual should be allowed to lead, speak at or address the service.[14]

The obvious effect of this strategy will be to sustain a clear distance between the church and gay movements. It is unlikely to find it easy to address the needs of members of the church with gay inclinations. Occasional expressions of 'pastoral' concern will not counter the overall message that it projects. Even introducing a badge, I ADMIT THAT ASPECTS OF MY IMAGINATIVE LIFE ARE INTRINSICALLY DISORDERED, may not guarantee gay people a welcome in such churches! It might, however, have the advantage of inviting non-gay church members to wrestle again with the Bible's teaching that all sexual imagination is disordered and needs an environment of grace for its transformation.

2 Conflict and discretion

In the years from 1990 to 1993 the Methodist Church in Great Britain found itself racked by a major debate on the question of homosexuality informed by the 1990 Report of the Conference Commission on Human Sexuality. Although this debate focused on particular resolutions to be presented to the 1993 Methodist Conference, it involved careful discussion at every level of the Methodist Church and resisted any attempt to protect the church from feeling responsible for the issues. The outcome of the debate was summarized as follows in *A Letter to the Methodist People* by Brian Beck, President of Conference:

> [The Conference] adopted a pastoral rather than a legal approach and decided to affirm both the traditional moral teaching of the Christian church, and the participation and ministry of lesbians and gay men in the church, while leaving decisions about particular cases to be taken by the appropriate committees against this background.

Despite continuing controversy, the outcome of this process is that decisions about the acceptance or discipling of lay people and the presentation of candidates for ordained ministry take place without a coherent statement of policy. The effect of this vacuum is to locate decision-making in the human and church processes that are in immediate contact with the individual or individuals concerned. People are dealt with by those who know them personally on the basis of particular judgments rather than a general denominational stance. This avoids, in the words of the 1990 Report, the danger of 'tak[ing] refuge in what we think are basic principles, before considering the lifestyle, sexuality and practice of actual human lives' (#42). This poses considerable difficulties for those who see a public stand 'against homosexuality' as a benchmark of loyalty to scripture but it has the merit of founding church life on human beings rather than disputed intellectual constructs.

A similar position exists in the Episcopal Church of the United States of America where extensive controversy has continued to leave decision-making to the internal processes of individual dioceses. The subject of the ordination of non-celibate homosexuals was a major one at the 1991 and 1994 General

Conventions. The 1994 General Convention failed to agree an authoritative resolution of the question by simultaneously giving a diminished status to a Pastoral Study presented by the House of Bishops that left some room for the pastoral recognition of gay relationships, and failing to adopt an 'Affirmation' of more conservative teaching. The same General Convention adopted motions affirming that sexual orientation should not be a bar to 'an equal place in the life, worship and governance of this Church' and 'to access to the selection process for ordination'. It also directed the appropriate bodies of the Church to act in support of equal protection under the law for 'homosexual persons' and also in the production of material to help parents understand their children's sexuality. It would appear that, to a greater extent than in British Methodism, opponents of any acceptance of gay 'relationships' see the issue as a battle between 'two religions'.[15] North American 'conservative' correspondents writing for the English Church papers appeared more concerned with the symbolic significance of 'practising' gay clergy than with resolutions addressing the suicide of young people wrestling with homosexual feelings.[16]

The primary integrity of this strategy is that it honours the ferocity of the disagreement within the respective churches while taking seriously the presence of gay people in the church. A scriptural defence could be mounted for a process that allows the mind of the church to be formed by Spirit-led discernment by local leaders trying to make sense of what God is doing in the lives of individuals (cf. Acts 11:1–18; 15:1–35). The manifest presence of the Holy Spirit in the lives of gay Christians rightly has a place in such discussion. The disadvantage of the strategy is that it contributes to a sense of vulnerability among the gay people concerned and to charges of incoherence and lack of scriptural principle. In the case of the Episcopal Church it has fed a strong undercurrent of hostility to the official processes of the Church that at times threatens its coherence and morale.

This approach may also avoid the difficulty of defining criteria to be used in the public processes or tribunals of the church. Attempts to exclude gay or 'practising gay' people from certain roles inevitably run into questions of definition and of the nature of the evidence required. Given the complexity of the emotional and imaginative make-up of individuals it is no easy matter to

define a person as homosexual, nor to articulate criteria by
which an intimate affectionate relationship between two people
is to be identified as gay. The question of sexual or genital
behaviour raises further difficulties. Relevant questions include
what limitations of process arise from a proper respect for
privacy, what actual evidence is required, and what precise
sexual behaviour is forbidden by the church's understanding
of scripture. One Anglican bishop is reported to believe that
sexual discipline needs to focus on the forbidden act of anal
intercourse. This may have the merit of trying to bypass
disputed questions of psychological or emotional identity, but the
prospect of ecclesiastical processes examining sexual behaviour
with such precision must bring delight to the editor of any tabloid
newspaper!

3   Gay self-assertion

It is not clear whether the primary factor behind the emergence
in the church of self-identified gay people and organizations has
been the growing confidence of secular gay movements, the
suffering that gay people have experienced within the church,
or a self-confidence born of an awareness of Jesus's love and
acceptance. Perhaps for a combination of all three reasons, gay
Christians with a variety of theological and ethical views have
begun to organize public expressions of Christian life and to
contribute to debate within the wider church. It is not surprising
that such initiatives have often been strongly resisted or have
found themselves forced to align themselves rather sharply with
particular theological or ethical positions. The horror with which
the Lesbian and Gay Christian Movement has been regarded in
many circles, the unsuccessful attempt in 1987 to remove its
entry from the Church of England Year Book, and the expensive
litigation undertaken in 1988 to remove its office from a London
church, are some indication of the resistance with which
attempts at self-articulation are met. The experience of LGCM
indicates the difficulty that gay people have in gaining access to
the processes of discussion in the wider church. When Tom
Hanks, a respected New Testament scholar and evangelical
missionary in South America, came out as gay he was summarily
ejected from membership of the Tyndale House Ethics Study
Group. In the face of such hostility, the resilience of such gay

Christians is remarkable. Pastor Joseph Doucé remarked to me that he thought that Christian gay organizations proved more long-lasting than their secular counterparts and attributed this to the long-term mindset encouraged by Christian theology and ministerial experience.

There is a common perception amongst British Christians that affirming gay movements are primarily associated with more 'liberal' or 'catholic' liturgical styles and theological positions. However, the reality in the English-speaking world is that there is considerable and increasing vitality among evangelical, reformed and charismatic gay Christian groupings. The Metropolitan Community Church, founded by the Reverend Troy Perry in Los Angeles in 1968, stands within the North American tradition of overt evangelical piety. In the early nineties Tom Hanks became Executive Director of Other Sheep which has an extensive and expanding ministry in the United States and Europe and, particularly, in many centres in South America.[17] Chris Glaser, for ten years Director of the Lazarus Project in the Presbyterian Church in the United States, has written a number of popular books which represent a mature and integrated approach to gay issues from within the Reformed tradition.[18]

Another expression of self-assertion by homosexual men can be seen in the role that some gay men have played in evangelical groups which offer personal support to people struggling with homosexuality, while upholding the position that genital acts between people of the same sex are always contrary to scripture. Perhaps the doyen of such groups in Britain is Martin Hallett, founder and director of the True Freedom Trust, whose candour and humility have played an important role in helping many evangelicals to a better understanding of homosexuality.[19] More will be said about these organizations in the next section but the hostility to which their ethical position gives rise in sections of the gay community should not obscure their importance as points at which gay people are giving their own account of their experience. In some ways their exposed position in the Christianity/homosexuality debate is not dissimilar from that of the *Church's Ministry Among the Jews* or *Jews for Jesus* in the relationship between the Jewish and Christian communities. The wider context makes it difficult for the mediating role played by such groups to be recognized.[20]

4 The therapeutic enclave

The various groups described in the last paragraph are an integral part of a strategy adopted by many evangelical churches. The essence of this approach is to create and support areas of safety in which people can seek to be open about their homosexual feelings without condemnation, while the church itself maintains a firm, even strident, opposition towards the emergence of a public gay identity.

While at least some of these groups are committed to opposing hostility to gay people, their effect is often to strengthen feeling against gay people in the wider evangelical movement that supports them. Campaigning literature of various anti-gay evangelical organizations often uses support for these groups as a way of giving credibility to their opposition to pro-gay reform. If these groups demonstrate that acceptance is an essential element in the growth of gay people towards emotional maturity, why are their sponsors then so hostile to moves that would encourage such acceptance elsewhere? Support for these groups often allows the churches themselves to remain satisfied with bland statements of concern that address none of the difficult issues facing the gay people in their orbit.[21]

These groups sometimes are selective in the presentation of 'expert' scientific evidence and find it difficult to admit, at least publicly, that there may be more than one way of reading the biblical evidence. In addition, they may place excessive trust in particular theories about the origin of homosexuality because they promise healing or behavioural change. The question of whether and what proportion of those who join these groups cease to be sexually attracted to people of the same sex remains in doubt. It seems clear that they can play a significant role where homosexual desire is not a major aspect of a person's make-up and they are able to offer genuine help where loneliness is leading to an addiction to anonymous sexual activity. The groups provide safe space for those whose sense of Christian identity is profoundly threatened by their awareness of homosexual feelings. However, firm evidence for a profound change in the pattern of people's erotic imagination is still lacking; inevitably part of the difficulty lies in the interpretive scheme that people bring to various claims or statistics.

5 The 'Via media' in the Church of England

A number of the strategies already mentioned are to be found
operating at different points in the Church of England. They
take their place within a framework of church law which has
yet to test the standing of committed gay relationships that
would not of themselves render the individuals involved liable to
prosecution under the criminal law.[22] More broadly the 'mind of
the Church' at the present time has been expressed in the 1987
General Synod motion 'that homosexual genital acts fall short
of this ideal [sexual intercourse within a permanent married
relationship], and are to be met by a call to repentance and
the exercise of compassion', and in the 1991 statement by the
House of Bishops *Issues in Human Sexuality*. This latter report
aims to promote an educational process within the church (1:9)
and sets its face against any 'general inquisition into the conduct
of the clergy' (5:18). Its position with respect to non-ordained
gay people who 'are conscientiously convinced that this way of
abstinence is not for them, and that they have more hope of
growing in love for God and neighbour with the help of a loving
and faithful homophile partnership' is:

> While unable, therefore, to commend the way of life just
> described as in itself as faithful a reflection of God's purposes
> in creation as the heterophile, we do not reject those who
> sincerely believe it is God's call to them. We stand alongside
> them in the fellowship of the Church, all alike dependent upon
> the undeserved grace of God. All those who seek to live their
> lives in Christ owe one another friendship and understanding.
> It is therefore important that in every congregation such
> homophiles should find fellow-Christians who will sensitively
> and naturally provide this for them. Indeed, if this is not done
> any professions on the part of the Church that it is committed
> to openness and learning about the homophile situation can be
> no more than empty words (5:6).

With respect to gay clergy the report takes a different position;
it deplores any discrimination against clergy on the ground
of marital status or sexual orientation (5:19) and sets its
face against clergy 'entering into sexually active homophile
relationships' (5:17). The reasons given for this judgment are

twofold: the importance of not obscuring the Church's allegiance to the 'God-given ideal' of marriage or celibacy (5:13), and the danger that the ministry of such clergy will not be acceptable to a significant number of people (5:14).

It is perhaps not surprising that the position that this report takes on both clergy and laity has been subject to serious criticism. In both cases the reasons given in the report need to be supplemented by aspects of the church's historic relations with the English nation. In the case of the laity, two main lines of thinking underlie the report's position of tolerance. The first is a realization that it is difficult to move directly from the pattern of homosexuality criticized in scripture to the loving and faithful relationships found among believing Christians today (2:23, 2:29). The second is a theologically grounded respect for an individual's 'free conscientious judgment' (5:6). Two long-standing features of historic Anglicanism probably also contribute to this position. The first is a tradition of legal pragmatism in the English Church by which the Church sees its ministry as being to the whole English people and therefore instinctively shrinks from a position of permanent conflict with one part of the population.[23] The second is a certain hostility of the English laity, greatly re-enforced at and after the Reformation, to the idea of their moral behaviour being subject to the jurisdiction of ecclesiastical courts.[24] That the position taken in 5:6 is not yet widely accepted, even among bishops, was demonstrated as early as 1992 when the Archbishop of Canterbury intervened to oppose the publication of prayers for lesbian and gay people.

Many people have criticized the implication of a 'double standard' in the different requirements the report makes of the clergy. However, this distinction can be defended from scripture (cf. 'husband of one wife', 1 Timothy 3:2; Titus 1:6). It is also of a piece with the classic strategy of the Western church articulated under Pope Gregory VII (1073–1085) which sought to preserve the faithfulness of a church deeply immersed in society by requiring a special consecration of the clergy.[25] An example of the impact of this strategy is the common acceptance that it is appropriate for lay people, but not clergy, to take up arms in war.

The policy may be defensible; it is less clear that it is

workable. An obvious difficulty is enforcement. The problem here includes the usual difficulties of definition and evidence. In the case of incumbents with the freehold it would also involve extended public trials in which the scandalous and immoral nature of such relationships would have to be established. More deeply, the policy fails to come to terms with the fact that a significant minority of the clergy of the Church of England are gay. They include many of the church's finest clergy, and it is precisely their homosexuality that has drawn them to Christ and gives them the insight and sensitivity that the Church of England values in their ministry. Often they are willing to undertake tasks from which other clergy shrink. Given the evidence that the Church of England now has of the stress that its policy causes to such clergy, it is hard to see how it can continue to justify not allowing them to address their own spiritual, emotional and relational needs in ways that seem appropriate to them. The policy does not sit easily with the hope that the clergy will minister out of a personal experience of the grace of Christ and model mature and responsible personal relationships.

Another aspect of the historic relationship of the Church of England with the English people emerges in the recent Health Education Authority's findings that most parents do not want the state or the clergy teaching sexual morality to their children.[26] One of the difficulties that the Church of England faces in gaining the trust of ordinary people and drawing them into its life is a long history of intimate involvement with the enforcement of laws governing sexual behaviour. There have been various strands to this history. In the early medieval period, while kings were still establishing the rudiments of national government, the clergy had responsibility for various areas of personal life including wills, marriage law and discipline in sexual matters.[27] Reformed and Puritan Christianity claimed the right to 'instruct the magistrate' and to discipline the personal lives of the populace.[28] In the nineteenth century the articulate middle classes used religious grounds to justify their attempt to regulate the social and sexual lives of the mass of the English people.[29] The resonance of this long history has a serious inhibiting effect on effective evangelism today. While some imagine that taking a 'firm moral stand' strengthens the Church's hand in evangelism, the reality is that while the majority of English people see the

Church of England as part of a national, moral police force they will not easily trust it with their intimate lives or find it a natural vehicle for personal faith in Christ.

Next steps

Conflict between the churches and gay people is not going to disappear in a day. For both groups profound questions of contested identity and the sources of joy and intimacy are at stake.

While it is important for the church's theological integrity that scriptural and theological questions are not ignored, there are two ways in which it can make progress in coming to terms with this new feature of the cultural and social landscape. The first lies in personal encounter and dialogue – getting to know the gay people within and outside its life, and becoming involved with gay groups within the community. The second way is to take steps to defend the humanity of gay people, to acknowledge that they are part of the community, to examine and act on questions of social justice, to work with gay people in addressing the results of stress, isolation and misrepresentation. One resolution of the 1993 Methodist Conference reads:

> Conference calls on Methodist people to begin a pilgrimage of faith to combat repression and discrimination, to work for justice and human rights and to give dignity and worth to people whatever their sexuality.

In 1992 the Tenth Assembly of the Conference of European Churches adopted a careful and detailed statement on racism and discrimination which explicitly includes 'sexual orientation'.[30] Responding to such exhortations will lead many churches into unfamiliar territory and give them some sense of how gay people experience society. It ought to set discussions about the sexual behaviour and relationships of gay people in a less confrontational context.

For gay people themselves the churches are likely to remain places of danger. Negotiating life within the church will remain difficult for gay people who find their love drawn out by the mysterious friendship of Jesus Christ. They ignore at their peril questions of spiritual authenticity, personal survival, security of employment, and the dangers of physical and emotional violence. They will need safe places in which to learn to distinguish the voice of Christ from the alien cultural commitments of the rest of the church. They are likely to experience the church of Christ as a garden infested with unseen dangers, or as a poisoned well. They will encounter simultaneously friendship and betrayal, the promise of intimacy and the threat of ostracism. The water of life will often come mixed with a much-prized local vintage which gives them little joy or nourishment but turns their friends in Christ against them. They may find themselves, like Jesus, suffering 'outside the gate' (Hebrews 13:12–13).

Chapter 12

The Uncharted Journey

There is no condemnation for those who are in
Christ Jesus.

St Paul, Romans 8:1

Sexual acts are acts of the imagination as well as acts
of the body. They function as symbolic discourse.

Bruce R. Smith[1]

In 1982 John Boswell gave the Fifth Michael Harding Memorial
Address to what was then the Gay Christian Movement;[2] its
contents are best indicated by the subtitle, 'Archetypes of Gay
Love in Christian History'. The lecture is attractive because
of the insight that it gives into John Boswell as a person and
a Christian; it is important because of the clarity with which
it addresses the question of homosexual ethics. This is how he
sets out the question:

> Everybody I think knows, or assumes, or guesses that hetero-
> sexual people fall short of their ethical standards . . . They don't
> understand what ethics gay people might even fall short of. Do
> gay people plan to be regulated by the same moral norms that
> regulate straight people? Many Christians I know who are very
> concerned about the issue and want to be very liberal-minded
> say, 'What are you proposing as a change in Catholic doctrine?
> Should gay people be allowed to do anything? Are they to be
> able to go to the baths, the bars and meet people on the street,
> and just have all the sex they want, while we are bound to
> be permanently faithful to a single person? It hardly seems
> fair, does it? . . .

Part of the ambivalence of the intellectual establishment in the United States is that they can't tell, when they read a book like Edmund White's *States of Desire*, whether the life of casual promiscuity it depicts represents a homosexual *ideal* or a failure of an ideal. Are they reading what gay people should do, what they do, or both, or neither? So they don't know how to fit it into their usual critical apparatus. They don't understand what would be a departure from homosexual ethics because they don't know what homosexual ethics would be. And neither do we.

Even gay Christians do not know what sexual ethics are for gay Christians. Or where we should start looking for them: or what they would be based on.

The way that John Boswell looks at this question, together with his analysis of some possible models from the traditional life of the church, remains, for all its brevity, one of the finest discussions of the topic. However, before a person can think about an ethical framework for their life, they have to discover who they are and where they belong. This first step is less analytical and more formative. It can be seen as finding a working 'script' for one's life – an understood pattern that gives subjective shape and meaning to a person's experience, expectations and relationships.[3] Identifying a script depends not only on what scripts seem to be available but also on aspects of one's make-up and circumstances that make one range of scripts more relevant than another. The important tasks of making ethical judgments, identifying sources of wisdom, and gaining access to the spiritual energy to live well, all have to take note of the earlier process of finding a script. They also need to take account of how finding a script has affected a person's view of themselves and their relationship to God and society.

Finding a script

Identifying a working script for one's life is a very different experience for straight and gay people.

1 The well-stocked shopping mall: the straight experience
Where a man and woman are attracted to each other and contemplate living together or marrying they will find that society

holds out to them a number of possible 'scripts' within which to explore their relationship. The tensions that notoriously surround the preparations for a wedding reflect this choice between available scripts as well as the difficulties the couple themselves may face in adapting whatever script they adopt to something that they can personally live with. The scripts on offer are not simply different views of the internal dynamics of a heterosexual relationship – of how 'love' works. They include different arrangements for income, employment and housing, different cultural perceptions of the appropriate emotional responses for men and women, and various possibilities for distributing domestic tasks and management. Equally, if less obviously, they include assumptions about how they will relate to other groupings: What is 'our' relationship to the cricket club or 'the in-laws'? Do we go to church as a couple or as two individuals? Is it still all right for Ken and Kevin to go out for a drink on Thursday nights?

It is interesting to ask where the scripts come from and how they are mediated to the couple. Family and class patterns are clearly important. Chat shows, popular magazines and well-known story lines all have an influence. Employment and accommodation possibilities, and for some the state benefit system, have a powerful effect and will differ for different people. In some cases the constraints of housing finance will be particularly important, for others it is the rules and procedures governing unemployment and housing benefit. For poorer people in Britain the rules governing access to public housing penalize those who do not cohabit or marry; the intrusiveness and expense of bureaucracy discourage the official registering of relationships, and the state's desire to limit social security payments means that any partnership that is more than fleeting is liable to be treated as equivalent to marriage.[4]

The churches continue to play a real, if contested, part in shaping the scripts on offer, both through their official teaching and through sponsoring symbolic celebrations of the married state. They have much less influence today than in the period when they had a monopoly on marriage law and were able to enforce its implications for personal wealth. In recent times church and state have seen state registration as an essential element in marriage. The widespread practice of cohabitation is leading some to rediscover other 'scripts' in the Christian tradition from before the time when Lord Hardwicke's 1753 Marriage Act required state registration.[5] While Christians in Britain still struggle to come to terms with 'irregular' forms of marriage which the church has accepted in medieval times and in other cultures, they are developing a greater confidence in handling the second marriages implied in the Western practice of 'serial polygamy'.

The availability of respected 'off-the-peg' scripts deeply conditions the experience and self-understanding of straight people. Although people may make serious misjudgments or may struggle to make do with a particular script, the script they choose is likely to bring with it a secure and positive social identity as well as social affirmation. It is also likely to come with ready-made ethical ground rules. Many straight scripts have a positive, if ambiguous, relationship with strong biblical images. In Western society the social affirmation of most straight scripts also implies a strong endorsement of the 'love' that is seen as having created the relationship in question.

An important tool in trying to understand the nature of this 'love' is provided in St Augustine's perception of the link between desire, the images that evoke and shape desire, and the social order created by desire. Popular accounts of human love tend to speak as if the only image to which a normal man or woman responds is that of the other sex. The reality, of course, is that a person's inner vision is shaped by the response that they make to both male and female images. This is part of the wisdom of older understandings that saw society as held together by bonds of gendered affection. A person's erotic imagination – meaning here not genital excitement but motivating desire – includes both male and female images. Despite the myth of heterosexual romantic love, people inevitably find themselves negotiating two gendered worlds – each evoked and ordered, on the Augustinian insight, by images of the gender in question. The invisibility of culturally affirmed images of male same sex affection in modern society, and their replacement by an assertive, competitive and isolated masculinity, naturally have an impact on the imaginative life of individuals as well as the political ordering of the community.

The formative images that people encounter and the way

they respond to them are an important part of what we call personality. 'Sin', that potent biblical word for human rebellion, alienation and disorder, may be present either in the images offered by society or in the way in which the person responds to these images. An individual may respond to the images that form society with admiration and devotion, or with pride, fear or envy. Jean Vanier, in his profound book *Man and Woman He Made Them*, discusses the way in which the 'heart' of the infant – its capacity to give and receive love – is drawn out, disciplined or crushed in the early encounters of its life.[6] (He opposes the common ideas that the infant is essentially selfish and only learns the ability to give freely and lovingly, or that the process of separation from its parents is necessarily harmful – it may facilitate growth or precipitate anguish and withdrawal.) It is part of the uniqueness of the individual that similar experiences shape their emotional and imaginative life differently. Obviously the sense of self and inner vision that emerges in early years affects the way people respond to the range of available social roles. Sin cannot be isolated to one part of the process of forming a person's life or to one outcome. While the social order tends to identify some recognized scripts as good and others as bad, the biblical vision of sin woven into the corporate and individual experience of humanity recognizes ambiguity and dignity in the vision that God places in each human being through these human processes.

2   *The ugly duckling: the gay experience*

Finding a script for a straight person is a process guided by the community; it probably leads to an outcome that confers a public 'righteousness'. For a gay person none of this applies. The loneliest journey made by most gay people is the one in which they perceive that they are different, that they are unable to relate to the scripts on offer in respectable Western society, and that the patterning of their imagination and affective life is viewed with horror and fear. The experience is beautifully evoked in Hans Christian Andersen's fairy story 'The Ugly Duckling' where one of a family of ducklings is perpetually awkward and ostracized. In the folk tale, when the ugly duckling grows up to be a swan, its beauty is recognized, it encounters others swans, and it flies away to a life of happiness. The reality

for many gay people is very different – in terms of the story
they are shot, battered, or put through rigorous attempts to
reprogramme their behaviour, long before they meet the world
of swans.

There is a common perception that gay men are only
interested in sex – and in sex without rules or relationships.
Probably the group for which this is nearest to being true
is deeply closeted men, often married, whose only outlet
for their responsiveness to the masculine is anonymous sex
that does not endanger their public gender identity. What this
public myth really demonstrates is the absence in the culture
of positive scripts of male same sex intimacy so that patterns of
affection characteristic of gay men are neither recognized nor
affirmed. It seems broadly true that the men who emerge as gay
in modern culture are characterized by a gentle sensitivity which
distinguishes them from the normal masculinity of the culture,
and that they have an imaginative responsiveness to the male
– they are attracted to men. This attraction is located in the
imagination before it finds any outworking in emotion, in the
quest for intimacy, or in the categories of activity, behaviour
and relationship which we call sexual. Public myths that raging
promiscuity is characteristic of gay men are based primarily on
the fact that sexual acts are seen as scandalous, while other
aspects of the lives and affections of gay people are invisible or
unrecognized.

Given the absence of accessible public scripts to which they
can easily relate, men with this emotional or imaginative
make-up tend to respond in a number of ways. Some simply
adopt one of the scripts on offer and do their best, often
with considerable violence to their inner selves, to play a role
acceptable in the culture. Others accept the message projected
by the culture about the disordered nature of their imagination
and see themselves as outcasts whose existence threatens the
social, or even the cosmic, order.

A more common response is to take one of the scripts off
the shelf, either of the accepted forms of masculinity or of a
pattern of relationships, and adapt it. This has many different
outworkings. It can be seen in lesbian and gay couples who
carefully conform to gender stereotypes borrowed from the
surrounding culture. It is also present in the various forms of

behaviour which point to a divided sense of personal identity. Other examples occur where gay male sexual behaviour mimics the divorce of sex from intimacy common in straight men, or where people see covenanted gay partnership as a form of marriage.

A fourth response occurs when people allow the particular patterning of their imagination to lead them to aspects and projects in the culture where their sensitivity and sense of beauty can find a creative outlet. Obvious examples are the way in which gay people are drawn to the arts and to the public liturgy of the church. Often their participation in such areas depends not only on an innate responsiveness to beauty but is also honed by a sensitivity to pain and an astuteness about the dynamics and undercurrents of society which reflect their own experience as marginal figures.

The fifth response is to search for others whose experience in society is similar to their own. Many gay people's accounts of their own lives recall the moment when they realized from a passing reference in a conversation or film, or from a chance encounter, that they were not alone. Such moments are the raw material out of which gay subcultures of various sorts grow. Although acting on such a discovery is often difficult and even messy, it is an essential step in the process by which people discover the possibility of different accounts of their identity and alternative scripts by which to live.

In his lecture, John Boswell records that as a child in Ankara, Turkey, 'he took it as a matter of course that some gentlemen would be interested in others' and his later surprise when his family went back to the United States at encountering 'an overwhelming and powerful negative reaction to the same sort of feelings'. This strong hostility in the West to same sex affection, to any erotic response to the masculine, and to any suggestion of a departure from normal aggressive masculinity, strongly colours the way in which most gay men see themselves. It lends an important tone to each of the five responses set out above – with the possible exception of the move into art and liturgy. The effect of this hostility is to sow deep within the self-understanding of many gay men a powerful negative emotional pattern which oscillates between self-doubt and self-hate. The hostility that has this result is not itself a simple phenomenon and the effects that it has in individuals are correspondingly complex. Part of the hostility is a strong gut horror at the unnatural and the unmasculine. Another element is family disappointment at the lack of children, with all the diffuse fear, frustration, and sense of pointlessness to which this can give rise.

This pervasive hostility not only affects the self-image of gay people, it influences other aspects of their lives. It can distort their imaginative life by introducing self-doubt, fear or envy into their relations with either men or women. It makes responding to danger a higher priority than articulating rules of sexual behaviour or relationship. It introduces a reactive and fragmentary element to any gay identity that emerges as gay people search for some sort of self-understanding and self-expression. Gay cultures have many of the characteristics of a resistance movement. When space and visibility are needed they must be able to assert themselves in a way that is recognizable and effective but disarming. However, the threat of danger and the vulnerability of individuals also require that the identity can be packed up and made to disappear so that ordinary life can continue unmolested. There are intriguing parallels with the experience of King David and his followers during the period when he was a vulnerable outlaw. For example, it is possible to read the curious incident of David's feigned madness in the court of Achish, King of Gath (1 Samuel 21:10–15), as either the brilliant ruse of a skilled campaigner or as simple humiliation resulting from craven but understandable fear. Many of the more problematic issues of an assertive gay identity bear some relation to the moral dilemmas faced by resistance groups.

The tally of the heroes in 2 Samuel 23:8ff. could provide a model for a similar roll-call among the gay movements. (Would Peter Tatchell be among the thirty or the three?!) What this odd comparison may illustrate is that the contested and fragmentary character of a public gay identity will significantly shape the way gay people articulate ethical issues that affect their own behaviour. It is not simply that ethical priorities and realities change in contested situations, although they do. It is also that the articulation of ethical issues and options is likely to be conducted in a way that does not expose gay people to the lurking hostility and condemnation which provide the normal background to their lives. John Boswell may be overstating his case when he claimed that gay people do not know what homosexual ethics are; it is perhaps more true that discussion of ethical issues is cast in such a way as to avoid overt condemnation or providing ammunition against particular individuals or sections of the gay community.

The way of grace

Given the highly contested nature of gay identity and the active disagreement in society on the morality of same sex sexual acts, it is perhaps surprising that there is significant agreement that gay people need to begin any thinking about their way of life by gaining a sense of their inherent value as human beings and by entering into relationships based on unconditional acceptance. This emphasis is common to the evangelical Christian groups that seek to provide safe space and healing for gay people, to campaigning groups which seek to assert a positive image for gay people in society, and to those various groups modelled on Alcoholics Anonymous which seek to help gay people and others work through compulsive addiction to drink, drugs or sex.[7] Although the way in which this is articulated varies considerably with different groups, the agreement on what a Christian would call the principle of grace is as impressive as it is generally unrecognized. Despite the different public stances taken by these groups their common acceptance of this principle is worked out in strikingly similar 'pastoral' strategies, namely the drawing of the individual into a supportive group in which their self-hate and emotional immaturity can be addressed, in which they can gain a sense of power and responsibility in addressing the difficult issues of their own lives, and in which they can make contact with the restoring goodness that God has hidden in his world.

Very near the heart of the Christian faith is the profound truth that loving acceptance has hidden within it a power to regenerate human beings and to enable them to establish healthy, self-controlled and emotionally mature relationships with others. This truth was embodied in Jesus's relationship with individuals and in the costly identification with human alienation that reached its mysterious resolution in his death. Its exposition is a central feature of St Paul's writing and, as discussed in Chapter 4:8, provides the context for the apostle's injunctions about sexual behaviour. The method of grace addresses three aspects of the inner life of gay people: the low self-image which they often absorb from the hostility and misunderstanding of society; the discovery of positive human relationships within which a person can gain a sense of perspective on their lives; the need that all human beings have to learn the patience, vulnerability and self-control that are the keys to maturity and intimacy.

It is not too surprising that there is little recognition of this common ground. Gay movements are too aware of the links between evangelical therapeutic groups and public opposition to gay people from the mass of evangelical Christians easily to disentangle the two. For their part some Christians may be nervous about so generalizing the principle of grace as to obscure the precious truth that grace has taken flesh in Jesus Christ. A more refined difficulty arises with the question of when the reality of sin in a fallen world makes the method of grace inappropriate. Probably all would agree that there are some sorts of human behaviour too destructive or heinously wicked for them to be tolerated without drastic action. The decriminalization of sexual activity between men over the age of eighteen, and the fact that few modern people now want to turn openly gay friends or relatives over to the criminal law, are signs that modern society does not see modern expressions of homosexuality in this light.

Another factor which obscures the common ground between these different groups is that for different reasons both Western Christianity and the modern gay movements give a very high symbolic significance to sexually designated genital activity. Later Christian tradition, for reasons set out in Chapter 3, not only developed a profound suspicion of sexual desire but also tended to treat sexual behaviour as the touchstone of authentic Christian discipleship. In the case of modern gay movements genital behaviour gains its primary symbolic significance not because it is the essence of the gay imagination but because Western hostility to any genital contact between men has made it the visible marker of a contested identity.

The current evangelical Christian strategy of public condemnation complemented by the sponsoring of therapeutic enclaves is an attempt to hold some middle ground. It reflects a gut feeling that the homosexuality is either too serious or too intractable for the scriptural principle of grace to be allowed to operate without drastic curtailment. This position is not without contradictions and may turn out to be inherently unstable. One sign of such instability is the common practice in evangelical presentations on homosexuality of deploring 'homophobia' and the ill-treatment of gay people. A sustained refusal to operate the method of grace must be driven by outrage sufficiently passionate to defend the severe criminal sanctions enacted against gay people in earlier times. Another possible indication that this strategy may be unstable can be seen in the consistency with which evangelical therapeutic groups criticize the irrational hostility and violence to which gay people are exposed, while themselves being unwilling to make common cause with gay people who differ from them on the morality of certain genital acts. There is an unsettling ambiguity in this stance, particularly as it is allied with a public approach to gay people that would be profoundly disturbed by any action that addresses the misrepresentation and injustice that gay people experience.

Of itself the way of grace throws little light either on the particularities of possible gay scripts or on ethical guidelines that might inform the way gay people live. However, at a deeper level, it illuminates many aspects of gay experience.

One example is the way that it accepts and harnesses anger. Anger is one of the least acceptable expressions of the modern gay identity. There is abundant evidence in scripture that anger is one of the most essential and creative of human emotions – it is human beings making contact with their value in creation and reaching out to God to lay claim to the faithfulness from him which grace leads them to believe is their due. Anger is a major element in many strands of scripture, not least in the laments of the psalms and in the insights and passion of the prophets. The fact that passionate anger finds such extensive expression in scripture is not a denial of faith; it arises precisely because God's unconditional commitment to his people creates an environment in which anger can be freely expressed. The articulation of anger in scripture may be dangerous but it is not barren. Occurring within the context of God's unconditional love for his people and his covenanted relationship with the creation, anger deepens our vision of justice and our perseverance in the face of evil. More importantly, anger brings us into contact with God, from whom we may be profoundly alienated. It enables us to meet and receive blessing from a God who in Jesus has identified with our alienation, our rebellion and with our thirst for life. One of the finest expressions of gay anger is this poem by A.E. Housman.

> The laws of God, the laws of man,
> He may keep that will and can;
> Not I: let God and man decree
> Laws for themselves and not for me;
> And if my ways are not as theirs
> Let them mind their own affairs.
> Their deeds I judge and much condemn,
> Yet when did I make laws for them?
> Please yourselves, say I, and they
> Need only look the other way.
> But no, they will not; they must still
> Wrest their neighbour to their will,
> And make me dance as they desire
> With jail and gallows and hell-fire.
> And how am I to face the odds
> Of man's bedevilment and God's?
> I, a stranger and afraid
> In a world I never made.
> They will be master, right or wrong;
> Though both are foolish, both are strong.
> And since, my soul, we cannot fly
> To Saturn or to Mercury,
> Keep we must, if keep we can,
> These foreign laws of God and man.

If there is a failure of faith in this poem it does not lie in the anger that drives it but in the pathetic and unresolved acquiescence of the last four lines.

For gay people, calls to repentance are often presented as calls to abandon a gay way of life or association with other gay people. If such calls make the language of penitence difficult for gay people they also raise the question of what repentance and holiness should mean for them. Again the way of grace is the key to these life-transforming realities. Repentance is one of the great New Testament words. New Testament repentance is not about moral self-improvement nor about adopting a more socially acceptable identity; it is about turning from the emptiness of idolatry to draw life from the reality and grace of God (cf. 1 Thessalonians 1:9–10). The heart of repentance for gay people lies not in contriving closer conformity with the accepted patterns of society, nor about making oneself more acceptable to God, but in refusing to believe the condemnation of one's deepest intuitions and therefore in opening one's heart and love to the God who offers us friendship in Jesus Christ. In the same way, holiness is not a set of stick-on moral qualities, it is the reordering of one's life that takes place through contact with the living God. None of this is to deny that turning to God will involve the drastic reordering of one's life. But it is to assert that mere conformity to social pressure creates barriers between us and God (cf. John 5:44). Holiness and repentance are about discovering the surprising acceptance and friendship of a generous and creating God.

Two other biblical terms which the idea of grace can open up are gentleness and wisdom. It has been part of the argument of this book that the modern gay identity is closely linked with an intuitive, affectionate and gentle masculinity to which modern Western culture is ideologically hostile. In scripture this quality of gentleness is not the same as weakness but rather a form of tender strength that arises as people experience love and accept their responsibility for others. If this quality of male gentleness is characteristic of gay men, it is also threatened by the hostility that they encounter and the self-hate which this easily generates. Within society at large the possibility of a male gentleness is undercut by the self-justifying competitiveness which the prevailing ideals impose on straight men. In both cases hope lies with the way of grace that found its fullest expression in the gentle strength of Jesus and his practice of friendship.

The New Testament letter of James contrasts two kinds of wisdom (James 3:13–18). One is characterized by an envious and self-regarding ambition and is described by the writer as 'earthly, unspiritual and devilish'. The other he describes as the 'wisdom from above' that is 'first pure, then peaceable, gentle, open to reason, full of mercy and good fruits, without uncertainty or insincerity'. There appears to be an echo here of the feminine attribute of God described in Proverbs 8 that is the source of order and delight in God's creation. It does not seem too far-fetched to see in these passages a contrast between the harsh acquisitive ideals of modern, materialistic society and the gentle order that is created when people turn to the caress of the divine wisdom. It is as true of gay men as of any other group that they may give their soul either to the grasping ambition of Mammon or to the tender and regenerating generosity of God. However, it may also be the case that the inward intuition that makes them gay has its origin in an instinctive rejection of the violent acquisitiveness of a society dedicated to Mammon.

Although the way of grace has little to say about the actual scripts or conceptual models that may be appropriate for gay men, there is one way in which the 'shape' of grace in the New Testament throws light on some of the choices that gay people face. As discussed in Chapter 4, a characteristic of the way grace works in the New Testament is that it resists the attempt of 'righteous' cultures to impose an identity on those on the margins of their life. Not only did Jesus find his friends beyond the pale of religious and law-abiding society, but the main conflicts of the post-resurrection church arose precisely from the controversial assertion that Gentiles did not have to conform their Christian discipleship to the predetermined patterns of Jewish culture and identity. Gay people cannot simply demand that God accept in its entirety a way of life formed in a situation of alienation, violence and rejection. Equally, their search for the way of godliness must not treat as normative the conventions, identities and social scripts pressed upon them by those in voices of modern society who claim to be the voice of 'righteousness'.

Sources of wisdom

People search for wisdom in ways appropriate to their temperament, context and education. One gay friend will never read this book, or probably any one of the books that has contributed to its making; his attempts to understand his life and to find goodness and happiness are naturally directed to people and communities, and depend on other styles of communication. Although people seek their access to wisdom in different ways, the argument of this book suggests certain directions to which gay people should turn in their search for models and guidelines for living. In giving a map of such sources of wisdom, it is natural for me to illustrate it with books I think important and accessible. The personal, even idiosyncratic, nature of the selection is not intended to impose on others or to dictate a style of communication but merely to stimulate a line of reflection. Many gay men have used various popular songs as a way of reflecting on their lives and seem to have found it an effective source of the insight that I have struggled to obtain by more laborious means!

1. *God and the Bible*. Much of this book has been devoted to exploring the contention that the scriptures should not be seen as a weapon against gay people but as a source of wisdom from a gracious and generous God who is actively seeking the friendship of gay people. At its centre is the free and beautiful figure of Jesus of Nazareth, identifying himself with human beings in the dignity and misery of their lives, forging in his own life of love and suffering a new way of living that is accessible to all (and particularly the outsider), and creating by his peculiar gift of friendship a community of acceptance and hope.

2. *The experience of gay people*. Ingrained cultural hostility to gay people and the contested character of a public gay identity mean that gay people need to be cautious about accepting any account of their experience or advice on how they should behave which originate from outside their own ranks. This is not to imply that the accepted wisdom of popular gay culture is either uniform or always correct; it suffers ferment and fashion as any other area of human life. It means that gay people, whatever their view of the moral status of genital sex, need to be open to those who have faced the challenges of survival, who have studied the dangers that gay people face in society, who have struggled to find their own voice in articulating what it is to be gay, and who have addressed the life issues that gay people experience.

Many people encounter these issues piecemeal in the popular gay press. For those more at home with books, and particularly for those who presume to pastor and advise gay people, there are three areas in which they need to take steps to be well-informed. The first is the state of the law as it affects gay people and the way it can impact on their lives. A useful British source is Caroline Gooding's *Trouble with the Law*.[8] But information on this subject can quickly go out of date.

The second is the sort of practical advice that has its origin in the attempt by gay people to live openly and happily in society. In this area there are no shortage of titles, often covering very similar ground. A popular British author is Terry Sanderson, author of *How to be a Happy Homosexual*, *Making Gay Relationships Work* and other titles.[9] Also useful is Malcolm Macourt's *How Can We Help You?* which is written as a guide to running a gay helpline, and therefore deals concisely with many issues as they arise for gay people.[10] To read one of these books should not be to give their advice infallible status. However, it is a way of gaining access to the experience and reflection of gay people about life in modern society.

The issues that face young gay people and their parents are illuminating and also need attention. A useful book is Terry Sanderson's *A Stranger in the Family: . . . how to cope if your child is gay*.[11] While many readers will disagree with some of the positions adopted in this book, it deals sensitively with the feelings of shock that parents may experience, assumes almost no prior knowledge in the reader, and engages judiciously with many of the concerns and fears that parents may have. It has a long and careful section on 'the religious dilemma confronted' which differs at many points from the positions explored in this book, but still gives people some access to different Christian viewpoints.

3. *Pre-modern Christian thinking on desire and friendship.*
Christians before the sixteenth century did not associate human desire primarily with the pursuit of heterosexual relationships and marital affection, and did not identify the home and the family as the prime context for friendship, intimacy and art. This provides an important counterbalance to the family-centred character of much modern Christianity. This rich tradition, often

associated with early and medieval monasticism, has much to give to the modern imagination as well as providing a different vision of society and neglected models of human relating. Some people's access to this world will be through music and architecture. My own recommended sources would be the writings of St Augustine of Hippo and St Aelred of Rievaulx – for the former starting with his *Confessions*, for the latter with his *On Spiritual Friendship*. These are not difficult to read, although the modern reader will initially find much that is alien and some that is wrong. A reader of Aelred moves with some sense of shock between the sweetness and depth of his feelings for his beloved Simon and his absolute assurance that God predestines many infants to eternal destruction.[12] But such a reader will return to both the Bible and the modern world with fresh eyes.

4. *Modern gay people finding hope in Jesus Christ.* In these cases the wisdom is to be found from listening in to what emerges as gay people engage with and respond to Jesus. Probably the best known of such figures in English circles is Jim Cotter. Some books have about them a sense of raw and moving encounter. One such is Thomas O'Neil's *Sex with God*, a cycle of lyric poems that move between sweetness, anger and joy. Another is Oscar Wilde's extraordinary *De Profundis*, written from prison as he reflected on prison itself, on art, on his own plight, on his anger at Lord Alfred Douglas – all in the light of the joy he found each day in reading the Gospels in Greek. Like St Paul's second letter to Corinth, the vulnerability and movement of the book make it as puzzling as it is powerful. Writers on Wilde disagree on whether it represents real faith, skilful irony or abject collapse. Nothing can hide the depth of Wilde's appreciation of Jesus; if Wilde's style keeps him from being captured by the reader that is simply of a piece with his understanding of art.

The second type of writing reflects the spirituality, pastoral concern and public reflections of gay people who have integrated their acceptance of their homosexuality with the theological tradition from which they write. One such is *On Being Gay*, a collection of articles by Brian McNaught, a Roman Catholic.[13] Its easy style and wide scope provide insight into a range of issues that have emerged in the dialogue between gay people and American secular and religious culture. In *Come Home!*

Chris Glaser writes with a similar integrated confidence but from within the American Reformed tradition. His beautiful bi-monthly cycle of meditative prayers, *Coming Out to God*, must lift the anger, introversion and despair of many. *The Word is Out* provides a year's worth of reflection on Bible passages from a gay perspective.

The question of sex

If the way of grace reveals surprising common ground between different interpretations of gay experience, and if exploring different sources of wisdom opens up what it is to live and pray as a gay person, the question of sexual behaviour – particularly male genital sex – immediately introduces very sharp divisions. Disagreement not only exists between those who rule out any genital sex and those who do not. It is also reflected in the careful discussion in many gay 'manuals' of whether 'open' relationships are possible, and of the pros and cons of anonymous or recreational sex.

Although the fact of radical disagreement is obvious enough, the interpretation of what is going on in such discussions is less so. Two factors have already been noted in this chapter: the different influences that make sexual behaviour symbolically important for the Christian tradition and for the assertion of a public gay identity; the casting of ethical discussion within gay sub-cultures in such a way that disagreement does not expose other gay people to danger from a hostile environment. A third element is closely related to what I have called the way of grace: ethical discussion tends to be cast in a way that affirms rather than condemns individuals out of a conviction that acceptance is the precondition for responsible and mature behaviour.

Another curious dynamic in such discussions is the question of how sexual acts relate to intimate or domestic relationships. Those who object to all sexual activity between people of the same sex find that the effect of their opposition is to make individuals opt for anonymous sex rather than stable public relationships. For the individuals concerned, anonymous sex offers less chance of being labelled as gay. It also can preserve a person's conscience because it does not involve an ongoing commitment to sin; for similar reasons women in some Roman Catholic countries prefer an occasional abortion to the continuing sin of contraception. Equally, those upholding this absolute position find that it focuses public attention on the least 'promiscuous' gay people: a position that asserts the sinfulness of certain *acts* has the effect of fuelling hostility against a set of *persons* in whose lives sexual activity may have a low, even non-existent, place.

In evaluating the moral status of sexual behaviour in the light of the Bible, three broad lines of approach seem to be possible. The first locates absolute moral rules in certain physical acts. What the scriptures forbid are certain unnatural acts. As discussed at various points, this position has a long and distinguished history within the church. In its classic form it prohibited all forms of non-procreative sexual acts by males, i.e. masturbation, contraception, oral sex, anal sex, any sex between people of the same sex, and sexual activity with animals. The modern form of this position tends to thin down the list of prohibited acts by noting the apparent silence of scripture on oral and anal sex and on contraception. Earlier exponents of this position would not have accepted this confident assertion of silence without protest. It is also interesting to note that many people who hold this position would not accept the argument that silence means freedom when evaluating the practice of abortion.

A second view locates absolute moral rules, not in the physical acts themselves, but in the gender of the persons involved in the sexual activity. This view has two advantages: it can appeal easily to the anti-gay texts discussed in Chapter 8; it removes the spotlight from any sexual activity practised by straight people. However, as an attempt to expound scripture it has serious weaknesses. It treats as irrelevant the high symbolic significance that Leviticus gives to bodily acts and 'discharges', and which lie at the heart of that book's teaching on sexual activity, but it then continues to appeal to verses in the same book as the basis for rejecting sexual contact between males. Although this position has considerable popular appeal among modern evangelicals, its basis in scripture or Christian tradition is not secure. It derives its sense of moral rightness from two related features of modern culture: one is a horror of gay people; the second is a cultural dis-ease at non-competitive intimacy between two unrelated males.

The careful discussion of the biblical material in part one of this book points to a third view, namely that sexual behaviour derives its meaning from the social order of which it is a part. This emerges clearly in the case of the prohibition of adultery in the Ten Commandments: what is forbidden is not certain physical acts that are intrinsically wrong but sexual acts which threaten social relationships that are central to the ordering of society.

In the course of the detailed discussion in part one, various nuances emerged which illuminate rather than contradict this fundamental assertion. The symbolic significance given to bodily acts and functions in a society reflects the social ordering of that society. The culture of a society to which one belongs – with its social order and symbolic understanding of the body – has a real, but not an absolute, claim on the members of that society. Again, there may be circumstances which would justify a group of people creating a sub-culture of resistance within their society.

This account of what scripture is saying has two immediate applications in evaluating gay sexual behaviour. The first is diagnostic. It explains many aspects of the sexual practices of gay sub-cultures, including some of the most controversial. Much gay sexual behaviour finds its interpretation in particular aspects of the place of gay people within the social order. Gay identity is heavily contested and therefore often fragmented rather than coherent: the natural outworking of this is fragmented sexual behaviour. Gay identity has the episodic character of a threatened resistance movement; the result is that gay sexual behaviour is often episodic and functions as a form of cultural resistance – it becomes both politicized and corporate. Society sees sexual acts by gay people as the symbolic heart of this contested identity; the consequence is that gay sexual activity can function as a form of imaginative catharsis – a potent way of getting the oppressor or the oppression out of one's head. There are strong social forces operating against the formation of publicly recognized and supported gay relationships; it is therefore understandable that many gay men find themselves trapped in a form of perpetual or recurrent courtship.

This biblical principle that sexual behaviour derives its meaning from the social order of which it is part also explains why there are different interpretations of the gay phenomenon. Many gay people see sex as the heart of what it is to be gay; this conviction mirrors society's seeing same sex sexual acts as the truly scandalous element of what it is to be gay. Again, many straight people articulate their objection to the new gay identity, and to the sexual behaviour to which it gives rise, by claiming that it marks a rejection of the complementarity of the sexes. Earlier chapters of this book have suggested a different interpretation: the conventional competitive masculinity of our culture has alienated the 'normal' male both from himself, from other men, and from women. On this view the men who emerge as gay, although perceived as aberrant, are involved in the recovery of a more affectionate and intimate masculinity and a consequent reconciliation with the feminine. While the way this works for individuals may be problematic and is certainly contested, the emergence of a gay identity is both a symptom of gender stress in the culture and one of the ways by which this stress is being addressed.

On this latter view, although sexual activity may be an important part of what it is to be gay, it is not in fact the heart of the gay vocation within the social process of modern society. Part of what makes individual people gay is their openness to male intimacy and the erotic potential of the masculine which the culture is set on denying. One result of this is that gay people have a natural role in rescuing desire, gentleness and intimacy from its limitation to the domestic sphere and restoring it to the public realm from which it has been driven.

If this interpretation is correct it has interesting results for evaluating gay sexual behaviour. It suggests that the primary questions to be asked of such behaviour are: does it support or undermine what gay people are themselves seeking? and, what has the gay imagination to give to society? It may also imply that, while the wider culture needs to focus on this second question, gay people themselves may be the best people to discern what patterns of behaviour are healthy and supportive in the lives of gay people.

The pursuit of friendship

Where a person senses that the scripts on offer are not going to work for them and begins to establish some stability or social continuity as a gay man, the natural tendency is to borrow and adapt scripts that govern the relationship of men and women in straight society. Given the invisibility of social scripts that affirm affectionate same sex relationships it is not surprising that gay people who are looking for stability, affection and intimacy tend to look to the pattern of marriage. While this is a natural move, often embraced with relief by the person's immediate family – 'we think of Kevin as a son-in-law' – it also marks the extent to which modern culture has abandoned the ancient idea of society as a network of friendships, held together by bonds of affection.

The scriptures do not limit the notion of covenant to the institution of marriage. The idea of covenant involves the creation of affectionate bonds that imply mutual responsibility and create the obligation of faithfulness – of an uncompromising commitment to the welfare of those involved and to the preservation of the bonds of affection. Covenant is used in scripture of marriage (Malachi 2:14), of political order and relationship (2 Samuel 5:3), of same sex friendships (1 Samuel 18:3; Psalm 55:20), as well as of the bonds between God and his people. Covenant creates kinship. Covenant points to the importance of affection and faithfulness in the ordering of society. Although the modern mindset limits publicly recognized social bonding to marriage and the obligations associated with parenthood, ancient societies regarded it as an essential and recurrent element in a wide variety of valid social relationships.

These ancient categories of affectionate and binding social bonding – seen, for example in covenant, extended kinship and friendship – provide the background for the particular possible archetypes for gay relationships which John Boswell identifies in the tradition of the pre-modern church.

One of the archetypes that John Boswell discusses is the formation of households, based on affectionate bonds that do not originate in marriage or biological relationship. This was the basic conception that gave rise to monastic communities with the abbot as 'father' to the brothers. The idea of the household is also central to the New Testament's idea of church (cf. Ephesians 2:19; 1 Timothy 3:15; 5:1,2). Both Acts and 1 Timothy provide evidence that this was worked out in a strong, if diverse, network of social bonding and mutual financial support.

'Woman, behold, your son.' . . . 'Behold, your mother!' (John 19:26,27)

Jesus's last words to Mary and John are not simply a moving personal aside; they embody an essential principle of church life – the love of friends creating bonds of kinship. While the style of many modern churches does not recognize this, or fails to extend such friendship to their gay members, it forms an essential element in the lives of many gay people. This is a (fictional?) example from an article in the *Gay Times*.[14]

Although at twenty-eight Andrew has been out of work for nearly two years and has little prospect of finding a job, he has carved out a reasonable life for himself. He lives in a council flat with Luke – another gay man. They are not a couple but get on well as flatmates and Luke accepts that he will pay a higher share of bills – so long as Andrew does more of the shopping, cooking and housework!

Andrew supplements his dole cheque by doing a few odd jobs and decorating work for gay men he knows. On the council estate he's also known as the one to see when your car won't start. Although Andrew never has any spending money he still manages to lead quite a social life.

Two or three days a week he 'buddies' for a man who has AIDS, and part of this involves preparing meals for them both which Andrew does not have to pay for. Two small perks of this work are that he can claim for a weekly bus pass, and his Terrence Higgins Trust card gets him into most gay clubs free. Tuesday night is free anyway at the local gay disco, and there are usually one or two friends there who will buy him a drink (on a bad night he might nick somebody's pint from the edge of the dance floor).

On Saturdays Andrew goes out to dinner with some rich queens he knows, and there's an unspoken agreement that he doesn't need to bring along a bottle of wine. On Sunday he usually kicks a ball around with the gay football club, or else visits his mum for a Sunday lunch. Andrew is currently going out with someone who seems fairly keen on him, and this guy is happy to pay for both tickets when they visit the cinema together. Sometimes Andrew wonders, if he did find a job, just how he'd fit working into his busy schedule!

Two of the other archetypes that John Boswell discusses draw attention to different emotional tones that may arise within these bonds of friendship. One is *paedeia*, the warm love that can exist between mentor and learner and was a recognized element of monastic life. It has obvious links with the social context of the book of Proverbs ('My son') and with some forms of Greek education.

The emotion that we identify as 'romantic love' flourished, and even gained its first cultural and poetic form in European culture, within the single sex institutions of the Christian church. Jonathan's response to David (1 Samuel 18:1) has something of this quality; there are clear similarities between the romantic love articulated within the Christian monastic tradition and the love often recorded between soldiers in pre-modern literature. The history of the interpretation of this 'emotion' in Western culture is complex and illuminating. In ancient cultures it often led to genital sex. Within the great flowering of medieval literature on love in the twelfth and thirteenth centuries it was mainly divorced from sexual activity. Within the monastic tradition it was affirmed and celebrated – and was used to describe the spiritual life and the love of God, for example in the writings of Bernard and Aelred. In the secular tradition of courtly love, the object of romantic love was another man's wife and its proper outworking was seen as chivalry rather than adultery. Dante regarded his encounter with the beauty of a young girl, Beatrice, as a moment of cosmic vision – as a revelation of the beauty in God and in the goodness of his creation.[15] None of these interpretations associated the experience of falling in love with marriage. Marriage was associated with the less intense bonds of affection that hold all society together, and with the particular task of bearing children.

Out of this cauldron of interpretations, and under the guidance of later medieval theologians, emerged the notion that the purpose and proper context for romantic love was marriage.

Taken with the Reformers' emphasis on companionate marriage, this created the mindset that saw 'good' desire as the love of a man and a woman on their way to marriage. Nineteenth-century science took this 'self-evident' interpretation as the basis of its exploration of the human psyche. The triumph of this interpretation of the sharp desire we feel when beauty is revealed to us has led to dreadful distortions in Western culture. It lies behind the idea that a concern for culture is displaced sexual desire. It has promoted distorted views of the place of affection, emotion and intimacy in marriage. It has caused some of the powerful intuitions of God experienced by young people to be categorized and dismissed as adolescent sexuality. It has led to intuitions of male beauty being derided as perverse.

A better starting point in thinking about romantic love would be to stay with the classical understanding: to see it as an intuition of beauty, a moment of revelation both about God and about creation. As an emotion it should be seen as an awakening – a summons to other emotions and other commitments. As a revelation of God it should lead to worship. As a revelation about creation it should lead to an appropriate engagement with the created order – possibly art, poetry or political endeavour; possibly, but not necessarily, to relationship with the person whose beauty has been seen. It may be appropriate for such a moment to lead to marriage, to friendship, or to some affectionate sexual relationship. The discernment of what outcome is appropriate cannot lie with the experience of romantic love itself; it must be discovered within creation and within responsible and affectionate society. For a gay man who finds himself 'falling for' another man, a society that interprets his insight as intrinsically perverse can offer him little guidance on how wisely to 'order his affections'.

Gay people have to address their human need for intimacy, affection and society in a cultural context that has little place for bonds of affection apart from marriage or for the intuitions of the beauty of God and creation which comes to them through romantic love. They cannot look to the culture to provide them with appropriate ways of living but have to discern their own ways of honouring their humanity and their sense of God. The various forms of affectionate bonding that occur among gay people, whether paired domestic partnerships or in more diffuse networks of friends, are neither a denial of masculinity nor necessarily a rejection of heterosexual marriage. The recognition of affection and desire that they represent, and their harnessing into real social commitments, are not contrary to the Christian vision of human life but close to themes and instincts that are an integral part of biblical and Christian tradition.

Hidden in the current clash between the gay movement and modern church culture about 'lifestyle' lie a question and a danger. The question faces the churches: What is it about their understanding of Jesus Christ that leads them to a poorer grasp of some fundamental Christian insights than the gay movement? The danger faces gay people: they may fail to hear in their experience of love and their intuitions of beauty the mysterious call of God.

Chapter 13

Over the Rainbow

Many that are first will be last, and the last first
Jesus, Mark 10:31

HIV/AIDS is an illness that will one day be conquered like TB or syphilis, or eliminated like smallpox. It is having its most terrible effects in Africa where it risks decimating whole age groups in nations struggling with other problems that have political or natural causes. However, the fact that this virus began its onslaught on prosperous Western societies by attacking gay people has had profound results for gay people and for wider Western culture.

The advent of AIDS has deeply affected gay communities. At an individual level the story has often been terrible – great suffering and poverty, rejection by hostile communities and bewildered families. However, its effect within the gay communities and on their relationship with wider society has been to transform both their self-understanding and their public image. It has led to a significant reordering of the symbolic map by which gay people recognize themselves and are understood by others. This symbolic reordering has occurred in three areas: it has shifted the focus from sex to people; it has revealed the human qualities present in the gay social vision; it has contributed to a new cultural dialogue with death.

The shift of focus from sex to people has occurred at many levels and for many reasons. Before the advent of AIDS, the social relationships, cultural contribution and social impact of gay people were invisible to wider society. In the public imagination gay people did not exist, except when sexual acts that violated its symbolic code came to light. On the whole this suited gay people well, as it lessened the chance of discrimination or violence. At the same time, as we have seen, it meant that gay people also tended to identify the core of their identity in sex rather than in a wider set of personal qualities. AIDS has changed both the image and the reality of gay people's lives. The suffering of people with AIDS, the need to provide proper support, and the importance of engaging the attention of the medical world and government, made gay visibility an important social priority. Whereas it had seemed to many people that it was dangerous to be recognized as gay, it became clear that gay invisibility was more dangerous. This not only affected the image of gay people, it also changed the way that the gay community functioned and saw itself. It led to a more integrated sense of identity, to a broadening of cultural focus, and to new maturity and skill in dealing with wider society.

This shift of focus also affected the image of gay people in straight society. Typical sentiments, not always articulated, were: 'However low they are, they do not deserve this.' 'It's nature taking its revenge.' 'It doesn't matter if it gets them, but suppose it were our Fiona.' 'I did not know that he/she/they were gay.' 'They do their charity fund-raising with style.' 'I never realized there were so many of them.' At some levels AIDS has increased hostility to gay people. It has also broadened people's understanding of what it is to be gay and made them aware that this strange identity includes friends and people they admire.

The second way in which AIDS has altered the symbolic map surrounding modern homosexuality is in making visible something of the gay social vision. Many people, even those deeply horrified at any homosexuality, probably admire the way in which the gay community has responded to AIDS. The qualities that this disease has brought to light may have matured under its onslaught but they were always present in what it was to be gay. They include: male tenderness, being at ease with the human body, sensitivity to vulnerability, realism about sexuality, deep acceptance of other people's weaknesses, refusal to dismiss anyone as 'unclean', artistic flair and creativity, intuitive grasp on how to engage society's imagination, sense of irony, genius for celebration, ability to move from gentle humour to well-crafted anger.

The third symbolic consequence of AIDS has been to thrust

the gay community into the centre of one of the most important tasks facing any culture: the way in which death is received, understood and celebrated. While death is an inescapable fact, the ways in which it is acknowledged, handled and allowed to interpret the meaning of existence, vary dramatically in different societies. For almost a millennium of Western history the Christian faith held the monopoly on how the cultural imagination engaged with death. The modern way of handling death is to call it 'natural' and ignore it as far as possible. Modern church life, despite the richness of its past theological and artistic tradition, has gone a long way towards accepting this view. Contemporary evangelical Christianity treats death as one of the accidents of life – to be responded to compassionately and passed over as quickly as possible. Something profound about the spirit that moves modern Christians is seen in how few recent popular Christian songs aim to prepare people for death.

Wrestling with death

The scriptures speak of death as 'the last enemy' (1 Corinthians 15:26), 'the king of terrors' (Job 18:14), as a power by which the forces that oppose God keep the human race in 'lifelong bondage' (Hebrews 2:15). Death is not simply an event in the life of an individual, it is a power that stalks the world, that destroys life and spreads a reign of fear (Romans 5:17; 8:2). However, this is not its only view of death. Death is also a summons from God (Luke 12:20), an instrument for containing human evil and pride (Psalm 49, Isaiah 14:1–21), a way of reversing human suffering (Luke 16:19ff.). Something of the dual character of death as both natural and terrible is caught in an aphorism of St Isaac of Syria.[1]

> Death is a dispensation of the Creator's wisdom. It will rule only a certain time over nature; then it will certainly disappear.

Jesus experienced the ferocity and reality of death. The first Christians saw his encounter with death as central to the meaning of his life and the key to the hope with which they confronted the hostile world of the Roman Empire (Colossians 2:13–14; Acts 17:6,7). The New Testament is alive with an understanding of resurrection. This is not simply a vivid metaphor for affirming all that is good in life – which is what it sometimes becomes in modern church life. It is a real conviction that there is another world of beauty and life which has broken into history and of which they already had a taste (Hebrews 6:5; 12:22–4).

It was the great achievement of the medieval church to give a rich, cultural expression to this understanding of death and to the reality of heaven. Although present in a very rich architectural and artistic tradition it is probably met by most people today through the translation of hymns produced by the Oxford Movement.[2] Many modern Christians tend to regard the medieval treatment of death as morbid and its portrayal of heaven as fanciful. There may be some truth in the charge of morbidity. The medieval imagination was often overwhelmed by an all-pervasive experience of death, interpreted the greatness of God in categories borrowed from the exercise of feudal authority, and may at times have been panicked by economic scarcity. Towards the end of the period it may also have lost the complementary grasp it once had on the beauty and goodness of creation.

The criticism that the great medieval hymns about heaven are fanciful has less to be said for it. It is interesting mainly for demonstrating the extent to which scepticism about the afterlife has captured Christians who think themselves orthodox. Many modern Christians are not far from the scepticism of the Sadducees of Jesus's day, who based their scepticism on the paucity of scriptural evidence about the character of the afterlife (Acts 23:8; Luke 20:27ff.). It is intriguing that, on this matter, both Jesus (Luke 20:34–8) and Paul (Acts 23:6; 24:15) sided firmly with the Pharisaic party in Judaism. Under Greek and Persian influences, this group had elaborated the more limited traditional views of life after death to provide a vivid picture of the last judgment, of hell and of paradise.

The success of the medieval vision was also its downfall. Not content with a vivid liturgical portrayal of the reality of death, the glory of resurrection and the beauty of heaven, it began to harness the whole elaborate machinery of Christian worship to the task of praying for full salvation for the imperfect Christian dead. The result was not only a dubious doctrine of purgation but an elaborate system of organization in which the power of the clergy and the financing of the church were based on such prayer. The understandable response of the Reformers was to cut back the whole luxuriant growth as far as they possibly could. Calvin and Knox argued that the best witness to the resurrection was to lay the body in the ground with dignity and in silence.[3]

Behind the response of the Reformers was the conviction that their whole culture needed to be exposed again to the scriptures, that faith in God needed to be generated again by a deep immersion in the Bible. The regeneration in the understanding of death that they hoped for did occur to some extent and can be seen in the fine but neglected pastoral teaching of the Puritans about death.[4] However, at a cultural level the policy of the Reformers was a failure. Before a new Christian culture could emerge to express a Christian understanding of death, other influences emerged which effectively gained the right to express the English understanding of death.

The new interpreters of death were the scientists, whose horizons were limited to what they could see, and the world of commerce, who had little interest in death except for the profit that could be made out of the grief and fantasies of the bereaved. Both groups found support for their position in new sceptical schools of philosophy. The result has been a new understanding of death which has continued to hold sway until very recently. The public handling of death has rested with the worlds of medicine and commerce, with the churches providing a twenty-minute religious slot to keep things 'decent'. The message that has gone out through all this is that death is natural and should be passed over as quickly as possible – a regrettable feature of biological life as unmentionable as personal hygiene. This understanding of death has been sustained in the culture partly by the apparent success of science in keeping many people alive to a reasonable old age: most people who die are people for whom death is 'appropriate'.

In the twentieth century the one major breach in this cultural perception that death is natural and happens to people who do not really matter any more has been death in war. A source of some embarrassment to both churches and politicians, the British people have insisted on proper liturgical acknowledgment of the death of the victims of war. More recently there have been other cracks in the modern attempts to contain and sanitize death. The intellectual and moral authority of science is under challenge. Bereavement counselling and the hospice movement are giving people the confidence to name and respond to death. Non-religious groups are threatening the churches' monopoly on funerals. Important as these signs are, they have not yet achieved a new cultural expression for death.

It seems likely that death is on the threshold of finding a new voice in our culture. From very different angles both the churches and the gay community have an interest in the emergence of this new voice. In the case of the churches, there are few signs that they recognize the slenderness of their toehold in the interpretation of death or the extent of the changes that may emerge. Nor do they appear to understand that the right to articulate death's new voice will not be conferred by British culture simply on the basis of tradition. If today's followers of Jesus are to play a part in the articulation of this new voice, they are going to have to be present with the people as they wrestle with death, and they are going to need the artistic sensitivity to interpret death as it is experienced today and to relate it to a Jesus that people can recognize as real. Fifteen minutes at the 'crem' are certainly not going to be enough.

AIDS, like war, is likely to play some part in articulating a new cultural voice for death. Gay people with AIDS have had a significant impact on medical practice by their determination to be taken seriously as people rather than be treated as mere units in the medical assembly line. This has occurred partly because of the age, professional skills and social background of many of those involved. It has also drawn strength from the experience of the gay movement in gaining a hearing in a reluctant and oppressive society. It is already clear that the same intuitions will operate in the handling of death from AIDS. Gay skills in art, in celebration, and in the voicing of anger, love and pain mean that the gay movement is well placed to play some part in articulating death's new voice.

There are many uncertainties for English society as it stands on the threshold of this rearticulation of death. It is likely that commercial concerns will play a significant part; as in the Victorian era there is money to be had in doing death well. It is unclear whom these commercial concerns will regard as their natural allies in the process. It is equally unclear whether the way in which gay people respond to death from AIDS will influence wider practice. Continuing hostility to gay people may mean that they will not be listened to. However, the success of the film *Four Weddings and a Funeral* may indicate that people detect more authenticity in the face of death from gay people than from conventional religion. In the end, death may be too powerful for people to trust a church that is afraid of reality and mess in human life. It is certain that it will be costly for the church to re-engage with death in our culture. Although it might be a bitter pill to swallow, one of the ways by which the church may learn how to give Jesus a place in the culture's rearticulation of death is attempting a reconciliation with gay people.

Gay paradise

One reason why AIDS may play a bigger part than, say, cancer or road deaths, in putting death back on the British cultural map is its link with sex. Throughout the twentieth century British culture has been involved in a complex dialogue as to the meaning of sex. Among the factors that have contributed to this have been the two World Wars and the arrival of reliable contraception. Many 'conservative' people are inclined to blame the 'permissive' sixties. However, the underlying movements are older and more complex. The seeds of the recovery of sexual pleasure can already be seen in the nineteenth century. Capitalism's removal of affection from public life and its tendency to disintegrate social bonds have heightened the link between sex and personal identity and weakened the link between sex and social bonding.

The advent of AIDS means that, in the same moment, the culture is forced to confront its understanding both of sex and death. Its association in the Western imagination with the contested sexual identity of gay people has naturally increased the tension – invading the cultural imagination while distancing it from 'ordinary' life. The link between sex and death should

not be seen as either new or surprising. In much popular presentation, sex is associated primarily with pleasure or recreation.
The main concern of moral reformers has been to re-establish
its link with responsible relationship. The categories of *pleasure*
and *relationship* do not exhaust people's instincts of what either
life or sex is about. Some of the deepest human concerns that
we associate with sexual behaviour and imagination are better
expressed by the ideas of *desire* and *immortality*.

Cultural developments in recent centuries mean that modern
people think about desire and immortality in very different
terms from the earlier Western tradition. The classic Christian
imagination saw the awakening of love, the sweetness of sexual
pleasure, and the fruitfulness of the sexual act as real but
partial anticipations of the true locus of human longings for
joy and immortality. The true and lasting fulfilment of these
hopes lay in heaven. In a curious way the modern denial of
heaven has simultaneously strengthened and weakened the
relationship between sex and human preoccupation with desire
and immortality.

In the case of desire, moves begun in the late Middle Ages,
structured into the social order from the eighteenth century by
the triumph of the market, and endorsed by nineteenth-century
science, have identified desire with heterosexual love. Contests
remain between those who wish to locate joy in physical pleasure
and those who locate it in intimate relationship. The elimination
of society and heaven – of the earthly and heavenly city, to
follow Augustine – from our vision of desire is hardly noticed.
One result of this contracted vision is cultural ferment as the
deep human longings for joy and immortality thrash around
without being ordered around an adequate and sustainable focus.
Another result is the denial of desire: human beings abandon
their intuition of God and settle for pleasure and 'relationship'.

The human longing for immortality has responded differently
to the loss of heaven from the modern imagination. The
re-imaging of desire and the rediscovery of non-procreative
sex have, if anything, weakened the link between sex and
the hope of immortality. That it has not altogether disappeared
emerges in the distress gay people sometimes encounter at the
ending of a family line. This is beautifully captured in Thomas
O'Neil's poem 'A Sexual Apology to my Father'.[5]

The same brooding Jesus
you once hung on my bedroom
wall made me this way.

But, oh, how I would have loved
to have extended your line,
to have held that gilded mirror
up to you, history's prize
for having given the gift of birth.
You would have seen your tiny face, dad,
giggling once again under
a Christmas tree,
slobbering on the wrapper
of a candy cane, and saying
things like, 'Wawayouhaha.'
His little pecker would have drawn
the same line so far into the future
we'd have lost sight of it
over the cemetery hill

where someday, you know,
we will be family again.

But I fell in love
with peckers, dad . . .

Although some sense of link between sex and the longing for
immortality remains, in the main modern people have divorced
the hope of immortality from either heaven or the fruitfulness
of the sexual act to the sphere of the public realm. Immortality
lies in the mark we make on history. Ultimate meaning is found
not in the heavenly city but in an isolated personal identity and
in the direction of history.

It is interesting to move from these modern reworkings of
the great themes of desire and immortality to an example of the
medieval imaging of heaven:

> Jerusalem, the golden,
>   With milk and honey blest,
> Beneath thy contemplation
>   Sink heart and voice opprest.

I know not, O, I know not
   What joys await us there,
What radiancy of glory,
   What bliss beyond compare.

They stand, those halls of Sion,
   All jubilant with song,
And bright with many an angel,
   And all the martyr throng;
The Prince is ever with them,
   The daylight is serene,
The pastures of the blessed
Are decked in glorious sheen.

There is the throne of David;
   And there, from care released,
The shout of them that triumph,
   The song of them that feast;
And they, who with their Leader
   Have conquered in the fight,
For ever and for ever
   Are clad in robes of white.

O sweet and blessed country,
   The home of God's elect!
O sweet and blessed country
   That eager hearts expect!
Jesu, in mercy bring us
   To that dear land of rest:
Who are, with God the Father
   and Spirit, ever blest.

The hymn takes as the symbolic heart of its contemplation of
heaven not a sexual but a political image – drawing on the
biblical and Augustinian theme of Jerusalem, the heavenly city.
Although this twelfth-century hymn by Bernard of Cluny derives
its form and much of its imagery from the culture of its day,
its roots in scripture, not least in the book of Revelation, are
easy to trace. However, like any response of the imagination
to the richness of scripture, it excludes elements of the biblical
picture and risks distortion in so doing. For example, in the book

of Revelation, the rich biblical imagery is firmly rooted in the present suffering of the first Christians and in the violence of their clash with the idolatry represented by political pretensions and commercial ruthlessness of the Roman Empire. Equally, heaven, in the New Testament, is not simply a beautiful future which we possess now in our imagination, but a reality that we enjoy now through our fellowship with Jesus Christ (Hebrews 10:19–25; 12:22–4).

A gay person turning to scripture and the Christian tradition for an image of heaven is in for some pleasant surprises. In heaven there is no marriage (Matthew 22:30; Luke 20:35); gay people will not find themselves on the margins of heaven because they are excluded from the socially validating institution of marriage. The biblical and traditional images of heaven are so preoccupied with style and public celebration as to be almost camp. While relentlessly political, they have more in common with a Gay Pride event than with the sobriety of English political life or the leisurewear informality of evangelical Christian life. Again, the vision of heaven is firmly rooted in a present experience of suffering, oppression and exclusion (Revelation 6:9–11; 13:16; 18). The hope of heaven does not rest on fitting in with the way of the world but on the Lion and the Lamb (Revelation 5:5) – on the beauty of a king who strives for justice and the love of a gentle friend who takes to himself our pain and failure.

It is interesting to ask why contemporary Christianity, particularly in its evangelical form, has lost its vision of heaven. The loss of a sense of heaven from modern culture has come about through a series of moves – economic, philosophical and scientific. However, one of the most powerful of these has been the diversion of human desire and social affection from God, the public realm and the world to come. While modern evangelical Christianity struggles to gain a hearing in society and to make an impact on issues that it regards as close to the heart of the gospel, it is largely ignorant of the extent to which it has bought into the modern project. Its recurrent anxiety over 'family issues' is a measure of how deeply it has sold its soul to the destructive idols of Western culture: the reduction of the sense of beauty to 'heterosexual love' and the elimination of bonds of affection in the search of prosperity through the market. Its hostility to gay people is not so much a sign of its loyalty to scripture as a mark of the extent to which it has not heeded St John's advice, 'Little children, keep yourselves from idols' (1 John 5:21).

Recovering a vision of heaven cannot be achieved simply by biblical exegesis, intellectual rigour, artistic passion or cultural nostalgia. It has to emerge as human beings in their diversity encounter the friendship of Jesus within the brokenness and confusion of human life. Restoring the fractured imagination of Western Christianity involves turning away from the idols that destroy and fragment our society. Reconciliation with gay people's experience of Christ is simply part of a more extensive act of healing that needs to take place.

Revelation 21:26 pictures the heavenly city as one in which all the glimpses of divine beauty dispersed in human culture will have their place. I am very aware that, in exploring the one strand of how gay men relate to the beauty of God reflected in creation, I have not begun to face the question of how my argument would illuminate the contribution of women, of lesbians, or of other alienated groups to the same task. It may be that the healing of the masculine imagination in the Western church would, of itself, have profound effects for others.

Jesus the outsider

The letter to the Hebrews gives us one of the tenderest portraits in scripture of the humanity of Jesus (2:9, 14–18; 5:7–10; 12:2–3) and one of the most beautiful images of the reality of heaven (12:22–4). It is written to a group of Christians whose experience of rejection and suffering (10:32–4; 12:4), and whose sense of being trapped between the two identities of Jew and Christian, are reflected in their forming a distinct group amongst the Christians in Rome (13:24). It seems that they were in serious danger of giving up on Jesus altogether (10:35).

The writer responds by pointing to Jesus as one who shares with them their experience of exclusion:

> Jesus also suffered outside the city gate in order to sanctify the people by his own blood. Let us then go to him outside

the camp and bear the abuse that he endured. For here we have no lasting city, but we are looking for the city that is to come (13:12, 13).

Gay people, in their experience of exclusion, need to know that they have in Jesus one who shares with them the same flesh and blood and 'is not ashamed to call them brothers and sisters' (2:11–15). The wider church of Christ needs to ask itself whether it is willing to follow his example.

Notes

Chapter 1

1 Grove Books, Nottingham, 1991.
2 Terry Sanderson, 'Gays and the Press', in *Coming On Strong*, eds Simon Shepherd and Mick Wallis, Unwin Hyman, 1989.
3 David T. Evans, *Sexual Citizenship*, Routledge, 1993, pp.125–46.
4 Madeleine Colbin and Jane Hawkesley, *Section 28: A practical guide to the law and its implications*, National Council of Civil Liberties, 1989. cf. *Homosexuality: A European Community Issue*, eds. Kees Waaldijk and Andrew Clapham, International Studies in Human Rights, Martinus Nijhoff Publishers, 1993, pp.120–1. See also *The Pink Paper*, 3 February 1995, pp.1, 3.
5 *The Pink Paper*, 2 February 1992, p.3.
6 *Independent*, 5 December 1990, p.5 (but cf. *Gay Times*, June 1991, p.16).
7 *Gay Times*, April 1990, p.9.
8 *Gay Times*, August 1990, p.5 (cf. *Gay Times*, April 1990, p.7).
9 My reasons for preferring the term 'gay' will emerge in Chapter 7.
10 *Sexuality and the Church*, Action for Biblical Witness to Our Nation, 1987, pp.76–7.
11 *Daring to Speak Love's Name*, ed. Elisabeth Stuart (subsequently published by Hamilton, 1992).
12 John D'Emilio, *Sexual Politics, Sexual Communities: The Making of a Homosexual Minority in the United States 1940–70*, University of Chicago Press, 1983, pp.231ff.
13 Some papers have been published as D. Altman et al., *Which Homosexuality?*, GMP, London, 1989.
14 Noted, e.g., in Stephen Jeffery-Poulter, *Peers, Queers & Commons: The Struggle for Gay Law Reform from 1950 to the Present*, Routledge, 1991, pp.263–7.
15 John Boswell, *Christianity, Social Tolerance and Homosexuality*, Chicago UP, 1980, pp.170–6, 272ff. cf. *Creeds, Councils and Controversies*, ed. J. Stephenson, SPCK, 1966, p.158.

16 Richard Plant, *The Pink Triangle*, Mainstream Publishing, Edinburgh, 1987.

17 For the emergence of the caricature, see George M. Marsden, *Fundamentalism and American Culture: The Shaping of Twentieth Century Evangelicalism 1887–1925*, Oxford University Press, 1980; for an analytical overview of the British movement, see D.W. Bebbington, *Evangelicalism in Modern Britain: A History from the 1730s to the 1980s*, Unwin Hyman, London, 1989.

18 *Ezra and Nehemiah*, IVP, 1979, p.71.

19 Constable, 1989.

20 *ibid.* p.41.

21 G.L. Watson, *A.E. Housman: A Divided Life*, Rupert Hart-Davis, London, 1957. Verses on pp. 15 and 223 from *The Collected Poems of A.E. Housman*, Jonathan Cape.

22 *Observer*, 24 October 1988.

23 For a discussion of this link from an evangelical perspective, see Roy McCloughry, *Men and Masculinity*, Hodder & Stoughton, 1992 and Roy McCloughry and Roger Murphy, *Men Without Masks*, Grove Books, 1994.

24 Diana Fuss, *Essentially Speaking: Feminism, Nature and Difference*, Routledge, 1989.

25 *Evangelical Christians and Gay Rights*, p.7.

26 David Holloway in *Daily Mail*, 23 February 1991.

27 From *Sex With God*, Indulgence Press, NY, 1989. 2nd edn, Wexford Press, NY, 1994.

Chapter 2

1 Anthony C. Thistleton, *New Horizons in Hermeneutics*, HarperCollins, 1992, pp.44–6.

2 David Bentley-Taylor *The Great Volcano*, Overseas Missionary Fellowship, 1965, p.127.

3 D. Kidner, *A Time to Mourn and a Time to Dance*, IVP, 1976, p.50; *Ecclesiastes*, Michael Eaton, IVP, 1983, p.94.

4 Act 3, Scene 3, lines 415–30.

5 Jeffrey Weeks, *Sexuality*, Routledge, 1989, p.15 (first published in 1986).

6 *The History of Sexuality*, Vol. 1, *An Introduction*, Robert Hurley, Allen Lane, London, 1979, p.105.

7 *Studies in the Psychology of Sex*, Vol. 1, 1936, cited in Jeffrey Weeks, *Sex, Politics and Society: The regulation of sexuality since 1800*, Longman, 1981, p.21.

8 *Which Homosexuality?* p.84.

9 Alan Bray, *Homosexuality in Renaissance England*, Gay Men's Press, 1982, p.68ff.

10 cf. 'Is there a class ethic in Proverbs?' by Brian W. Kovacs, *Essays in Old Testament Ethics*, eds. J.L. Crenshaw and J.T. Willis, Ktav Publishing, NY, 1974, pp.171–89.

11 Ivan Illich, M. Boyars, *Gender*, London, 1983, p.178.

12 Peter Brown, *The Body and Society*, Faber, 1990, pp.14ff. (first published 1988).

13 'A Simple Way to Pray for Master Peter, the Barber', quoted in *The Minister's Prayer Book*, ed. J.W. Doberstein, Collins, 1964, p.450.

14 On pre-industrial households see *Homosexuality in Renaissance England*, p.44–6. For an Indian Christian's reflection on the non-residential extended family in the West see Peter Pothen, *Unpackaging the Family*, Grove Ethical Studies, No. 87, 1992.

15 Wayne Meeks, *The Moral World of the First Christians*, SPCK, 1987 pp.20–1; Peter Brown, *op.cit.*, p.17.

16 Ivan Illich, *op.cit.*,. pp.22–6; 30–1; 60ff.

17 *Sex, Politics and Society*, p.24ff.

18 BBC, 13 April 1986.

19 Roy McCloughry, *op.cit.*,. p.154.

20 *Sex, Politics and Society*, p.201ff. See ch. 7, n.2, p.258.

21 cf. Matt 3:9; 4:22; 8:21,22; 10:34–8; 12:46–50; 13:54–8; 19:10–12; 19:16–30. In addition to parallels in other Gospels note: Mark 13:12; Luke 4:22–30; 5:11; 6:32–5; 9:61,62; 10:38–42; 11:27–8; 12:49–53; 14:12–14; 14:26,27; 18:29; 20:34–6.

22 *The Body and Society*, pp.216–20; 262ff. St Augustine, *Confessions* VIII 14–20.

23 'The importance of Roman Portraiture for Head Coverings in 1 Corinthians 11:2–16', David W.J. Gill, *Tyndale Bulletin*, Vol. 41.2, November 1990, p.257.

24 'The Church and Polygamy', David Gitari, *Transformation*, Vol. 1.1, 1984, pp.3–10.

25 *ibid*. p.6.

26 A Statement by the House of Bishops, Church House Publishing, 1991, pp.18 cf. #2.10 on p.9.

27 David Gitari, *op.cit.*,. p.7.

28 L.W. Countryman, SCM, 1988.

Chapter 3

1 *Freedom to Choose*, Richard Bauckham, Grove Books, 1991.

2 *Sexual Behaviour in Britain*, Kaye Wellings, Julia Field, Anne Johnson and Jane Wadsworth, Penguin, 1994, pp.157–8.

3 'The Importance of Roman Portraiture for Head Coverings in 1 Corinthians 11:2–16', David W.J. Gill, *Tyndale Bulletin*, Vol. 41.2, November 1990, pp.245–60.

4 Rom. 12:4,5; 1 Cor. 12:12–31; Eph. 1:22,23; Col. 1:18, etc.

5 cf. *Purity and Danger*, Mary Douglas, Routledge and Kegan Paul, 1966; also *Natural Symbols*, Barrie & Rockliff: The Cresset Press, 2nd edition 1973. See also *Face Values*, ed. Anne Sutherland, BBC, 1978, chapter 3.

6 Lev. 11:44–47. The commentary *The Book of Leviticus* by Gordon Wenham, Hodder & Stoughton, 1979, is the most useful known to this writer and draws extensively on Mary Douglas's work.

7 1 Macc. 1:50, 2 Macc. 6. *Natural Symbols* pp.60–4.

8 Acts 10:9ff., 15:4–20. cf. Eph. 2:13–3:11.

9 Luke 14:7–14.

10 Diana de Marly, *Fashion For Men: An Illustrated History*, B.T. Batsford, 1985, pp.56–7.

11 *ibid*. p.71 cf. p.40.

12 *ibid*. p.102, 119.

13 *ibid*. p.117–19.

14 *ibid*. p.119, 144–5.

15 'If the bishop has a wet dream let him not offer, but let the presbyter offer. Nor let him partake of the mystery, not as if he were polluted, but because of the honour of the altar.' *The Testamentum Domini*. ed. Grant Sperry-White, Alcuin/GROW, 1991, p.18. This 'church order' probably dates from Asia Minor *c*.AD 350–70.

16 cf *Liturgical Portions of the Didascalia* ed. Sebastian Brock and Michael Vasey, Grove Books, 1982, chapter 26, pp.31–3.

17 Gordon Wenham, *op.cit*., p.222–3.

18 Halsbury's Laws of England Vol. 11(1), 4th edition, 1990, pp.379–80. (Consensual heterosexual anal intercourse was decriminalized for the first time in the 1994 Criminal Justice and Public Order Act with an age of consent of eighteen, the same as for gay men.)

19 Jeffrey Weeks, *Coming Out*, Quartet Books, 1977, p.13.

20 *ibid*. p.14–15.

21 John Boswell, 'Rome: the Foundation', chapter 3, *Christianity, Social Tolerance and Homosexuality*, Chicago UP, 1980. David F. Greenberg *The Construction of Homosexuality*, Chicago UP, 1988, pp.154–60. The concepts are explored starkly for the similar culture of ancient Athens in *One Hundred Years of Homosexuality*, David M. Halperin, Routledge, 1990, pp.29–38.

22 Boswell, pp.74–8; Greenburg, pp.157–8. On Roman terms for the 'active', i.e. inserting, role in oral sex, see Boswell, p.21 note 41, p.50 note 20.

23 D.S. Bailey, *Homosexuality and the Western Christian Tradition*, Longmans, 1955, pp.115–18.

24 *Contraception*, J.T. Noonan, Belknap Harvard, 1986, pp.25, 44–5, 92, 104, 542.

25 Jeffrey Weeks, *Sex, Politics and Society*, pp.187–94, 259–60. The story is vividly documented in *Making History 5/Birth Control*, Television History Centre and Channel 4, 1988.

26 *The Lambeth Conference 1930*, SPCK, 1930, pp.43–6.

27 Peter Brown, *The Body and Society*, pp.399ff. See also Paul Ramsey's

fine essays 'Augustine and "the Presiding Mind"' and 'Sex and the order of reason in Thomas Aquinas', made available to me by David Attwood.

28 Peter Brown, pp.131–3.
29 *ibid*. pp.405–8, 416–22.
30 Noonan, p.537. (This somewhat changed the grounds for forbidding contraception – see pp.542ff.)
31 Peter Brown, *op.cit.*, pp.59–60.
32 *ibid*. pp.47–9.
33 *ibid*. pp.52–5.
34 Jim Cotter, *Pleasure, Pain and Passion*, Cairns Publications, 1988, p.20.
35 *Sex, Politics and Society*, pp.48–51. Bruce R. Smith, *Homosexual Desire in Shakespeare's England*, p.87. *Unauthorised Sexual Behaviour during the Enlightenment*, ed. R.P. Maccubbin pp.43–7.
36 *Sex, Politics and Society*, pp.24–32, 201–17.
37 *St Francis*, SCM, 1982, pp.3–47.

Chapter 4

1 *Marilyn Monroe and Other Poems*, Search Press, 1975, p.74.
2 cf. Oliver M.T. O'Donovan, *On the Thirty-Nine Articles*, Paternoster, 1986, pp.54–6.
3 Oliver M.T. O'Donovan, *Resurrection and Moral Order*, pp.159–60.
4 *Dirt, Greed and Sex*, pp.72–6. cf. pp.104–9.
5 *Presbyterians and Human Sexuality 1991*, pp.3–4, 9–10.
6 *ibid*. p.3.
7 *New Horizons in Hermeneutics*, HarperCollins, 1992, pp.7,27–8, chapters XI, XIL.
8 *ibid*. chapters XI, XII.
9 *ibid*. pp.25–6, 331–8, 617–19.
10 *ibid*. pp.7, 28–9, 613–17.
11 'Misogyny and Mary Whitehouse', chapter 7 in Simon Shepherd, *Because We're Queers*, Gay Men's Press, 1989.
12 Gordon Wenham, *The Book of Leviticus*, Hodder & Stoughton, 1979, p.169.
13 *ibid*. p.174.
14 *Dirt, Greed, and Sex*, p.86.
15 For a useful discussion, see *Sexual Dissidence*, Jonathan Dollimore, Clarenden Press, Oxford, 1991, p.174ff.
16 *Paradoxes of Paradise*, The Almond Press, 1983, p.29ff.

Chapter 5

1 *Sexual Behaviour in Britain*, Kaye Wellings, Julia Field, Anne M. Johnson and Jane Wadsworth, London, Penguin, 1994, p.8.

2 e.g. Jeffrey Weeks, *Coming Out*, Quartet Books, 1977; John D'Emilio, *Sexual Politics, Sexual Communities*, University of Chicago Press, 1983; David T. Evans, *Sexual Citizenship*, Routledge, 1993.

3 e.g. *Sex, Politics and Society*. See ch. 7, n.2, p.258.

4 e.g. *Hidden from History*, ed. M.B. Duberman et al, Penguin 1991; *The Gay Past*, ed. S.J. Licata & R.P. Petersen, Harrington Park Press NY 1985; 'Unauthorised Sexual Behaviour During the Enlightenment', ed. R.P. Maccubbin, *Eighteenth Century Life*, 1985, Vol IX, n.s., 3.

5 Chicago University Press.

6 *Sexual Dissidence: Augustine to Wilde: Freud to Foucault*, Oxford University Press, 1991.

7 Greenberg pp.110–16, 141–2, 148; *Same-sex Unions in Pre-modern Europe*, John Boswell, Villard Books, NY, 1994, pp.61–5, 96–7.

8 *Christianity, Social Tolerance and Homosexuality*, pp.231–2.

9 Greenberg, *op.cit.*, p.25.

10 *ibid*. p.28.

11 *ibid*. p.50.

12 *ibid*. pp.26–40.

13 cf. e.g. *Construction of Homosexuality*, pp.37–40; G. Herdt and R.J. Stoller, *Intimate Communications: Erotics and the Study of Culture*, Columbia University Press, 1990.

14 *Construction of Homosexuality*, pp.40–65.

15 cf. Channel 4's *Ladyboys* in 1992, somewhat sourly reviewed in *Gay Times*, December 1992, p.88.

16 *Which Homosexuality?* D. Altman et al., GMP, 1989, p.84.

17 Greenberg, *op.cit.*, pp.66–77.

18 *ibid*. pp.89–123.

19 Routledge, London and New York, 1993, chapter 1, particularly pp.33–5.

20 *Hidden From History*, pp.17–53.

Chapter 6

1 St Augustine, *Confessions*, translated by Henry Chadwick, Oxford University Press, 1992, p.106, Book VI xii(21).

2 'Friendship', *New Dictionary of Christian Ethics and Pastoral Theology*, eds D.J. Atkinson, D.H. Field, IVP, 1995, pp.398–9.

3 *Paul VI: The First Modern Pope*, Collins, London, 1993, pp.33–51.

4 cf. *The Sunday Times*, 22 October 1993 before the publication of *The Expense of Glory: A Life of John Reith* by Ian McIntyre, HarperCollins, 1993.

5 Plato, *The Symposium*, translated and introduced by Walter Hamilton, Penguin Classics 1951, p.21.

6 *ibid*. p.12, cf. pp.22–7.

7 The subject is complex. See the detailed discussions in Greenberg pp.141–60; *Hidden from History*, pp.32–4; pp.44ff.

8 *Same-sex Unions in Pre-modern Europe*, John Boswell, Villard Books, NY, 1994, p.74ff.
9 *ibid*. Chapter 3.
10 *Christianity, Social Tolerance and Homosexuality*, pp.84–6.
11 *ibid*. p.75.
12 *ibid*. pp.133–4.
13 Aelred of Rievaulx, *On Spiritual Friendship*, translated by Mary E. Laker with a fine introduction by Douglass Roby, Cistercian Publications, Kalamazoo, Michigan, 1977.
14 cf. the criticisms of Greenberg, *op. cit.*, p.229, p.264 n.118, and R.W. Southern, *Saint Anselm*, Cambridge University Press, 1990, pp.148–53.
15 *Christianity, Social Tolerance and Homosexuality*, pp.131–2, 362–3.
16 Greenberg, *op.cit.*; Boswell, *op.cit.*, pp.218–41, 255–60, 261–8.
17 Boswell, *op.cit.*, pp.221–6.
18 *On Spiritual Friendship*, 1:57–61.
19 *ibid*. 3:87.
20 cf. J. Leclercq, *Monks and Love in the Twelfth Century*, Oxford University Press, 1979.
21 *Same-sex Unions in Pre-modern Europe*, pp.372–4.
22 *ibid*. pp.151–2.
23 *ibid*. pp.240–3.
24 *ibid*. p.182.
25 see extensive discussion in e.g. *ibid*. pp.21–4, 68–9, 98–100, 192–3, 221.
26 *ibid*. p.185.
27 *ibid*. pp.259–60.
28 *ibid*. pp.264–5.
29 *The Construction of Homosexuality*, pp.302–46.
30 *Christianity, Social Tolerance and Homosexuality*, Chapter 10.
31 e.g. 'The myth of lesbian impunity: capital laws from 1270 to 1791', Louis Compton *The Gay Past*, pp.11–25; 'A lesbian execution in Germany 1721: the trial records', translated Brigitte Eriksson, *The Gay Past*, pp.27–40; 'Sodomy and Heresy in early modern Switzerland', E. William Monter, *The Gay Past*, pp.41–79; 'Sodomy in the Dutch Republic during the eighteenth century', Arend H. Huussen, *Hidden from History*, pp. 141–9.
32 *Christianity, Social Tolerance and Homosexuality*, pp.127–8; *Construction of Homosexuality*, pp.218–34.
33 Leonardo Boff, *St Francis*, SCM 1982, Chapter 2.
34 'Conceptions of homosexuality and sodomy in Western history', A.N. Gilbert, *The Gay Past*, Alan Bray, pp.57–68; *Homosexuality in Renaissance England*, Gay Mens Press 1982, pp.13–32; cf. also Bruce R. Smith, *Homosexual Desire in Shakespeare's England*, Chicago University Press 1991, pp.41–55.
35 *Homosexuality in Renaissance England*, pp.67ff.
36 *ibid*. pp.48, 68–9.
37 '"Writhing Bedfellows": 1826 – Two young men from ante-bellum South

Carolina's ruling elite share "extravagant delight"', M.B. Duberman, *The Gay Past*, pp.85–101.

38 *The Pink Triangle*, R. Plant, Mainstream Publishing, 1987; cf. also the play *Bent* by Martin Sherman (1979) and Martin Sherman's review of Plant in *Gay Times*, June 1987, p.61. cf '"Stigmata or Degeneration" – Prisoner Markings in Nazi Concentration Camps', E.J. Haerberle *The Gay Past*, pp. 135–9; 'The Pink Triangle: R. Lautmann, 'The Persecution of Homosexual Males in Concentration Camps in Nazi Germany', *The Gay Past*, pp. 141–60.

39 Plant, *op.cit.*, p.181.

40 *ibid.* p.17.

41 *ibid.* p.19.

42 Phillip Stubbes, quoted in Smith, p.155.

43 Smith, *op.cit.*, pp.235ff.

44 *ibid.* p.24.

Chapter 7

1 Leiden lecture, 7 September 1994.

2 D.F. Greenberg, *The Construction of Homosexuality*, Part II (pp.301–499); 'The Birth of the Queen: sodomy and the emergence of gender equality in modern culture, 1660–1750', Randolph Trumbach, *Hidden from History*, pp.129–40; 'Gender and the Homosexual Role in Modern Western Culture: the 18th and 19th Centuries Compared', Randolph Trumbach, *Which Homosexuality?* pp.149–69; Alan Bray, *Homosexuality in Renaissance England*, Gay Men's Press, 1982; Jeffrey Weeks, *Coming Out: Homosexual Politics in Britain from the Nineteenth Century to the Present*, Quartet 1977; Jeffrey Weeks, *Sex, Politics and Society: The Regulation of Sexuality Since 1800*, Longman, 1981; John D'Emilio, *Sexual Politics, Sexual Communities: The Making of a Homosexual Minority in the United States 1940–1970*, The University of Chicago Press, 1983; David T. Evans, *Sexual Citizenship: The Material Construction of Sexualities*, Routledge 1993.

3 *Hidden from History*, pp.129–35; *Which Homosexuality?* pp.156–7.

4 *Which Homosexuality?* p.157.

5 Bray, *op.cit.*, Chapter 4.

6 *Hidden from History*, p.134.

7 cf. 'Sodomy in the Dutch Republic During the Eighteenth Century', Arend H. Huussen, *Hidden from History*, pp.141–9.

8 Bray, *op. cit.* pp.112–14. See also n. 18, pp.134–5.

9 *Which Homosexuality?* p.154.

10 Greenberg, *op.cit.*, pp.356–68.

11 *ibid.* pp.368–83.

12 *Gay Times*, November 1992, pp.18–20.

13 *Wall Street Journal* quoted in *The Independent*, 9 August 1994, p.24.

14 *Homosexuality: A European Community Issue, op.cit.*, pp.18–20 cf pp.289–316.

15 cf. *Sex, Politics and Society*; Greenberg pp.397–9.

16 *Sex, Politics and Society,*. pp.102–3.

17 Caroline Gooding *Trouble with the Law?* Gay Men's Press 1992, p.223. See ch.10,n.9,p262.

18 *Fundamentalism and American Culture*, pp.14ff.

19 Chapter 9, 'The Medicalization of Homosexuality'.

20 Jeffrey Weeks, *Coming Out*, pp.25ff; *Sex, Politics and Society*, Chapter 8.

21 Greenberg, *op.cit.*, p.409.

22 *ibid*, p.351.

23 Ian Kennedy, *The Unmasking of Medicine*, George Allen & Unwin, London, 1981, pp.8ff.

24 *Sex, Politics and Society*, p.103.

25 Richard Plant, *The Pink Triangle*, p.107, cf. pp.28ff, 45ff.

26 *ibid*. pp.54–69.

27 *ibid*. pp.148–9, cf. '"Stigmata or Degeneration" – Prisoner Markings in Nazi Concentration Camps', E.J. Haerberle, *The Gay Past*, pp.135–9; 'The Pink Triangle: The Persecution of Homosexual Males in Concentration Camps in Nazi Germany', R. Lautmann, *The Gay Past*, pp.141–60.

28 cf. *Sex, Politics and Society*, pp.152–6; Jonathan Dollimore, *Sexual Dissidence*, Chapters 11,12.

29 Elizabeth R. Moberley, *Homosexuality: A New Christian Ethic*, James Clarke & Co, 1983.

30 ed. Anne Sutherland, *Face Values*, BBC, 1978, Chapter 7.

31 cf. John Boswell, *Christianity, Social Tolerance and Homosexuality*, p.43, n.6; Bruce R. Smith, *Homosexual Desire in Shakespeare's England*, p.18, n.29; *Gay Times*, August 1993, p.65.

32 cf. *Gay Times*, June 1994, pp.20–1.

33 cf. John D'Emilio, *Sexual Politics, Sexual Communities: The Making of a Homosexual Minority in the United States 1940–1970*.

34 S Jeffery Poulter, *Peers, Queers & Commons: the Struggle for Gay Law Reform from 1950 to the Present*, S. Jeffery–Poulter, Routledge 1991.

35 cf. *Homosexuality: A European Community Issue*, European Human Rights Foundation 1993.

36 *Sexual Behaviour in Britain*, pp.213–18, 226–7.

37 *Sexual Dissidence*, Clarendon Press, Oxford, 1991, Chapters 1 and 2.

38 George Steiner, *A Reader*, Penguin, 1984, p.194.

39 Joseph P. Goodwin, *More Man Than You'll Ever Be! Gay Folklore and Acculturation in Middle America*, p.33.

40 *Sexual Citizenship*, p.96–7.

41 *op.cit.* p.34.

42 cf. Frank Browning, *The Culture of Desire*, Vintage Books, New York, 1993/1994, Chapter 2.

43 Greenberg, *op.cit.*, pp.313–14.

44 *Sex, Politics and Society*, pp.32–3, 57–95.

Chapter 8

1 W.M. Swartley, 'The Bible Argument on Slavery', quoted in *Slavery, Sabbath, War and Women: Case Issues in Biblical Interpretation*, Herald Press, 1983, p.37.
2 *Freedom to Choose*, Grove Books 1991, p.12.
3 Section 2:29, p.18.
4 *Spiritual Friendship*, 1:57–61.
5 D.F. Greenberg, *The Construction of Homosexuality*, p.96.
6 cf. *Hidden from History*, ed. M.B. Duberman et al., p.134.
7 cf. John Boswell, *Christianity, Social Tolerance and Homosexuality*, p.29, p.81, p.245 n.7; W.L. Petersen, *Vigiliae Christianae*, p.191 n.12(2); Bruce R. Smith, *Homosexual Desire in Shakespeare's England*, p.195.
8 *The Shadow of the Galilean*, SCM, 1987, p.106.
9 *One Hundred Years of Homosexuality*, Routledge, 1990, Chapter 4.
10 John Boswell *op.cit.*, p.134, n.41; cf. p.46.
11 'A Tango in the Morning with Jesus', *Sex With God*, Indulgence Press, NY, 1989, p.56.
12 *On Spiritual Friendship*, 1:69–70.
13 cf. 'The myth of sodomy' in Chapter 2. See also John Boswell, *Same-Sex Unions in Premodern Europe*: 'Jewish Perspectives', pp.365–71.
14 cf. 1 Corinthians 6:9; 1 Timothy 1:10.
15 e.g. Matthew 27:25; 1 Thessalonians 2:16.
16 cf. Chapter 3: 'Bodies and boundaries'. Chapter 4: '4. Discernment and scripture', '8. The method of grace', '7. Respect for creation.' '9. The shape of grace'.
17 cf. Leviticus 20:10 with John 8:5.
18 cf. Galatians 2:14–17; 3:1–3; 5:2–6.
19 cf. Greenberg p.97.
20 cf. Obadiah; Isaiah 63:1–6.
21 *Theological Dictionary of the New Testament*, ed. G. Kittel trans. G.W. Bomily, Eerdmans, Grand Rapids, Vol III, pp.1101–4.
22 cf. Greenberg, pp.94–106.
23 *ibid.* p.95.
24 'Romans 1: Entropy, Sexuality and Politics', Michael Williams, *Anvil*, Vol. 10:2, 1993, pp.105–110.
25 cf. Neil Elliott, *The Rhetoric of Romans: Argumentative Constraint and Strategy and Paul's Dialogue with Judaism*, JSOT Press Sheffield 1990.
26 cf. *The Interpretation of the Bible in the Church*, The Pontifical Biblical Commission, Rome, 1993, pp.42–4.
27 Helpfully set out in *Gay/Lesbian Liberation: A Biblical Perspective*, G.R. Edwards, Pilgrim Press, NY, 1984, pp.85–100.
28 Greenberg, *op.cit.*, p.350.

29 *Homosexuality and the Western Christian Tradition,* Longmans, 1955, p.xi, 37–40, 168ff.
30 *Christianity, Social Tolerance and Homosexuality,* p.109.
31 cf. 'Relations natural and unnatural: A response to John Boswell's exegesis of Romans 1', Richard B. Hays, *The Journal of Religious Ethics,* Vol. 14:1, 1986.
32 C.E.B. Cranfield, *Romans,* Vol. 1, T.&T. Clark, 1975, p.127; J.D.G. Dunn, *Romans 1–8,* Word Books, Dallas, 1988, p.65.
33 Pages 34–5, 39–40.
34 'Sexuality, Symbol, Theology and Culture: A Reply to Francis Bridger', Peter Reiss, *Anvil,* Vol.1:1, 1994, pp.29–43.
35 Hays, *op.cit.,* p.200.
36 *New Horizons In Hermeneutics,* pp.44–6.
37 *Slavery, Sabbath, War and Women,* pp.31–64.
38 cf. Jacques Ellul, *The New Demons,* Seabury Press, Mowbray, 1975.
39 pp.59–61.
40 cf. D. Sherwin Bailey, pp.38–40.
41 John Boswell, *Christianity, Social Tolerance and Homosexuality,* p.106; L.W. Countryman, *Dirt, Greed and Sex,* pp.117, 202.
42 Boswell, *op.cit.,* p.114, 341ff.
43 Countryman, *op.cit.,* p.117–20;127–8.
44 'Homosexuals or Prostitutes?', David F. Wright, *Vigiliae Christianae,* 38 (1984), pp.123–53.
45 *Sexuality and the Church,* ed. Tony Higton, ABWON, 1987, p.41.
46 W.L. Petersen, *Vigiliae Christianae,* 40 (1986) pp.187–91; David F. Wright, *Vigiliae Christianae,* 41 (1987) pp.396–8.
47 Hays, *op.cit.,* p.206–7.
48 'Defining sodomy in Seventeenth-Century Massachusetts', Robert F. Oakes, *The Gay Past,* pp.79–83.
49 Richard Bauckham, *Jude, 2 Peter,* Word Biblical Commentary 50, Word Books, Waco, Texas, 1983, p.54, cf. pp. 46–7; 50–3.
50 *Slavery, Sabbath, War and Women,* pp.31–7.

Chapter 9

1 Gilbert Herdt and Robert J. Stoller, *Intimate Communications,* Columbia University Press 1990, Chapter 2.
2 *ibid.* Chapter 9.
3 *ibid.* Chapter 10.
4 cf. Vincent J. Donovan, *Christianity Rediscovered,* SCM, 1978, pp.16–21; 56–7.
5 cf. Chapter 5.
6 cf. Michael Charlesworth, *Behind the Headlines,* Greenbank Press, Somerset, 1994, pp.80–5.
7 D.F. Greenberg, *The Construction of Homosexuality,* pp.145, 149–50,

404–8; cf. John Boswell, 'Revolutions, Universals and Sexual Categories' in *Hidden from History*, pp.23–30.

8 Greenberg, *op.cit.*, p.66.

9 cf. Chapter 4:10.

10 Greenberg, *op.cit.*, pp.400ff.

11 *ibid.* pp.400–3.

12 Jeffrey Weeks, *Sex, Politics and Society*, pp.40, 48–50.

13 Greenberg, *op.cit.*, p.401.

14 *ibid.* pp.411–15.

15 *ibid.* pp.415–18.

16 *ibid.* pp.418–21.

17 *Sex, Politics and Society*, p.129.

18 Greenberg pp.421–30.

19 *ibid.* p.427.

20 *ibid.* pp.430–1.

21 Yale University Press.

22 cf. pp.35–7; Chapter 5.

23 *ibid.* Chapter 2.

24 cf. Friedman, pp.91–3; 205–13.

25 *ibid.* pp.xi; 136–40; 170–2.

26 cf. also Richard Green, *The 'Sissy Boy' Syndrome and the Development of Homosexuality*. Yale University Press 1987.

27 cf. Friedman, pp.15–21; 192ff.

28 cf. *ibid.* pp.238–40; 244–5.

29 *ibid.* Chapter 16.

30 James Clarke & Co, 1983.

31 'Is the Distant Relationship of Fathers and Homosexual Sons Related to the Sons' Erotic Preference for Male Partners, or to the Sons' Atypical Gender Identity, or to Both', K. Freund and R. Blanchard, *Homosexuality, Masculinity and Feminity*, ed. Michael W. Ross, Harrington Press, NY, 1985, pp.7–25.

32 G.D. Comstock, *Violence against Lesbians and Gay Men*. Columbia University Press, 1991, pp.90–4.

33 Jeff Konrad, Monarch Publications, 1993.

34 *ibid.* cf. pp.13; 181–3; 195–6; 235–9.

Chapter 10

1 Quoted in Bruce R. Smith, *Homosexual Desire in Shakespeare's England*, Chicago University Press, 1991, p.42.

2 *Gay Times*, December 1993, p.38.

3 *Gay Times*, February 1991, p.11.

4 *The Pink Paper*, 14 June 1992, p.3.

5 *The Pink Paper*, 9 May 1993, p.14.

6 *Gay Times*, August 1993, p.7; *The Pink Paper*, 16 July 1993, p.1.

7 *The Pink Paper*, 7 February 1993, p.1.

8 *Gay Times*, November 1990, p.21; December 1990, p.18; January 1991, p.20.

9 Caroline Gooding, *Trouble with the Law: A Legal Handbook for Lesbians and Gay Men*, GMP, 1992, pp.28–34; 299–300. *Homosexuality: A European Community Issue*, eds. Kees Waaldijk and Andrew Clapham, European Human Rights Foundation, 1993, pp.104–12.

10 *Homosexuality: A European Community Issue*, pp.216ff.

11 David Crawford, *Easing the Ache: Gay Men Recovering from Compulsive Behaviours*, Plume USA, 1991.

12 *Gay Times*, June 1994, pp.30–1.

13 'Homosexual in law' in *Coming on Strong*, pp.180ff.

14 cf. *Gay Times*, November 1994, pp.40–3; October 1994, pp.36–7; cf. also *The Independent*, Tuesday 18 December 1990, p.12.

15 cf. *Gay Times*, May 1994, p.32; June 1994, p.25.

16 *Gay Times*, July 1994, pp.27–8.

17 Marc E. Burke, *Coming out of the Blue*, Cassell, 1993, pp.191ff.

18 *Trouble with the Law*, pp.218–31.

19 cf. *Coming on Strong*, pp.180–1.

20 cf. *Gay Times*, February 1994, pp.20–1.

21 *Trouble with the Law*, pp.219–20. For a recent reference to magistrates accepting that a car could be a private place see *Gay Times*, January 1995, p.23.

22 *Trouble with the Law*, p.224.

23 *ibid*. p.214.

24 *ibid*. p.222.

25 *The Pink Paper*, 18 March 1994, pp.1,3.

26 'Gays and the Press' in *Coming on Strong*, pp.242ff.

27 Quoted in *The Independent*, 25 November 1991, p.14 – an informative article with both statistics and stories.

28 *Mental Illness: Sometimes I think I can't go on any more . . .* p.6.

29 *Gay Times*, February 1991, p.16.

30 Burke, *op.cit.*, pp.167ff.

31 *Gay Times*, November 1994, p.33.

32 e.g. Hosea 2,4; Isaiah 1:21ff; 46–7; Jeremiah 2,5; Ezekiel 8–9; 16; Revelation 12–13; 17–18.

33 Seabury Press, 1975; Mowbray.

34 SCM, 1982.

35 Matthew 23:37; 1 Thessalonians 2:7; Boff, *op.cit.*, pp.33–4.

36 cf. *Gay Times*, November 1992, pp.18–20.

37 cf. David Evans, *Sexual Citizenship*, Routledge, 1993, chapters 4 and 5.

38 cf. 'Lesbian and Gay Men in the European Community Legal Order' in *Homosexuality: A European Community Issue*, pp.7–69.

39 cf. the useful *Human Rights: Our Understanding and Our Responsibilities*, Church of England Board of Social Responsibility, GS 324, 1977.

40 *Pastoral Care of Homosexual Persons # 10*; *Issues in Human Sexuality*

4.8; CARE Briefing Paper, 1992, *Homosexual rights – the issues examined*, 'Conclusion'.

41 *The Independent*, 11 March 1992; *Church Times*, 13 February 1992.

42 *The Times*, 21 June 1994, p.8.

43 *The Pink Paper*, 28 October 1994, pp.1,14–15.

44 *Declaration on Religious Liberty* in *Vatican Council II: The Conciliar and Post Conciliar Documents*, ed. Austin Flannery, pp.799ff. See also articles in *Law and Justice: The Christian Law Review* No. 82/83, 1984; also 'Toleration, Religious' in *New Dictionary of Christian Ethics and Pastoral Theology*, eds. D.J. Atkinson and D.H. Field, Leicester, IVP, 1995, pp.851–2.

45 pp.84–5

46 *Godparents and Kinship in Early Medieval Europe*, J.H. Lynch, Princeton University Press, 1986.

47 cf. 'A conversation about pornography', Richard Dyer in *Coming on Strong*, pp.198–212.

Chapter 11

1 *Report of Proceedings*, General Synod, 12 July 1992, p.340.

2 cf. Philip Hacking, *Church of England Newspaper*, 8 April 1993, p.16.

3 cf. Aidan Kavanagh, *On Liturgical Theology*, Pueblo, NY, 1984.

4 D.F. Greenberg, *Construction of Homosexuality*, Chicago 1988, pp.289ff.

5 Diane Karay Tripp, 'Daily Prayer in the Reformed Tradition: An Initial Survey', *Studia Liturgica*, Volume 21, 1991, pp.76–107; 190–219.

6 cf. Francis Penhale, *Catholics in Crisis*, Mowbray, 1986, p.6.

7 *Church Times*, 13 January 1995, p.3.

8 *Clergy Under Stress*, Mowbray, 1990, pp.65; 83ff.

9 *ibid.* pp.ix, 84.

10 p.34–5 (Chapter 2); pp.39–40 (Chapter 8(d)).

11 cf. *On The Way*, Church House Publishing, 1995, pp.70–3.

12 Stephen Jeffrey-Poulter, *Peers, Queers & Commons*, Routledge, 1991, pp.33, 36, 70. cf. *The Tablet*, 3 July 1993, p.856.

13 *Some Considerations Concerning the Response to Legislative Proposals on the Non-Discrimination of Homosexual Persons*, Congregation for the Doctrine of the Faith, *L'Osservatore Romano*, 29 July 1992, p.5. cf. also *Gay Times*, October 1992, pp.24–6.

14 *Church of England Newspaper*, 26 August 1994.

15 cf. Bishop Clarence Pope, *Church Times*, 26 September 1991.

16 cf. *Church of England Newspaper*, 16 September 1994, p.8.

17 319 N. 4th Street, Suite 902, St Louis, MO 63102, USA.

18 *Come Home! Reclaiming Spirituality and Community as Gay Men and Lesbians*, HarperSanFrancisco, 1990; *Coming Out to God: Prayers for Lesbians and Gay Men, Their Families and Friends*, Westminster/John Knox Press, 1991; *The Word is Out*, HarperSanFrancisco 1994.

19 cf. *I am Learning to Love*, Martin Hallett, Marshall Pickering, 1987.

20 cf. Tony Green, 'Souls in Conflict', in *Capital Gay*, 16 December 1994. (Tony Green is Secretary to a Commission of Enquiry investigating the 'ex-gay' movement.)

21 cf. *Homosexuality: Finding the Way of Truth and Love*, Christopher Townsend, *Cambridge Papers* 3:2 (c/o 41 London Road, Stapleford, Cambridge CB2 5DE).

22 *Moore's Introduction to English Canon Law*, Third Edition, Timothy Briden and Brian Hanson, Mowbray, 1992, pp.119–22.

23 cf. R.E. Rodes, Jr, *Ecclesiastical Administration in Medieval England: The Anglo-Saxons to the Reformation*, University of Notre Dame, 1977, pp.xi–xiv.

24 R.E. Rodes, *Law and Modernization in the Church of England: Charles II to the Welfare State*. University of Notre Dame 1991, pp.23ff;114ff.

25 *Ecclesiastical Administration in Medieval England*, pp.32–45.

26 *Church of England Newspaper*, 4 November 1994, p.1.

27 *Ecclesiastical Administration in the Medieval England*, pp.129ff.

28 cf. *Lay Authority and Reformation in the English Church: Edward I to the Civil War*, University of Notre Dame, 1982, pp.137ff; 181.

29 *Sex Politics and Society*.

30 GS Misc 402, pp.15–17.

Chapter 12

1 *Homosexual Desire in Shakespeare's England*, Chicago 1991, p.15.

2 *Rediscovering Gay History*, available from the Lesbian and Gay Christian Movement, Oxford House, Derbyshire Street, London E2 6HG.

3 cf. *Homosexual Desire in Shakespeare's England*, pp.15–16, cf. footnote 23, p.274.

4 cf. Michael Vasey, 'Cohabitation: one law for the rich and one for the poor', *Church of England Newspaper*, 29 May 1992. Reprinted in *Living Together: a challenge for the Church*, CEN Books, 1992.

5 *Law and Modernization in the Church of England*, *op.cit.*, p.117.

6 Darton, Longman & Todd, 1985, pp.36–7, cf. pp.11–26.

7 cf. David Crawford, *Easing the Ache: Gay Men Recovering from Compulsive Behaviours*, Plume, 1991.

8 GMP, 1992.

9 Published by GMP. North American equivalents appear to be books by Wes Muchmore and William Hanson, *Coming Out Right, Coming Along Fine*, etc., Alyson Publications.

10 Bedford Square Press for the National Council for Voluntary Associations, 1989.

11 The Other Way Press, 1991.

12 *Mirror of Charity*, *op.cit.*, cf. 1:34; 1:15.

13 St Martin's Press, NY, 1988.

14 'Queers, beers and shopping: myths about the Pink Pound', Bill Short, November 1992, p.20.

15 cf. Charles Williams, *The Figure of Beatrice: A Study in Dante*.

Chapter 13

1 *Heart of Compassion*, ed. A.M. Allchin, Darton, Longman & Todd, 1989, p.52.
2 e.g. *Hymns Ancient & Modern Revised*, 466, 278, 279.
3 *The Liturgy of Christian Burial*, Geoffrey Rowell, Alcuin/SPCK, 1977, pp.81–2.
4 '"Precious in the Sight of the Lord . . .": the theme of death in puritan pastoral theology', David Sceats, *Churchman* 1981, pp.326–39.
5 *Sex with God*, Indulgence Press, NY, 1989; 2nd edn Wexford Press, NY, 1994.

Index